# THE COMPLETE GUIDE TO

THE BABY-SITTERS CLUB

**Other books by
Ann M. Martin**

# THE COMPLETE GUIDE TO

## Ann M. Martin

AN
**APPLE**
PAPERBACK

SCHOLASTIC INC.
New York Toronto London Auckland Sydney

Cover art by Hodges Soileau

ISBN 0-590-92713-2

12 11 10 9 8 7 6 5 4 3 2       6 7 8 9/9 0 1/0

Printed in the U.S.A.      40

First Scholastic printing, September 1996

*The author gratefully acknowledges*
*David Levithan*
*for his help*
*with this book.*

*Thanks also to*
*Kim Dooley, Janet Vultee, Veronica Ambrose,*
*Olivia Ford, and Charles Agvent*
*for their assistance in compiling and fact-checking*
*the entries in this book.*

# Key

•

Each fact in *The Complete Guide to the Baby-sitters Club* is followed by a reference that includes the book number and page number where the fact can be located. For example, "(#34-p.24)" means that the fact can be found in book #34 (*Mary Anne and Too Many Boys*) on page 24. Because of space limitations, only one reference for each fact has been included.

Regular BSC series books are denoted by their number. Other books are listed as follows:

CB = *Claudia's Book*
CL = *The Baby-sitters Club Chain Letter*
DB = *Dawn's Book*
KB = *Kristy's Book*
LB = *Logan Bruno, Boy Baby-sitter*
LS = *Logan's Story*
M# = *Mystery*
MAB = *Mary Anne's Book*
SB = *Stacey's Book*
SecS = *The Baby-sitters Club Secret Santa*
ShS = *Shannon's Story*
SM# = *Super Mystery*
SS# = *Super Special*

# Contents

•

# ● Contents ●

# ● Contents ●

# ● Contents ●

# ● Contents ●

# ● Contents ●

# THE COMPLETE GUIDE TO

# CLUB
# FACTS

•

# CLUB FACTS

●

**TIME/PLACE:**
Meets every Monday, Wednesday, and Friday, 5:30-6:00 in Claudia's room (#4-p.2). Girls can walk into Kishis' house, don't have to ring bell (#76-p.26).

**MEMBERS:**
Kristy, Mary Anne, Stacey, Claudia, and Dawn are thirteen and in eighth grade now at Stoneybrook Middle School (#10-p.1). Mallory and Jessi are eleven and in sixth grade, also at SMS (#14-pp.1, 12). Kristy, Mary Anne, Stacey, Claudia are original BSC members; Dawn joins club (#4-p.166), followed by Logan (#10) and Shannon (#11). Stacey moves back to NYC (#13). Mal and Jessi join the BSC originally to replace Stacey (#14-p.127) and are made official members (#15-p.11). Stacey rejoins club when she moves back to Stoneybrook (#28). Logan questions whether he can be an associate member and still do sports; quits (LS-p.115), then rejoins (LS-p.133). Club goes down to six members once Dawn leaves for six-month stay in CA (#67-p.140). Wendy Loesser is made a BSC member (#68-p.62), then quits (#68-p.125). Shannon becomes alternate officer (#68-p.127). Mal has to drop out because of mono (#69-p.51) and is made an honorary member (#69-p.55); rejoins club after mono is gone (#73-p.139). Dawn returns to club from CA (SS#12; #81-p.24). After big fight, Stacey quits—and is fired by Kristy—leaving another opening in the club (#83-p.127). Stacey is let back into club after asking to rejoin; is put on probation (#87-p.138). Dawn moves back to California for good, which means the BSC needs a new member; Dawn is made honorary member (#88). Anna and Abby Stevenson are asked to join the club; Anna says no because of time constraints, but Abby says yes and becomes alternate officer (#89-p.143). Abby takes over as president and treasurer when Kristy is away in Hawaii and Stacey is in New York City (#99-p.49).

**HISTORY:**
Kristy got idea for BSC on first Tuesday afternoon of seventh grade (#1-

3

p.1). First meeting was on a Friday (week and a half after Kristy's idea) (#1-p.54). Kristy misses meeting when her dog, Louie, is sick and dying (#11-p.111). Kristy is so worked up about the success of the We ♥ Kids Club that she forgets to call the BSC meeting to order (a BSC first) (#72-p.54). Hardly has to advertise anymore (M#19-p.14). Mary Anne has never made a baby-sitting scheduling mistake (#21-p.14; #34-p.6). Jeff, Jordan, Byron, and Adam join as Baby-sitters-in-Training, who earn a quarter of what the Baby-sitter earns (#98-p.69). Friday meeting changed to Thursdays (#100-p.26). Club is disbanded in 7-2 vote (with Jessi and Mal against and the rest of the club for dissolving the BSC) (#100-p.78). Then, a few weeks later, the club reforms in a unanimous vote, with a probation period declared (#100-p.149).

## OFFICERS AND DUTIES:

**PRESIDENT:** (Kristy)
Makes sure meetings begin exactly on time and are conducted in businesslike fashion, comes up with new ideas to promote club, attract clients (#43-p.24), i.e., summer play group, Mother's Day event, Kid-Kits (#44-p.23). Always asks if there is any club business or new business to begin meeting (#48-p.31; #49-p.20). Wears a visor, and a pencil over one ear, sits in director's chair during meetings (#54-p.18).

Gives a Look if a member is late for a meeting (#61-p.12).

**VICE-PRESIDENT:** (Claudia)
No real duties, but holds this title because club meetings take place in her room (only member with her own telephone and private line) (#45-p.24); she sometimes takes calls from parents during non-meeting times; gives junk food to members at meetings, as well as sugar-free snacks for Stacey (#43-p.24).

**SECRETARY:** (Mary Anne)
Keeps record book up-to-date and in order. Has never made a baby-sitting scheduling mistake (#21-p.14; #34-p.6).

**TREASURER:** (Stacey, then Dawn [#14-#27], then Stacey [#28-#83], then Dawn [#84-#87], then **Stacey** [#88 on])
Collects dues from members each Monday; keeps money in manila envelope (#52-p.16) (a dollar from each, #53-p.36); grumbling from members on dues day is tradition (#65-p.21); records expenditures and earnings in back of record book; doles out money for Claud's phone bill, gas money for Charlie to bring Kristy and Abby to meetings, club parties, Kid-Kit supplies, etc. (#43-p.25; M#25-p.21). Dawn is a good treasurer in Stacey's absence (#86-p.19).

**ALTERNATE OFFICER:** (Dawn, then Shannon [#68-p.127 to #80], then Dawn [#81-#84], then Shannon

[#84-#87], then Dawn [#88], then Shannon [#89], then **Abby** [#90 on])
No real responsibilities, takes over job of member who is absent from a meeting, must be familiar with all duties, answers telephone a lot (#43-p.25).

**JUNIOR OFFICERS:** (Jessi and Mallory)
Take a lot of the afternoon jobs because they are not allowed to sit at night unless they're taking care of their own siblings (#43-p.26).

**ASSOCIATE MEMBERS:** (Shannon and Logan)
Reliable sitters who don't go to meetings regularly but can take a job if none of the members are available (#43-p.26).

**HONORARY MEMBER:** (Mal [#69-73], Dawn [#88 on])
Non-practicing member of the BSC (#69-p.55).

## CLUB POSSESSIONS:

### CLUB RECORD BOOK:
Contains clients' names, addresses, phone numbers, rates paid, allergies, and other special info about children, and all schedules of baby-sitting jobs (#43-p.24). Also has all of the sitters' individual schedules (#71-p.22). Mary Anne is in charge of entire record book except for Stacey's treasury section (#48-p.28). Mary Anne has not made one error

in book yet (#21-p.14; #34-p.6; #63-p.24).

### CLUB NOTEBOOK:
More like a diary (#4-p.7); all members must write description of every job and read each other's entries about clients and handling of sticky situations (#43-p.26). Kristy and Mal like to write in it (#31-p.37). Most don't like to write in it but enjoy reading it (#48-p.26).

### MYSTERY NOTEBOOK:
A record of the BSC's detective work, reporting strange occurrences and keeping a list of suspects and clues (SM#2-p.3-4). Mal compiles it from past notebook entries (SM#2-p.86).

### FLIERS:
First got the word out by distributing fliers; still pass them out once in a while if they feel like they need extra business. The fliers tell about the club and tell parents when and where to call (M#1-p.36). BSC plans to make fliers that will inform clients of the BSC rules (#81-p.121).

### KID-KITS:
(Kristy's idea) Medium-sized boxes full of toys, books, stickers, art materials, and games the members used to play; puppets, great for rainy baby-sitting days (#45-p.28). Kits are not brought to every job, because they want them to be a treat for the kids (#53-p.60). Each member has one (can decorate it with glitter and other "stuff," like paint

and fabric, #54-p.14); kids and parents love them; kids love playing with other people's toys (#48-p.27).

*Members' Additions to Kid-Kits:*
*Stacey's:* *The Dancing Cats of Applesap* (Charlotte enjoys, #43-p.5).
*Mal's:* Packed with books, games, her old toys, crayons, coloring books, stickers, scissors, and glue (#47-p.26). Books include *Angelina Ballerina* (M#3-p.81).
*Jessi's:* An office kit made out of a plastic box with colored pencils, Magic Markers, pens, erasers, paper clips (red, white, and blue), blunt scissors, tape, memo pads, rubber bands, stickers, animal stamps, writing paper, and envelopes (#56-p.60).
*Kristy's:* Includes an old rag doll, some dinosaur figurines, a few small puzzle books, an old yo-yo.
*Claudia's:* Decorated with acrylic paints; mermaids painted on the top; inside there are blocks, baby puzzles, teething rings, rattles, books, including *Muggie Maggie* by Beverly Cleary (M#2-pp.107-108). Is more like an Art-Kit, filled with art supplies (#85-p.8).
*Dawn's:* Includes Jeff's old Wiffle Ball (M#2-p.118), makeup crayons (#81-p.55).
*Mary Anne's:* Includes little coloring books that Suzi Barrett loves (M#16-p.48).
*Shannon's:* Contains coloring book, mini-Frisbee, *Esio Trot,* and *Tiffky Doofky* (#89-p.53).
*Abby's:* A shoebox from a new pair of cleats (#90-p.27).

## PAST CLUB EXPERIENCES:

### BOOKS #1–#20:
Has the first BSC **pizza party** (#1). Deals with the **Phantom Phone Caller** (#2). Battles with its short-lived competitor, the **Baby-sitters Agency** (#3). Sits at **Elizabeth and Watson's wedding** (#6). Forms a **summer playgroup** for clients (#7). Throws Mary Anne a **surprise party** (#10). Throws Stacey a **good-bye carnival party** (#13). Becomes involved in the **Little Miss Stoneybrook pageant** (#15). Has a period of **bad luck** because of chain letter Mary Anne receives in the mail (#17). Sits for clients in **New York City** (#18). Exchanges **practical jokes** with Betsy Sobak (#19).

### BOOKS #21–#40:
Holds **BSC elections** (#22). Sponsors a **"mother's day off"** for the moms of their clients (#24). Searches for **lost Tigger** (#25). Sets up informal **Saturday art class** (#26). Throws **going away party for Derek Masters** (#27). **Tutors** Buddy Barrett (#29). Helps clients with their **Science Fair projects** (#36).

### BOOKS #41–#60:
Organizes **pet show** for charges (#42). Enacts **Operation Help** — plan that gives money to Zuni elementary school that burned down (#44). Takes a four-week **infant-care class** and earns certificates (#45).

Makes a float for the **Stoneybrook Baby Parade**, with theme of The Old Woman Who Lives in a Shoe (#45). **Volunteers** for various organizations and people in the community for a month (Jessi's idea) (#48). Organizes **Valentine's Day Masquerade Party** (#51). Plans **Mini-Olympics** for all charges (#55). Helps kids form a band, **All the Children of the World** (#56). **Save the Planet Class**: Taught by Dawn and Stacey for six weeks (#57); kids organize **Green Fair** (#57).

**BOOKS #61–#80:**
Organizes famous people to donate things for **school auction** (#62). Goes to **Shadow Lake** with Kristy's family and goes to dance at lodge there (#63). BSC gets **anonymous notes** and invitation from Rodowskys, Arnolds, and Braddocks, who want to thank BSC for being best baby-sitters (#63). **Goat-sits** for Elvira Stone (#65). Mary Anne teaches a **sewing class** for charges (#66). Arranges **going away party** for Dawn (#67). Films movie, *Snow White and the Seven Zorbs*, for Dawn in CA (#68). Puts together **Thanksgiving food baskets** for residents of Stoneybrook Manor (#69). Watches as some charges act out the **BSC Follies** (#75). Begins a **Friendship Campaign** for Natalie Springer (#78). Staffs competing **haunted houses** (#79). Some BSC members help out with the **Kids**

**Can Do Anything Club** at SES (#80).

**BOOKS #81–#100:**
BSC organizes a **kids' talent show** in neighborhood (#83), which Stacey skips. Helps settle the **Barrett/DeWitts** into their **new house** (#84). Helps kids audition for Claudia's **radio show** (#85). Runs **Camp BSC**, with a circus theme, in Dawn and Mary Anne's yard for two weeks (#86). Plans **going away party for Dawn** and **Christmas in Summer** for an injured James Hobart (#88). Puts together booths for **Stoneybrook Arts Fund Carnival** (#90). Organizes **BSC family Thanksgiving dinner** (#91). Helps out with the **Stoneybrook Manor Christmas Boutique** (#92). Helps start an SMS chapter of **Students Against Drunk Driving** after Amelia Freeman's death (#93-p.96). Puts together a *Record Wreckers* book and show for neighborhood kids to make wacky "world" records (#95). Deals with disgruntled kids after neighborhood parents **ban television** and the kids decide to make their own show (#96). As members earn money for SMS trip to Hawaii, Jeff, Jordan, Byron, and Adam are made **Baby-sitters-in-Training**, until they find the job too much to handle (#98). In order to make money for trip to Hawaii, holds the **Official BSC Fourth of July Pre-Fireworks Festival** (#98). Under Abby's leadership,

puts together the BSC Mexican Festival (#99).

## MYSTERIES #1–#20:
Competes in **Sitter of the Month contest,** voted upon by clients (M#2). Helps with **Heritage Day Projects,** makes fund-raising booth for historical society using cardboard cutouts (M#5). Helps kids with their **Readathon** projects (M#13). Sets up **day care center at Washington Mall** (M#14). Puts together *A Day in the Life of Stoneybrook* for Dawn (M#16). Plans a **kids' holiday party** with a sleigh ride (M#18). Helps out cleaning up the **arboretum** (M#19). Works on the **Free Babar** movement, including Elephant Walk fund-raiser (M#20).

## MYSTERIES #21–#25:
Participates in **Mrs. Goode's Cookware Battle of the Bakers,** both competing and setting up a **day care center** (M#21). Deals with **Ghostbuster Mania** (M#22). Helps set up the **Greenbrook Club** (M#23). Campaigns to **save Miller's Park and Ambrose's Sawmill** (M#24). Holds a **scavenger hunt** for neighborhood kids (M#25).

## SUPER MYSTERIES #1–#2:
While Claudia, Kristy, Dawn, and Mary Anne are at **Randolph Mansion,** Jessi and Mal help organize the BSC on Wheels portion of Stoneybrook's **Celebrate America!** Day Parade (SM#1). Jessi helps charges track down the **man with the blue tattoo** (SM#2).

## SUPER SPECIALS #1–#13:
Goes on a cruise on the **Ocean Princess** (SS#1). Spends the summer as CITs at **Camp Mohawk** (SS#2). Goes with the entire SMS student body to **Leicester Lodge** in Vermont (SS#3). Dawn and Claudia get **stranded on Nine O'Clock Island** in storm; hold press conference after they are found (SS#4). Wins the Jack-O'-Lottery and **goes to California** to visit Dawn's father and brother (SS#5). Heads to **New York** with Stacey (SS#6). Gets caught in a big **blizzard** (SS#7). Takes a summer vacation to Watson's cabin on **Shadow Lake** (SS#8). Works on the SMS production of *Peter Pan* (SS#9). Takes a trip to **Sea City,** where they experience **Hurricane Bill** (SS#10). Recalls some of their most important **memories** (SS#11). Attends the simultaneous **weddings** of **Mr. Schafer and Carol** and **Mrs. Barrett and Mr. DeWitt** (SS#12). While some BSC members are in **Hawaii,** others help with **Mrs. Stone's farm camp** (SS#13).

## READER REQUESTS, PORTRAIT COLLECTIONS, AND SPECIAL BOOKS:
Puts together a booth on safe-sitting for local **health fair** (LS). Helps their

charges deal with **EJ the bully** (LB). In celebration of Mother's Day, the BSC plans both the **Make Your Own Mother's Day Giftathon** (ShS) and a **Mother-Daughter Softball Game** (ShS). Sends revealing **chain letter** and throws party for hospitalized Kristy (CL). Reunites Eliza Stanley with her long-lost sister as part of **Santa's Helpers** program (SecS).

## BSC RULES:

### MEETING PROCEDURES/RULES:

Kristy sits in **director's chair** with **pencil over ear** and **green visor** on head (#17-p.19). Mary Anne, Dawn, Stacey, and Claudia usually sit on bed; Mal and Jessi sit on the floor (#19-p.80). Claudia also has desk and chair, Stacey sometimes sits there, and Claudia has a digital clock and princess phone. **Whoever is closest to phone answers**, takes information (including number of children being sat for, as of #81), hangs up, then Mary Anne checks record book and assigns job and client is called back. Has **answering machine** (CL-p.18). Not club policy to let clients **request** particular sitters (#56-p.51). Refer to themselves as the **BSC** (#61-p.7). Meetings must begin with **club business**, not personal business (M#19-p.33). Claud provides **junk food**, and sugar-free snacks for Stacey and Dawn (#62-p.14). Every job that comes along must be **offered** to all the members of the club before someone takes it (#3-p.161). Sometimes hold **emergency meetings**, i.e., called one to discuss the mystery of the old Hennessey house (#35-p.98). Two **unofficial meetings** were held for the first time to discuss volunteer projects, one in Dawn and Mary Anne's barn (#48-p.71), the other in Jessi's room (#48-p.101).

### JOB RULES:

Members are **never on the phone for very long during a job** in case parents may be trying to reach them (#46-p.119). Members **rarely miss meetings** (#51-p.18). Members make it a point to be **a little early for jobs** (M#5-p.83). When baby-sitting, they try to be the ones who **answer the phones** (M#6-p.60). When clients are new in town, BSC members always **ask someone to come to the door with them** the first time, just to get a sense of what the family is like (M#10-p.49). The Baby-sitters **always leave notes when they take charges outside**, even if the parents aren't going to be back for hours (M#16-p.60). BSC rule is that there has to be **more than one sitter if there are more than four kids** (#81-p.86). When talking to clients on the phone, they ask **the number of children they will be sitting for** (#81-p.144). If a sitter is going to be late to a meeting and doesn't tell anyone about it first, she/he will lose privileges (i.e., jobs won't be assigned to him/her if there's a choice) (#12-p.48).

**MISCELLANEOUS:**

Members have **club T-shirts** (#45-p.34). Celebrations are often capped with **Pizza Toasts.** A **group hug** is a BSC tradition (M#9-p.122). Club uses the word **"dibble"** to mean cool (#54-p.17). **"Chilly"** means mega-cool (M#8-p.37).

# THE BSC MEMBERS

•

# KRISTY (KRISTIN) AMANDA THOMAS

•

**BIRTHDAY:**
August 20, born at 4 A.M.

**AGE:**
Thirteen (#10 on)

**NARRATOR OF BOOKS:**
#1, #6, #11, #20, #24, #32, #38, #45, #53, #62, #74, #81, #89, #95, #100, M#4, M#9, M#15, M#19, M#25, *Kristy's Book*

**BSC POSITION:**
President

**CURRENT ADDRESS:**
Now lives at 1210 McLelland Road, Stoneybrook, CT 06800 (SS#2, p.89).

**PERSONAL INFO:**

**PHYSICAL DESCRIPTION:**
Small for her age (#2-p.122); shortest girl in eighth grade (#19-p.4); five feet tall (#92-p.17). Big brown eyes and long brown hair (#2-p.15). Has three-inch scar from appendix operation (CL-p.30). Is left-handed (KB-p.129).

*Clothing/style:* Ears not pierced (#21-p.6). Looks and acts younger than Claudia and Stacey (#2-p.15). Never wears makeup, doesn't do much with hair (#65-p.19). Always wears the same jeans (#14-p.23), all fall the same outfit: jeans, turtleneck, sweater, and sneakers (#11-p.4). Only one in club who does not wear bra (before Jessi and Mal joined) (#10-p.28). Owns only about three dresses (M#4-p.123). Shaves her legs for the first time (SS#7-p.193).

**PERSONALITY TRAITS:**
Talkative (#1-p.4); bossy (#14-p.23); rarely cries (#13-p.30). An extrovert (#31-p.10). Is always punctual (M#19-p.12). Can outrun practically anybody in the eighth grade (#73-p.19). Is a "dog person" (M#3-p.89). Her version of a hug is a little punch on the arm (M#5-p.91). A major sports fan (M#25-p.1). A big Mets fan (M#14-p.10). Throws her fist into the air and says "Yess!" when she's pleased (M#15-p.16). Has a sense of humor about her big ego (LS-p.100). Is only opinionated when she knows she's right (#95-

p.4). Her friends call her the Idea Machine (#95-p.5). Not a huge movie fan (#95-p.34). With her large family, Kristy has to *work* in order to get attention (M#24-p.13).

**FAMILY:**
*Parents/Stepparents:* Mother, Elizabeth Thomas Brewer, divorced Kristy's dad, married Watson Brewer (#6-p.142). Mom is one of Kristy's heroes (M#19-p.6). Father, Patrick Thomas, ran off to CA and remarried (#1-p.16); infrequently hears from him, on her birthday or Christmas (#45-p.2). Sometimes Kristy hates him and wishes he were dead (CL-p.4). Stepfather, Watson Brewer, very rich (#6-p.2), divorced, has two kids (#1-p.18). *Stepsister and Stepbrother:* Karen, age 7 (#38-p.4; age 6 in #6-p.2), and Andrew, age 4 (#6-p.1). Live with Kristy's family every other month. *Siblings:* Charlie, age 17 (#7-p.53); Sam, age 15 (#6-p.5); and David Michael, age 7 (#24-p.4). *Adopted sister:* Elizabeth and Watson adopted Emily Michelle Thomas Brewer, Vietnamese, age two and a half (#45-p.3). *Grandparents:* Nannie, Kristy's maternal grandmother, in her seventies, lives with Kristy's family to help take care of Emily Michelle (#26-p.3).

**CHILDHOOD EXPERIENCES:**
Had lived at Bradford Court since birth, next to Mary Anne and across from Claudia (#1-p.7), where Perkinses now live (#7-p.139). Phone from old address on Bradford Court: KL5-4378 (#1-p.45). Wasn't a fussy baby; a crier, not a mover (KB-p.16). Mrs. Frederickson was first grade teacher (MAB-p.22); Mrs. Jeffries was second-grade teacher (MAB-p.58). In fifth grade, got into a lot of trouble for talking back to the teacher and pouring Yoo-Hoo down Alan Gray's shirt; teacher sent a note home to her parents (#70-p.68). Attended Camp Topnotch at age ten (KB-p.86).

**ROOM:**
Has portable color TV that Watson gave her (#95-p.67). Walls of room covered with Olympic posters and posters of gymnasts and football players (#4-p.21). Has queen-sized bed (#10-p.24).

**LIKES:**
Loves sports (#4-p.21). Likes baseball (#20-p.3). Likes being a businesswoman (#13-p.107). Likes anchovies (#38-p.138). Loves Chinese food, especially chicken with cashews (#1-p.48). An animal lover (SS#11-p.23). Likes being in charge (M#25-p.2).

**DISLIKES:**
Hates crying (#12-p.75); can't stand snobs, cabbage, blood, people who chew with their mouths open, and

squirrels (#11-p.1). Hates bagpipes, thinks they sound like twenty mean cats fighting over one piece of fish (#45-p.118). Thinks smoking is for losers (#74-p.75). Hates dressing up (M#9-p.78). Thinks people should never wear bikinis (SS#8-p.63). Hates the nickname "Crusty" (#100-p.89).

**MEDICAL:**
Broke ankle during summer when she was 11 (#1-p.123). Is in the hospital with appendicitis (CL-p.2); stays in Room 237 of Stoneybrook General Hospital (CL-p.3). Is left with a three-inch scar (CL-p.30). Comes down with a staph infection (CL-p.14).

**BABY-SITTING AND CLUB EXPERIENCES:**

**GENERAL:**
Can now baby-sit until ten on weekends, nine-thirty weeknights (#4-p.56). Has saved a lot of money from sitting (#56-p.5). Fire is what she fears most when baby-sitting (#11-p.38). Has talent for making money and likes being a business-woman (#13-p.107).

**BSC ROLE:**
President. Starts the meetings exactly on time; sits in director's chair, wears visor, and a pencil over one ear at meetings (#17-p.19). Always asks if there's any new club business at the beginning of every meeting (#48-p.31; #49-p.20).

**CLIENTS:**
Favorite kids to sit for are her own siblings. Likes baby-sitting for Newtons because Jamie is fun, Lucy is adorable, and Mrs. Newton is well-organized (#53-p.20). Papadakises are one of her favorite families to sit for; Mrs. Papadakis is very thorough (#62-p.68).

**HISTORY:**
Got idea for club on first Tuesday afternoon of seventh grade (#1-p.1). Misses meeting when Louie is sick and dying (#11-p.111); is late for BSC meetings during her class president race (#53-p.136). Is late for another meeting when Shannon is dognapped (M#7-p.52). First club job was to baby-sit for Mrs. McKeever's St. Bernards, Buffy and Pinky (#1-p.68). Earns perfect score on written and practical exams for infant-care class (#45-p.47). Volunteers for a month to help at the day care center as part of Jessi's idea for BSC members to do community service (#48-p.37). Is so worked up about the success of the We ♥ Kids Club that she forgets to call the BSC meeting to order (a BSC first) (#72-p.54). First sitting job was for David Michael when she was ten (SS#11-p.31).

### SCHOOL-RELATED EXPERIENCES:

#### CLASSES:
In eighth grade (#10 on). In social studies at the same time Mary Anne is in math (M#13-p.111). Ms. Griswold is science teacher (#53-p.128). Mr. Fiske is English teacher (#45-p.35). Mrs. Simon is English teacher (#53-p.68) for other semester. Is in Anna's math class and Abby's English class (#89-p.80). Likes social studies (M#25-p.13).

#### EXTRACURRICULAR ACTIVITIES:
Runs for class president (#53-p.36) with Claudia as campaign manager, who thinks up symbol "K+" for her (#53-pp.44-45). Decides to drop out of race for president because of other responsibilities (#53-pp.140-141). Wins serious recognition award at Awards Night (M#4-p.131). Tries out for the girls' softball team (#74-p.30); makes it and decides that she'll probably stick with it, even after the "initiation" incident (#74-p.135). Title character in *Peter Pan* (SS#9). Helps start chapter of Students Against Drunk Driving at SMS (#93-p.96).

#### GETTING TO SCHOOL:
From new residence on McLelland, she has to take bus to school (#10-p.13). Backpack has lots of compartments—Kristy puts homework in one of the outside compartments, her notebooks in another, and then adds her books to a third compartment as she needs them during the day (M#25-p.13).

#### GRADES:
Straight A's on report card (#6-p.38); gets mostly A's and a few B's (#20-p.102); fails the same science test twice during race for class president. (#53-p.118); Ms. Griswold calls her parents about bad grades (#53-p.128).

#### LUNCH:
Brings lunch to school often: peanut butter and jelly sandwich, apple, Doritos, box of fruit juice (#5-p.34). She and Mary Anne decide bringing bag lunches looks too babyish for eighth grade (#10-p.17). Usually makes funny, disgusting comments about school food, which she sometimes eats; orders hot lunches (#17-p.1).

### SOCIAL ACTIVITIES:

#### DANCES:
Goes to **Final Fling** with Alan Gray (#6-p.34) and goes stag to **Remember September** dance (#10-p.88). Goes to **Halloween Hop** with Bart, dressed as lobsters (#38-p.133); there Bart kisses her on cheek and she falls in love (#38-p.134). Goes to **Valentine Dance** with Bart (#51-p.102). Goes to **Spring Dance** at Community Center with Bart (#63-p.114). Goes to **Spring Dance** at school alone because Bart couldn't make it (#65-p.124). Dances at

Leicester Lodge Dance with Jay Marsden (SS#3-p.221). Dresses as Amelia Earhart for **Mischief Night Masquerade** (M#22-p.134).

**FRIENDS:**

Best friend is Mary Anne (#45-p.11). She and Mary Anne could see into each other's bedrooms, had secret code using flashlights (#1-p.10). They strung paper cup telephones, or sailed paper airplanes with messages through windows (#6-p.20). Kristy was jealous at first of Mary Anne and Dawn's friendship (#5-p.36). At first she is hurt that Mary Anne gets a make over, but tells her she really likes her New Look (#60-p.128). Hasn't had much time to spend with Shannon (#61-p.26); thinks Shannon is trying to steal her friends (#61-p.112); apologizes to Shannon and will ask her to come to regular BSC meetings now and then (#61-p.133).

**BOYS/BOYFRIENDS:**

*Bart Taylor:* Has gigantic crush on Bart Taylor (#20- p.29). She and Bart have a lot in common, both like anchovies (#38-p.138). Kristy hardly ever sees him during the week, just for fun (SS#7-p.52). Is sent anonymous love letters from Bart (#38-p.37). Bart kisses her on cheek at Halloween Hop and she falls in love (#38-p.134). Bart talks to Kristy in her room for the first time (#38-p.98) and gets stranded at her house during blizzard (SS#7-from p.52). Says she's not ready for a "real" boyfriend (#45-p.11); is sort of going out with Bart. Calls Bart from New Year's Eve sleepover and says, "Happy New Year, Bart-Man" (#50-p.38). Bart kisses her in front of everyone at awards ceremony (M#4-p.131). Kristy sometimes still feels shy around Bart (M#9-p.80). Insists she's "not into that boyfriend-girlfriend stuff" (M#16-p.39), but they are hanging-out-and-going-to-dances-and-parties steady (sort of) (#95-p.16). Kristy and Bart are caught kissing, and Kristy is grounded (#95-p.67). Kristy then breaks up with Bart, even though she feels rotten doing it (#95-p.85). She calls Bart again and says they should just be pals, not boyfriend and girlfriend (#95-p.117). Bart reluctantly goes along with it and disinvites Kristy from the April Fools' Dance at SDS (#95-p.128). In the end, Bart and Kristy are still friends—they see each other in the neighborhood and do Krushers/Bashers things, but they don't talk on the phone much anymore, or get together for catch and hitting practice. And they never go to the movies (#95-p.135).

**KRISTY'S KRUSHERS:**

Kristy's name for the kids' softball team she coaches. Coaching outfit: Krushers T-shirt, blue jeans, sneakers, and baseball cap with collie on it (#20-p.108), in memory of her dog, Louie (#53-p.28). Has to cancel Krushers practice to keep up with workload during class president race (#53-p.85). Has practice and baby-sits at same time—a disaster (#63-pp.76, 82). *See more about Krushers under KID GROUPS.*

**NON-BSC TRAVEL:**
Has never been on big vacation before trip to Bahamas (SS#1-p.2). Owns her own skis (SM#2-p.125).

**MISCELLANEOUS:**
Orders "fil-it mig-nun" at the Hard Rock Cafe (#18-p.35). Can touch her nose with her tongue (#16-p.19). Never has been hit in the face with a pie (#19-p.1). If she could be any animal, she'd be a dog (M#11-p.11). Has never seen an R-rated movie (SS#1-p.128). Kristy's Cardinal Rule of Business is *There's no such thing as too much business* (#95-p.24).

# CLAUDIA LYNN KISHI

•

**BIRTHDAY:**
July 11, born at 4:36 A.M.

**AGE:**
Thirteen (#10 on)

**NARRATOR OF BOOKS:**
#2, #7, #12, #19, #26, #33, #40, #49, #56, #63, #71, #78, #85, #91, #97, M#6, M#11, M#16, M#21, *Claudia's Book*

**BSC POSITION:**
Vice-President

**CURRENT ADDRESS:**
Has lived at 58 Bradford Court, Stoneybrook, CT 06800, since she was born, across the street from where Kristy used to live (#1-p.7); personal phone number used by BSC and clients, KL5-3231 (#1-p.45).

## PERSONAL INFO:

**PHYSICAL DESCRIPTION:**
Five feet, four inches. Second generation Japanese-American (#92-p.19) with long, silky, jet-black hair; dark eyes, creamy skin (#1-p.26); never had a pimple (#18-p.17). Looks just like Mimi did when she was twelve (#33-p.134). *Clothing/style:* Does something different with hair almost every day (#4-p.6). Has pierced ears (#14-p.22), gets another hole in right ear (#21-p.131). Uses makeup (#14-p.22). Wears exotic outfits (#1-p.25) that she can throw together in a minute; once went to school with glitter in her hair (#20-p.7). Dedicated to never wearing exact same outfit twice (even if it means only wearing different earrings) (#63-p.19). Favorite art class outfit: black jeans, giant bright blue T-shirt, and snake bracelet worn above elbow (#7-p.4). Wears lots of jewelry, especially the pieces she's made.

**PERSONALITY TRAITS:**
Outgoing, lots of friends (#7-p.3). Fashion-conscious, dresses in the absolute latest trendy clothes (#3-p.8). Loves junk food; munches more when she's stressed (#61-p.113); is not supposed to be eating any (M#10-p.6). Not a morning person (#76-p.47); likes to sleep late

**19**

(SB-p.146). Generally grumpy at the beginning of the week (#78-p.2). Must buy her own trendy clothes (#1-p.26). To her, the most ordinary thing can be an object of art (#100-p.18).

**ABILITIES:**
Can't spell to save her life (M#9-p.122). A terrible singer (LB-p.15). Not a fast reader, unless she's rereading a Nancy Drew mystery (#33-p.93). Can understand some Japanese but can't really speak it (ShS-p.38). Practically a champion skier, has her own equipment (SS#3-p.12). Also a good sailor (SS#4-p.8).

**FAMILY:**
*Parents:* Mr. John Kishi, partner in investment firm in Stamford (#7-p.6); Mrs. Rioko Kishi, head librarian at local library (#7-p.6). *Sister:* Janine, age 16, has IQ of 196, always correcting Claudia (#1-p.27). Claudia sometimes feels inferior to Janine, who is much smarter (#11-p.15). *Grandmother:* Mimi, with whom she was very close and used to live with, died (#26-p.63). Claud gets Mimi's pearl pin that she may never wear but will always keep (#26-p.129). *Cousin:* Claudia is godmother to her newborn cousin Lynn (#97-p.45). *Worries:* Thinks she's adopted since she doesn't look like anyone in her family (#33-p.46); searches for her parents but

discovers she's not adopted (#33-p.131) and that she looks exactly like Mimi looked when she was young (#33-p.132-4).

**CHILDHOOD EXPERIENCES:**
Born 7 lbs., 7 oz.; announcement was in the *Stoneybrook Gazette* (CB-pp.13-4). Cokie Mason, Alan Gray, Pete Black, Kristy, and Mary Anne were in her kindergarten class (CB-p.29). Only Kristy and Mary Anne show up to her sixth birthday party (CB-p.45). Russ and Peaches lived in Stoneybrook until she was seven; would take her to the park (#78-pp.8-9). On Claudia's eighth birthday Mimi dressed up in a kimono to take family to Japanese restaurant but it was closed so they ended up at a sleazy pizza joint (#26-p.76). Gave up dressing stuffed animals in third grade; always felt different from other kids (#13-p.22). Still has rag doll named Lennie (#10-p.41) with yarn braids (#13-p.20). Is sent to the Stamford Alternative Academy for part of fourth grade but is allowed to return to SES after her parents see she's miserable at SAA (CB-p.121).

**ROOM:**
Hangs single-framed picture of her and Mimi at about the same age over her desk (#33-p.135); walls of room covered with her art (#4-p.21). Stashes snacks in bedroom (#3-p.9), which is always messy (#19-p.13).

**20**

Hollow book is her best hiding place (#12-p.71). If Claudia's room ever caught fire, it would turn into one huge S'More because of all her hidden snacks (SS#13-p.12). Claudia paints little stars and moons on her ceiling, as well as a purple polka dot cow jumping over a silver moon (#78-p.2). Clock is on Claudia's desk (#79-p.13). Is the only BSC member with her very own phone, with a private line (M#7-p.14). Has a dressing-table mirror (M#11-p.30).

### LIKES:

Really into art (#1-p.7) and reading mysteries (#1-p.8). Likes boys (#11-p.15). Favorite mysteries are Nancy Drews (#7-p.6), which she has to hide because parents think she should be reading more worthwhile things (#19-p.13). Loves art classes (#7-pp.1, 2). Junk-food addict (#3-p.9). Started liking Bach (#56-p.1). Thinks nose jewelry looks cool, even though she'd never wear any (#75-p.10). Chocolate chips are her favorite (#78-p.11). Loves to string beads (M#6-p.48). Loves to shop (M#10-p.2). Absolutely loves spaghetti (SS#5-p.21).

### DISLIKES:

Hates school (#7-pp.1, 2). Hates foreign languages (#21-p.62) and has no interest in sports (#31-p.12).

### MEDICAL:

Had the chicken pox at seven (#11-p.99); couldn't go to the circus be-cause of it (#24-p.46). Breaks her leg; her fully decorated cast without a white patch on it (#19-p.134) is taken off by Dr. Rivera (#19-p.135), though few months later she still has pain now and then, especially if rain is on the way. Has type O blood (LS-p.39).

## BABY-SITTING AND CLUB EXPERIENCES:

### GENERAL:

Can baby-sit until nine-thirty on school nights (#2-p.54). Money she makes from baby-sitting goes to art supplies first, then jewelry and accessories; hasn't saved much (#56-p.5). Parents have threatened to make her quit the BSC if it takes too much time from her studies (#71-p.25).

### CLIENTS:

Decides to wear jeans whenever baby-sitting Rodowskys (#12-p.34), her spill-proof, accident-proof outfit (#63-p.56); likes baby-sitting Rodowskys—Mrs. Rodowsky always has something not too healthy to eat (#63-p.56). Jamie Newton calls her "Claudee" (#56-p.122). Sat for three-year-old named Skip in New Hampshire (#8-p.135). Is Rosie Wilder's favorite sitter (#49-p.80). Claud decides to stay in club on condition she never has to sit for Betsy Sobak (#19-p.131). Sits for the

Hills, likes Sarah because she's artistic (#50-p.66). Helps Shea Rodowsky with homework, and he helps her (#63-pp.99, 101-102).

## HISTORY:
First club job was to baby-sit for Jamie Newton and his cousins (#1-p.74). Never got over the experience of sitting for Jamie's cousins; stories of baby-sitting terrors are always of special interest to her (#11-p.70). Betsy Sobak's practical joking causes Claud to fall from broken swing and break right leg severely enough to require week-long stay in hospital (#19-pp.37-47).

## SCHOOL-RELATED EXPERIENCES:

### CLASSES/ATTENDANCE:
In eighth grade (#10 on). Takes remedial math and a help session in the resource room (#12-p.11). Mrs. Hall is Claudia's English teacher (#12-p.2). Gets bored at school (#63-p.28). So bored from being home after she broke her leg that she wanted to go back to school (#19-p.104); missed three weeks of school (#19-p.106). Takes two summer school courses: math, with Mr. Davies, and photography, with Mr. Geist (M#16-pp.2,8). Mr. Geist inspires her; is the best teacher she's ever had (M#16-p.86). English and spelling are her least favorite subjects (#86-p.18). Absolutely can't stand science (#33-p.1). Ms. Bernhardt is her social studies teacher (#97-p.10).

## EXTRACURRICULAR ACTIVITIES:
Wants to work on the scenery for class play, *Mary Poppins* (#53-p.35). Is Kristy's campaign manager (#53-pp.44, 45). Becomes Personals columnist for *SMS Express*; gets her own old-looking, beat-up desk in the *Express* office (#71-p.49). Becomes overnight celebrity as columnist (#71-p.87). Starts second column, "Claudia Advises" (#71-p.118).

## GRADES:
IQ above average but doesn't do well in school (#2-p.3); a C- student (#12-p.88). Was tested for learning disabilities but doesn't have any (#63-p.50). She has to keep grades up to stay in club (#19-p.24). Earns 94% on math test (#40-p.31); Shawna Riverson cheated off of her (#40-p.79). Mrs. Hall tells Claud she's in danger of failing unless she improves spelling and vocabulary (#63-p.5). Stacey tutors her (#63-p.100), as does Shea (#63-p.149); Claudia passes English (#63-pp.31, 33); says she won't mind trying resource room if she needs help again (#63-p.150).

## HOMEWORK:
"Sort of a family rule" that someone has to help her with homework each night (#19-p.24).

## LUNCH:
Never brings lunch to school, also refuses to buy the "revolt-o" hot

lunch; usually eats a sandwich (#12-p.45).

**SKILLS AND ABILITIES:**
Learns how to use computer (#71-p.60).

# SOCIAL ACTIVITIES:

**DANCES:**
Goes to **Final Fling** (#6-p.34) and **Remember September** dance (#10-p.88) and **Halloween Hop** (#17-p.82) with Austin Bentley. Goes to **Halloween Hop** with Woody Jefferson (#38-p.130). Goes to **Valentine Dance** with friend (#51-p.22). Goes to **Spring Dance** at Community Center with Austin Bentley (#63-p.146). Dances fox-trot with Shea Rodowsky at **Spring Dance** at Community Center (#63-p.149). Goes to **Spring Dance** at school with Austin Bentley (#65-p.124). Goes to **Winter Wonderland Dance** with friend Iri Mitsuhashi (SS#7-p.14). Dresses as giant Twinkie for **Mischief Night Masquerade** (M#22-p.135).

**FRIENDS:**
Stacey is only best friend she's had (#13-p.22). Seems older than Kristy and Mary Anne (#1-p.8). Has argument with Stacey about tutoring (#63-p.94); Stacey ends up reading Claudia's personal journal that slanders Stacey, instead of reading journal intended for tutoring sessions (#63-p.130); she and Stacey apologize (#63-p.141). Goes to Fire Island

with Stacey; becomes mad at her for lying about Robert and for ditching her to spend time with him (#76-p.98). They make up (#76-p.158).

**BOYS/BOYFRIENDS:**
**Trevor Sandbourne** is her sort-of boyfriend (#3-p.80). **Timothy Carmody** is her cruise secret admirer (SS#1-p.120); kisses her (SS#1-p.211). Wants to impress **Terry**, in California; they go on a date to Italian restaurant and Claudia acts "intellectual" (SS#5-p.66); in the end, learns she can just be herself. Thinks she's in love with him (SS#5-p.234) but geography tears them apart (SS#5-p.252). Thinks **Arthur Feingold** has gorgeous hair (#50-p.33). Thinks **Ron Belkis** (seventh-grader) is cute (#51-p.39). Goes on date at Rosebud Cafe with **Brian Hall**, who she met through Personals (he was "Good Listener"); the date doesn't pan out though; he's rather dull and unartistic (#71-p.100). Goes on date with **Richard Brompton** ("Rock" in his personal ad); he spends whole time quizzing her on Japanese culture and showing her his tattoo; he does not get a kiss good night (#71-p.128). Has third ill-fated Personals date with **Kurt**, who is boring (#71-p.137).

**IDEA OF THE PERFECT BOY:**
Doesn't care if he's Japanese-American (#71-p.3); must be funny, handsome and taller than her, athletic, sensitive, easy to talk to, a good lis-

tener, artistic, a good dresser; must have muscles (not too many and not too few) (#71-p.6). Must be a good speller, uncritical, and crazy about her (#71-p.8). No tattoos (#71-p.129).

**ART:**

Has studied in school at the Stoneybrook Arts Center and in NYC, where art teacher was McKenzie Clarke (#49-p.123). Makes pot on vacation, begins pottery classes (#8-p.135). Mrs. Baehr is pottery teacher (#43-p.57). Taking two art classes (#12-p.20), one on Wednesday afternoon (#16-p.20); Mrs. Baehr enters her piece as work-in-progress in show sponsored by new gallery (#12-p.135); wins honorable mention, would have won first prize if finished (#12-p.139). Begins giving art classes with Mary Anne on Saturday morning (#26-p.35). Volunteers for a month to help teach art class with Mr. Renfrew at Community Center for seven-year-olds (#48-pp.39, 80). Andy Warhol's paintings of Campbell's soup cans and Del Monte peaches inspire her to paint a series of pop art pieces, all of junk food (#49-p.7). Has her first art show of junk food paintings (Claudia Lynn Kishi's Disposable Comestibles, A Pop-Art Multi-Media Extravaganza) in Kishis' garage (#49-pp.128, 129). Is making mobiles, also doing a still-life painting, a charcoal sketch, jewelry with beads, sequins, and lace (#56-p.9). Makes clip-on earrings for Mary Anne (#58-p.15). Always makes her own valentines and Christmas cards (#73-p.13). Has her photos of sand castles shown at the Beach Glass Gallery in Davis Park; they receive a "wonderful response" (#76-p.150); three of them are sold, at twenty dollars a piece (#76-p.158). Uses her father's old Minolta to shoot photographs (M#16-p.2). Knows how to develop own film (M#16-p.98). Takes classes at the Fine Arts League of New York (SS#6-p.2). When Claudia is deep in the throes of creativity, she's not great company—she's more or less in her own world (#99-p.36).

**NON-BSC TRAVEL:**

She and Janine have never been to Japan (#33-p.4). Goes to Vermont in the mountains at the beginning of summer vacation (#34-p.12). Owns her own skis (SM#2-p.125).

**MISCELLANEOUS:**

For years thought the famous singer's name was Elbow Presley (#25-p.117). If she could be any animal, she'd be a wildly colored jungle parrot (M#11-p.13). Made an honorary trustee of the Stoneybrook Museum after finding coin thieves; gets her picture in the *Stoneybrook News*; Mr. Snipes wants her to set up an exhibit of local student work (M#11-p.133). Insists that brown M&M's taste best (M#13-p.92). Has never seen an R-rated movie (SS#1-p.128). Is pretty sure that parents want her to marry someone Japanese and have Japanese children (SS#2-p.166). Charm bracelet contains Hershey's Kiss, little crayon, silver crane, and book charms (M#21-p.1-3). Subscribes to the "Kishi Scientific Ener-joy Theory," which states that if you eat what you like, you become happy, and the energy from your joy burns off calories (#92-p.19).

# STACEY (ANASTASIA) ELIZABETH McGILL

•

**BIRTHDAY:**
April 3, born at 2:22 A.M.

**AGE:**
Thirteen (#6-p.24 on)

**NARRATOR OF BOOKS:**
#3, #8, #13, #18, #28, #35, #43, #51, #58, #65, #70, #76, #83, #87, #94, #99, M#1, M#10, M#14, M#22, *Stacey's Book*

**BSC POSITION:**
Treasurer (#1-p.43)

**CURRENT ADDRESS:**
89 Elm Street, Stoneybrook, CT 06800 (SS#5 -p.101)

**BIRTHSTONE:**
Diamond (M#1-p.7)

## PERSONAL INFO:

**PHYSICAL DESCRIPTION:**
Very pretty, tall, and quite thin with huge blue eyes framed by dark lashes and fluffy blonde hair that's been permed (#1-p.32); dresses like a model (#4-p.6). Has diabetes (see *Medical*). Has hair cut to just above shoulders, looks older (#7-p.13). Wears hair pretty much the same each day (#43-p.12). After she dresses up for fancy dinner, father says she looks like her mother (#58-p.96). *Clothing/style:* Wears nail polish (M#3-p.17). Has both ears pierced (#58-p.14). Has great pulled-together-looking outfits but doesn't wear same clothes all the time, likes to experiment with new looks (#63-p.19). Can put small braids in her hair, with Claudia's help for the back (M#2-p.41). Reading on a bus usually gives her a headache (SS#2-p.10).

**PERSONALITY TRAITS:**
Sophisticated, smart, outgoing, very grown-up, sensitive (#11-p.16). Not a morning person (#76-p.47). Is part workaholic (like her father) and part laid back (like her mother) (SB-p.2). Likes to dress nicely and look good (SB-p.3). Not afraid of scary movies or ghost stories (M#18-p.52). Nonconfrontational, like her father; would rather side-

step an issue than fight about it (#99-p.96).

**FAMILY:**
*Parents:* Maureen McGill and Edward McGill, divorced: Stacey lives with mother in Stoneybrook on Elm Street and father lives in NYC (#28-p.101). No sisters or brothers (parents couldn't have any more children (#3-p.19). Dad has awful baby name for her, "Boontsie" (#43-p.31). *Divorce:* Stacey informs her mother that she will not be caught in the middle of her parents' problems any more (#43-p.137). Has feelings of resentment over their divorce (#58-p.81); wishes they were still happily married (#58-p.82). Dad sends alimony and child care payments regularly (#65-p.4). It "makes sense" to Stacey that her parents would be divorced (SB-p.2). *Other:* Of Scottish-American and French-American descent (#13-p.7).

**CHILDHOOD EXPERIENCES:**
Born in Mt. Sinai Hospital in NYC with a smile on her face (SB-p.13). First steps at ten months (SB-p.14). Started talking before the age of two (SB-p.17). Moved from Greenwich Village at age of three (SB-p.18). Grew up in NYC on Upper West Side (#3-p.19), lived in tenth-floor apartment (#13-p.14), had own bedroom with windows that looked out onto Central Park (#3-p.19). Had many nightmares

around the age of four (SB-p.22). Was taken to the Plaza for her fourth birthday (SB-p.23). At five, was on Cinderella's float in Macy's Parade (SB-p.39). Knew how to navigate the subways by the age of ten and bought all her own clothes by the age of twelve (M#18-p.6). Parents took her to psychotherapist before diabetes was diagnosed (#3-p.17). Had to give up soccer tryouts (SS#11-p.65).

**MOVING EXPERIENCES:**
First moved to Stoneybrook in August before seventh grade (#2-p.12) to 612 Fawcett Avenue (#1-p.29) because parents were protective, thought she needed a "peaceful little town" because of her diabetes (#1-p.151). She and her parents moved back to NYC to 14 West 81st St., Apt. 12E (SS#2-p.3) when father was transferred (#13-p.13); phone there: JK5-8761 (#13-p.139). After parents split up, she and mother moved back to Stoneybrook (89 Elm Street) and father moved to East 65th St. in NYC. Has been in hospital quite a few times (#19-p.50), once missed a whole month of school (#19-p.108). Goobaw, an old teddy bear that's missing one eye and most of his fur and is rubbed bare, has always been a comfort to her (#35-p.29). Amelia Jane was ratty ten-year-old doll Stacey once loved (#13-p.108) that is sold to Jenny Prezzioso at yard sale (#13-p.109).

## ROOM:

Has pig collection in room (#51-p.34). Posters of New York at night, Empire State Building, and map of Manhattan on walls of room (#4-p.21). Curtains are lace; bed is brass with a blue satin quilt. Also has secondhand bureau that Stacey and her mom painted white, a desk, and a flower-patterned rug (SB-p.1). Hangs framed painting of counterfeit "Stacey" bill by Claudia over her bed; it's a large red, white, and blue bill, with a great sketch of her in the middle (M#10-p.161).

## LIKES:

Loves numbers and is great at math (#19-p.18). Favorite movie: *Mary Poppins*; has seen it 65 times (#6-p.96). Bloomingdale's is favorite store (#13-p.25) but now finds it always crowded and too hot (#18-p.38). Likes snow (#51-p.1). Loves pigs (#51-p.34). Joyce is her favorite hair stylist at the salon in Washington Mall (#60-p.43). Likes to do "city things" like going to museums and plays, or just walking on crowded streets (SB-p.3). Sometimes likes to clean house (M#1-p.1). Favorite breakfast is blueberry pancakes (M#1-p.1). Loves to sleep late (M#1-p.52). Loves to shop (M#10-p.2). Loves the Marx Brothers (#91-p.7).

## DISLIKES:

Doesn't like doctors and her strict diets (#11-p.16). Can't stand to see people barf (#18-p.106). Not a huge pet lover (although she does like Carrot) (M#22-p.111). Hates to iron (#34-p.75).

## JOBS:

Works at Kid Center at Bellair's for summer (#87-p.49).

## MEDICAL:

*Diabetes:* reveals to club she is a diabetic (#1-p.150); is a brittle diabetic (severe form), gives herself insulin shots every day (#43-p.2) and stays on strict diet. Must test her blood to see if she needs insulin (#43-p.3); diabetes definition: pancreas doesn't make enough insulin, so blood sugar is uncontrollable (#62-p.17). Can't eat desserts and sweets but can eat fruit (#51-p.9). Doesn't want to be treated any differently because she is sick (#94-p.76).

*Diabetes-related incidents:* BSC friends thought she was anorexic when they first met her (#61-p.68). In NYC, had fainted and gone into insulin shock at school; also wet bed, went to therapist (#3-p.21). Wets bed at sleepover at Laine's (SS#11-p.58), which is tip-off to diabetes diagnosis. Has been hospitalized because of it, once missed a whole month of school (#19-p.108). Dr. Frank is Stacey's specialist in Stoneybrook (#3-p.27). After bingeing on chocolate for a week, becomes tired, very thirsty (#43-p.53); while visiting Dad in NYC, blood sugar gets very high and she is hospitalized (#43-p.62). Doctors change insulin because her body is changing; she feels better (#43-p.110). Volunteers for a month at a diabetes clinic talking to kids with diabetes (#48-pp.38-39). Talks to Dana Cheplin about her diabetes (#94-p.76).

## BABY-SITTING AND CLUB EXPERIENCES:

### GENERAL:
Can baby-sit until ten on weekends, nine-thirty on weeknights (#4-p.56). Not usually allowed to sit on both the afternoon and the evening of a school day (#3-p.115). Gives babysitting tip: never count on being able to do homework at a job (#61-p.74).

### CLIENTS:
She and Charlotte Johanssen are very close (#65-p.26); call themselves "almost sisters." Henry and Grace Walker are her favorite NYC clients (#28-p.2). First baby-sitting job is for Alice O'Connell on Pine Island while Mr. McGill is taken to hospital (SB-p.125). Never stopped sitting for Charlotte, even when she wasn't in BSC (M#21-p.7).

### HISTORY:
Used to put up signs in laundry room of NYC apartment in order to get sitting jobs (#1-p.33). First club job was to baby-sit for David Michael (#1-p.58). Is first BSC member to baby-sit for the Gianellis (#52-p.71). Quits/is fired from club (#83); is let back in on probation (#87-p.138).

## SCHOOL-RELATED EXPERIENCES:

### CLASSES/ATTENDANCE:
In eighth grade (#10 on). Great at math (#19-p.18). Has Ms. Gonzalez for science class, but not at the same time as Dawn; not too good at science (#57-p.9, 29). Once missed a whole month of school while in hospital (#19-p.108). Is in high school level math class upon return to Stoneybrook (#28-p.138). Has Mr. Zizmore for math; current unit is pre-algebra (#58-p.42). Math is last class of day (#65-p.8). Has crush on Wes Ellenburg, the student teacher who takes over Zizmore's last month of math class (#65-p.42); has highest average in math class during Wes's student teaching (#65-p.84). Ms. Levine is homeroom teacher (#70-p.10). Doesn't like gym class in the middle of the day because it leaves her all sweaty and gross (#70-p.71). Mr. Fiske is English teacher (M#10-p.130). Takes Math for Real Life class with Mr. Schubert (M#14-p.1). Takes project work class with Mr. Withum, the last class of the day (M#14-p.9). Ms. Bernhardt is her social studies teacher; she is in Abby's class (#97-p.12).

### EXTRACURRICULAR ACTIVITIES:
Auditions to be a cheerleader (#70-p.111) but doesn't make the squad (#70-p.130). Plays Mrs. Darling in *Peter Pan* (SS#9). On the decorations committee for the Mischief Night Masquerade (M#22-p.23).

#### GETTING TO SCHOOL:
She and Mal use code on school mornings: white towel on Mal's patio means she wants to walk to school with Mary Anne, Dawn, and Stacey; red towel means Mal has to walk her brothers and sisters to school (#51-p.53).

#### GRADES:
Mr. Zizmore says she's his star student (#65-p.6).

#### SKILLS AND ABILITIES:
Learning how to use computer (#71-p.60). Knows how to do a slip stitch (M#4-42).

## SOCIAL ACTIVITIES:

#### DANCES:
Goes to **Snowflake Dance** (#3-p.166) and several other dances (#6-p.33) with Pete Black. Goes with Howie Johnson to **Remember September** dance (#10-p.88) and a few other dances (#13-p.3); attended dance committee meetings (#10-p.21). Goes to **Halloween Hop** with Kelsey Bauman (#38-p.130). Goes on double date with Austin Bentley, Laine Cummings, and Pete Black to **Valentine Dance** (#51-p.101). She and Laine argue, leave dance early (#51-pp.109-116). Is going to **Winter Wonderland Dance** with Austin Bentley (SS#7-p.45). Goes to dance at **Shadow Lake** with Sam (SS#8-p.208). Goes to **January Jamboree** with Sam Thomas (#60-p.132). Goes to **Spring Dance** at Community Center with Sam Thomas (#63-p.115). Goes to **Spring Dance** at school dateless (#65-p.124). Dances at **Leicester Lodge Dance** with Pierre D'Amboise (SS#3-p.222). Dresses as Morticia Addams for **Mischief Night Masquerade**; goes with Robert Brewster, who dresses as Gomez Addams (M#22-p.135).

#### FRIENDS:
Claudia is best friend in Stoneybrook; she and Claud met first day of school of seventh grade when Claud stepped on her notebook and they were dressed similarly (#13-p.31). Introduced to Kristy and Mary Anne (#1-p.32). Laine Cummings was best friend in NYC (#43-p.11) until she and Laine have fight when Laine spends winter vacation in Stoneybrook; now Laine is her ex-best friend (#51-p.135). Dawn drives her crazy with Save the Planet class and science project—too preachy (#57-p.91); Dawn apologizes, they reconcile (#57-p.129-130). Has argument with Claud about tutoring (#63-p.94); Stacey ends up reading Claudia's personal journal, which slanders Stacey, instead of reading journal intended for tutoring sessions (#63-p.130). She and Erica Blumberg had always been friendly (#65-p.83). Takes Claudia to Fire Island, doesn't tell her about Robert; Claudia stops speaking to her, has a miserable time (#76-p.98). Soon, though, they're back together (#76-p.159).

# ● The BSC Members ●

**BOYS/BOYFRIENDS**

*Robert Brewster:* Goes on coffee shop date with Robert (#70-p.80) and he later quits the basketball team because he shares her dissatisfaction with SMS sports program. Robert is steady boyfriend (#76-p.2); she meets him secretly on Fire Island, then is found out by her father. After Robert sees that she's lied to her father and to Claudia, he doesn't want to having anything more to do with her; she's heartbroken (#76-p.148). Soon, though, they're back together (#76-p.154). They usually go out on one date a week, Friday or Saturday night (M#18-p.23). He calls her Toots after she tells him that was what her neighborhood grocer in NYC called her (#87-p.2). Mrs. McGill's rule is that Robert can be over when adults aren't around, as long as he and Stacey stay in the kitchen (#94-p.3). Stacey learns that Robert has been seeing/kissing Andi Gentile (#99-pp.113–114) and breaks up with him (#99-p.148).

*Sam Thomas:* Likes Sam Thomas (Kristy's brother) (#1-p.85); they date sometimes (#58-p.6). Initially get together at Shadow Lake (SS#8-p.208). Goes to January Jamboree with him (#60-p.132). She and Sam like each other a lot but have drifted apart recently (#65-p.11). Lies to Sam, says she already has a date for the Spring Dance (#65-p.93). She and Sam decide to see other people as well as each other (M#10-p.8). She sees him with Kathy while she's with Terry (M#10-p.101). He calls to say he still likes her; she still likes him; they plan a date (M#10-p.164). Sam still likes Stacey, but he thinks of her as a friend, someone who is fun to goof with; likes to flirt with her—it keeps him in practice for his next girlfriend (SM#2-p.185).

*Toby:* First kiss in the Tunnel of Luv at Sea City with Toby (#8-p.121). Toby wins bear for her and gives her shell; they promise to write to each other (#8-p.126). Meets Toby again at Sea City while sitting for the Pike kids with Mary Anne (#34-p.68); goes out with him, then he dumps her (#34-p.116).

*Wes Ellenburg:* Has huge crush on Wes Ellenburg, student teacher for Mr. Zizmore; gives him poem (#65-pp.94, 97); tells him she loves him (#65-p.108); dances with him at Spring Dance (#65-p.127); he tells her age difference is too big—they'll be just friends (#65-p.132).

*Others:* **Pete Black** is her sort-of boyfriend; they sit together at lunch and talk on phone (#3-p.25). Then he falls for Dorianne (#6-p.33). Stacey has crush on **Ross Brown**, he likes her, too (#43-p.105). **Pierre D'Amboise** is world's cutest guy; they meet after she tailgates him on skis at Leicester Lodge (SS#3-p.83). He becomes her "first meaningful crush" (SS#3-p.86). They kiss (SS#3-p.95), they dance, they exchange addresses (SS#3-p.224). **Terry Hoyt** is cute (M#10-p.9). They go out on date (M#10-from p.94), bump into Sam and Kathy (M#10-p.101). Terry

kisses her good night (M#10-p.105).
She's sad when he says he must
move away to be with his father;
there's no way for them to keep in
touch; they kiss again (M#10-p.159).
**RJ Blaser** asks her out to movie (#70-
p.5); they don't have much in common, although Stacey does get to
bask in the glow of his popularity
(#70-p.35). Gets number from **Ethan**,
cute fifteen-year-old artists' helper
to the Walkers, in NYC (#99-p.142).

**NON-BSC TRAVEL:**
Trip to Sea City was first time she
was away from parents since she

got diabetes two years ago (#8-
p.17). When she was seven, the
McGills went to a dude ranch.
Eight: went with the Cummingses
to San Francisco. Nine: Ireland and
Scotland. Ten: Pine Island, ME. Also
went to St. Thomas Resort (SB-p.94).

**MISCELLANEOUS:**
If she could be any animal, she'd be
a lion or a panther (M#11-p.13).
Wants to save up money so she can
buy a red convertible sports car
when she's old enough to drive
(#94-p.81). Once dyed her hair red
(CL-p.8).

# MARY ANNE SPIER

•

**BIRTHDAY:**
September 22

**AGE:**
Thirteen (#10-p.139 on)

**NARRATOR OF BOOKS:**
#4, #10, #17, #25, #30, #34, #41, #46, #52, #60, #66, #73, #79, #86, #93, M#5, M#13, M#20, M#24, *Mary Anne's Book*

**BSC POSITION:**
Secretary

**CURRENT ADDRESS:**
177 Burnt Hill Road, Stoneybrook, CT 06800, phone: 555-8456 (#71-p.105)

**PERSONAL INFO:**

**PHYSICAL DESCRIPTION:**
Five feet and a half-inch tall. Petite, neat, and precise, brown eyes (#14-p.23); ears not pierced (#21-p.7). Second shortest to Kristy in eighth grade (#17-p.4). Used to wear her mousy brown (#2-p.15) wavy (#10-p.39) hair in braids, per father's instructions (#1-p.5). Was finally allowed to let hair down sometimes (#4-p.140). Gets hair cut short by Joyce from salon in Washington Mall, loves the new style (#60-pp.43, 46). Wears wire-rimmed glasses (#3-p.9) for reading (#51-p.15). *Clothing/style:* Now wears makeup (blush, eyeliner, lipstick), which her dad allowed her to buy during her makeover (#60-p.48). Has some jewelry but used to wear no makeup (#10-p.39). Dresses "sort of conservatively" (#66-p.6); wears clip-on earrings (#52-p.14); gets a bra (#10-p.27). Taking more of an interest in clothes (#15-p.5). Never tans, must cover herself completely when at beach to avoid burning (#34-pp.16, 41). Look is "neat preppy casual" (#79-p.3). Always wears little "Mary Anne" necklace around her neck (M#5-p.36). Looks and behaves like her mother (M#5-p.107).

**PERSONALITY TRAITS:**
Quiet, shy (#1-p.4). Not self-assured (#17-p.9). Cries easily and often (#13-p.30); Logan sometimes calls

her the "Town Crier" (#98-p.26). Whisper the words "Old Yeller" to her and her eyes well up (#100-p.3). Perceptive and honest, sees the best in people (#62-p.18). Can be as stubborn as she is shy (#62-p.43). Well-organized, has the neatest handwriting in club (#7-p.7). Looks and acts younger than Claudia and Stacey (#2-p.15). She's the youngest of the five older club members (#10-p.14). Usually stays calm in emergencies (#18-p.95). Can sound schoolteacherish, wants to be a teacher (#7-p.116). Tries to put others first, then learns how to balance others' needs with her own (#66-pp.8,154). Gets spooked if you say "boo" to her in broad daylight (M#18-p.52). Saves letters and other sentimental things in cedar box her grandmother gave her (SS#11-p.117). Finds it hard to study with music playing (#31-p.100). Doesn't get angry very often, but when she does, she's an expert with the silent treatment (#31-p.118). The thought of dancing in front of people paralyzes her (#93-p.2). Wishes she were more outgoing (#93-p.9).

**FAMILY:**

*Parents/Stepparents:* Mother, Alma Baker Spier, died when Mary Anne was a baby (#27-p.15); Mary Anne barely remembers her mother (#10-p.6); Richard Spier is strict (#1-p.5) and a neatnik (#30-p.78); has rule that phone conversations be limited to ten minutes (#10-p.105). Richard Spier marries Dawn's mother, Sharon Schafer (#30-p.145), who used to be his Stoneybrook High sweetheart (#31-p.3); Mary Anne and her dad move into Schafers' house because it's bigger than the Spiers (#31-p.7). Calls Dawn's mom "Sharon" (#31-p.3). *Pet:* Gets a gray tiger-striped kitten from the Stoneybrook Animal Shelter named Tigger after the tiger in *Winnie the Pooh* (#10-p.129). Tigger sleeps with her every night in the same spot (#31-p.63); has zillion aliases, like Mousekin (#64-p.8). Visits **grandmother**, Verna Baker, in Maynard, Iowa (M#5-from p.126), after learning she had lived with grandparents for eighteen months after her mother's death. *Other:* Family makes chore chart, dinner schedule, and promises to be more honest with each other to ease adjustment of moving in together (#31-pp.140-142). Always wanted a sister, especially a twin (#5-p.36; #30-p.68). She and Dawn want their parents to have another baby (#52-p.40); later decide that another baby would be too rough on their parents; also don't want another pet (#52-p.136).

**CHILDHOOD EXPERIENCES:**

Had lived at Bradford Court since she was born (#1-p.7). Mother dies shortly after her birth. Spent first birthday with maternal grandparents, the Bakers, after her mother died (M#5-p.61); stays with them until she is eighteen months old

(M#5-p.62). Mr. Spier and the Bakers have a custody fight, which is resolved without much fuss or bitterness (M#5-p.106). Mrs. Frederickson was first-grade teacher (MAB-p.22); Mrs. Jeffries was second-grade teacher (MAB-p.58); Ms. Ellison was fourth-grade teacher (MAB-p.88). Had never been away from home until trip with Pikes and Stacey (#8-p.12). Father used to only let her talk on the phone if it was about homework, and made her come straight home from school (#81-p.17). Has an antique doll named Lila and a white teddy bear named Snowman.

### ROOM:

Room was decorated in pink and white and looked like a nursery (#4-p.20); had pink-framed pictures of family, Alice in Wonderland, and Humpty Dumpty (#4-p.21) until Kristy and Dawn helped her redecorate room; takes off babyish stuff and puts up posters and photographs, stencils picture frames (#5-pp.31-32).

### LIKES:

Likes yellow and navy blue (#4-p.20). Likes movie stars, animals (#11-p.15), especially Tigger, who keeps her company when she's lonely (#10- p.125). Cam Geary is her favorite star (TV) (#31-p.47). Likes Cam Geary's singing (#50-p.32). *Pollyanna* is her favorite Hayley Mills film (#30-p.5). *Little Women*

is one of her favorite books (#17-p.28). Has read *Wuthering Heights* three times, *To Kill a Mockingbird* many times (#41-p.36). Adores books by Megan Rhinehart (#46-p.43), has read all of them (#46-p.61). Checking mailbox is sometimes highlight of her day (#17-p.12), getting mail is her favorite thing (#25-p.11). Likes sewing and knitting (#31-p.14). Likes Schafers' old house (#13-p.39). Has a crush on NYC, her dream is to live there some day (#18-p.12). On his wedding day, Richard gives Mary Anne a pearl necklace that belonged to her mother (#30-p.140). Loves old movies, rock and roll, and the latest TV shows (M#13-p.1).

### DISLIKES:

Hates crowds, being the center of attention (#11-p.15). One of her biggest fears is confronting and dealing with people she doesn't know (#4-p.103). Hates sports (#26-p.10). Hates the color pink (#4-p.20). Does not like how Sharon cleans house (#31-p.142). She and Kristy hate bagpipes (#45-p.119). Doesn't like to dance; walks around and talks to people during dances (#51-p.76). Not the type of person who likes to camp out (SS#10-p.93). Hates cooking (MAB-p.145).

### JOBS:

Says she'll volunteer at the children's room in the public library every once in a while (M#13-p.137).

**MEDICAL:**

Badly sprains ankle in biking accident (#86-p.100).

## BABY-SITTING AND CLUB EXPERIENCES:

### GENERAL:

Can stay out until nine-thirty weeknights, ten on weekends (#4-p.154). Has never made a baby-sitting scheduling mistake (#21-p.140; #34-p.6; #61-p.23).

### CLIENTS:

Loves to sit for the Perkins kids (#22-p.52). Baby-sits for kids at the next farm over when in Maynard (M#5-p.130).

### HISTORY:

First club job is to baby-sit for the Brewers (#1-p.88). Scariest baby-sitting experience when Jenny Prezzioso gets fever of 104 and ambulance takes her to hospital (#4-p.121). Volunteers for a month as part of Jessi's idea for club to do community service; helps with her parents' friends' son who has brain damage (Frankie) (#48-p.40). Becomes BSCO (BSC Outcast) after Logan is discovered baby-sitting with her at the Kuhns' (#79-p.95).

## SCHOOL-RELATED EXPERIENCES:

### CLASSES/ATTENDANCE:

In eighth grade (#10 on). School locker #132, homeroom 216, about as far from locker as you can get (#10-p.15). Mr. Blake is Dawn and Mary Anne's homeroom teacher, room #216 (#10-p.15). Kristy is in her eighth-grade social studies class (#10-p.17). Can't stand home ec. class; is in danger of failing (M#4-p.9). Wins Most Improved Home Ec. Student Award (M#4-p.130) Ms. Frost is her math teacher (M#13-p.110). Classes are in this order: English, math, gym, social studies, lunch, science, study hall, and French (#10-p.16). Locker combination is 33 right—21 left—36 right (#93-p.12). Mrs. Simon is her English teacher (#93-p.17), as is Mrs. Belcher (for a different semester) (MAB-p.151).

### EXTRACURRICULAR ACTIVITIES:

Takes sewing lessons on Saturday afternoons in exchange for doing chores with Mrs. Towne (#66-p.46).

### GETTING TO SCHOOL:

Being on time to school is important to her (M#24-p.1). Walks (#51-p.53).

### GRADES:

Had a little trouble in English and panicked (CL-p.20).

### LUNCH:

Brings lunch to school: peanut butter and jelly sandwich, apple, Doritos, box of fruit juice (#5-p.34); doesn't bring lunch to school anymore because she and Kristy decided it looks too babyish for eighth grade (#10-p.17).

## SOCIAL ACTIVITIES:

### DANCES:

Goes with Logan: to **Remember September** dance , dances with him and loses her shoe, gets so embarrassed she can't dance for the rest of the night (#10-pp.90-92); to **Fifties Fling** (#10-p.130); to **Halloween Hop**, dressed as cats (#17-p.84). Tells him she's too shy to dance (#51-pp.76-77); goes to **Valentine Dance** and he doesn't pressure her to dance (#51-p.105). Also with Logan, goes to: **January Jamboree** (he wears a tux) (#60-p.132), **Spring Dance** at Community Center (#63-p.114), **Spring Dance** at school with Logan (#65-p.124). Dresses as Dorothy for **Mischief Night Masquerade** (M#22-p.134).

### FRIENDS:

Kristy is best friend (#1-p.4), grew up together on Bradford Court (#4-p.1). Meets Dawn on her second day of school at SMS, two weeks after she moved from CA (#4-p.31). Dawn is other "new" best friend (#5-p.5). Kristy was jealous of Mary Anne and Dawn's friendship at first (#5-p.36). After Dawn moves to California, she writes Mary Anne constantly, and they talk on the phone a lot (#93-p.5).

### BOYS/BOYFRIEND:

*Logan Bruno:* First meets Logan during lunch first month of eighth grade (#10-p.36). Feels like she

could be in love with Logan (#10-p.117). First date is the Remember September Dance (#10-p.75).Never had a boy in her bedroom. Father demanded Mary Anne and Logan meet at the party (and dance) instead of Logan coming to her house (#10-p.108). Feels like Logan is taking over her life (#41-p.61). He gives her bracelet with tiny gold hearts linked together (#41-p.108); Mary Anne gives it back to him and breaks up, wants to be independent (#41-p.137). She and Logan are good friends (#42-p.43). She starts dating him again, their boyfriend-girlfriend relationship resumes; he now gives her "space" (#46-p.138). Logan loves her new look, new haircut (#60-p.62). "Tigger" is one of his nicknames for her (#71-p.105).

*Other Boys:* Exchanges rings with **Alex** at Sea City; wears it on chain around neck (#8-p.134). He was first boy she was interested in, sees him again when sitting for Pikes (#34-p.67); he gives her big purple hippopotamus (#34-p.96); she thinks she's falling in love with him, but she's loyal to Logan; Alex has girlfriend back home, so they end vacation as "friends forever" (#34-p.122). Goes out with boy named **Bob** in Maynard, Iowa; is the grandson of one of her grandmother's friends; he's very cute, but they don't have much in common (M#5-p.132). BSC members spreading rumors about a boy named

Chris from SHS who supposedly likes her (#60-p.78). Another rumor is that **Carlos Mendez** invited Mary Anne to the Winter Dance at SHS (#60-p.88).

she was four (#17-p.23). If she could be any animal, she'd be a koala (M#11-p.15). Wants to live in NYC as an adult (#1-p.33).

**MISCELLANEOUS:**
After getting chain letter she falls out of her bed for the first time since

# DAWN READ SCHAFER

•

**BIRTHDAY:**
February 5

**AGE:**
Thirteen (#9-p.12 on)

**NARRATOR OF BOOKS:**
#5, #9, #15, #23, #31, #37, #44, #50, #57, #64, #67, #72, #77, #84, #88, #98, M#2, M#7, M#12, M#17, *Dawn's Book*

**BSC POSITION:**
Honorary member (#88 on); was alternate officer of the club (#5-p.73).

**CURRENT ADDRESS:**
22 Buena Vista, Palo City, CA 92800

**CURRENT SUMMER ADDRESS:**
177 Burnt Hill Rd., Stoneybrook, CT 06800

## PERSONAL INFO:

**PHYSICAL DESCRIPTION:**
Tall, five feet, five inches; pale blonde hair, almost white, hanging straight and silky to her rear end; pale blue eyes (#4-p.31). Gets freckles if she stays out in sun too long (#15-p.6). On thin side (#30-p.19). *Clothing/style:* Gets ears pierced, two holes in each (#21-p.132). Dresses how she feels (#11-p.17), a unique style the BSC calls "California casual" (#54-p.16); likes to look trendy but be comfortable (#58-p.16). The only kid in school who could get away with wearing clogs (#21-p.60). Looks best in summer colors (blue, yellow) (#77-p.37). Wears Thrash's snake ring on a chain around her neck (M#12-p.145).

**PERSONALITY TRAITS:**
Sensitive but says what she thinks (#62-p.20). Confident, an individual (#11-p.17). Very neat (#29-p.97); has clean room (#9-p.12). Rarely gets angry; sometimes pouts or feels cross, but doesn't often scold. Doesn't eat meat (#66-p.5). Not afraid to take a stand (#66-p.5). Believes in psychic experiences and ESP (#67-p.47). Can't read maps too well; can barely tell left from right (SS#2-p.179).

**FAMILY:**

*Parents/Stepparents:* Mother and father, Sharon and Jack Schafer, divorced (#4-p.44). Father lives near Anaheim, California (#23-p.35), in Palo City. Father started calling her "Sunshine" when she was little and the name stuck (#23-p.2). Sharon marries Mary Anne's father, Richard Spier (#30-p.145), who used to be her Stoneybrook High School sweetheart (#31-p.3); Mary Anne and her dad move into Schafers' house because it's bigger than the Spiers' (#31-p.7). Dawn calls Mary Anne's dad "Richard" (#31-p.3). Mr. Schafer announces engagement to Carol Olson; Dawn is upset (#72-p.72) and runs back to Stoneybrook (#72-p.87). Carol and Mr. Schafer call off their engagement after fighting (#72-p.134). They get back together later (#77-p.143) and are married (SS#12-p.140). Dawn has grown to like Carol (M#17-p.5). *Grandparents:* Mother's parents still live in Stoneybrook (#5-p.1). *Brother:* Jeff (ten), misses father and goes back to CA to live with him (#15-p.112). *Stepsister:* Dawn gives Mary Anne a silver barrette as new sister gift (#30-p.146); also gives her a pin in shape of a cat as new sister gift (#31-p.136). Mary Anne is upset and mad when Dawn announces she's leaving for CA for good, but they make up in the end (#88-p.125). *Other:* Family makes chore chart, dinner schedule, and promises to be more honest with each other to ease adjustment of moving in together (#31-p.140-142). She and Mary Anne wanted their parents to have a baby (#52-p.40) but change their minds, don't even want another pet (#52-p.136). Spiers and Schafers have family feud during trip to Boston (#64-p.83). Dawn returns to live in CT (#81-p.24). Moves back to CA for good (#88-p.126) but will spend summers in Stoneybrook.

**CHILDHOOD EXPERIENCES:**

Won a baby contest in L.A. when she was two (#15-p.24). Used to have a bird named Buzz who once flew into a bowl of mashed potatoes (M#7-p.25). In California, went to Camp La Brea (SS#2-p.132).

**ROOM:**

*In CT:* Lives in farmhouse built in 1795 (#15-p.6) on Burnt Hill Road, which has barn with secret passage that leads right to her bedroom (#44-p.2). Room has a small, round window near the ceiling; is well lit (#4-p.43). *In CA:* Carol gives her director's chair with the word *Dawn* on the back in the middle of a gold star (#72-p.36).

**LIKES:**

Loved eighty-degree Christmases in CA (#5-p.2). Likes health food, baby-sitting, sunshine, ghost stories (#11-p.17); favorite collection of ghost stories is *Spirits, Spooks, and Ghastly Tales* (#23-p.24). Loves Hayley Mills; favorite film is *The Parent*

*Trap* (#30-p.5). Loves getting phone calls (#30-p.8). Only member of club who likes green peppers (#26-p.75). Likes brown rice and tofu (#46-p.10). Favorite restaurant is Cabbages and Kings (#50-p.147). Loves tofu and vegetable curry, and seaweed salad (M#7-p.58). Making food is one of her favorite hobbies (#81-p.39). Honey granola snaps are one of Dawn's favorite cookies (#93-p.8).

**DISLIKES:**

Hates cold weather (#5-p.2); doesn't mind it when snow is falling (#50-p.41). Hates red meat (#19-p.8) and junk food (M#17-p.2). Doesn't eat sugar (#46-p.10). Hates it when Richard switches lights on and off to wake her up (#64-p.77), hates waking up early (#64-p.78). Hates good-byes (#34-p.21).

**BABY-SITTING AND CLUB EXPERIENCES:**

**GENERAL:**

*In Stoneybrook:* Has to be home by nine on weeknights, ten on weekends, unless she is baby-sitting late (#67-p.57); doesn't allow kids to "play guns." Must leave her house by 5:24 P.M. in order to make it to meeting on time (#70-p.55).

**CLIENTS:**

*In Stoneybrook:* Sits for Barretts often, they live nearby (#58-p.36). Her favorite client at Baker Institute is Kendra, who has cerebral palsy

(#48-p.103); is first BSC member to sit for Norman and Sara Hill (#50-p.41). She and rest of club members help Norman begin to tackle his weight problem (#50-p.157). Used to think the Barrett kids were the Impossible Three, now they're some of her favorite charges to sit for (#57-p.19). *In CA:* Whitney Cater gives her half of a Best Friends necklace (#77-p.81).

**HISTORY:**

Used to baby-sit all the time in California; started sitting when she was nine (#4-p.164). Moved to Stoneybrook four months after BSC had started (#18-p.19). Mary Anne introduces Dawn to club members (#4-p.164) and asks her to join club because they have so many clients (#4-p.166). Kristy asks her to become the official alternate officer (#5-p.73). Replaces Stacey as treasurer (#13-p.128) until Stacey returns (#29-p.28). Volunteers for month at Baker Institute in Stamford for physically disabled kids (#48-p.38); teaches after-school ecology class to kids she sits for (#57-p.28). Is interim secretary while Mary Anne is in Iowa (M#5-p.135) and is interim treasurer while Stacey is in NYC (M#8-p.28).

**SCHOOL-RELATED EXPERIENCES:**

**CLASSES/ATTENDANCE:**

In eighth grade (#10 on). *At SMS:* Mr. Blake is her and Mary Anne's homeroom teacher, room #216 (#10-p.15). Shawna Riverson is in Dawn and Mary Anne's homeroom, locker next to Dawn's (#40-p.63). Math is not one of her strengths (#57-p.14). Mrs. Gonzalez is her science teacher (#57-p.1). In modern living class she pretend-marries Aaron Albright, whom she doesn't like; have child-egg named Skip (#52-p.95). *At Vista:* Mr. Swanson is English teacher (#98-p.1).

**EXTRACURRICULAR ACTIVITIES:**
*At SMS:* Teaches Save the Planet class (#57-p.39); Mrs. Gonzalez asks Dawn to co-chair recycling center, which they've organized at SMS (#57-p.143). Plays Wendy in *Peter Pan* (SS#9).

**GETTING TO SCHOOL:**
*In CA:* Walks most days to school with Sunny; routine is for Dawn to pick Sunny up; they try to change the route as often as possible (M#17-p.92).

**LUNCH:**
Always brings her own (SS#9-p.28). Her natural peanut butter with honey and banana sandwiches are wrapped in wax paper—more environmentally safe (#62-p.28).

## SOCIAL ACTIVITIES

**DANCES:**
Goes stag to **Remember September** dance (#10-p.88). Goes to **Halloween Hop** stag (#38-p.130). After going to **Winter Wonderland** dance with Price Irving (SS#7-p.26), she thinks they don't have anything in common (#51-p.40). Goes to **Valentine Dance** with friend (#51-p.22). Goes to **January Jamboree** with Pete Black, their first date together (#60-p.130), wears a black velvet dress with a sheer bodice, hair in a French braid (#60-p.130). Goes to **Spring Dance** at Community Center with Pete Black (#63-p.146). Goes to **Spring Dance** at school alone (#65-p.124).

**FRIENDS:**
Met Mary Anne on her second day of school, fourth day in Connecticut (#5-p.33). Mary Anne is best friend (#5-p.5) and now her stepsister (#30-p.145). Her "old best friend" was Sunny Winslow in California (#5-p.5). Mary Anne introduces Dawn to rest of club members (#4-p.164). Kristy was jealous of Dawn and Mary Anne's friendship at first (#5-p.41), but Kristy and Dawn work it out; Kristy asks Dawn to become the alternate officer of the club (#5-p.73). Drives Stacey crazy by preaching about saving the earth during their science project (#57-p.91); she apologizes, they reconcile (#57-pp.129-130). After Dawn moves to California, she writes Mary Anne constantly, and they talk on the phone a lot (#93-p.5).

**BOYS/BOYFRIENDS:**
Has crush on **Travis** (#37-p.21); he tried to change her too much (#37-

p.122), so she breaks up with him (#37-p.126). Writes **Lewis Bruno** (Logan's cousin) at Mary Anne's suggestion and plans to see him when he visits Stoneybrook (#37-p.136). Wears lots of makeup and dresses more trendily to impress Lewis when he visits in January (#50-p.58), then tones down; double dates with Lewis, Mary Anne, and Logan (#50-p.147). She and Lewis kiss in front of antique shop; she can't imagine ever wanting to kiss anyone else (#50-p.151). She and Lewis continue to write each other, plan to see each other over summer (#50-p.152). Thinks **Dave Griffin** (eighth grader) is cute (#51-p.40). **Parker Harris**, who she meets on cruise, is her first real boyfriend (SS#1-p.96); kisses her on the cheek (SS#1-p.154). Has amazing overnight crush on **Price Irving** (SS#7-p.26) but then thinks they don't have anything in common (#51-p.40).

### DAWN'S THEORY OF SHOPPING:
Rule number one: Never shop with best friends if you have something truly important to buy; rule number two: If you have to buy it during the holiday season, multiply rule number one by ten. (SS#12-p.7).

### ENVIRONMENTAL ISSUES:
Dawn is outspoken about environmental issues (#57-p.1). Carries a string bag wherever she goes (#77-p.34). Always tells take-out places not to pack the food in Styrofoam and not to send plastic forks (#86-p.78).

### MISCELLANEOUS:
Nervous on her first trip to NY (#18-p.28). If she could be any animal, she'd be a dolphin (M#11-p.17). Taking surfing lessons (M#12-p.2), is a grommet (an inexperienced surfer) (M#12-p.86). Has never seen an R-rated movie (SS#1-p.128). A pretty good skier; her father took her to Vail (SS#3-p.104). Always uses chopsticks with Thai food (#72-p.75).

# ABBY (ABIGAIL) STEVENSON

•

**BIRTHDAY:**
October 15

**AGE:**
Thirteen

**NARRATOR OF BOOKS:**
#90, #96, M#23

**BSC POSITION:**
Alternate officer (#89-p.143 on)

**CURRENT ADDRESS:**
1206 McLelland Road, Stoneybrook, CT 06800. Lives two doors down from Kristy, next door to Mrs. Porter (#89-p.7)

## PERSONAL INFO:

**PHYSICAL DESCRIPTION:**
Hair and eyes are deep brown, almost black; has long, thick hair, so curly it is almost in ringlets; wears glasses or contact lenses (#89-p.62). Nearsighted (M#23-p.4). Has a pointy face (#90-p.10). Has asthma (#89-p.63, see *Medical*). Has many allergies (#89-p.67, see *Medical*). Couldn't carry a tune in a bucket (#96-p.1).

**PERSONALITY TRAITS:**
Has a wild sense of humor, which grows on you (#89-p.63). Tends to wander off when she's not the center of attention (#89-p.72). A natural athlete (#89-p.77). Assistant coach of the Krushers (#89-p.132). A good mimic (#89-p.144). Likes to jam to Aretha (#90-p.4). Is into environmental issues (#90-p.49). Jewish (#96-p.5); must learn some Hebrew for becoming a Bat Mitzvah (#96-p.6). Is One Tough Cookie; stands up to Kristy and is as firm in her opinions as Kristy is; loves jokes, especially puns; speaks a little Yiddish (SM#2-p.30). Plays on soccer team; runs miles when not practicing soccer, to keep her competitive edge (SM#2-p.30). Is great at skiing (SM#2-p.45). Plays softball in the summer; bikes, runs, plays tennis (M#23-p.2). Dedicated to having fun (M#23-p.4). Cooks using the "every pot in the house" method (M#23-p.6).

**FAMILY:**

*Parents:* Mother is Rachel (#89-p.64). Father, Jonathan (#90-p.122), died in a car crash when Abby was nine (#89-p.71). Has twin *sister*, Anna, who is about eight minutes older than Abby (M#23-p.4). Mom, Abby, and Anna move to Stoneybrook from Long Island (#89-p.70). Abby is home alone a lot of the time (M#23-p.3). Family is not demonstrative (M#23-p.5).

**LIKES:**

Loves to be outside, working up a sweat (M#23-p.2). Is more into Motown than Mozart (M#23-p.4). Likes puns, the worse the better (#96-p.3).

**CHILDHOOD EXPERIENCES:**

Moves to Stoneybrook from Long Island (#89-p.70). After her father died, it felt wrong to laugh and to be alive (#90-p.6) until one day she found herself laughing and realized it was okay (#90-p.7). In Long Island, middle school principal had a British accent, a huge pot belly, and a tendency to twist his hair into knots whenever he spoke (#89-p.70). Was the star forward, leading scorer, and co-captain of the soccer team (#90-p.4). Had a housekeeper in Long Island (#90-p.7). Used to go up to Lake Placid every winter to ski (SM#2-p.45).

**MEDICAL:**

*Asthma:* Has gotten used to it; often it looks worse than it is (#89-p.112).

Has two kinds of inhalers—a prescription one for when her attacks get really bad, and a regular over-the-counter one for times when she gets a little short of breath (#90-p.8). Has had a couple of asthma attacks before, which were fixed by a trip to the emergency room (#90-p.34). After she has an attack while babysitting, is taken to the ER and given a shot of epinephrine, and is then checked for her skin coloring, her heart rate, her respiration, etc. (#90-pp.34-35). Doesn't like talking about her asthma; is counting on outgrowing it and some of her allergies when she grows older (#90-p.39). Has attacks maybe a couple of times a year, and usually knows when they are coming on (#90-p.40).

*Allergies:* Abby is allergic to: dogs, dust (#89-p.67), kitty litter (but not cats) (#89-p.69), feathered pillows (M#22-p.19). Also, certain foods, including: tomatoes (#89-p.69), shellfish (#89-p.70), cheese (#90-p.11), milk (#90-p.49). Is outrageously allergic to pollen (M#23-p.2). Allergies are always worse during times of stress and hay fever season (#89-p.68). Wears surgical mask sometimes if it's really dusty (M#22-p.106).

**BABY-SITTING AND CLUB EXPERIENCES:**

Joins the BSC (#89-p.143) and is officially welcomed (#89-p.145). Takes over as president while Kristy is in Hawaii; in her own way is as dynamic and persuasive as Kristy (#99-p.53).

## SCHOOL-RELATED EXPERIENCES:

Goes to SMS, in eighth grade (#89-p.76). Is in Kristy's English class (#89-p.80). Calls the school bus the "Wheeze Wagon" (#90-p.2). Plays on a soccer team (#90-p.41) with her lucky pair of cleats (#90-p.42). Has Ms. Frost for math (#96-p.13). Is suspended for three days after inadvertently obtaining a copy of a math test on the night before the exam (#96-p.64). Ms. Bernhardt is her social studies teacher; she is in Stacey's class (#97-p.12). Doesn't try hard, but is always the best in gym class (#89-p.78) .

## SOCIAL ACTIVITIES:

### DANCES:
Dresses as Lucy Ricardo for the SMS **Mischief Night Masquerade** (M#22-p.134).

### MISCELLANEOUS:
Becomes a Bat Mitzvah (#96-p.115). Owns her own skis (SM#2-p.125). Hebrew name is *Avigail* (#96-p.115), which means "father's light—his joy" (#96-p.116).

# JESSI (JESSICA) DAVIS RAMSEY

•

**BIRTHDAY:**
June 30

**AGE:**
Eleven (#16-p.3 on)

**NARRATOR OF BOOKS:**
#16, #22, #27, #36, #42, #48, #55, #61, #68, #75, #82, M#8

**BSC POSITION:**
Junior officer

**CURRENT ADDRESS:**
612 Fawcett Avenue, Stoneybrook, CT 06800 (Stacey's old house) (#14-p.29).

## PERSONAL INFO:

**PHYSICAL DESCRIPTION:**
Five feet, two inches tall; wears size 6 shoes (#47-p.125); does not wear a bra (#16-p.19). Black, beautiful, long-legged, thin, graceful (#14-p.13); huge dark brown eyes (#16-p.3) with long lashes (#14-p.14); has eyeglasses just for reading (#14-p.39). Skin is color of darkish cocoa (#16-p.3). Moves gracefully no matter what she's doing (#80-p.15). Singing voice is so bad it peels wallpaper (#75-p.60). *Clothing/style:* Gets ears pierced with Mal, has one hole in each ear (#21-p.130). Needs braces (#17-p.17). Has white sweatshirt that says "ABT" (American Ballet Theatre) (#55-p.4). Not allowed to wear miniskirts (M#2-p.67).

**PERSONALITY TRAITS:**
Terrible letter writer (#16-p.11). Is very good at languages (#16-p.1).

**FAMILY:**
*Parents:* John and Janice Ramsey. Jessi calls mother "Mama" and father "Daddy" (#16-p.3). *Siblings:* sister Rebecca (Becca), age eight and a half, brother John Philip (Squirt), age fourteen months. *Aunt:* Aunt Cecelia moved in with Ramseys when Mrs. Ramsey returned to work (#36-p.7). She and Becca don't like Cecelia in the beginning: they short-sheet Cecelia's bed, fill her slippers with shaving cream, and

**47**

put a rubber spider on her pillow (#36-p.56); they learn to love and appreciate Cecelia (#36-p.137).

### CHILDHOOD EXPERIENCES:

Lived in Oakley, NJ, where there were more black people in her neighborhood and school than there are in Stoneybrook (#36-p.4). Went to Oakley Elementary (#16-p.4). Family moved to Stoneybrook because father's company transferred him (#14-p.35). Used to pretend that she and Becca were twins (#21-p.36). Used to say "Rabbit, Rabbit" on first day of month for good luck but nothing happened when she stopped saying it (#17-p.122).

### ROOM:

Her room has ballet posters, stuffed animals, collection of ceramic horses, and books (#48-p.101).

### LIKES:

Jokes; ballet; wants to be a ballet dancer (#14-p.36). Likes horses and reading (#14-p.38), especially horse stories by Marguerite Henry (#29-p.12); favorite horse story is *Impossible Charlie* (#14-p.39) by Barbara Morgenroth. Also likes Lynn Hall (#30-p.21). She and Mal like mysteries, not horror stories, like the *Green Knowe* books by L.M. Boston or *Tom's Midnight Garden* (#48-p.12). Likes sitting with family at dinner (#16-p.7). Likes to make endless gum-wrapper chains (#30-p.21). Good joke teller, good with children

(#16-p.11). Likes junk food as much as Claudia does but tries not to eat too much of it (#16-p.101).

### DISLIKES:

Used to think boys are a giant pain (#16-p.14); hates anchovies (#26-p.75) and green peppers. Thinks basketball is a great big bore (SS#8-p.81).

### BABY-SITTING AND CLUB EXPERIENCES:

#### GENERAL:

Not allowed to baby-sit on evenings (#19-p.16), except for her sibs, which she loves to do (M#2-p.68). Sometimes gets "the Look" from Kristy because she's occasionally late for meetings on Fridays after ballet class (#61-p.12). Loves babies, even likes to change their diapers (#45-p.85).

#### CLIENTS:

Mrs. Braddock teaches Jessi some American Sign Language before she sits for Matt (#16-p.35-37). Knows sign language better than other BSC members, so usually sits for Matt Braddock (#40-p.58). Marnie Barrett has a huge crush on her these days (#100-p.32).

#### HISTORY:

She and Mal decide to start their own baby-sitting club because club members give Mal too many tests to be in BSC (#14-p.73); call it Kids Incorporated (#14-p.80). BSC doesn't want to compete for business and they realize they were unfair to Mal, so they ask Jessi and Mal to come to BSC meeting (#14-p.119). Jessi sits for Jackie Rodowsky as test to join BSC (#14-p.128). She and Mal are made official junior members of the club (#15-p.11). First steady baby-sitting job is for Haley and Matt Braddock (#16-p.50); BSC is first place in Stoneybrook, besides Mal's house, where Jessi feels completely accepted (#22-p.95). Volunteers for Mr. Katz's Kids Club at SES when Ms. Simon goes away for month (#48-p.32). BSC has meeting in her room for first time (#48-p.101). Makes office kit especially for Caitlin Lowell to add to her Kid-Kit, but Mrs. Lowell, a racist client, does not let Jessi in the front door to baby-sit her kids (#56-pp.61-62).

## SCHOOL-RELATED EXPERIENCES:

### CLASSES/ATTENDANCE:
Was a new student in Mal's sixth-grade homeroom; homeroom teacher is Mrs. Frederickson (#14-pp.12, 13); in Mal's eighth period science class (#14-p.18). She and Mal have Ms. Walden for gym class, who takes them to the community pool complex for swim lessons during class (#55-p.28). Has gym Mondays and Wednesdays (#59-p.111). Switches fourth period lunch with fifth period, misses gym class in exchange for synchronized swim-

ming program at the community pool complex run by Ms. Cox fourth period (#55-p.35). Paired with Elise Coates, a pretty raven-haired girl in synchronized swimming (#55-p.37); she and Elise decide not to continue with synchro class (#55-p.138). Has computer programming for her Short Takes class (#75-p.2) during third period (#75-p.8). Mr. Williams is English teacher (#14-p.16).

### EXTRACURRICULAR ACTIVITIES:
Is assistant choreographer/dance captain for the Sixth Grade Follies (#75-p.77). Becomes sixth-grade correspondent for the *SMS Express*, assistant choreographer for *Peter Pan* (SS#9).

### GENERAL:
Only black girl in sixth grade; one of about six black students at SMS (#14-p.13).

### LUNCH:
She and Mal have different lunch period from rest of club members (#46-p.39).

## SOCIAL ACTIVITIES:

### DANCES:
Goes to **Halloween Hop** stag (#38-p.130). Goes to **Valentine Dance** with Curtis Shaller because Quint lives in NYC (#51-p.22). Goes to **Spring Dance** at Community Center with Curtis Shaller (#63-p.115).

Goes to Spring Dance at school alone (#65-p.124). Dresses as a cowgirl for Mischief Night Masquerade (M#22-p.134).

**FRIENDS:**

Mallory is best friend; Keisha was best friend (and cousin) in Oakley (#16-p.4). Mallory introduces herself to Jessi outside of Jessi's house the first week they are in Stoneybrook (#14-p.32). Was jealous of Mal when she took riding lessons; friendship suffered eight weeks of bad communication, but best friends again (#54-pp.124-126). Jessi and Mal sometimes pretend that they're horses (M#3-p.8); they also always recommend books to each other (M#3-p.124).

**BOYS/BOYFRIENDS:**

*Quint:* Meet at Lincoln Center (SS#6-p.75). Quint gives Jessi her first kiss (SS#6-p.211). Thinks Quint has wonderful eyes; they like each other (#50-p.33). He lives in NYC (#51-p.22). They met at New York City Ballet production of *Swan Lake*; he was sitting next to her (M#8-p.3). Quint is first boy Jessi's kissed (M#8-p.3). Writes Quint (#61-p.86); he suggests scholarship idea for underprivileged kids in dance class (#61-p.100-101). Long-distance romance with Quint has been fun, but maybe they're better off friends (M#8-p.3). After much thought, they mutually agree to just be friends, figuring they're too young for a long-distance relationship (M#8-p.129).

*Other boys:* Likes **Curtis Shaller** (#63-p.8); has gone to two dances with him (M#8-p.3). Flirts with **Daniel** at Shadow Lake—they have nothing in common, decide to just be friends since they already have significant others (SS#8-pp.82,218).

**BALLET EXPERIENCES:**

Always able to wake up before alarm at 5:29 A.M. and go to *barre* in basement to practice (#16-p.2). Played Clara in *The Nutcracker Suite* (#14-p.71); gets into advanced class at Stamford Ballet School (#14-p.95) Tuesdays and Fridays (#16-p.33); a tougher ballet school than in Oakley (#16-p.7); considered to be one of the best schools on the East Coast, not counting the professional ones in NYC (#61-p.2). Can dance *en pointe* (#55-p.3). Wants to be a professional ballerina (#55-p.3). Mme Noelle is teacher (#16-p.22); older woman (#27-p.21). Gets starring role of Swanilda in *Coppèlia* (#16-p.26). Class dances in toe shoes, she's youngest and newest of twelve girls in class (#16-p.23). Gets part as one of the swan maidens in professional production of *Swan Lake* at SCC (#27-p.127). Gets the lead as Princess Aurora in *Sleeping Beauty* (#42-p.11). Favorite part of dance is Rose Adagio (#42-p.113). Takes Level Three class with Mme Noelle, which temporarily conflicts with BSC meeting. (#100-p.23).

**BALLET TERMINOLOGY:**

*arabesque penché:* raise one leg way up behind you while leaning forward for balance (#61-p.5).

*assemble:* basic jump (#61-p.46).

*bourée with port de bras:* tiny steps on toes while moving arms gracefully up and down (#61-p.5).

*demi pliés:* half knee bends; when done in fifth position, they're harder (#61-p.61).

*echappé:* small jumps (#61-p.93).

*grand battement:* warm-up exercise meant to loosen the hips and hamstring muscles (#61-p.2).

*jeté:* jump from one leg to the other (#61-p.117).

*pas de chat:* "step of the cat," jump in the air, touch toes together lightly, come down softly (#61-p.5).

*pirouettes:* turns (#61-p.5).

*tour jeté:* a type of graceful jump (M#10-p.83).

**NJ VISITS:**

Goes back to Oakley to visit Keisha (#67-p.21); finds Keisha and Oakley to be very different (#67-p.83). Hawaii is the farthest away from home she's ever traveled (SS#13-p.2).

**MISCELLANEOUS:**

Would like to name her daughter Mary Rose (#52-p.133). If she could be any animal, she'd be a horse (M#11-p.18).

# MALLORY (MAL) PIKE

•

## PERSONAL INFO:

**BIRTHDAY:**
May 2

**AGE:**
Eleven (#14-p.1 on)

**NARRATOR OF BOOKS:**
#14, #21, #29, #39, #47, #54, #59, #69, #80, #92, M#3

**BSC POSITION:**
Junior officer

**CURRENT ADDRESS:**
134 Slate Street, Stoneybrook, CT 06800

## PERSONAL INFO:

**PHYSICAL DESCRIPTION:**
Five feet, one inch tall (#92-p.17). Wears glasses all the time; has chestnut brown hair and blue eyes; the only one in family with curly hair (#14-p.3); has freckles across her nose (#14-p.4); doesn't like her nose, which looks like her grandfather's (#59-p.6). Wants contacts but not allowed to get them until she's fifteen (#14-p.4). Does not wear bra (#16-p.19). Wants desperately to grow up and look older; parents say she's not old enough for miniskirt and glittery sweatshirt (#19-p.9). Gets a haircut and braces (#21-p.134). Has to wear braces for two years (#28-p.142); has the clear, plastic kind (#47-p.3). *Clothing/style:* Gets ears pierced (one hole in each ear) (#21-p.129). Has sweatshirt that says "I'd rather be writing my novel" (#14-p.31). Looks really good in autumn colors, like orange-red and gold (#77-p.37).

**PERSONALITY TRAITS:**
Level-headed and practical (#13-p.59). Klutzy, uncoordinated (#59-p.28). Keeps a journal (#14-p.5). Mopes well; goes to a fat sycamore in playground to do so (#14-p.66). Wants to be an author and illustrator of children's books (#36-p.13).

**FAMILY:**
*Parents:* John and Dee Pike. *Siblings:* Adam, Byron, and Jordan (identical triplets, ten years old); Vanessa (nine); Nicky (eight);

Margo (seven); Claire (five). *Pets:* Frodo is pet hamster (#22-p.139). *Other:* Starts the Pike Club meetings with siblings to talk about ways to save money while Dad is not working (#39-p.40). Sometimes walks siblings to school (#51-p.53). Is last one home from school (#59-p.1). Always being asked to babysit siblings, has little privacy (#59-p.4). Needs time for writing so she goes on strike to avoid her siblings (#47-p.104).

**ROOM:**

Mal shares a room with Vanessa (#14-p.5).

**JOURNAL:**

Journal is plain old composition book, with mottled black-and-white cover; doesn't write in journal every day, just whenever she feels like it. Only writes when she feels an urgency—which is often. Also, she likes to write when good things happen. Journal is hidden underneath mattress (#29-pp.2-3).

**CHILDHOOD EXPERIENCES:**

Gets straight A's for the first time in fourth grade; had crush on fourth-grade teacher, Mr. Barnes (#29-p.96).

**LIKES:**

Loves to read, write, and draw (#17-p.16). Loves kids (#54-p.23). Likes writing in the club notebook (#54-p.14). Favorite poems are *Wynken, Blynken, and Nod; The Owl and the Pussycat;* and *Jabberwocky* (#19-pp.89-90). Likes horses (#14-p.38) and reading horse stories, especially those by Marguerite Henry (#29-p.12), Barbara Morgenroth, and Lynn Hall (#30-p.20). Favorite horse story is *A Morgan for Melinda* (#14-p.39). She and Jessi like mysteries, not horror stories, like the *Green Knowe* books by L. M. Boston or *Tom's Midnight Garden* (#48-p.12). Ear-piercing boutique is her favorite shop in Washington Mall (#21-p.4). Has read *Black Beauty* many times (#54-p.4). Her dream horse is pure white Arabian with long mane and brown eyes (#54-p.6). Loves finding new great words, like "pandemonium" (#59-p.1). Likes archery, makes archery team (#59-pp.128, 135). Loves attics (M#3-p.83).

**DISLIKES:**

Hates wearing glasses; has begged parents for contacts (#47-p.3); not into gym class at all (#55-p.27); hates gym jumpsuit (#59-p.30) but likes gym after she makes archery team (#59-p.138). Hates her nose, which she got from her grandfather (#29-p.3). Dislikes Nan White, Janet O'Neal, Valerie, and Rachel from school because they said mean things about her dad when he wasn't working (#39-p.49). Hates it when a good book ends (#80-p.9).

**JOBS:**

Hired as Henrietta Hayes' assistant for three weeks (#80-p.66).

**MEDICAL:**

Gets chicken pox for second time (#31-p.40); has scars from it in "unmentionable" places (#31-p.144). Sprains ankle in potato sack race (#55-p.92), stays on crutches longer than she has to so she doesn't have to be in SMS Sports Festival. Had intended to pretend to hurt herself (#55-p.138). Comes down with mononucleosis (#69-p.27). Prone to mosquito bites (SS#8-p.43).

**BABY-SITTING AND CLUB EXPERIENCES:**

**GENERAL:**

Likes writing in the club notebook (#54-p.14). Compiles the club mystery notebook (SM#2-p.86).

**CLIENTS:**

First started baby-sitting for siblings (#14-p.4). Always being asked to baby-sit siblings, has little privacy (#59-p.4).

**HISTORY:**

She and Jessi decide to start their own baby-sitting club because club members gave Mal too many tests to be in BSC (#14-p.73). Call it Kids Incorporated (#14-p.80). BSC doesn't want to compete for business and realize they were unfair to Mal, so they ask Jessi and Mal to come to BSC meeting. (#14-p.119). Sits with Claudia for Newtons as final test to join BSC (#14-p.128). Officially inducted into BSC as junior member with Jessi (#15-p.11). Hosts her first BSC sleepover in rec room (#39-p.135). As part of BSC volunteer work, Mal helps counselors at a recreation program at park after school and on weekends for a month (#48-p.40). Her parents make her quit the BSC until she has recovered from mono (#69-p.49); the BSC makes her an honorary member until she returns (#69-p.55). Allowed to sit again, for her sibs (#72-p.105). Rejoins BSC (#73-p.139).

**SCHOOL-RELATED EXPERIENCES:**

**CLASSES/ATTENDANCE:**

In sixth grade (#14-p.12). Homeroom desk has big E.L. carved in upper corner and heart carved in lower corner (#14-p.12). Jessi was a new student in Mal's sixth-grade homeroom; teacher is Mrs. Frederickson (#14-pp.12, 13) and in Mal's second period English class, fifth period lunch, and her eighth period science class (#14-p.18). Mal has gym third period; gym class held on Mondays and Wednesdays (#59-p.111); math fourth period and lunch fifth period (#14-p.16); French sixth period and study hall seventh period (#14-p.18). Ms. Walden is her and Jessi's gym teacher (#55-p.28). Math and science are her two hardest subjects (#47-p.6). Math teacher is Mr. Zizmore (#59-p.103). Is asked to join creative writing class that meets Tuesdays and Fridays (#47-p.43). Ms. Walden calls her "Pike" (#59-pp.59, 129); Mal likes archery, is good at it (#59-pp.128, 130-131). Misses a whole lot of school due to mono. Loves English class; Mr. Williams is English teacher (#80-p.1). Writes *The Early Years*, a play based not-loosely-enough on her life (#80-p.75).

### EXTRACURRICULAR ACTIVITIES:
Wins race for secretary of sixth grade (#53-p.145). Makes archery team, most members of which are from seventh and eighth grades (#59-p.135). Apprentice costume designer for *Peter Pan* (SS#9).

### AWARDS/DEMERITS:
Wins Young Author's Day contest for Best Overall Fiction in the Sixth Grade (#47-p.137). First time for detention when she refuses to play volleyball in gym class (#59-p.67).

### GETTING TO SCHOOL:
Uses code on school mornings for Stacey to see from her house: white towel on patio means she can walk with Stacey, Dawn, and Mary Anne to school; red towel means she has to walk her siblings to school (#51-p.53).

### GRADES:
Has never failed a subject in school (#59-p.87). Gym has never been her strong point (#55-p.25). Once copied off of Jessi's paper during a test (CL-p.11).

### LUNCH:
Mal and Jessi eat at different lunch than rest of the BSC (M#25-p.39). Mal and her siblings buy lunch every day or make their own (#14-p.16).

## SOCIAL ACTIVITIES:

### DANCES:
Dances at **Leicester Lodge Dance** with Justin Price (SS#3-p.215)—her first dance with a boy (SS#3-p.221). Goes with Ben Hobart to: **Halloween Hop** (#38-p.130); **Winter Wonderland Dance** (#51-p.22); **Valentine Dance** (#51-p.102); **Spring Dance** at Community Center (#63-p.115); **Spring Dance** at school with Ben (#65-p.124). Dresses as ballerina for **Mischief Night Masquerade** (M#22-p.134).

### FRIENDS:
Used to want a best friend (#14-p.15); now Jessi is best friend (#16-p.5). Mallory introduces herself to Jessi outside of Jessi's house the first week the Ramseys are in Stoneybrook (#14-p.32); have homeroom, English, science, and lunch together (#14-pp.14-18); exchange favorite horse stories with each other (#14-p.39); join BSC together (#14-p.136). Jessi's parents don't allow her to take riding lessons, she becomes jealous of Mal. Their friendship suffers eight weeks of bad communication, but they

reconcile at end (#54-pp.124, 126). Jessi and Mal sometimes pretend that they're horses (M#3-p.8); they also always recommend books to each other (M#3-p.124).

## BOYS/BOYFRIENDS:

*Ben Hobart:* Admits she has crush on Ben Hobart (#32-p.62); studies with him (#32-p.109); Ben asks her to go to the movies (#32-p.144). Is "becoming an item" with Ben (M#2-p.11); he thinks she's a "bonzer sheila"—a terrific girl/kangaroo (M#2-p.29). Has short-lived disagreement with Ben at the library (#51-pp.74-75). Has never kissed him (#69-p.30). Doesn't speak to Ben after he's mad that she has to bail out on caroling date; after much confusion, they get back together and go caroling (SS#12-p.169).

*Toby:* Stacey's Sea City ex; Mal falls in love with him (SS#10-p.144), but then decides that they should just be friends (if that) because her heart lies more with Ben (SS#10-p.218)

## HORSE EXPERIENCES:

Takes horseback riding lessons English style (Beginning Equitation (#54-p.133) at Kendallwood Farm at ten A.M. on Saturdays and agrees to pay for half the cost of the eight beginner lessons (#54-pp.12, 36). Lauren Kendall is her riding instructor (#54-p.39). Had gone trail riding at Camp Mohawk; had ridden Western style before but that felt clunky compared to the English saddle (#54-p.42). Pax is name of white Arabian horse she likes, is slightly gray, looks marbled, has delicate nostrils (#54-pp.43, 45). Decides she may continue to take lessons in a few years, too scared after her fall; loves horses from a distance now (#54-pp.141, 149).

## MISCELLANEOUS:

Talks in her sleep (#34-p.129). If she could be any animal, she'd be a horse (M#11-p.18). Joins six-week-long writing group at Stoneybrook Public Library (#100-p.69).

# LOGAN BRUNO

•

**BIRTHDAY:**
January 10

**AGE:**
Thirteen

**NARRATOR OF BOOKS:**
*Logan's Story* and *Logan Bruno, Boy Baby-sitter*

**BSC POSITION:**
Associate member of club (#10-p.139 on)

**CURRENT ADDRESS:**
689 Burnt Hill Rd., Stoneybrook, CT 06800; phone: KL5-1018 (#10-p.108).

**PERSONAL INFO:**

**PHYSICAL DESCRIPTION:**
Blue eyes, average height, average build (LS, p.3). Has blondish brown (#17-p.7), curly hair (#25-p.42); looks like his mother (#25-p.42). Gentle and normal-sized (#79-p.9). Has southern accent (#17-p.8). Looks exactly like Cam Geary, according to Mary Anne (#10-p.20).

**PERSONALITY TRAITS:**
Funny, understanding (#17-p.8). A take-charge kind of guy, sometimes even bullheaded, the opposite of Mary Anne (LS-p.3). Not at all jockish (#79-p.9). Sometimes has a hard time being in a room full of girls (M#11-p.69). Is a big Mets fan (M#14-p.10). Not a morning person (LB-p.2). Is always hungry (M#24-p.112).

**FAMILY:**
*Parents:* Lyman and Louise Bruno. *Siblings:* Nine-year-old sister, Kerry, and five-year-old brother, Hunter. *Cousin:* His cousin Lewis visits him for winter break (#50-p.87).

**CHILDHOOD EXPERIENCES:**
Used to live in Louisville, Kentucky. Moved beginning of eighth grade (#10-p.20). Didn't want to move (SS#11-p.118). He and cousin Lewis used to spend their summers on a horse farm outside of Louisville (#50-p.140).

**LIKES:**
Mary Anne (#10-pp.117-118). Sports, particularly football, baseball and

track (LS, p.3). Likes kids (#17-p.8). Loves to sleep (#86-p.28).

midnight on Fridays and Saturdays (#10-p.37).

**DISLIKES:**
Hates putting on cologne, but sometimes he does it for Mary Anne, anyway (LB-p.107).

**JOBS:**
Works at Rosebud Cafe (#67-p.113) as a busboy. The youngest busboy there (SS#10-p.156). Calls it the Road Spud (SS#10-p.130). Boss doesn't like him getting phone calls or talking to friends while at work (SM#1-p.103). Other buspeople include Geraldine Breslin and Carlos (SM#1-p.109).

**BABY-SITTING AND CLUB EXPERIENCES:**

Sits for siblings, used to sit for Louisville neighbors, even babies (#10-p.37). Goes on first BSC job with Mary Anne to sit for Jackie Rodowsky (#10-p.49). Made an associate member of the BSC, doesn't have to come to meetings or pay dues (#10-p.139), (LS, p.5). Got teased by friends about belonging to BSC (LS, p.5). Can't replace Dawn as regular member because football practice is becoming really intense (#67-p.69). Quits the BSC for a very short while, because he doesn't have enough time for BSC and sports (LS-p.115). Can stay out to ten-thirty on weeknights, maybe

**SCHOOL-RELATED EXPERIENCES:**

In Stacey's eighth-grade homeroom and English class (#10-pp.19-20). Plays on school baseball team (#25-p.20); not performing up to coach's standards (#25-p.138). Sometimes eats lunch with BSC (#62-p.25). Member of the football team (#67-p.69) and volleyball team (#73-p.6). Eats lunch with BSC half the time and with his guy friends the other half (SS#9-p.29). Gets caught up (and caught by) the Badd Boyz, who he later turns in to the police (LB-p.86).

**SOCIAL ACTIVITIES:**

**DANCES:**
(see *MARY ANNE SPIER, Dances*)

**FRIENDS:**
Friends with Austin Bentley (LS, p.6), Pete Black, and Rick Chow.

**GIRLS/GIRLFRIEND:**
*Mary Anne:* First meets Mary Anne (gives her warm smile) and rest of club members during lunch in first month of eighth grade (#10-p.36). Goes to surprise party for Mary Anne at Stacey's, tells Mary Anne she's different from other girls, has good sense of humor (#10-p.118).

Mary Anne fell in love with Logan when she saw him for the first time on the first day of eighth grade (#10-p.20). Dresses in tux for romantic candlelight dinner for Mary Anne, gives her bracelet with gold hearts linked together for Valentine's Day (#41-p.108). Mary Anne breaks up with him (feels like Logan is taking over her life) and gives back bracelet (#41-p.137). He and Mary Anne still friends (#42-p.43). He and Mary Anne resume their relationship; he now gives her "space" (#46-p.138). Loves her new look, new haircut (#60-p.62). Carries a box of tissues when they go to movies together (#72-p.17). "Tigger" is one of his nicknames for her (#71-p.105). Hires horse-drawn buggy to convey her home after Sea City sojourn (SS#10-p.221). Thinks Mary Anne's sensitivity and shyness are the coolest things about her (LS-p.3). Would never dream of calling Mary Anne's father anything but "Mr. Spier" (LS-p.16). Candlelight dinner at Renwick's is ruined after Logan confesses that Nicky Cash ticket he has might have been stolen (LB-p.118).

*Other girls:* Goes out with **Cokie Mason** a few times because he misses having Mary Anne around (#46-p.106).

**SPORTS:**
Plays on school baseball team (#25-p.20); not performing up to coach's standards (#25-p.138). Football practice is really intense (#67-p.69). Likes football a lot, but doesn't take it too seriously—he's in it for fun, not to be recruited (LS-p.2). Volleyball tournament keeps him away from Mary Anne (M#13-p.4). Volleyball team made it to the state tournament (#73-p.6). Coach Mills might make him back-up quarterback (#79-p.34). Believes anyone can do well at sports (#79-p.59). Makes the SMS track team; runs the hundred-yard dash (LS-p.125). Ties county all-time record in track practice (LB-p.5).

**VACATIONS:**
Goes to Aruba with family instead of Leicester Lodge (SS#3-p.3). Goes to baseball camp (SS#8-p.15).

**MISCELLANEOUS:**
If he could be any animal, he'd be a hawk, so he could fly (M#11-p.19).

# SHANNON LOUISA KILBOURNE

•

**BIRTHDAY:**
March 17

**AGE:**
Thirteen

**NARRATOR OF BOOKS:**
*Shannon's Story*

**BSC POSITION:**
Associate member (#11-p.145 on)

**CURRENT ADDRESS:**
Lives across the street from Kristy on McLelland Road, next door to the Papadakises and the Kormans (#11-pp.9, 29).

**PERSONAL INFO:**

**PHYSICAL DESCRIPTION:**
Thick, curly, blonde hair, blue eyes, interesting-looking, high cheekbones, wears black mascara every morning, has a cute nose (#38-p.35). Isn't going to be really tall (ShS-p.4).

**PERSONALITY TRAITS:**
Takes tap lessons, occasionally (#67-p.128). A real Achiever; fluent in Spanish and French (#70-p.60). An animal lover (SS#11-p.23). Is funny as well as studious (M#23-p.19).

**FAMILY:**
*Parents:* Ted and Kathy Kilbourne (M#5-p.109). Parents call her "Shanny" as a nickname (ShS-p.9). Has two *sisters:* Tiffany (eleven) and Maria (eight) (#11-pp.35-36); they and Shannon all go to Stoneybrook Day School (#11-p.36). Has *dog*, Astrid of Grenville, a pedigreed Bernese mountain dog (#11-p.29).

**ROOM:**
Across from Tiffany's room; has a Stoneybrook Day pennant on the wall, neat stacks of books on the desk, and a poster from a summer camp production of *Oklahoma* (#70-p.67). Has a Dream Machine clock-radio (ShS-p.41).

## BABY-SITTING AND CLUB EXPERIENCES:

Baby-sat for Papadakises and Delaneys before joining BSC (#11-pp.35, 58). Kristy asks her to join BSC as associate member; doesn't have to come to meetings (#11-p.144). Sometimes watches Maria, so can't attend BSC meetings (#38-p.46). Buddy Barrett has crush on her (#38-p.90). Can't replace Dawn as regular member because of after-school tutoring project (#67-p.69). When Honor Society dinner committee is over, however, she decides to take Dawn's place (temporarily) as alternate officer (#68-p.127). Shea Rodowsky might have a crush on her (M#14-p.100).

## SCHOOL-RELATED EXPERIENCES:

Goes to Stoneybrook Day School with siblings (#11-p.36). Must wear uniform to school (ShS-p.14). Involved in a lot of clubs after school (#89-p.31); Honor Society. Starts after-school tutoring project for the Honor Society (#67-p.69). Acts and sings in plays (#70-p.60). A member of the Stoneybrook Day debate team; it's one of the best in the state (M#18-p.71). Aside from regular classes, like English and algebra, takes philosophy and psychology (SS#11-p.175) and joins the astronomy club as its only eighth-grader (SS#11-pp.176,185) after being asked to try out by her science teacher, Mr. Katz (SS#11-p.179). Is elected vice-president of the astronomy club and has been chosen to play one of the leads in a drama club production of *Arsenic and Old Lace;* is thinking of joining the Spanish Club, too (#89-p.51). Not crazy about math in the way that Maria is (ShS-p.7). Madame DuBarry is her French teacher (ShS-p.20). Deliberately fails a French final so she won't have to go on Paris trip with her mom (ShS-p.90).

## SOCIAL ACTIVITIES:

### FRIENDS:

She and Kristy were mean when they first saw each other waiting for their buses (#11-pp.10-11); she and Kristy are introduced (#11-p.29). Was jealous of Kristy because of BSC (#11-p.135); gives Kristy one of Astrid's puppies and David Michael names it "Shannon" (#11-p.136). Has more time on her hands; Kristy didn't have time to hang out with her, so she spends time with other BSC members (#61-pp.26, 42); Kristy thinks she's stealing her friends, apologizes to her, and will ask her to regular BSC meetings now and then (#61-pp.112, 132-133).

### DANCES:

Goes to Spring Dance at Community Center with boy from her school (#63-p.146).

**CAMP EXPERIENCES:**
Attends Camp Erie as a camper (SS#2-p.214) and as a CIT (SS#8-p.15). Attends drama camp (SS#10-p.16). Attends Camp Azure Hills (SS#10-p.225).

**MISCELLANEOUS:**
Has won a drama plaque, a framed Honor Society certificate, and an archery trophy from summer camp, among other things. If she could be any animal, she'd be a cat (M#11-p.19).

# BSC FAMILY MEMBERS

•

# The BREWERs and the THOMASes

●

**HOUSE:**

*Indoors:* Live in mansion (#5-p.21) on McLelland (#2-p.133) with three floors (#6-p.2) and nine bedrooms (#5-p.38), gigantic living room containing grand piano, a little tree, three couches, five armchairs, a long glass coffee table, several end tables, a crystal chandelier, small Oriental rugs instead of carpeting— looks almost like a hotel lobby (#5-p.56). Living room also has floor-to-ceiling windows looking out on front lawn (#5-p.60). Family room is always on the messy side (#11-p.51). Kitchen, which Kristy adores, has all the modern conveniences but looks old and country with a big parson's table and two long benches; countertops covered with blue and white tiles, copper pots hang from walls, curtains match wallpaper (#11-p.6). Mudroom is where they get dressed for winter weather (#81-p.5) and where Shannon's leash is hung (#95-p.10). David Michael, Karen, Andrew, and Emily Michelle all share a bathroom (SS#7-p.195). Ghost of Ben Brewer (Kristy's great-grandfather) is said to haunt bedroom on third floor (#62-p.97) as well as attic. Boo-Boo won't go above second floor, perhaps because of Ben Brewer's ghost (#29-p.71). Kristy finds Nannie's old pink bowling ball, which Karen uses as doorstop in her playhouse (#62-p.101). Watson's library is a dark, peaceful, comfortable place, with cushy leather chairs, thick rugs, china lamps, a big wooden desk, and shelves and shelves of books; room has a nice smell to it, Lemon Pledge and musty books (M#19-p.29); wood and brass stepladder makes upper shelves accessible (M#19-p.30). Charlie installs intercom system for Watson while he's recuperating (#81-p.76).

*Attic:* The entire fourth floor of the house—room after room (#29-p.73)—and is big with rafters that Kristy has to duck under (#62-p.99); attic is filled with old furniture, all covered in white sheets (#29-p.74). Also contains brass doll's bed and rocking horse (#29-p.74).

*Outdoors:* Big backyard with great climbing tree, playground set, and tons of outdoor games in garage (#55-p.54). Watson has rose garden (#1-p.93). Garden has daffodils (M#4-p.98).

*Location:* House is three miles from Kishis' house (#7-p.9); Kristy figures it would take a half hour each way via bike (#5-p.102). Train station is exactly four minutes away (SS#6-p.17).

*House rules/customs:* Twice a week a cleaning woman comes in (#11-p.5). Watson's List of Forbidden Foods is posted on the refrigerator, right next to the week's menus and snacks (#81-p.76). Shopping list and schedules posted on bulletin board (#81-p.77). Strict rule about girl-friends/boyfriends—they are not allowed into the house unless adults are present (#95-p.11). Kids get story time after bath time before going to sleep (#81-p.70). Watson and Elizabeth subscribe to both the *Stoneybrook News* and *The New York Times* (M#25-p.79).

*Cars:* Watson has old black Ford, emergency car parked in shed at back of property; in garage are red sports car, fancy new car, and Thomases' green station wagon (#8-p.86); station wagon has four-wheel drive (SM#2-p.182).

## ELIZABETH (EDIE) THOMAS BREWER:

### PERSONAL INFO:
Thirty-seven "or something" (#16-p.106). Tries to spend a little time alone with each kid every day (#1-p.16). Married to Watson Brewer (#6-p.142); diamond on engagement ring is very big (#1-p.140). Plays tennis with Mrs. Crane (M#3-p.23).

### JOB:
Works full-time for a big company in Stamford (#1-p.16); company symbol is a sun (#1-p.39).

### EXPERIENCES:
Has never forgiven Patrick for leaving the family, but never sat around whining about how badly he treated them (M#15-p.3). She and Watson adopt Vietnamese child, Emily Michelle (#24-p.127). Wants to get pregnant but thinks she's too old (#16-p.106). Hobby is to go to estate sales with Watson and find interesting things for their yard and house (#21-p.77). Had labor pains (with Kristy) during Yankees game (KB-p.14). Elizabeth and Patrick had just moved to Stoneybrook around the time that Mary Anne's mother died (M#5-p.113).

## WATSON BREWER:

### PERSONAL INFO:
Going bald (#1-p.18). Is a millionaire, was divorced, has two kids by previous marriage (Karen and Andrew), who live with their mother but spend every other month with their dad. Shares household chores equally and is a better cook than Kristy's mom (#11-p.5). Kristy initially thinks he's okay but can sometimes be a jerk (#6-p.3). Best friend is Tom Fielding (#6-p.53). Doesn't like to admit defeat (#81-p.7). Says "resume yourself" instead of "sit down" (SS#4-p.185).

### HOBBIES AND INTERESTS:
Likes baseball almost as much as Kristy (#20-p.3); good at organizing and running things (#20-p.29). Is a gardening fanatic (M#25-p.4). Goes to estate sales with Elizabeth; likes to find interesting things for their yard and house, like a birdbath, a chandelier, a lampshade (#21-p.78). Helps a lot with the Krushers; Kristy jokingly calls him her "assistant manager" (M#4-p.21). Umpires sometimes (#89-p.42). Has high-powered binoculars for bird watching (M#18-p.118). Loves books (#81-p.78). Watson and Elizabeth sometimes go to very fancy affairs wearing tuxes and evening dresses (#61-p.76).

### JOB:
Is CEO of Unity Insurance, which has its main offices in Stamford (#81-p.3). After heart attack, decides to turn work duties over to a vice-president (#81-p.99); will work at home for three hours a day and spend the rest of the time with the family (#81-p.152).

### MEDICAL:
Has a mild (#81-p.43) heart attack (#81-p.29); will have to exercise, start a healthy-heart diet, and cut out stress (#81-p.43).

### EXPERIENCES:
Marries Kristy's mom, Elizabeth (#6-p.142). He and Kristy's mom adopt Vietnamese child, Emily Michelle (#24-p.127). Makes scholarship contribution of two full scholarships every year to the Stamford Ballet School for less privileged students (#61-pp.123-124), called the Watson and Elizabeth Brewer Dance Scholarships (#61-p.134). Loans Kristy his expensive Nikon (M#16-p.37). Stays in hospital after minor heart attack (#81-from p.63). Gets welcome back party upon his return (#81-p.75). Becomes Mr. Mom (#81-from p.99).

## LISA ENGLE (FORMERLY LISA BREWER):

### PERSONAL INFO:
Karen and Andrew's mother, marries Seth Engle (#6-p.35). Karen and

Andrew live with their mother but spend every other month with Watson (used to be every other weekend and every other holiday and two weeks in summer [#21-p.78].) Calls Andrew "Andy-Pandy" (#7-p.78). She and Seth live in "the little house" (as Karen calls it) and have a dog named Midgie (#81-p.81) and a cat named Rocky. Fills in for Seth's assistant at workshop (SM#1-p.13). Address is 12 Forest Drive in Stoneybrook (SecS-p.17).

## EMILY MICHELLE THOMAS BREWER:

### PERSONAL INFO:
Adopted Vietnamese girl (two years old at the time of adoption) (#24-p.127). Two and a half (#45-p.3). Dark, shiny hair, bangs across forehead, smooth skin (#24-p.139). Hair is short (#29-p.70). Calls David Michael "Davie" (#62-p.33). Was adopted through an agency called Love Bundles (#33-p.67). Favorite game is Shark Attack (#45-p.4), doesn't play by rules (#59-p.97). Uses high chair (M#2-p.32). Plays with troll dolls (M#15-p.7). A slow, one-step-at-a-time stair-climber (#29-p.73). Is not the world's best walker—on the slow side (#33-p.60).

### SPEECH/DEVELOPMENT:
Favorite word is "cookie" (#26-p.102). "Language delayed," because she heard only Vietnamese for two years, so family spends hours talking and reading to her (#29-p.70). Lately, favorite word is "tylis", which means "stylish" (M#19-p.7). Sometimes tutored by Claudia (SS#8-p.109).

### EXPERIENCES:
Has nightmares, is afraid of everyone (#33-p.35) until Claudia tutors her; Emily now trusts people, but still cries out in the night sometimes (#33-p.139). New word is "puway, puway," which means put away (#61-p.78); Nannie trying to teach her to put away her toys (#61-p.78); she's been putting away other people's things, too (#61-p.79). Says "ball," and "how" for "house"; says "ballel" for "bottle" (#62-pp.40-41).

## ANDREW BREWER:

### PERSONAL INFO:
Four years old (#6-p.1) [three (#1-p.120)]. Shy (#5-p.55). Mother calls him Andy-Pandy (#7-p.78). He and Karen live with their mother every other month; arrangement was pretty loose (#6-p.4). Sucks thumb (#55-pp.61, 131). Liked Louie but is afraid of other dogs (#8-p.85); likes Shannon the puppy (#62-p.4). Adores Karen (#16-p.80). Can swim (SM#1-p.157).

### EXPERIENCES:
Had tonsillitis (#16-p.82).

## KAREN BREWER:

### PERSONAL INFO:
Seven years old now (#38-p.4) [six (#5-p.55), five (#1-p.87)]. Has freckles (#2-p.66); talks too much (#5-p.55). Blonde, blue eyes, thin (#21-p.82). Has blue glasses for reading, pink ones for everything else (#81-p.81). She and Andrew live with their mother every other month; arrangement was pretty loose (#6-p.4); she calls herself and Andrew "two-two" for two houses, two families, etc. (#62-p.7). Must wear earplugs when she swims (SS#1-p.41). Attends Stoneybrook Academy, a private school (#11-p.36). Likes to tell stories. Very protective of Andrew (#16-p.80); fearless, with wild imagination (#20-p.3) Takes spelling seriously (#20-p.56). In art class at Community Center Tuesdays and Fridays after school (#48-p.39). Best friends with Nancy Dawes and Hannie Papadakis, inseparable, call themselves the Three Musketeers (#61-p.38). Loves to help in the kitchen (M#3-p.95).

### TOYS/GAMES/POSSESSIONS:
Has a stuffed cat named Moosie (#15-p.133) that's kept at her father's house (#41-p.80). Has a stuffed cat named Goosie that's identical to Moosie, which is kept at her mother's house (#41-p.80). Tickly is Karen's blanket (#15-p.133) that she ripped in half to keep one piece at each house. Likes to play "Let's All Come In," a hotel game using costumes in second-floor bedroom; favorite character is Mrs. Mysterious, for which she dresses all in black (#5-p.58). "Going Camping" is one of her favorite games (#37-p.70). *The Witch Next Door* is her favorite book (#30-p.90).

### EXPERIENCES:
Began kindergarten but was put in first grade at Christmastime because she's very smart, reads like crazy (#5-p.55). Now in second grade. She thinks the Brewers' attic is haunted by old Ben Brewer (#5-pp.54, 64). Names their neighbor, Mrs. Porter, "Morbidda Destiny" because Karen thinks she's a witch (#1-p.93). Got her hair destroyed once at Gloriana's House of Hair, she thinks it should be called Gloriana's House of Horror (#60-p.32). Wants to be thirteen, copies Kristy (#74-from p.25); says she loves boys with green eyes (#74-p.60). Plays right field for the Krashers (M#9-p.7). Is mad when her mother won't let her stay at Watson's house after his heart attack (#81-p.83). Summer at Camp Mohawk is her first time away from home alone (SS#2-p.69). Went to circus camp once with her friends (#86-p.31).

## BEN BREWER:

Watson's deceased great-grandfather, whom Karen thinks is haunting their attic (#5-p.64) and the third floor (#29-p.2); a recluse who ate fried dandelions (#11-p.138). Karen believes that Ben Brewer was haunted by a headless ghost, and after he died, both he and the headless ghost continued to haunt the attic and the third floor (#29-p.72).

### OTHER BREWERS/ENGLES:

#### GRANNY AND GRANDAD:
Karen's maternal grandparents; home is in Nebraska (SS#10-p.187). Grandad deceased.

#### SETH ENGLE:
A carpenter (SM#1-p.20). Works in workshop, has assistant (SM#1-p.13).

## THE THOMASes

When they lived on Bradford Court, house was not that big; had four bedrooms but David Michael's was more like a closet (#5-p.37). Had awards wall in den for trophies (#6-pp.40-41).

### see ELIZABETH (EDIE) THOMAS BREWER

### MR. PATRICK THOMAS:

#### PERSONAL INFO:
Never calls kids, divorce not friendly (#11-p.75). Doesn't send much child support money (#1-p.16). Can be a jerk, forgot Kristy's twelfth birthday (#1-p.16). Job involves horses (M#4-p.100). Hated the responsibilities that went with being a father (M#4-p.100). Claudia hadn't liked him very much (CB-p.127). Was a big Yankees fan (KB-p.14). Once was a sportswriter (KB-p.135).

#### EXPERIENCES:
Ran off to California and remarried (#1-p.16). Has split from his California wife (KB-p.117). Separated from Elizabeth Thomas not long after David Michael was born (#11-p.8). David Michael got a birthday card from him from Petaluma, CA (M#4-p.99). Argued a lot with Elizabeth during marriage; one day he just quit his newspaper job and headed out west, without even telling his wife/children (KB-p.54). Sent Kristy and sibs an occasional postcard, always signing it "P." for Patrick (KB-p.116). Revisits Kristy; makes her keep it a secret (KB-from p.116) before skipping out again (KB-p.137). Was player for minor league baseball team (KB-p.118). Sends Kristy a Christmas card (SecS-p.30).

### DAVID MICHAEL THOMAS:

#### PERSONAL INFO:
Seven years old (#6-p.3 on). Allergic to chocolate (#1-p.81). Has dark curls (#1-p.6). Wary of little girls

(#1-p.23). A champion whiner (#6-p.18). Emily calls him "Davie" (#62-p.33). Slowpoke (#11-p.4). Newer dog, Shannon, spends lot of time in David Michael's room (#62-p.4). Does not like to play "Let's All Come In" (#15-p.32). Charlie, Sam, and Kristy are responsible for watching him until Mom comes home (#1-p.6). Kristy is a second mother to him (#15-p.31). Watson has taught him crawl stroke, so he can swim (SS#1-p.59). A klutz (#20-p.54). Loves bugs (#24-p.4). Owns Polaroid camera (M#2-p.35). Dreams of being a great athlete (M#4-p.22). Is supposed to brush his teeth every night, no exceptions (M#9-p.89). Not allowed to ride his bike farther than two blocks from his house (#81-p.109). Catches for the Krashers (M#9-p.7).

### FRIENDS:
Frankie is a friend (#5-p.99); Linny Papadakis is a good friend (#62-p.6), who calls him "Big D" (#89-p.8). Carver Ensign is David Michael's new friend; not allowed to visit without parental supervision (#47-p.95).

### EXPERIENCES:
Was attached to their dog, Louie; says, "He was my best friend" at Louie's funeral (#11-p.126). Digs up a corner of the yard every now and then, looking for buried treasure (M#15-p.7). Has been bitten by the acting bug (#81-p.5); gets part of rooster in *The Brementown Musicians* (#81-p.45).

## SAM THOMAS:

### PERSONAL INFO:
Fifteen (#6-p.5 on) [fourteen and freshman, #1-p.9]. Member of math club (#1-p.11). Has dark curly hair, sparkly blue eyes, and a few freckles (#1-p.83). Sophomore (#24-p.4). Used to share room with Charlie in Thomases' old house (#6-p.2). Champion practical joker (#23-p.19). Likes anchovies (M#9-p.125). Sometimes can be really obnoxious (M#10-p.8). Loves to play/follow baseball (M#19-p.11). Plays intramural basketball at SHS (#81-p.34). Doesn't even shave yet (SS#8-p.44).

### JOBS:
Delivers groceries for A&P, as he did last summer (#6-p.39); works there part-time during school year also (#62-p.2).

### GIRLS/GIRLFRIENDS:
Girls are practically the only thing on his mind (#11-p.5). Likes Stacey (#1-pp.85-86); can tell he likes Stacey because he has teased her endlessly (#63-p.8); they date sometimes (#58-pp.6, 133). They get together at a dance at the Shadow Lake lodge (SS#8-p.208). He and Stacey like each other a lot, but have drifted apart recently (#65-p.11). Still likes Stacey, but he thinks of her as a friend, someone who is fun to goof

with; likes to flirt with her—it keeps him in practice for his next girlfriend (SM#2-p.185). Liked Monique, a sophisticated private school girl (#11-p.5). Takes Tamara, a high school freshman with spiky yellow hair, to movies (#2-p.99). Goes to January Jamboree with Stacey (#60-p.132). Goes to Spring Dance at Community Center with Stacey (#63-p.115). Stacey lies to him, says she already has date for Spring Dance at school (#65-p.93), so he goes with Amanda Martin from Stacey's class (#65-p.110). He and Stacey have decided to see other people as well as each other (M#10-p.9). Once brought rubber tarantula to a dance with Stacey (M#10-p.7). Has been calling and dating a girl named Kathy (M#10-p.67); he and she bump into Stacey and Terry (M#10-p.101). Has been having problems with his girlfriend (SM#2-p.14)—they break up (SM#2-p.185).

**EXPERIENCES:**
Is a camp counselor for a summer (SS#10-p.111). Used to play baseball; team made the playoffs (CB-p.128). Childhood best pals were Ricky and Randy Jones (KB-p.36).

## CHARLIE THOMAS:

**PERSONAL INFO:**
Seventeen, got driver's license (#6-p.5 on). [sixteen and a junior, #1-p.9]. Plays varsity football at Stoneybrook High (#1-p.9). Likes to be punctual (#61-p.76). Had shared a room with Sam for years; at Watson's they each have own room (#6-p.2). Will be in college next year, bosses around siblings (#22-p.44). Remembers holding Kristy as a baby (M#9-p.79). Loves to play/follow baseball (M#19-p.11). Plays intramural basketball at SHS (#81-p.34). Shaves (SS#8-p.114). Sarah is his girlfriend (#95-p.11).

**CAR AND DRIVING:**
First car: sort of gray, fenders rusting, scratches, dents (#30-p.96), called the Junk Bucket (#42-p.101). Is a good driver (SM#2-p.44). Friends with Travis, whom Dawn used to like, (#37-p.13). Excellent driver in rainstorm; terrific with the kids in the Haunted Mansion (M#9-p.49). Drives Kristy to club meetings and sitting jobs in their old neighborhood and gets gas money from club treasury (#7-p.16).

**EXPERIENCES:**
Has summer job (#7-p.53). Lands a job on the set of *Little Vampires*, as a gofer for the assistant-assistant stage manager (M#15-p.24). Used to play baseball; team made the playoffs (CB-p.128). Kristy catches him kissing his girlfriend (#95-p.11). Childhood best pals were Randy and Ricky Jones (KB-p.36).

## ● BSC Family Members ●

### NANNIE:

**PERSONAL INFO:**
Kristy's maternal grandmother who moves in with them to help take care of Emily Michelle (#26-p.8). In her seventies, bowls, volunteers at hospital, sews, a terrific cook; used to live in apartment forty-five minutes away (#6-p.59). Is a gardening fanatic (M#25-p.4). Usually wears pants (#63-p.106). Drives old car painted pink called the Pink Clinker (#6-p.61). Never used to come to Thomases empty-handed (#6-p.61). Can be very firm regarding discipline (#6-p.108). Has tons of friends (#45-p.3). Member of bowling league; is great at baking, but doesn't do it that often (M#4-p.32). Favorite CD is Frank Sinatra (#81-p.4). Has old cedar steamer trunk in which she keeps old letters, pictures, and other things she's saved over the years (#81-pp.111, 151). Favorite book is *The Mayor of Casterbridge* (SS#1-p.73).

**EXPERIENCES:**
Moves into the Brewer household (#26-p.8). Feels left out when Watson becomes Mr. Mom (#81-from p.102). Announces that she's moving out, to an apartment in Waterford Gardens complex outside of Stoneybrook (#81-p.109); moves out (#81-p.111). Moves back into the Big House once she realizes that she's needed and loved (#81-pp.142,150).

### THOMAS/BREWER PETS:

**BOB:**
Pet hermit crab that travels back and forth with Andrew (M#19-p.9).

**BOO-BOO:**
Watson's cat, gray with big yellow eyes, seventeen pounds, bites and scratches if provoked (#1-p.89). Old and cranky (#13-p.76). Fat (#30-p.13). Gets stuffed in a pillow cushion by Lou McNally (Papadakis foster child) (#62-p.116). Won't set foot above the second floor, perhaps because of Ben Brewer's ghost (#29-p.72).

**CRYSTAL LIGHT THE SECOND AND GOLDFISHIE:**
Karen and Andrew's goldfish (#45-p.4). Karen announces that they are getting married (M#2-p.34).

**EMILY JUNIOR:**
Named after Emily Michelle; Karen's pet rat, gets entered in BSC pet show wearing Mickey Mouse ears (#42-p.145). Travels back and forth with Karen.

**SHANNON:**
Female puppy of Astrid's given to Kristy and David Michael by Shannon (#11-p.130). David Michael names her after Shannon Kilbourne (#11-p.136). A ball of brown and white fluff (#11-p.131). David Michael's puppy (#11-p.136; #18-p.130). Bernese mountain dog (#30-

p.13). Will be the size of a St. Bernard; clever and loyal (#42-p.62). Barks whenever David Michael blows in her ear; is the sweetest and most gentle puppy Mary Anne's ever seen (M#5-p.31). Brewers have a dog run for her, a wire that stretches across the front yard with a chain attached (M#7-p.55). Shannon is dognapped (M#7-p.54). Speaks when you tell her to (#86-p.128).

## LOUIE:

Deceased. Was the family's collie (#1-p.9). Wasn't a purebred, his grandfather was a sheep dog (#7-p.96). Didn't like dark places; liked car rides (#5-p.97). Died of old age (put to sleep at vet's), arthritis, blindness (#11-p.122); Karen's idea to give him funeral (#11-p.122); dig grave and bury his leash and dog dishes in it, set up cross with "Louie Thomas, REST IN PEACE" on it (#11-pp.123-126). Was David Michael's "best friend" (#11-p.126).

## OTHER THOMAS/BREWER RELATIVES:

## GRANDMA:

Kristy's other grandmother (#6-p.120). A widow (SS#1-p.215).

## ROBIN:

A cousin who has diabetes (#1-p.150). Lives in western Connecti-cut (SS#1-p.3). Sends Kristy a chain letter that was sent to Robin by her friend Margie (CL-p.2).

## AUNT COLLEEN AND UNCLE WALLACE MILLER:

Kristy's favorite aunt and uncle (#6-pp.36, 51). Colleen is Kristy's mother's youngest sister, a younger version of Nannie, busy and active with wild streak, understands Kristy so well it's almost scary (#6-p.66).

## ASHLEY MILLER:

Nine (#6-p.51), on crutches, broke leg roller-skating (#6-p.67).

## BERK MILLER:

Six, a boy (#6-p.51). Has outdoor allergies (#6-p.72).

## GRACE MILLER:

Five (#6-p.51).

## PETER MILLER:

Three (#6-p.51).

## AUNT THEO AND UNCLE NEAL MEINER:

Theo is Kristy's mother's younger sister; Neal wears clashing clothes, smokes cigars, talks too loudly; not Kristy's favorite relative (#6-p.63). Uncle Neal breaks his leg, so Meiners can't come to Stoneybrook for Thanksgiving (#91-p.34).

## LUKE MEINER:

Ten (#6-p.51). Skinny and little for his age, thatch of thick unbrushed dark blond hair; serious brown eyes (#6-p.64).

**EMMA MEINER:**
Eight (#6-p.51). Tiny; messy blonde ponytails and sparkling brown eyes (#6-p.64), bundle of energy (#6-p.65).

**BETH MEINER:**
One (#6-p.51). Ordinarily screams when stranger comes too near (#6-p.65). Loves her Walk-a-Tot chair; usually takes two naps, and a bottle of soy milk to bed with her—she's allergic to cow's milk. (#6-p.74).

**FAITH AND PIERSON CHAMBERS:**
Watson's aunt and uncle; live at 21 Nappanee Court, Harrisport, PA 00241; give Watson the cabin on Shadow Lake (SS#8-p.1).

# The KISHIs

**GENERAL:**

Both Mr. & Mrs. Kishi left Japan for the U.S. when they were very young; are very conservative (#1-p.26). Parents love Claudia and Janine equally; good grades and artistic talent are given equal weight (M#6-p.78).

**HOUSE:**

Live at 58 Bradford Court. Basement is finished, carpeted, and heated (#26-p.36). Mr. and Mrs. Kishi keep a locked box full of cash for emergency money in the bottom drawer of desk in the den; Claudia knows about it (#33-p.133). Goldmans live next door (#2-p.108). Russ and Peaches move in temporarily; the Kishis must move some of the den furniture to the living room in order to make space (#78-p.39). The Braddocks live nearby (M#6-p.69). Claudia turns the bathroom between her room and Janine's into a temporary darkroom (M#16-p.4), which has no windows (M#16-p.10). Family has a cordless phone (M#21-p.62).

**MR. JOHN KISHI:**

**PERSONAL INFO:**

Claudia's father, not as strict as Mr. Spier (#1-p.8); enjoys mowing the lawn (M#6-p.69). Plays golf (M#6-p.72). Has been married for twenty-one years (#1-p.46). Every morning he comes downstairs as soon as he stumbles out of bed to make himself and Mrs. Kishi coffee; they're caffeine addicts (#7-p.5). Born in Japan (#13-p.7). His idea of a good time is doing the crossword in the Sunday *New York Times* (#97-p.4).

**JOB:**

Partner in investment firm in Stamford (#7-p.6). His eyes light up when he talks about stocks and bonds (#97-p.4).

**EXPERIENCES:**

Once dropped a chicken on floor at dinner party with the Pikes (#26-p.80).

## MRS. RIOKO KISHI:

### PERSONAL INFO:
Claudia's birth date is her ATM code (M#16-p.126). Has been married for twenty-one years (#1-p.46). Needs coffee (#7-p.5). Born in Japan (#13-p.7).

### JOB:
Head librarian at Stoneybrook Public Library (#7-p.6). Very organized (#78-p.5). Was certified to teach elementary school in Connecticut (#33-p.45).

### EXPERIENCES:
Delivers eulogy at Mimi's funeral (#26-p.86). Insists on accompanying Claudia to meet her date at Rosebud Cafe (#71-p.92). Has a habit of shouting last-minute instructions to Claudia as she goes down the block (#78-p.5). Comes up with idea for library crafts fair to raise funds (M#6-p.48). Wanted to keep Mr. Kishi all to herself after she first met him (M#6-p.126).

## JANINE KISHI:

### PERSONAL INFO:
Claudia's sixteen-year-old sister (#7-p.2) [fifteen and sophomore in #1-p.26]. Has straight black hair cut in an old-fashioned Dutch-Boy style; wears black wire-rim glasses; wearing her particular clothes (wool skirt, knee socks, loafers, etc.)
looks like a twelve-year-old (M#6-p.51). Likes school; junior; wears blah clothes (#7-p.2). Looks a lot like Mr. Kishi (#33-p.132). Best friend is fourteen-year-old math nerd [now fifteen] who graduates early from high school (#1-p.27). Sticks to herself, almost no friends, all she cares about is her computer; always uses big words (#7-p.3). Room is precise: shoes in a line, clothes in order by color and item, cleans her room every Saturday morning (#63-p.71); has computer in room (#65-p.45). Likes to cook (#78-p.76). Kristy and Mary Anne avoid her as much as possible (#4-p.4). Is taking French class (#97-p.6).

### GENIUS:
Takes classes at Stoneybrook University, has IQ of 196, always correcting Claudia (#1-p.27). Taught herself to read before she went to kindergarten (M#11-p.3). Is great at helping Claudia study (M#16-p.133). Never misses the bus; her homework is always done on time (M#6-p.32). Was awarded most accomplished science student at community college where she's been taking classes for two years (#33-p.8). Signs up for "numbers cruncher" job as part of summer work/study program (M#16-p.5); is working with Professor Woodley (M#16-p.9).

### BOYFRIEND:
Has a boyfriend, Jerry Michaels, a high school student who's in ad-

vanced placement classes at the college with her; he likes her as she is, not with any "new look" (M#6-pp.124-5). Jerry practically has to beg her to take time off for picnics and hikes (M#21-p.4). Jerry sends her notes in the mail (M#6-p.136).

**EXPERIENCES:**
Wears makeup for the first time that Claudia can remember (M#6-p.33). Gets makeover from Claudia (M#6-from p.51). Is grounded for the first time for being late to dinner and lying about the reason (M#6-p.66).

## MIMI YAMAMOTO:

**PERSONAL INFO:**
Claudia's maternal grandmother (#1-p.136) who dies during night in the hospital (#26-p.63) on a Wednesday (#26-p.92). Claudia was very close to her. Came to U.S. when 32 (#26-p.4); quiet, patient, polite, had gentle, rolling accent (#2-p.4). Began living with Kishis after Janine was born and after her husband died following Claud's mom and dad's marriage (#7-p.5). Older sister was Hideyoshi (#97-p.3).

**EXPERIENCES:**
Had written her own obituary (#26-p.126) and labeled objects, except jewelry, with names of people who should inherit them (#26-p.129). Claudia gets pearl pin, which she won't wear but will always keep (#26-p.129). Had stroke one night in July (#7-p.48); stayed in hospital long time; Dr. Marcus was one of Mimi's doctors (#7-p.88); recovered well, physical therapy helped her walk and talk (#10-p.3); can't use right hand because of stroke (#11-p.13), limps (#19-p.22). Speech is difficult, says and does weird things (#26-p.2-3). Started watching *Wheel of Fortune* daytime reruns when recovering from stroke, got hooked on it (#19-p.75). On Claud's eighth birthday, Mimi dressed up in kimono and took the family to a Japanese restaurant, which turned out to be closed; instead went to a sleazy pizza joint where Mimi had her first pizza (#26-p.76). Taught Mary Anne how to knit (#78-p.32). Mary Anne invited her to first-grade tea party (MAB-p.40). Mary Anne visits her gravestone, which has a small bouquet of wildflowers on it and a picture of a crane etched into the simple headstone (M#5-p.49).

## RUSS BENEDICT:

**PERSONAL INFO:**
Claudia's uncle, by marriage. Caucasian (#33-p.6). Lived in Stoneybrook until Claudia was about seven; would climb trees with her. (#78-p.9). Has red hair, freckles, and a big friendly grin; Claudia thinks his grandparents came from Ireland (#78-p.8). Has long-lost relatives from Ireland who come to visit for Thanksgiving (#91-p.41).

**EXPERIENCES:**

After huge storm seven years ago, Russ drove over with broken ankle in golf cart to make sure Mimi was okay (#26-p.79). Decides to move back to Stoneybrook (#78-p.28). Is very sad after Peaches has miscarriage; thinks they might wait a while before trying to have another baby (#78-p.128).

**HOUSE:**

Looks like something out of *Better Homes and Gardens*. A perfect Cape Cod-style house, with a white picket fence, big backyard with a climbing tree, and huge front porch (#78-p.133). Master bedroom has a big bed; the sleeper couch is in the room next to it. Bright corner room with gleaming hardwood floors is study/guest room (#78-p.134). Backyard barbecue (#78-p.135).

**PEACHES (MIYOSHI) BENEDICT:**

**PERSONAL INFO:**

Claudia's aunt; Peaches is Mrs. Kishi's sister; Russ thought of the name Peaches, and it stuck (#33-p.6). Carefree and fun, more kid-like than her sister (#78-p.5). Her sense of humor is similar to Claudia's (#97-p.6). Lived in Stoneybrook until Claudia was about seven; would hang from monkey bars in park (#78-p.9). Works for an

advertising firm and is always coming up with wacky ideas for selling toys and weird household products (#78-p.29). Gets a perm (SS#9-p.197). Dr. Zuckerman is her physician (#97-p.34).

**EXPERIENCES:**

Once fell down stairs and an ambulance had to be called (#26-p.80). Doesn't have any kids, but Claud wishes they did (#33-p.6). Is two months pregnant (#78-p.12). Decides to move back to Stoneybrook (#78-p.28). Decides to leave job (#78-p.29). Has miscarriage (#78-p.126). Office will send her freelance work to do at home (#78-p.134). Has baby, Lynn (#97-p.35).

**LYNN BENEDICT:**

**PERSONAL INFO:**

Born in May (#97-p.35). Named after Claudia's middle name (#97-p.36). Almost named Agnes (#97-p.37). Claudia is her godmother (#97-p.45). Wears cloth diapers (#97-p.65).

**EXPERIENCES:**

Christened at the First Congregational Church in Stoneybrook (#97-p.138).

# The McGILLs

•

**GENERAL:**
Stacey and her mom live at 89 Elm Street, her father lives at 321 East 65th St., Apt 2F, NYC, NY 10000 (SS#5-p.195). The three of them first moved to Stoneybrook from NYC on Upper West Side (lived in tenth floor apartment) in August before Stacey's seventh grade; address was 612 Fawcett Avenue (#1-p.29); (#3-p.19); (#13-p.14). Parents can't have any more children and are very protective of her and constantly searching for a miraculous cure for her diabetes (#3-p.19); they thought she needed a "peaceful little town" like Stoneybrook because of her diabetes (#1-p.151). Father worked in Stamford, heading branch of a company (#13-p.12). She and her parents moved back to NYC to 14 West 81st St., Apt. 12E (SS#2-p.3) when father was transferred (#13-p.13); phone there: JK5-8761 (#13-p.139). After parents split up, she and mother moved back to Stoneybrook (89 Elm Street) and father moved to East 65th St. in NYC.

House on Elm St. was run-down and small, but Stacey and mom fixed it up (SB-p.8).

**HOUSE:**
Their house on Elm Street has two sets of stairs, low doorways, wavy panes of glass, and floors that tilt a little (#29-pp.19-21). House dates back to the 1880s (#28-p.8). At least six families have lived in house the past ten or so years (#29-p.65). The McGills' new backyard is back-to-back with the Pikes' (#28-p.88). House has bathtub resting on claw feet, a bedroom with dormer windows (#28-p.89). Doorway to attic is next to doorway for upstairs bathroom (#29-p.18). Attic is on third floor, with light switch at the bottom of the stairs (#29-p.18); it is small but crammed with stuff (#29-p.19). Mrs. McGill has exercise machine in the basement (#83-p.48). Stacey hangs portrait of Sophie, of mystery diary fame, over the living room mantelpiece (#29-p.139).

**APARTMENT:**

Father's address is 321 E. 65th St., Apt. 2F, NYC, NY 10000 (CL-p.3). Apartment is old and classy, with brick walls and a cozy little fireplace (#76-p.15). Building is prewar, with a southern exposure (#28-p.100). Desk in office corner has computer, printer, and fax machine (#76-p.16). There are two bedrooms, one for Stacey whenever she visits; also, there's a futon that unrolls into an extra bed (M#8-p.35); couch in the living room opens into a double bed (SS#6-p.45). Apartment building doesn't have a doorman (SS#6-p.44).

**EDWARD MCGILL:**

**PERSONAL INFO:**

Stacey's father. Stacey is "all he has" (#58-p.65). Pays alimony and child support (#58-p.4) regularly (#65-p.4). Takes a two-bedroom apartment on East 65th St. in a prewar building with southern exposure and woodburning fireplace (#28-p.100). Has awful baby name for Stacey: "Boontsie" (#43-p.31). Often beats around the bush rather than being direct; has trouble talking about his emotions (#76-p.3). Not a morning person (#76-p.47). McGills had been married for fifteen years (#1-p.46). Right before Stacey's diabetes diagnosis, the McGills learned they couldn't have

any more children (#3-p.19). Stacey loves doing things in Manhattan with him (#94-p.4). Non-confrontational, would rather sidestep an issue than fight about it (#99-p.96).

**JOB:**

A workaholic (#76-p.2). Gets promotion to vice-president of the company with a raise and bigger office (#58-p.6); company honors him with a dinner at fancy hotel on Madison Avenue, which Stacey attends. Mr. Davis (president), and Mrs. Barnes (executive vice-president) give him a plaque (#58-pp.97, 100-101).

**EXPERIENCES:**

Breaks ankle on vacation to Pine Island (SB-p.123). Stacey has to leave NYC early, and he gets upset (#58-p.105); Stacey plans special award ceremony and certificate for the Fantastic Father Award (#58-p.138). Hires visiting nurse from Stamford, Miss Koppelman, to stay with Mrs. McGill when she has pneumonia (#58-p.109). Took Stacey to see her first Broadway play, *Annie* (#28-p.106). Goes on vacation to Fire Island with Stacey (#76-p.50). Has secret rendezvous with Samantha Young, the first woman he's dated since divorcing Stacey's mother (#76-P.112); is still seeing her (#99-p.117).

## MAUREEN MCGILL:

### PERSONAL INFO:

Stacey's mother; likes to travel and read, likes dogs and can sew (#24-p.124). Very close friends with Mrs. Pike (#58-p.5). Uses flat voice whenever she talks about Stacey's father (#76-p.2). Speaks French (M#18-p.1). McGills had been married for fifteen years (#1-p.46). Right before Stacey's diabetes diagnosis, the McGills learned they couldn't have any more children (#3-p.19). Loves *I Love Lucy*; favorite episode is when Lucy poses as the Maharincess of Franistan (SS#7-p.151).

### JOB:

Is a buyer at Bellair's department store (#76-p.5); has her own office (M#10-p.29) and gets a great employee's discount (#99-p.35). Used to work part-time in the children's clothing department at Macy's (SB-p.38).

### EXPERIENCES:

Liked Stoneybrook better than her husband liked it (#26-p.84). Goes hunting for full-time job, doing temporary work (#58-p.4); collapses during interview, taken to hospital for pneumonia, goes home for recovery (#58-pp.44, 47); Stacey arranges "Mom-sitters" to care for her when Stacey's not there (#58-p.59). Gets into argument with longtime friend, Laine Cummings' mother (#51-p.119) but expects to patch things up (#51-p.123). Spent junior year of college abroad in Paris; fell in love with Jean-Paul, whose father was a famous chef (M#18-p.1). Is lonely while Stacey is "super-sitting"; misses having someone special to spend Valentine's Day with (#94-p.133).

## OTHER MCGILL RELATIVES:

### BEVERLY AND LOU SPENCER:

Stacey's aunt and uncle in NYC (#3-p.139).

### JONATHAN SPENCER:

Beverly and Lou's child (#3-p.139).

### KIRSTEN SPENCER:

Beverly and Lou's child (#3-p.139).

### CARLA AND ERIC MCGILL:

Stacey's aunt and uncle in NYC (#3-p.139).

### CHERYL MCGILL:

Carla and Eric's child (#3-p.139). Stacey likes Jonathan and Kirsten more than she likes Cheryl (#3-p.139).

# The SPIERs

•

**GENERAL:**
Mary Anne's dad, Richard Spier, and Dawn's mom, Sharon Porter Schafer Spier, marry (#30-p.145); Mary Anne and Richard move into Dawn and Sharon's house because it's bigger (#31-p.7) at 177 Burnt Hill Road, Stoneybrook, CT 06800.

**HOUSE:**
*Indoors:* Old farmhouse (#23-p.4). Has a secret passage (#15-p.6) that goes from Dawn's bedroom to the barn (#23-p.5). Kitchen and bathrooms had been remodeled, but there was still the old outhouse in the backyard with cobwebs in it (#5-p.26). Narrow stairways (#13-p.39) and hallways, low ceilings (M#5-p.33), big brick fireplace, wobbly panes of glass in window; has a garage (#13-p.41). Doorway leads to the attic; light switch is at top of steep, narrow flight of stairs (M#5-p.34). Weak sunshine comes through a dusty window at one end of the attic (M#5-p.52), which has many boxes and a big chair (M#5-p.60).

*Outdoors/barn:* Mr. Spier hangs hammock in the backyard (#66-p.103). Mary Anne rakes leaves in the front yard (#80-p.56). Front porch has a roof (M#9-p.40). Barn has bales of hay sitting around, rope to swing on (#5-p.67); barn is divided into two rows of horse stalls—tools have been removed, but here and there a nameplate remains, as do old feeding troughs, hayloft, ladder (#5-pp.70-71).

*House history:* Built in 1795 (#23-p.4); house used to be a stop on the Underground Railroad (#30-p.7). In 1810, the owners, the Mullrays, who owned a home past the Smythe property and a small farm called Wood Acres (Dawn's house), fell deeply in debt to banker Mathias Bradford. Old Man Mullray and family moved to Peacham, Vermont, except for thirty-year-old son Jared, who wasn't right in the head and who mysteriously disappeared. Legend has it that Jared's ghost still haunts Wood Acres in search of trinkets and things he could sell to pay back Mr. Bradford

(#9-pp.88-91). Sharon purchased the house in run-down condition— nobody had lived on the property for two years (#5-p.67).

*Location:* They live near the Barretts (#58-p.36).

*House rules/customs:* Family makes chore chart, dinner schedule, and promises to be more honest with each other to ease adjustment of moving in together (#31-pp.140-142). Put Christmas tree up the day after Thanksgiving (#93-p.1).

### MARY ANNE'S OLD HOUSE:
Mary Anne and her dad used to live at 59 Bradford Court in Stoneybrook. Mary Anne's mother died when she was a baby and she has no biological siblings (#1-p.5; #27-p.15). Their basement was dark and cold with a cement floor that leaked when it rained (#26-p.36). They almost always ate in the kitchen (#30-p.43). The mail didn't come there until five (#17-p.12).

## MR. RICHARD SPIER:

### PERSONAL INFO:
Mary Anne's father, Dawn's stepfather. Forty-two (#4-p.111). First wife, Mary Anne's mother, died when Mary Anne was a baby (#27-p.15). Very strict (#1-p.5) but warm and caring (#66-p.4). Wears glasses (#4-p.161); gets contact lenses (#5-p.108). Hates asking for favors (#25-

p.71); not a sports fan (#30-p.136); totally unathletic (#64-p.7). Can't stand being interrupted (#30-p.44). Always feels a little uncomfortable around kids (#34-p.20). Dawn calls him "Richard" (#31-p.3). He uses words like "spiffy" (#60-p.31). Owns an old Brownie camera (M#16-p.37). Hates it when people use words like *yeah, shut up, hey,* and *gross* (#4-p.16). Says grace before dinner (#4-p.16). A mashed potato and meat loaf kind of guy (#86-p.7). Mentions of Mary Anne's mom make him sad (MAB-p.8).

### JOB:
Has own law firm in Stamford, begun four years ago (#4-p.111). Law firm is merging with another firm, which means he'll have to travel more (#86-p.10). Used to work at Thompson, Thompson and Abrams (#5-p.111).

### ORGANIZATION/ROUTINES:
A neatnik (#30-p.78). Particular about vocabulary (#4-p.16). Had a rule that phone conversations be limited to ten minutes (#10-p.105). Systematic; arranges books by genre and clothing by color (#31-p.59-60); he color codes his socks; likes sheets to have hospital corners (#64-p.5). Always gets up early, around six, and drinks one-and-a-half cups of coffee; reads paper in methodical order—first, business news, then (in this order) international news, national news, and local news (#31-p.60). Always buttons

his coats and sweaters and shirts the same way, from bottom to top, because that way he won't waste any time making a mistake (#66-p.4); alphabetizes bathroom cabinet (#66-p.4). Shops with a boxful of coupons and a calculator (#67-p.59). Files his socks (#81-p.20).

### HOBBIES/INTERESTS:

Likes jazz music (#60-p.49). Likes driving to Stamford and visiting museums, play matinees, going out for fancy meals (#31-p.62). Has always loved Boston for its chowder and historic sites (#64-p.56).

### EXPERIENCES:

Was devastated after wife Alma died; knowing he wasn't going to be able to take care of Mary Anne for a while, he sent her to the Bakers' house in Iowa; once he got back on his feet, he wanted Mary Anne back. When she was eighteen months old, she was returned reluctantly—there was a custody fight, but it was resolved without much fuss or bitterness (M#5-p.106). Mary Anne's resemblance to Alma is a comfort now, not a painful reminder (M#5-p.107). Marries Sharon Schafer (#30-p.145). Sharon was his SHS sweetheart (#4-p.111). Likes Logan (#60-p.6). On his wedding day to Sharon, he gives Mary Anne a pearl necklace that belonged to her mother (#30-p.140). Used to live on Taylor Street; moved several months before Mary Anne was born (#5-p.112). Goes on

two-week business trip to Cincinnati (#86-p.11).

## SHARON EMERSON PORTER SCHAFER SPIER:

### PERSONAL INFO:

Dawn's mother, Mary Anne's stepmother (#31-p.7). Forty-two (#4-p.107). Pretty with short, curly hair light as Dawn's (#4-p.41). Works (#9-p.13). Her lawyer is a woman (#15-p.18). Does not like cats (#30-p.47) but is getting used to Mary Anne's kitten, Tigger (#52-p.8). Mary Anne calls her "Sharon" (#31-p.3). Always tells Jeff to write, has received one letter in six months (#64-p.134). Rarely gets angry, but when she does, her face turns bright red (#64-p.123). Misses Dawn a whole lot ever since Dawn returned to CA (M#24-p.6).

### DISORGANIZATION/ROUTINES:

Absentminded (#5-p.10), disorganized but nice (#13-p.40), isn't much of a cook (#11-p.61); has been known to leave her gloves in the freezer, her keys in the bathroom soap dish (#60-p.5), or hedge clippers in the bread drawer, or high heels in the refrigerator (#64-p.5). Never owned a vacuum cleaner before the Spiers moved in (M#5-p.6).

### FOOD:

Vegetarian, eats and makes health food for Dawn and Jeff (#5-p.68) and tried to convert Mary Anne and

Richard to vegetarianism but it didn't work (#31-p.62). Does not drink coffee (#31-p.60). Always tells take-out places not to pack the food in Styrofoam and not to send plastic forks (#86-p.78).

**HISTORY:**

Grew up in Stoneybrook (#4-p.44); was Richard Spier's SHS sweetheart (#4-p.111) but her parents disapproved of him (#5-p.107), thought he wouldn't be a success, so they sent her to college in CA (#50-pp.4-5). Went to college in California, where she met Dawn's dad (#31-p.4). Married Dawn's dad about sixteen years ago (#31-p.3). They lived in Palo City (#72-p.2). She divorced him and moved back to Stoneybrook because she had always liked it and she wanted to be closer to her parents, who still live in Stoneybrook (#5-p.1).

**HOBBIES/INTERESTS:**

Likes movies, shopping, going to park for a picnic (#31-pp.61-62). Loves jewelry (#30-p.47).

**EXPERIENCES:**

Marries Richard Spier (#30-p.145). A romantic, saved a rose Richard had given her the night of their senior prom, pressed it in her yearbook (#5-p.9). Dated Theodore "Trip" Gwynne (#9-pp.81-83); Dawn and Jeff called him Trip-Man (#9-p.81); they didn't like him very much. Mary Anne buys Sharon a charm that is replica of the Stoney-

brook High ring for her birthday (#30-p.78). She and Richard don't want to have another baby but offer to give Dawn and Mary Anne another pet, but girls say no thanks (#52-pp.135-136).

**ALMA BAKER SPIER:**

Died of cancer (#1-p.46) when Mary Anne was a baby. Mary Anne has no real memory of her (M#5-p.48). Died very shortly after her illness was diagnosed (M#5-p.113). Was a lovely person, very welcoming to the Thomases when they moved in (M#5-p.113). Had a bright, sunny disposition, like Mary Anne (M#5-p.53). Mary Anne looks and behaves just like her (M#5-p.107). Made a great applesauce cake (M#5-pp.113-115). In childhood, was sensitive and shy and loved animals (M#5-p.127). Cherry-chocolate cake recipe becomes contest-winner, named Alma's Memory Cake (M#21-p.142). Was a terrible cook, but loved sewing, knitting, and other handiworks (MAB-p.146). Middle school grades were all A's (MAB-p.146).

**VERNA AND BILL BAKER:**

Mary Anne's maternal grandparents; address is Box 127, Old County Road, Maynard, Iowa (M#5-p.52). Mary Anne spent her first birthday with them; stays with them until she is eighteen months old (M#5-p.62). They fight Mr. Spier for custody, but dispute is resolved (M#5-p.106). They haven't spoken with Mr. Spier for quite a while (M#5-p.77). Gave Alma a very happy childhood (MAB-p.127). House sits in the middle of a huge field of corn (M#5-p.126). Mary Anne's bedroom is entirely pink; the decorations are from nursery rhymes (MAB-p.134).

### VERNA BAKER:

Mary Anne goes to visit (M#5-from p.126). Verna doesn't farm her land herself but rents it out to farmers down the road; is very curious about Mary Anne and feeds her well and often (M#5-from p.126). Mary Anne is very eager to return next summer (M#5-p.139). Verna finds Alma's famous cherry-chocolate cake recipe for Mary Anne (M#21-p.92). Mary Anne calls Verna "Grandma Baker" (MAB-p.8). A fabulous cook (MAB-p.126). Cries easily (MAB-p.131). Friends are Marion, Ethel, and Janet (MAB-p.136).

### BILL BAKER:

Bill dies of a coronary, making Verna's desire to see Mary Anne more acute (M#5-pp.77-78). Had a positive attitude and something good to say about everything and everybody (MAB-p.132). Always used to say "what you see is what you get" (MAB-p.133).

### GRANNY:

Dawn's grandmother (#5-p.109); early sixties, never sends anyone home empty-handed (#9-pp.86-87); Sharon's mother, she and Pop-Pop still live in Stoneybrook (#5-p.1); Sharon moved back to Stoneybrook because she wanted to be close to her parents (#5-p.1). Lives at 747 Betrand Drive (SS#2-p.173). Is relatively organized; doesn't like Dawn to say "jeez" (SS#11-p.212). Has lived in Stoneybrook her whole life (M#23-p.50).

### POP-POP:

Dawn's grandfather, a banker (#4-p.158); Sharon's father, still lives in Stoneybrook (#5-p.1). Lives at 747 Betrand Drive (SS#2-p.173). Is relatively organized (SS#11-p.212). Has lived in Stoneybrook his whole life (M#23-p.50).

### OTHER SPIER RELATIVES:

#### GRANDPA SPIER:
Richard's father was a mailman in Stoneybrook (#4-p.158). Deceased (#31-p.4).

#### AMY PORTER:
Dawn's second cousin; Dawn hasn't seen Amy since she was in diapers; now she's six and almost four feet tall and learning to read; comes to Stoneybrook for three-week visit

while her parents go to London; misses parents and tries to run away (#87-from p.50). Has freckles and reddish-brown hair, tied with a bow (#87-p.57)

**ED PORTER:**
Son of Granny's cousin; Amy's father; an executive at a meat packing plant; lives in Chicago (#87-p.51). A loud, bearlike guy (#87-p.57).

**ROCHELLE PORTER:**
Ed's wife and Amy's mother (#87-p.52). Elegant and sweet (#87-p.57).

**SPIER PETS:**

**TIGGER:**
Mary Anne's gray tiger kitten (#10-p.129), named after Tigger from *Winnie the Pooh*. Had worms (#11-p.69); likes to bat the phone receiver off hook (#18-p.134). Sleeps with Mary Anne every night in same spot, sheds (#31-p.63). Favorite toys are plastic balls with bell inside, which he keeps losing behind fridge (#25-p.2). Was missing for five days (#25-p.130). Mary Anne has other nicknames for Tigger (#26-p.75); calls him "Mousekin" (#64-p.8); calls him "Tiggy" (#65-p.30) and "Munchkin" (#30-p.41).

# The SCHAFERs

•

**IN STONEYBROOK:**
Live at 177 Burnt Hill Rd., Stoney-brook, CT 06800. *(for description of house, see THE SPIERS).*

**IN CALIFORNIA:**
Live at 22 Buena Vista, Palo City, CA 92800 (SS#2-p.57), near Ana-heim (#23-p.35) (the same one Dawn, Jeff, and Sharon used to live in); house is cool with "terra-cotta floors and skylights in almost all the rooms" (#23-p.34). House is one floor, long and wide, shaped like a square (#23-p.34); airy, open, like a square-edged U around a yard; al-most all the rooms have glass sky-lights (#72-p.8). Long, tiled hall leads to the kitchen (M#12-p.2). Hired a housekeeper, Mrs. Bruen, who keeps the house bright and sparkling (#23-p.34). John Wayne Airport is close to their house; LAX is almost an hour away (#72-p.84). Green couch faces the TV/VCR (M#17-p.8). Carol puts framed pic-tures of Mickey Mouse in the bath-room (SS#12-p.73).

**SHARON PORTER SCHAFER SPIER, See THE SPIERS**

**MR. JACK (JOHN) P. SCHAFER:**

**PERSONAL INFO:**
Dawn's dad, divorced (#5-p.1). Blond (#23-p.63). Superorganized (#5-p.10), he and Sharon weren't right for each other (#5-p.10). Has nickname for Dawn, "Sunshine" (#23-p.1). Marries Carol Olson on December 17 in beach wedding (SS#12-p.132). Is one of the nicest guys in the world, too nice some-times (#72-p.9). A great cook (#72-p.10). Always uses chopsticks with Thai food (#72-p.75).

**EXPERIENCES:**
Jeff and Dawn visit him for the first time after divorce toward the end of the summer (#13-p.38). He and Carol announce their engagement (#72-p.70) then fight and call it off (#72-p.133). After some disastrous other dates, Mr. Schafer proposes to Carol again, with Jeff and Dawn's blessing (#77-p.143); she says yes

(#77-p.143). Marries Carol (SS#12-p.140). Honeymoon in Puerta Vallarta (SS#12-p.200).

## JEFF SCHAFER:

### PERSONAL INFO:
Dawn's younger brother (#5-p.1). Ten years old (#15-p.112), in fifth grade (#11-p.64) [nine (#9-p.42)]. Has spiky sun-bleached hair (#64-p.33). Pretty relaxed about things, like Dawn and mother; has active imagination (#64-p.6). Is practically vegetarian (#73-p.5). Hates getting up early even more than Dawn does (#64-p.78). Doesn't believe in ghosts (#9-p.70). Thinks girls are gross (#98-p.2). Fairly responsible, not allowed to have friends over if Dawn isn't there (#9-p.42). Plays soccer (#64-p.35). Taught Dawn how to climb ropes (#15-p.111). Always uses chopsticks with Thai food (#72-p.75). Hangs out with skateboarding buddies (M#12-p.53). Claims his room is an organized pigsty — Mrs. Bruen is not allowed to move or touch the clutter on his floor (SS#5-p.244). Friends with Jordan, Adam, and Byron; calls them JAB (#98-p.59).

### LIKES/INTERESTS:
Mexican food is favorite (#64-p.53). Loves vending machines, photo booths, and machines that plasticize things (#15-p.109). Loves sports (#64-p.7). His favorite shirt is green-and-white-striped T-shirt (#64-p.32); favorite frozen yogurt is double chocolate chip (#64-p.34). Considers himself a major "Deadhead" (#68-p.121). Loves to create elaborate Halloween costumes (M#17-p.2). Is compiling/writing *Jeff's Off-the-Wall, Krazy, Explode-Your-Sides Sense of Humor (a.k.a. The Jeff Schafer Book of Funniest Jokes Ever Told, Volume One)* (#98-pp.2,58).

### EXPERIENCES:
Born in Palo City but moved to Stoneybrook when parents divorced (#72-p.2). Moved back to California to live with his father (#15-p.112) because he missed him (#11-p.65) and because he had problems at school (#11-p.60) and hated most things about Connecticut (#15-p.13); was always getting into fights with Jerry Haney (#64-p.2). Ms. Besser was his teacher at SES (#15-p.15). Joined basketball team in CA, practically the star player (#30-p.9). Helps Dawn sit for Carol's friends' kids in CA and does a great job with Gregory, who has colic (#34-p.89). Comes back to Stoneybrook for winter vacation (#50-p.5); visits Stoneybrook for week (#64-p.4); didn't get along with Richard because he's not as athletic as Jeff (#64-p.68). Has only sent one letter to Mom in six months (#64-p.134). Gets "O's" (for "Outstanding") instead of A's on book report (#67-p.12). Wants to be a stand-up comedian (#72-p.8). Has to be rushed to the hospital with a ruptured appendix; is kept in hospi-

tal for more than a week, but recovers fully (LS-p.33). Joins the BSC as a Baby-sitter-in-Training (#98-p.64) but then decides it takes too much time — there are better things to do, like Rollerblading (#98-pp.122-3).

## MS. CAROL OLSON:

### PERSONAL INFO:
Age: thirty-two or so (#67-p.3); marries Dawn's father on December 17 in beach wedding (SS#12-p.132). A painter (SS#5-p.42). Keeps her own last name (SS#12-p.207). Initially Mr. Schafer's girlfriend who rubbed Dawn the wrong way (#34-p.82). Tries to be hip, has tons of energy, pays a lot of attention to Jeff and Dawn; tends to go overboard (#72-p.10). Drives a red Miata (#72-p.69) convertible (M#17-p.22). Uses fork to eat Thai food (#72-p.75).

### LIKES/INTERESTS:
Favorite dish is Mr. Schafer's *chimichangas* (#72-p.10). Likes MTV (M#12-p.6). Loves lava lamps (SS#12-p.73).

### EXPERIENCES:
Dawn first hears about her (#31-p.73). Brought her college friend's kids (Carol doesn't have any children) to the house in CA for Dawn to baby-sit: Julie (three) and Gregory (eight months) (#34-p.83); didn't keep a secret about Stacey's CA misadventures, which caused Dawn to respect her (SS#5-p.214); Mr. Schafer is thinking about marrying Carol (SS#5-p.215). She and Mr. Schafer announce engagement (#72-p.70), then fight and call it off (#72-p.133). Then they get back together again; he proposes with Jeff and Dawn's blessing, and she accepts (#72-p.143). She and Mr. Schafer cook a lot together (M#17-p.8). Honeymoon in Puerta Vallarta (SS#12-p.200).

## MRS. BRUEN:

Mr. Schafer's housekeeper; house is bright and sparkling since she's been there (#23-p.34). Day off is Friday (#72-p.81). Keeps the house spotless and is a wonderful cook (M#17-p.5). Nicholas is her newest grandson; she has been spending a lot of time at her daughter's house lately, helping to take care of him (M#17-p.6).

## GRANNY AND POP-POP, see THE SPIERS

**91**

# The STEVENSONs

•

**GENERAL:**
Live two doors down from Kristy at 1206 McLelland Road, next door to Mrs. Porter (#89-p.7). Move to Stoneybrook from Long Island (#89-p.70) with all new furniture and decoration (#90-p.7). Kids are enrolled at SMS because neither Stoneybrook Day nor Kelsey have an orchestra for Anna to play in (#89-p.76). Not normally a demonstrative family (M#23-p.5).

**HOUSE:**
Dark, carved-wood front door; a humongous porch with a swing; a chimney and U-shaped driveway and new wood shingles and a small side extension with a bay window (#89-p.31). Have recycling bin and only buy frozen dinners in recyclable containers (#90-p.49).

**MRS. RACHEL GOLDBERG STEVENSON:**

**PERSONAL INFO:**
Has extremely short brown curly hair, with squarish face and dark hazel eyes (#90-p.11). Very organized (#96-p.80). Drives a minivan (#89-p.60). Family is Jewish, of Eastern European origin (SM#2-p.30).

**JOB:**
An executive editor of a publishing house in New York City (#89-p.71). A workaholic, especially since her husband died (M#23-p.4). Has an assistant at work (#89-p.64). Commutes to work via train (#90-p.115). Usually gets home from work later than 6:45 P.M. (M#23-p.8).

**EXPERIENCES:**
Before husband's death, had started training as a chef at the Culinary Institute of America; taught cooking at a local college (#90-p.5). Stopped cooking after he died (#90-p.7). Did not mention husband's name for a long time after the funeral (#90-p.6).

**MR. JONATHAN STEVENSON:**

**PERSONAL INFO:**
Died in a car crash when the twins were nine (#89-p.71). Was killed in-

stantly, hit by a truck; truck driver only had a broken arm (#90-p.6). Worked in environmental engineering and urban planning (#90-p.5). Wore glasses, and went to the first Woodstock (with a ticket) (#90-p.68). Played the harmonica (#90-p.121).

## ANNA STEVENSON:

### PERSONAL INFO:
Abby's twin; hair and eyes are deep brown, almost black; her hair is cut shorter than Abby's, with bangs; wears glasses or contact lenses (#89-p.62). Nearsighted (M#23-p.4). Has a pointy face (#90-p.10). Is about eight minutes older than Abby (M#23-p.4). Isn't athletic (#96-p.1). Doesn't have asthma or allergies (#96-p.2). Doesn't like public speaking—playing the violin in public is much easier (#96-p.8). Has close bond with Abby—sometimes, they can be in different places and will have intuitions about each other that end up being true (#89-p.79). Quiet (#89-p.80).

### SCHOOL:
In eighth grade at SMS (#89-p.76). Is in Kristy's math class (#89-p.80). Mrs. Pinelli is her orchestra teacher (#95-p.6). Hebrew name is *Hannah* (#96-p.115). Her music class sends tapes to kids in Mexican orphanage (#99-p.52).

### MUSIC:
Music is her life; most of her friends are from orchestras or other groups she plays in (M#23-p.4). Plays piano, but main instrument is violin (#89-p.72). Also plays harmonica (#96-p.2). Practices violin for two-hour stretches; loses track of time when she practices (#89-p.79). Takes private lessons (M#23-p.4). Is first chair in SMS orchestra (#96-p.2). Played a solo with the high school orchestra in Long Island; has won violin competitions (#89-p.82). Likes to practice a couple of hours each school day before dinner (#89-p.144).

### FRIENDS:
Has two best friends from Long Island: Corley has been best friend since kindergarten and is the queen of the note passers (#90-p.62), while Roxanne is a music maven, trumpet player, who has known Anna since third grade and would make Anna play fiddle when they jammed (#90-p.63). Becoming good friends with Shannon (#90-p.87). Has friend, Lauren, from the orchestra (#96-p.122).

### EXPERIENCES:
Asked to join the BSC, but declines because of time constraints (#89-p.143); offer is always open (#89-p.144). Becomes a Bat Mitzvah (#96-p.115).

# ● BSC Family Members ●

## OTHER STEVENSON RELATIVES:

### GRANDFATHER DAVID AND GRANDMOTHER RUTH STEVENSON:
Abby's paternal grandparents (#96-p.101). Abby and Anna have never been close with them (#96-p.102).

### GRANDPA MORRIS AND GRAM ELSIE GOLDBERG:
Abby's maternal grandparents (#96-p.101). Anna and Abby have been close with them, especially since Grandpa had triple bypass heart surgery the year before the Stevensons moved; Grandpa is better now, though still a little weak (#96-p.102). Gram Elsie wears her silver gray hair short, like Mrs. Stevenson; her eyes are so dark they almost seem black; she is tiny, much smaller than Grandpa (#96-p.109).

### AUNT JUDITH:
Mr. Stevenson's younger sister (#96-p.101). Is nicer than her husband (#96-p.105).

### UNCLE SAUL:
Aunt Judith's husband (#96-p.101). A lawyer, the kind of lawyer who never answers any question with yes or no; he frowns a lot and all his suits look exactly the same (#96-p.105).

### SARAH:
Aunt Judith and Uncle Saul's five-year-old daughter (#96-p.101).

### LILLIAN:
Aunt Judith and Uncle Saul's four-year-old daughter (#96-p.101).

### AUNT ESTHER AND UNCLE MORT:
Abby's paternal great-aunt and great-uncle (#96-p.101). They both are very enthusiastic and energetic (#96-p.105).

### MICAH:
Esther and Mort's son (#96-p.101).

### JANET:
Micah's second wife (#96-p.101). Is a doctor and is on call the weekend of Abby and Anna's Bat Mitzvah (#96-p.102).

### AARON, BETTE, JONATHAN:
Micah and Janet's children, aged six, four, and two (respectively) (#96-p.101).

### ELI:
Micah's seventeen-year-old son from his first marriage; doesn't attend Bat Mitzvah; mother lives in Baltimore (#96-p.102).

### COUSIN JEAN:
Mrs. Stevenson's first cousin, who has just gotten divorced (#96-p.102).

### AMY AND SHEILA:
Cousin Jean's two little kids (#96-p.102).

# The RAMSEYs

●

**GENERAL:**
Very close family (#22-p.3). Joined Stoneybrook Community Pool Complex (#55-p.12). Everyone in family is naturally thin except for Cecelia (#61-p.10). Some Ramsey rules: no miniskirts, short phone calls, and no watching horror movies (M#2-p.67). Family has a station wagon (#86-p.107).

**HOUSE:**
Moved into Stacey's old house, 612 Fawcett Ave., Stoneybrook, CT 06800. House in Stoneybrook is much bigger than one in Oakley; parents set up practice area in basement for Jessi; has mirrors, mats and a *barre* (#16-p.5). Mr. and Mrs. Ramsey planted rose garden in backyard, work on it every weekend (#48-pp.89-90). Around the corner from the Johanssens (M#18-p.26); you can see the back of their house from the Johanssens' (M#18-p.27). Have answering machine that allows you to monitor room noise (M#18-p.115). House has a fenced-in backyard and at least two picnic tables and a fir tree (#7-pp.97-98).

**IN NEW JERSEY:**
Lived in Oakley, New Jersey (#14-p.35), on Wagner Lane (SS#2-p.233). Father was transferred to Stamford by company (#16-p.4). In Oakley they lived on the same street as Jessi's grandparents, three aunts, two uncles, and seven cousins (#14-p.36). Neighborhood in Oakley had black and white families, but her street had all black families (#16-p.4); small town (#16-p.4). Family once went to Mexico for a week on vacation (#16-p.1).

**MR. JOHN PHILIP RAMSEY:**

Jessi's dad. Transferred to Stamford by company, which also found their house for them; got big raise and promotion (#16-p.4). Deep voice (#16-p.8), sounds like James Earl Jones (#55-p.4). Jessi calls him "Daddy" (#16-p.3). Picks Jessi up from ballet (#61-p.12).

## MRS. JANICE RAMSEY:

Jessi's mother. Jessi calls her "Mama" (#16-p.3). She and Jessi are very close, wakes up when Jessi wakes up to practice ballet in basement at 5:29 A.M. (probably doesn't know that Jessi knows she wakes up at same time) (#16-p.2). Returns to work in advertising (what she used to do before the children), five days a week, nine to five (#36-p.6). Best necklace is made of shiny black beads called jet (M#8-p.23).

was once stranded on an island during a sailing trip with friends (SS#4-from p.51). Helps Jessi play mean tricks on Aunt Cecelia (#36-p.56). Natalie Springer becomes practically inseparable from Becca and Charlotte (#78-p.137). After the rest of the Ramseys leave Stoneybrook for a weekend, Becca throws a tantrum (M#8-from p.53), "runs away" back to her house, with Mary Anne in tow (M#8-p.95); ends up having a good enough time at the Pikes she doesn't want to leave (M#8-p.124).

## BECCA (REBECCA) RAMSEY:

### PERSONAL INFO:

Jessi's younger sister, eight (#16-p.3). Younger version of Jessi except her eyes aren't as dark as Jessi's and her legs aren't long like Jessi's (#16-p.3). Shy, kind, thoughtful, sensitive (#48-p.2). Has stage fright (#16-p.3). Has hard time getting up in morning (#16-p.6). Big imagination (#22-p.2). A member of the Kids Can Do Anything Club (Kids Club, for short) (#48-p.2). Charlotte Johanssen is her best friend (#75-p.53); friends with Danielle Roberts (#48-p.88). Has twelve Barbies (#48-p.90). Has rock collection (#16-p.118).

### EXPERIENCES:

Last year in second grade she fainted while playing a flower in *Little Red Riding Hood* (#15-p.26);

## SQUIRT (JOHN PHILIP) RAMSEY JR.:

### PERSONAL INFO:

Fourteen months old (#16-p.3). Got his nickname because he was only five pounds, eight ounces when born at Oakley General Hospital (smallest in hospital) and nurses nicknamed him Squirt (#16-p.4). Born in late June (SS#11-p.104). Was a crier as a baby (SS#11-p.109). Gigantic brown eyes (#14-p.33). Extremely bright (#16-p.4). Just learned to walk (#22-p.2); has a wheelie walker but doesn't really need it (#82-p.6). Is into everything, going through "the terrible twos" before he's two (#59-p.51); learning to feed himself (#25-p.60); newest trick is pretending to sneeze (#25-p.65). Latest favorite food is macaroni and cheese (#59-p.52).

**SPEECH/DEVELOPMENT:**
Says four real words so far (#16-p.6). Says "who" for shoe and "whing" for swing (#48-pp.1, 10); "no" is one of his new words (#59-p.54); loves to swing (#48-p.1). Says "ah-*den*" for "again" (#75-p.13). Calls his belly button "ba"; likes to show it off (M#1-p.91).

**EXPERIENCES:**
Goes to talent show in Pikes' backyard with Jessi and Becca (#54-p.144).

## AUNT CECELIA:

**PERSONAL INFO:**
Mr. Ramsey's older sister who moves in with the Ramseys to help out when Mrs. Ramsey returns to work. About fifty or so (#75-p.12). Smells funny, can be bossy (#36-p.7). Always looks as if she's just been eating a lemon (SS#4-p.64). Not naturally thin (#61-pp.10-11). Has an old Volkswagen (SS#4-p.65). Husband Steven died, misses him very much (#36-p.51). Has children (#36-p.59). She and Jessi have been getting along pretty well (#82-p.5).

**EXPERIENCES:**
Used to live in Oakley, then moved to Queenstown, CT, before moving to Stoneybrook (SS#4-p.64). Forbids Jessi to attend one of the BSC meetings (#36-p.105). Short-sheets Jessi's and Becca's beds to get even with them (#36-p.136). Jessi and Becca

think that she's planning to marry Mr. Major, but really they are just good friends in another couple's wedding party (#82-p.98).

## OTHER RAMSEY RELATIVES:

**KEISHA:**
Jessi's cousin and best friend from Oakley (#14-p.36); lived across street from Ramseys (#14-p.71), at 8320 Wagner Lane (SS#2-p.233); has same birthday as Jessi (#16-p.4), which is June 30. Makes surprise appearance at *Coppèlia* (#16-p.139). Has new haircut, wears makeup, and spends every Saturday at the mall with her new friend Jennifer (#67-p.82).

**KARA:**
Keisha's two-year-old sister. Jessi baby-sat for her (#14-p.73).

**YVONNE:**
Jessi's aunt, and mother of Keisha and siblings, who lived across street from Ramseys in Oakley (#14-p.73).

**BILLY:**
Jessi's cousin, Keisha's brother (#14-p.73).

**RAUN:**
Jessi's cousin who lived down the block from her in Oakley (#14-71).

**ISAAC:**
Jessi's cousin, Raun's brother (#14-p.71).

**GRANDMA AND GRANDPA:**
Lived next door to Jessi in Oakley (#14-p.71). Travel to see Jessi dance in *Coppèlia* (#16-p.128).

**GRANDMOTHER:**
Would say the most hurtful things; at first, Jessi thought she was mean, but then she realized that she just wasn't comfortable making small talk (M#3-p.126).

**RAMSEY PETS:**

**MISTY:**
Baby hamster from the Mancusis; girls' first pet (#22-p.138). Has patches of golden brown and white fur, shiny black eyes (#25-p.63). Frodo's sister (M#7-p.22).

# The PIKEs

•

**GENERAL:**
All Pikes have blue eyes and dark chestnut brown hair, though Mallory is the only one with curly hair (#14-p.3) and hers is more reddish (#73-p.1). All kids get chicken pox except Mal (who already had it, and later gets it again (#31-p.40), (#11-p.107); Margo had worst case (#11-p.101). Great-grandfather had ten brothers and sisters, all of whom had names that started with "P" (M#5-p.40). Sitting for the Pike kids is not for the fainthearted: sitters have to be part traffic cop, part referee, and part camp counselor; if a sitter survives a job with them, he or she can sit for anyone (#95-p.43).

**RULES/CUSTOMS:**
Mrs. Pike insists on two sitters if more than five kids are being watched (#14-p.9). There are almost no rules at the Pike house, but Nicky has to stay within two blocks of the house when by himself (#9-p.44). Bedtime for anyone nine or older is now ten P.M. (#29-p.63). The eight Pike kids can eat whatever they want (#9-p.73). They all like spaghetti (#16-p.62). Always use Johnson's Baby Shampoo (#9-p.115). The sitter sometimes does chores at their house and gets higher wages (#9-p.112). The kids hold their breath near graveyards so souls won't possess them (#17-p.122). Family has had a lot of picnic lunches at Carle Playground (#24-p.53). It is Pike family tradition to listen only to classical music on Thanksgiving (#69-p.125) and to do Secret Santas for Christmas (#92-p.112). Whenever the Pikes take a family trip, they have to take two cars (M#11-p.40). Kids begin a lending library out of their rooms, open weekdays three-thirty P.M. to six P.M., weekends ten A.M. to five P.M., not during meals (#36-p.47).

**HOUSE/POSSESSIONS:**
Address: 134 Slate Street, Stoneybrook, CT 06800, not too far from Bradford Court (#4-p.93); have lived there over twelve years (#29-p.65). House has rec room on bottom floor (#47-p.34). Have two station wagons (#8-p.22) and get up early (#8-p.41). Have Nintendo in

rec room (#54-p.81) but don't have Game Boy (#59-p.108). Trees prevent Mal and Stacey from seeing into each other's back windows (#29-p.6). The (new) neighbors the Pikes spy on have a foreign accent (#13-p.59), are French (#13-p.64), and the woman has long, dark hair (#13-p.63). Basement has big sink, and Mr. Pike's workbench (#72-p.108). Backyard fence has daffodils poking up around borders (#73-p.1). Back screen door leads to kitchen (#73-p.123). The McGills' new backyard is back-to-back with the Pikes' (#76-p.8). Mrs. Murphy is neighbor (M#3-p.104). Yard has an apple tree (M#8-p.92) and cherry tree at end of driveway (#31-p.83). Family owns a Polaroid (M#16-p.37).

### SEA CITY:

They rent a large, rambling, old-fashioned gingerbread-looking house in Sea City that's yellow with white trim, has carved woodwork, and three floors (#8-p.33); also has a white wicker swing on the big front porch (#34-p.36); the lifeguard stand is in front of the house; Vanessa and Mal stay in the pink bedroom and Stacey and Mary Anne (who baby-sit for them in Sea City) stay in the yellow room (#8-pp.33-35). House also has a room with a window seat on the third floor, one of Mary Anne's and Mal's favorite places to "curl up in" (#8-p.34). Always take both station wagons to Sea City (#34-p.23) and stop at Howard Johnson's, the halfway point (#34-p.26); the billboard with the three-dimensional purple cow is a favorite landmark they look for every year (#34-p.34). Pikes have Barf Bucket for car sickness (#8-p.24) and decide who will do what to prepare for trip home by drawing names from chore hat (#8-p.124). One Pike rule in Sea City is that no one can go in the water before nine A.M. or after five P.M., since lifeguards are only on duty from nine to five (#34-p.66).

## MR. JOHN PIKE:

### PERSONAL INFO:

Mal's dad. He and wife are tennis nuts, like to go to see tennis matches (#31-p.80). Friends in NYC include the Sombergs and the Wileys (SS#7-p.34).

### JOB:

Gets laid off, finds new job at Metro-Works, smaller firm, lower salary (#39-p.127); used to be a corporate lawyer for big company in Stamford (#14-p.3).

### EXPERIENCES:

Burns his hand cooking for sick household (#31-p.108) and will have a scar (#31-p.144).

## MRS. DEE PIKE:

### PERSONAL INFO:

Mal's mom. Lots of energy, loves kids, patient, funny, hardly ever yells, organized (#5-p.3). Not a fanatic about house cleaning (M#3-p.4). Very close friends with Stacey's mom, Maureen McGill (#58-p.5). Had ears pierced when she was twelve (#21-p.111). She and husband are tennis nuts, enjoy seeing tennis matches (#31-p.80). Only goes to the beauty shop for special occasions (#69-p.124).

### JOB:

Trustee of public library (#5-p.3). Got job as a temporary to help out after Mr. Pike lost job, will continue to work once or twice a week (#39-p.136); works as a secretary but only goes to the office when agency calls (#88-p.38); used to not work (#14-p.3).

### EXPERIENCES:

Injures knee playing tennis (#31-p.108).

## ADAM, BYRON, AND JORDAN PIKE:

### PERSONAL INFO:

Ten years old, identical triplets (#8-p.13) [nine #4-p.92]. In Little League (#20-p.48). Always wear different clothes (#21-p.2). Sleep in bunk beds, which have two tops (#59-p.110). Triplets hate to get their hair cut (#14-p.7). Speak in Pig Latin, which they taught to Mal, when they need private language (#21-p.71); also speak backwards (M#9-p.43). Go to soccer practice (M#11-p.77) and ice hockey practice (#5-p.2). Jeff Schafer is friends with them; calls them "JAB" (#98-p.59).

### EXPERIENCES:

Had viral pneumonia at same time (#31-p.57). Start ABJ Incorporated, an odd-job service, when their dad gets laid off (#39-p.88). Don't snitch on each other when a window is broken while playing ball, call themselves The Three Musketeers (#40-p.46). All three form a Green Patrol, "arrest" anybody who is not being ecologically conscious in the house, go overboard (#57-pp.60, 70). Triplets get traded with Hobart boys for one night, Mal's idea (#59-p.107); triplets were great, Hobart boys were raucous (#59-pp.117-118). Triplets' new friend is Scott Danby (#64-p.59). Make a "clubhouse" out of a big cardboard box (M#7-p.40). Decide that they are too old for baby-sitters (#73-p.8); organize their own kickball league, to mixed results (#73-p.42). Join the BSC as Baby-sitters-in-Training (#98-p.63), but then decide it takes too much time and they have better things to do (#98-pp.122-123).

*Adam:* Has been complaining that they don't have enough Nintendo games (#59-p.108).

*Byron:* Has a lot of fears—afraid to go in haunted house and into ocean, though he can swim (#8-p.66). Doesn't like it when he can't see the bottom of the ocean (#8-p.104). Quieter than other triplets, more serious, sensitive (#8-p.137). Loves to eat (#11-p.106). Has idea to start the lending library (#36-p.42). Isn't into sports as much as other two (#40-p.71). Adores snakes and other slithery things (M#13-p.29).

*Jordan:* Takes piano lessons (#5-p.130). Admires Spuds Diamond, coach on the Olympics, acts like him (#55-p.87). Is very ticklish (M#3-p.25). Invents Secret Agents game and proclaims himself Head Spy (#13-p.62).

## VANESSA PIKE:

### PERSONAL INFO:

Nine (#8-p.13), [eight #4-p.92]. Wears glasses (#14-p.3). Rhymes everything, going to be a poet (#8-p.14). Loses tooth in candy bar (#17-p.72). Keeps a fat notebook full of her poetry (#21-p.33); not athletic, favorite activity is sitting somewhere in private and writing poetry; has volumes of poetry so far (#31-p.79). Super competitive (#76-p.142). A dud at sports (#80-p.6). Shares room with Mal (#80-p.48). Dusting is the only cleaning job she likes to do, which she does dreamily (M#3-p.31). Is the slowest person Mary Anne's ever met; Mrs. Pike

sometimes has to wake her twenty minutes before the other Pike kids in order for her to get ready on time (SS#1-p.21). Doesn't talk in rhyme when she's upset (#96-p.72).

### EXPERIENCES:

Takes violin lessons (#5-p.2). Skids on bike into cherry tree at end of driveway and sprains ankle (#31-p.83). Has crush on Chris at ice cream parlor in Sea City (#34-p.79); writes him poems, but he thinks they're from Mal; decides not to correct the mistake and writes one last poem pretending it's from Mal (#34-p.127). Dresses as one of The Three Stooges with Charlotte Johanssen and Haley Braddock to cheerlead Krushers' World Series (#38-p.110). Acts as "Miss Vanessa"—styles hair on playground to earn money while Dad is laid off (#39-p.118). Temporarily becomes ex-best friends with Haley after the two of them wear the same swimsuit to Stoneybrook Day Camp (#76-p.59). Puts together scary haunted house (#79-p.119). Her essay wins the Channel 3 "Old-fashioned Christmas Contest" (#92-p.29).

## NICKY (NICHOLAS) PIKE:

### PERSONAL INFO:

Eight (#8-p.13) [seven #4-p.92]. Third-grader (#79-p.3). Wears glasses (#14-p.3). A champion hider (#9-p.118). Has a coin collection (#9-p.132). Is a pest because he wants to be "one of the guys" but triplets don't always let him play with them (#8-p.137). Hates girls (#14-p.2); rarely nice to his sisters (#20-p.65). Ms. Farnsworth is teacher (#44-p.10). Likes Marilyn Arnold, and she likes him (#51-p.128). Pretty fast runner; likes sliding into base (M#7-p.7). Can't play first base without his lucky penny (M#7-p.120). Doesn't believe in "wasting" clean clothes by changing too often (M#11-p.41). Gets a haircut; the triplets say he looks like a cactus (M#16-p.31).

**EXPERIENCES:**
Tells Dawn she's his favorite sitter (#9-p.137). The only Pike to break a bone, falling out of tree (#8-p.61). Breaks finger in two places playing volleyball with Buddy (#14-pp.8-9). Rebreaks finger plus two others in gym (#31-p.78). Can go to his hut, secret passageway at Dawn's house, only if he tells person in charge that he's going (#23-p.114). Starts paper route, makes more money than ABJ, Inc. (#39-p.131). Plays on the Krashers (M#7-p.120). Pitches for the Krashers (M#9-p.7). Wins third-grade Readathon, surprising Mary Anne (M#13-p.142).

## MARGO PIKE:

**PERSONAL INFO:**
Seven (#8-p.13) [six #4-p.92]. Gets carsick (#8-p.28) and airsick (SS#1-p.8); weak stomach (#16-p.64);

needs the Barf Bucket on family trips. Has pigtails (M#11-p.87). Going through bossy phase (#14-p.2). She's crazy about her teacher, Ms. Cook (M#3-p.28). Has been obsessed with weddings lately (M#4-p.39). Doesn't like Oriental food (SS#7-p.184).

**EXPERIENCES:**
Throws up on merry-go-round at Sudsy's (#24-p.104). Almost gets sick at Trampoline Land in Sea City (#34-p.102). Jordan taught her how to play "Chopsticks" on the piano (#15-p.52). Can't carry a tune (#15-p.53) but can peel a banana with her feet (#15-p.55). Gets bronchitis (#31-p.108). Shoplifts a small ring and two packs of gum from Pembroke's Party Store (#68-p.76), then confesses her deed to her mother and pays back the store (#68-p.104). Promises to visit all of her new friends at Stoneybrook Manor at least once a month (#69-p.114).

## CLAIRE PIKE:

**PERSONAL INFO:**
Youngest Pike kid, five (#8-p.13) [four #4-p.92]. Goes to morning kindergarten, but can stay for the second session as well (SS#7-p.75). Sometimes runs around house naked (#4-p.92). Calls parents "Moozie" and "Daggles" (#8-p.21). Silly, attaches "silly-billy-goo-goo" to people's names (#14-p.2). Huggable and affectionate (#14-p.3).

Wears watch on right wrist though she can't tell time (#15-p.95). Has temper (#20-p.59), throws baseball tantrums, even when it's a game on television (#20-p.66). Noodle is Claire's mop-horse (#54-p.4). Best friends with sister Margo (#51-p.25). Likes to "help" in the kitchen (M#3-p.2) Has favorite dress that the Pikes call the Lucy Dress because it looks like something Lucy from the Peanuts comic strip would wear; striped blue and black with a flouncy skirt; Claire has worn it practically every day for the past six months (M#3-p.146). Her softball blow-ups are famous (M#7-p.48). Still believes in Santa Claus but is a little suspicious (#92-p.69).

### EXPERIENCES:

Gets bronchitis (#31-p.108). Promises to visit all of her new friends at Stoneybrook Manor at least once a month (#69-p.114). Protests the younger kids' exclusion from the Krashers (M#7-p.49). Made junior assistant equipment manager of Krashers, with Suzi and Patsy (M#7-p.87). Sees *Annie* and wants to be a star (M#11-p.20). Gets a "promotional video" at the mall (M#11-p.47); sends it out to an agent, who rejects her (M#11-p.135). Comes down with a case of vampire phobia (M#15-from p.42); is cured after dressing up as witch and "scaring" a vampire (M#15-p.116). Has new stuffed bear, Thomas (SS#10-p.25).

### PIKE PETS:

### FRODO:

Hamster, family's first pet, got it from the Mancusis; sibling to Misty (#22-p.139). Jessi watches him for Pikes when they go to Sea City, he gets loose; Jessi discovers Squirt had put it in Misty's cage (#34-pp.108,113). Gets dyed green and entered in pet show (#42-p.150). "Mr. X" threatens to do something to him, so the Pikes protect him (M#2-from p.81).

### POW:

Full name is Pow Barrett Pike (#86-p.1). Adopted by the Pikes from the Barretts after it is found that Marnie is allergic (#71-p.80). A basset hound (#5-p.46). Big, brown eyes; is patient, good-natured (#71-p.40). Short, stubby legs are compensated for by big strong chest, thick tail, and deep bark (#73-p.43). Gets entered in pet show, covered with pink ribbons (#42-p.150). In talent show with Buddy and Suzi as trainers; lazy, does not move after going through hula-hoop and eating T-bone steak Buddy used for bait (#54-p.147). Can roll over, play dead, and bark exactly three times on command; likes to watch *Scooby-Doo* on TV (#71-p.135); Barretts visit him every single day (#71-p.148).

### SARGE:

Cat, mentioned by Mary Anne in passing (#1-p.99). Since deceased.

## OTHER PIKE RELATIVES:

### UNCLE JOE:

Mr. Pike's uncle; lives in Stoneybrook Manor. Is in the early stages of Alzheimer's disease (#91-p.10). Has rugged face, clear blue eyes (M#3-p.31). Is thin, kind of bent over; hair is white, wears little spectacles with wire rims; wears starched white shirt buttoned all the way to the neck (M#3-p.52). Voice is dry, papery (M#3-p.53). A very confusing guy—can be so gruff and cranky, but also seems so frail and alone (#92-p.66). Used to go fishing, play tricks with Mr. Pike (M#3-p.10). Comes to stay with the Pikes for a month, lives in the den (M#3-p.11). Sometimes gets a little depressed (M#3-p.12). Can't stand dirt on his hands; is pretty standoffish (M#3-p.54). Not the easiest person to be around (#92-p.10). Makes odd little collections (like piles of scrap paper) (M#3-p.100). Goes back to SM (M#3-p.110). Has good, lucid days (M#3-p.154). Doesn't like crowds (#92-p.12). Hates to leave his room (#92-p.10). Mr. Connor is his roommate (M#3-p.152). Doesn't pay attention to loud TV, but uses it to drive Connor out of the room (#92-p.65). At Thanksgiving party, blows bubbles with kids (#69-p.108).

### MARIE AND PHIL STRAUSS:

Mrs. Pike's cousins, live in an apartment in NYC, invite the Pikes for Thanksgiving and the Macy's Parade (#69-p.3).

### MAL'S GRANDPARENTS:

All live pretty far away (M#3-p.32).

# The BRUNOs

•

Address: 689 Burnt Hill Rd., Stoneybrook, CT 06800 (#25-p.49). Got an upright piano from Barrett/DeWitts for Hunter's lessons (SS#12-p.226). Buys new computer with CD-ROM (#94-p.115).

## MR. LYMAN BRUNO:

Not a real macho-type, but old-fashioned; isn't thrilled about Logan's BSC membership but figures it's okay if Logan's simply doing it for Mary Anne (LS-p.15). Member of the Chamber of Commerce softball league (LB-p.7).

## MRS. LOUISE BRUNO:

In the 1960s, used to sleep with picture of Paul McCartney under her pillow (LB-p.27).

## KERRY BRUNO:

Logan's ten-year-old sister (#46-p.12) [nine, #25-p.20]. Has Logan's eyes and nose; hair is blonde, thick, and straight, looks like mother (#25-p.42). Had Tigger in her closet when kitten was missing (#25-p.131).

## HUNTER BRUNO:

Logan's five-year-old brother (#25-p.20); same dark blond, curly hair as Logan; looks like father (#25-p.42); allergic to dust, wheat, milk, strawberries, and seafood (#25-p.48). Also allergic to mold, pollen, animal hair (LS-p.11). Usually has a stuffed-up nose (#46-p.12). Kindergarten teacher thinks he's a piano prodigy; is going to start taking piano lessons (SS#12-p.226). Has a plastic dinosaur named Tricera Tops (LS-p.85).

## LEWIS BRUNO:

Logan's cousin from Louisville, KY; fourteen, fantastic-looking (#37-p.102). He and Logan spent summers on horse farm two hours outside of Louisville (#50-p.140). Brown eyes, 5'10", hates grits (#37-pp.132-133); writes Dawn, looking forward to meeting her (#37-p.137). Visits Logan's family during winter break (#50-p.56); Mary Anne, Dawn, and Logan meet him at airport; has short wavy, dark hair; looks taller than 5'10", thin, handsome, great smile (#50-p.87). Goes on double dates with Dawn, Mary Anne, and Logan to see *Gone With the Wind* (#50-p.109) and to Cabbages and Kings restaurant; goes bowling with them (#50-p.147). Has gone bowling with Logan lots of times, fathers were in same league (#50-p.147). Loves the food Dawn makes (#50-p.141). Tells Dawn he liked her the way she was in her letters and picture before her "sophisticated makeover" (#50-p.137). He and Dawn kiss (#50-p.150); plan to see each other over summer, continue to write (#50-p.153).

# The KILBOURNEs

•

**GENERAL:**
Live across the street from Kristy on McLelland Road, next door to Papadakises (#11-pp.9, 29). The three Kilbourne kids go to Stoneybrook Day School (#38-p.35). Go to family reunion (M#5-p.109). Mrs. Bryar is housekeeper (ShS-p.104).

**HOUSE:**
TV room is a large, wood-paneled room just past the kitchen, with a large Haitian-cotton couch facing a huge TV set; next to the TV is a cabinet with glass shelves above and drawers below; the top two shelves have Shannon's awards, and the third shelf has Maria's (#70-p.64). Maria's bedroom has pink wallpaper with a heart pattern, stuffed animals propped up all over the place, and framed swim team photos over her desk (#70-p.66). Tiffany's room, a pigsty, is across the hall from Shannon's (#70-p.67).

**MR. TED KILBOURNE:**

Not very tall; has dark hair and brown eyes (ShS-p.4). A workaholic; a lawyer with a big firm; also has Rotary Club meetings and board meetings and jogging and lunches and dinners with clients (ShS-p.11). Had been a serious gardener when Shannon was a kid (ShS-p.6). Has a beeper (ShS-p.104).

**MRS. KATHY KILBOURNE:**

Some people think Shannon and Mrs. Kilbourne look alike, but Shannon thinks her mom looks more like Tiffany; has thick, blonde hair, cut short; eyelashes are incredibly dark; tall (ShS-p.4). Tends to move at hyper-speed (ShS-p.5). Chaperones SDS field trip to Paris (ShS-p.103). Is thinking of getting a job again (ShS-p.142).

**TIFFANY KILBOURNE:**

**PERSONAL INFO:**
Eleven (#61-p.108). Blonde hair, blue eyes, and high cheekbones (#70-p.60). Tall, with incredibly dark eyelashes (ShS-p.4). Must

wear uniform to SDS (ShS-p.3). Used to be quiet but has recently turned into a brat (#70-p.23). Doesn't get along with Maria (#70-p.59). Doesn't do too well in school; never does homework; teacher sends notes home to parents (#70-p.66). Room is a pigsty (#70-p.67).

**EXPERIENCES:**
Goes with Shannon and Maria to the Kormans when Claud is sitting; they build a snow village (#61-p.109). Takes up gardening as a hobby (#70-p.108). Is raising spinach in her garden (ShS-p.2).

## MARIA KILBOURNE:

**PERSONAL INFO:**
Eight (#11-p.36). Has dark, reddish-brown hair and hazel-brown eyes (#70-p.60; ShS-p.4). Hates anything athletic; likes homework (#38-p.46). While it looked like she was going to turn into a bookworm, she's become outgoing and athletic (#70-p.59). Just started tap dancing (#83-p.68). Is crazy about math (ShS-p.7). Member of the SDS Junior Swim Team (ShS-p.45). Likes Word Searches (#70-p.108).

**EXPERIENCES:**
Goes with Shannon and Tiffany to Kormans when Claud is sitting; build snow village (#61-p.109). Has won trophies for swimming butterfly stroke; holds SDS record for breast stroke (#70-p.64).

## KILBOURNE PETS:

**ASTRID OF GRENVILLE:**
Pedigreed Bernese mountain dog (#11-p.29). Has puppy which Shannon gives to the Brewers; David Michael names it Shannon (#11-p.136).

# BSC Clients

•

# The ADDISONs

•

**GENERAL:**
Dawn was first to sit for them; parents shuttle kids from class to class to gain time for themselves; they call Claud to give Corrie art lessons once a week (#26-p.23), own blue Camaro (#26-p.134).

**SEAN ADDISON:**

**PERSONAL INFO:**
Ten (#26-p.23); takes tuba lessons (#26-p.40).

**EXPERIENCES:**
Rehearses for talent show in Pikes' backyard playing "Old MacDonald Had a Farm" on his tuba (#54-p.84); in talent show, supposed to be first act but goes on second because he temporarily loses tuba (#54-pp.145, 147). Burned books because he hated Readathon; feels ignored and abandoned; is a very mixed-up kid (M#13-p.133).

**CORRIE ADDISON:**

**PERSONAL INFO:**
Nine (#26-p.23); pretty with brownish-blonde hair cut straight across forehead in bangs; long, dark lashes; small for her age; no color in her cheeks (#26-p.37). Likes art (#26-p.40) and Nancy Drew, makes papier-mâché puppet of her (#26-p.44). Timid (#26-p.119), feels close to Claud (#26-p.105), and decides to give puppet to her instead of to her mother (#26-p.119).

**EXPERIENCES:**
Goes to Green Fair with her mother (#57-p.136).

**MRS. ADDISON:**

**EXPERIENCES:**
Takes Corrie to the Green Fair; is very impressed (#57-pp.136-137).

# The ARNOLDs

•

## GENERAL:

House is always well-decorated for Christmas (M#18-p.42) and other holidays (M#22-p.71). Christmas tree looks like something out of a picture book (M#18-p.44). Don't subscribe to cable-movie channels (#97-p.51).

## MARILYN AND CAROLYN ARNOLD (TWINS):

### PERSONAL INFO:

Eight (#30-p.33); identical twins who used to dress alike and who attend SES, were seven (#21-p.19). In second grade (#51-p.44). Used to have brown hair; wear silver rings on right pinkies and beaded ID bracelets on left wrists (#21-p.23). Communicate in nonsense twin talk; like to read (#21-p.62). Marilyn's nose is slightly more rounded than Carolyn's, whose cheeks are fuller (#21-p.87); after Mal and twins confront Mrs. Arnold they become more individualistic in appearance and manner (#21-p.137).

### EXPERIENCES:

Bedroom was split into identical halves (#21-p.26). They have trouble getting along until Mary Anne suggests they have separate rooms; Marilyn moves into sewing room and Carolyn into old guest room (#30-p.117). Twins, Rodowsky boys, and Braddocks send nice anonymous notes to BSC, treat them to surprise lunch at Rosebud Cafe for being great baby-sitters (#63-pp.131, 134). Twins go to Spring Dance at Community Center, dance with two of the triplets (#63-p.147). Take tennis lessons, dressed in whites (#67-p.29). Take gymnastic lessons; turn basement into mini-gymnastic center (M#12-p.45). Are frightened by *Horrorville* movies (#97-p.79) until they see "The Making of *Horrorville*" (#97-p.83) and decide to make their own movie, *The Twins Who Mutilated Their Baby-sitter* (#97-p.118).

# ● BSC Clients ●

## MARILYN:

### PERSONAL INFO:
Has tiny mole under right eye (#21-p.72), the more dominant twin, hair has grown out an inch or two and she wears simpler clothes (#30-pp.34-35). Her room (the old sewing room) is now all yellow (wallpaper, bedspread, rug) (#30-p.120). Likes Nicky Pike, gives mushy 3-D Valentine's Day card to him at Masquerade Party (#51-p.128). Says "You've got to or I'll go crazy mad out of my mind" when she wants one of her baby-sitters to do something for her (SB-p.156). Has a very good ear for songs (#86-p.71). Practices piano for half an hour each day (#21-p.25); is an excellent player, has taken lessons since she was four (#21-p.62).

### EXPERIENCES:
Gozzie Kunka is pretend-friend Marilyn makes up (#30-p.38). Plays piano with Shea in band performance that BSC organizes (#56-p.94); plays "If I Were a Rich Man" with Shea and rest of kids during performance (#56-p.132). Practicing Bach's "The Well-Tempered Clavichord" for piano recital (#60-pp.96-97). Watches over Carolyn after she sprains her ankle (M#12).

## CAROLYN:

### PERSONAL INFO:
Has tiny mole under left eye (#21-p.72). Tone deaf (#21-p.53). Gets haircut (very stylish with longer curls down the back of her neck) and trendier clothes (#30-p.35). Has become very fashion-conscious — it would kill her to wear the same thing two days in a row (#30-p.68). Room now has shaggy blue rug, bedpread printed with little black and white cats with matching curtains, and a wastebasket with pointy cat ears and a furry tail; two pillows in the shape of cats, blue-and-white-striped wallpaper (#30-p.121; M#12-p.78). Likes James Hobart, gives 3-D card to him at Masquerade Party (#51-pp.48,129). Likes puzzles (#21-p.27) and science (#21-p.49). Wants to be a scientist (#66-p.9); carries an official-looking notebook and a pen in order to write down data (#66-p.10).

### EXPERIENCES:
Plays out a *Back to the Future* fantasy; becomes like the mad scientist from the movie, makes her own time machine in their basement (#60-pp.10, 35, 37); sells tickets to kids to take a ride (#60-p.100); kids get their money back; Mary Anne helps her distinguish between reality and fantasy (#60-p.126). Badly sprains her ankle, must use crutches (M#12-p.49); is consequently watched over by Marilyn.

## MRS. LINDA ARNOLD:

Heads up fund-raising project at SES and needs sitter for eight weeks, Tuesday and Thursday, three-thirty P.M. to six P.M. (#21-p.20). Wears too many accessories that are too cute (#21-p.24). Redecorated kids' new rooms quickly (#30-p.119). Hair is permed (#68-p.19) Wears contact lenses (#79-p.115). Throws herself into the holiday season (M#18-p.42); bakes dozens of cookies (M#18-p.43).

## MR. JACK ARNOLD:

Reads *The Time Machine* to Carolyn (#60-p.35); participates in Underwear Race (#67-p.46).

## OTHER ARNOLD RELATIVES:

### AUNT ELAINE AND UNCLE FRANK:
Gave twins jump sticks for their birthday (#21-p.96).

# The BARRETTs and the DeWITTs

•

**FAMILY HISTORY:**
Barretts recently divorced. Mal calls the kids "The Impossible Three" (#5;#47-p.6); not so impossible anymore; some of Dawn's favorite kids (#57-p.19). Barrett kids get along with mother's boyfriend, Franklin DeWitt, very well (#64-pp.14, 28); Barrett kids don't like DeWitt children at first couple of encounters (#64-pp.43, 68); two families call a peace (#64-p.120). Seven kids share the same bizarre taste in food (#77-p.56). Mrs. Barrett and Mr. DeWitt announce plans to marry (#77-p.90). Wedding will be in December (#77-p.92). Kids don't react too well; the Barretts try to "DeWitt-proof" the house (#77-p.95). The De-Witts/Barretts decide to look for a new, bigger house; the kids bond (#77-p.118). Natalie and Franklin show the kids a house in Greenvale (M#17-p.49); but the kids do *not* want to leave Stoneybrook (M#17-p.76); Natalie and Franklin promise to stay in Stoneybrook (M#17-p.104); the DeWitt kids have a grandmother living nearby (M#19-p.84). Dawn is under instructions not to let the Barrett kids talk to their biological father if he calls (#5-p.89).

**NEW HOUSE:**
48 Chestnut Drive (SS#12-p.55). Very little front yard, no porch, four bedrooms (including a basement bedroom) (M#17-pp.107-108). No chimney (SS#12-p.52). Is kind of small (#84-p.24). Mr. and Mrs. De-Witt announce they're going to build an addition to the house (#84-p.100). At groundbreaking ceremony, kids announce the changes they want made: two big bedrooms next to each other, one for Buddy and Taylor, one for Lindsay and Suzi; Madeleine, Marnie, and Ryan will still each have rooms of their own (#84-p.123).

**OLD HOUSE:**
On Slate Street, three houses down from the Pikes, toward Dawn's house (#5-pp.21, 136). House isn't as messy anymore (#57-p.21); their house was a pigsty (#5-p.44). House has a front porch (#77-p.52). The Murphys and the Spencers are their

neighbors (#5-p.129). Buddy's room is decorated in "Early American Ninja Turtle" style (M#17-p.45).

## BUDDY (HAMILTON) BARRETT, JR.:

### PERSONAL INFO:
Eight (#13-p.96) [seven #5-p.22]. Third-grader (#79-p.6). Skinny, big knobby knees (#5-p.119). Wasn't reading at proper level (#29-p.34) but Mal tutors him successfully (#29-p.132). Picky eater (#24-p.109). Active and lively (#25-p.95). A mischief maker (SS#12-p.142).

### EXPERIENCES:
Mr. Moser is third grade reading teacher (#29-p.34). Buddy says he hates flash cards almost as much as he hates Mr. Moser (#29-p.51). After Mal's successful tutoring, Buddy is moved from lowest reading group (the Crows) to the middle reading group (the Robins) in his class (#29-p.142). Has crush on Shannon Kilbourne (#38-p.90). Likes *Dragon Warriors*, a TV show that comes on at eight (#25-p.97). Is "The World's Greatest Animal Trainer" in talent show held in Pikes' backyard (#54-pp.85, 86, 146). Sings in All the Children of the World, which BSC helps organize (#56-p.65). In Save the Planet class (#57-p.36); he and Billy work animal booth at Green Fair (#57-pp.85, 138). Figures out that the moondust they ordered through the mail is a lie (#58-p.73); he and other kids do traveling salesmen show to earn money (#58-pp.114-115); he and Suzi perform a "Mother's Helper" play (#58-p.124). Gets into fights over his participation in Mary Anne's sewing class; goes overboard in proving his masculinity (#66-p.90). Substitutes for Matt at second base for the Krashers (M#9-p.7). Ring bearer at mother's wedding (SS#12-p.142).

## SUZI BARRETT:

### PERSONAL INFO:
Five (#13-p.96) [four #5-p.11]. Round-faced, pigtails (#5-p.11), fat round tummy, pudgy (#5-p.119). Has a fit if Mary Anne shows up without little coloring books in her Kid-Kit (M#16-p.48). Likes to dance the baloney dance (SS#12-p.210).

### EXPERIENCES:
Is Buddy's assistant in talent show in Pikes' backyard (#54-pp.85, 146). In cross-country race in Mini-Olympics (#55-p.132). In Save the Planet class (#57-p.36); she, Karen, and Andrew make "Think Green, My Kids Care" buttons (#57-p.85); their booth gets temporarily smushed (#57-p.132). Orders moondust through the mail (#58-p.73); she and Buddy perform "Mother's Helper" play during traveling salesmen show (#58-p.124); keeps moondust instead of selling it with rest of stuff (#58-p.128). Made ju-

nior assistant equipment manager of Krashers, with Claire and Patsy (M#7-p.87).

## MARNIE BARRETT:

### PERSONAL INFO:

Two (#13-p.97) [one and a half #5-p.22]. Curly blonde hair and blue eyes (#5-p.43). Allergic to chocolate (#5-p.85). Sometimes fusses when mother leaves (#58-p.112). Cries sometimes; talks or sings when she wakes up from nap; makes "ham face" when happy (#5-p.48). Hates her playpen (#67-p.57). Highly allergic to cat and dog dander (#71-p.45). Room is made "dust-free" (#71-p.76). Has a huge crush on Jessi (#100-p.32).

### EXPERIENCES:

Once ate so much Kleenex she threw up (#58-p.39).

## MRS. NATALIE BARRETT:

### PERSONAL INFO:

Marries Franklin DeWitt (SS#12-p.156). Gorgeous, like a model, with chestnut curls; wears a lot of perfume (#5-p.44). Thirty-three, with lines on face and a few gray hairs (#5-p.88). Has a great figure and is always wearing elegant outfits (M#4-p.90). Disorganized, never gives instructions to sitters (#5-p.85); often calls for sitters on wrong day or after BSC meetings (#62-p.60). Happier and life has straightened out, so kids have settled down some (#64-p.11). Wears *Passion* perfume (#66-p.88). A nervous driver (SS#10-p.45). Has part-time job (#57-p.21).

### EXPERIENCES:

Marries Franklin DeWitt (SS#12-p.156). Kids like Franklin (#64-pp.14, 28); she and Franklin take all of their kids to petting zoo in Lawrenceville; turned into a disaster (#64-pp.44-45, 50). She makes Italian dinner for DeWitt family (#64-p.63). Shows Mary Anne a beautiful engagement ring that sparkles on her third finger (#77-p.91). Used to play intramural sports in college (ShS-p.123).

## MR. FRANKLIN DEWITT:

### PERSONAL INFO:

Mrs. Barrett's new husband (SS#12-p.156); very tall with auburn hair and wire-rimmed glasses (#64-p.16); gets along with Barrett kids well (#64-pp.14, 28). Has four kids about age of Barrett kids (#64-p.27). Is a very prompt and organized person (#77-p.51).

### EXPERIENCES:

Marries Mrs. Barrett on December 17 (SS#12-p.156). Kids weren't too interested in meeting Barretts for the first time (#64-p.43); kids reconcile and get along well (#64-pp.120-121).

**119**

# ● BSC Clients ●

## LINDSEY DEWITT:

**PERSONAL INFO:**
Eight (#64-p.42). Favorite food is Italian (#64-p.63). Hates olives (#64-p.69). Is a mischief maker; flower girl at father's wedding (SS#12-p.142)

## TAYLOR DEWITT:

**PERSONAL INFO:**
Six (#64-p.42). Hates onions (#64-p.69). His teacher is Mrs. Jody Andrews (#100-p.34).

## MADELEINE DEWITT:

**PERSONAL INFO:**
Four (#64-p.42). Teacher is Miss Raymond (#100-p.35). Always says her tummy hurts (#100-p.36).

## RYAN DEWITT:

**PERSONAL INFO:**
Two (#64-p.42).

## MR. HAMILTON BARRETT:

Lives in Milwaukee now (SS#12-p.50). Only supposed to speak to Buddy, Suzi, and Marnie on alternating Tuesdays (#5-p.123). Used to live in apartment near Stoneybrook (#5-p.91).

## OTHER BARRETT RELATIVES:

**BUDDY'S AUNT:**
Lives in Alaska (M#9-p.79).

**GRAM, GRAMPS, GEE-MA, AND GEE-PA:**
Buddy's names for his grandparents (#5-p.94).

**RANDI:**
Mrs. Barrett's sister, maid of honor (SS#12-p.149).

**ANDREA AND JENNIFER:**
Mrs. Barrett's bridesmaids (SS#12-p.149).

**GREG:**
Usher at Mrs. Barrett's wedding; walks down the aisle with Stacey; Mr. McGill's age (SS#12-pp.152-153).

## BARRETT PETS:

After Pow leaves, they quickly acquire gerbils, hermit crabs, and fish (#71-p.148). Animals are kept in the playroom (M#16-p.30).

**POW:**
See *the Pikes.*

**MR. TURTLE:**
Presumably a turtle (M#16-p.30).

**FRISKY:**
Gerbil, who isn't very frisky; mostly, he sleeps (M#16-p.30).

**120**

# The BRADDOCKs

•

**GENERAL:**
Moved to neighborhood (#16-p.20). Whole family knows sign language (#16-p.35). Own station wagon (#86-p.101). Mr. Braddock owns a camcorder, which the kids use to shoot a movie for Dawn (#68-p.108). Mr. and Mrs. Braddock host a picnic for hearing-impaired children (M#16-p.41).

**HOUSE:**
The "finished" section of the Braddocks' basement is surrounded by walls of wood paneling. Behind the walls are a few small rooms (#79-p.131). Live near the Kishis (M#6-p.69).

## HALEY BRADDOCK:

**PERSONAL INFO:**
Nine (#16-p.20); small, short blonde hair with tail; brown eyes, dark lashes, heart-shaped face with dimple in right corner of mouth (#16-p.33). Wears a pendant made of clay painted red with an H scratched in it that Matt made in art class and gave to her last Christmas (#16-p.96). Super competitive (#76-p.142).

**EXPERIENCES:**
Becomes friends with Vanessa Pike (#20-p.60). Dresses as one of the Three Stooges with Vanessa and Charlotte Johanssen to cheerlead for Krushers' World Series game (#38-p.110). Dresses as Mme Leveaux, queen of the Gypsies, to tell kids' fortunes for money (#44-p.101); wins telescope for most creative fund-raising idea (#44-p.120). Goes to Valentine's Day Masquerade Party (#51-p.46). Enters the funny-face race in Mini-Olympics run by BSC (#55-pp.80-81). Temporarily becomes ex-best friends with Vanessa after the two of them wear the same swimsuit to Stoneybrook Day Camp (#76-p.59). On the Krashers (M#7-p.86).

## MATT (MATTHEW) BRADDOCK:

**PERSONAL INFO:**
Seven (#16-p.20), uses American Sign Language (#16-p.32). Pro-

121

foundly deaf (#16-p.35). One of the best players on Kristy's Krushers (#53-p.99). His laugh sounds like a cross between fingernails on a blackboard and a goose honking (#16-p.48). Attends School for the Deaf in Stamford (#16-p.109), entered when he was two (#16-p.110). Ms. Frank is Matt's teacher (#16-p.111). On the Krashers (M#7-p.86). Goes to soccer practice (M#11-p.80).

**EXPERIENCES:**
Becomes friends with Pike boys (#20-p.60). Goes to Valentine's Day Masquerade party (#51-p.46). Finds missing Jake Kuhn, gets some glory for it (M#4-p.122). In Wiffle Ball Derby at Mini-Olympics (#55-p.81). Plays tom-toms, can feel the beat, in kids band BSC organizes (#56-p.48). Buys useless stuff through maga-zines with other kids, performs pantomime as part of traveling salesmen show to earn money back (#58-p.117).

## MRS. CAROLYN BRADDOCK:

Teaches Jessi some signs before she sits for Matt (#16-37); works with deaf adults at Community Center (#16-p.90). Gets Mal and Jessi jobs at Stoneybrook Day Camp through her friendship with the director, Adele Lebeque (#76-p.55). Is at home during the day (#86-p.29).

## MR. BRADDOCK:

His mother is in a nursing home in New Haven (#58-p.120).

# The CHEPLINs

•

## GENERAL:

*NOTE: The BSC will probably not be sitting for the Cheplins anymore.*

Live on Acorn Place (#94-p.26). House is small and brick, with bright blue shutters; it is set on a thickly wooded hillside that leads down to a stream; looks cozy, like a house from a fairy tale. Slate walkway leads to front of the house. Brass front door knocker is shaped like a woodpecker (#94-pp.29-30). Small, narrow kitchen, set behind a brick wall, is visible from hallway; in between the kitchen and the living room is a hall with spiral stairs leading to the second floor; it is a shadowy, cluttered house (#94-pp.30-31). Second floor is smaller than the first, with two bedrooms nestled around a tiny, square hallway; inside the kids' room, a thin, blue plywood wall separates Adam's space from Dana's; Adam's side is a clutter of toys, books, and clothing; Dana's side is neat (#94-p.57).

## DANA CHEPLIN:

### PERSONAL INFO:
Eight years old, has just been diagnosed with diabetes (#94-p.33). Attends the Miller School; needs to be picked up at bus stop at 3:15 P.M. sharp (#94-p.32). Her best friend is Mandy (#94-p.51). Can touch her nose with her tongue (#94-p.58). Takes piano lessons with Mrs. Kleinsasser (#94-p.82).

### EXPERIENCES:
Uses glucose test kit (#94-p.57). Stacey suspects she uses her diabetes to try to get her own way and make friends guilty (#94-p.74). When Dana's blood sugar level is dangerously low, Stacey takes her to Dr. Johanssen, who says Dana's insulin dosage will probably have to be adjusted (#94-p.111).

## ADAM CHEPLIN:

### PERSONAL INFO:
Six years old (#94-p.35). Attends the Miller School; needs to be picked

~~up at bus stop at 3:15 P.M. sharp~~
(#94-p.32). Lisps; a chatterbox (#94-p.50). Likes grape jelly the best (#94-p.52). It's hard to keep up a conversation with Adam because he does most of the talking (#94-p.53). One of his friends is Moira (#94-p.77).

## MRS. CHEPLIN:

### PERSONAL INFO:
A freelance photographer and a book designer; has recently taken a job as an art director for a magazine in Stamford (#94-p.31). Divorced (#94-p.83). Pays almost twice as much as other sitting clients pay (#94-p.35). Doesn't appreciate what Stacey does and only looks to find fault (#94-p.87).

### EXPERIENCES:
Leaves Stacey long work list, asking her to fold laundry, empty the dishwasher, clean Adam's room, put stamps on envelopes, defrost meat, and empty wastebaskets, among other things (#94-pp.70-71). Finally, Stacey calls her and says she won't be their regular sitter anymore (#94-p.140).

## MR. CHEPLIN:

### PERSONAL INFO:
Lives in Chicago; divorced wife after she wouldn't move to Chicago as well; calls kids every night and will visit in spring; kids will live with him during summer. He lives in an apartment building with a pool (#94-p.83)

# The CRAINEs

•

**GENERAL:**
Kids are usually taken care of by Aunt Bud, but after she breaks her leg, the BSC is called in (M#3-p.23). Mal doesn't have to knock on door when she's expected (M#3-p.78). Girls have large selection of toys (#62-p.82). Jessi takes them for a walk to see SMS; girls are very impressed (#62-p.85).

**HOUSE:**
High Street (M#3-p.85); porch wraps around the front and side of house (M#3-p.35). Attic doesn't have any lights, has angled walls, one tiny window, a lot of boxes and old furniture (M#3-pp.63-64), an opening in the rafters that leads outside, and a Ghost Cat (M#3-p.65), as well as a dressmaker's dummy, an old hat, and a bookshelf filled with dusty old books (M#3-p.84).

**MARGARET CRAINE:**

**PERSONAL INFO:**
Six (M#3-p.37). Has a Simpsons sleeping bag (M#3-p.41).

**SOPHIE CRAINE:**

**PERSONAL INFO:**
Four (M#3-p.37). Has a Barbie sleeping bag (M#3-p.41).

**KATIE CRAINE:**

**PERSONAL INFO:**
Two and a half (M#3-p.38). Has a Muppet Babies sleeping bag (M#3-p.41).

**MRS. CRAINE:**

**PERSONAL INFO:**
Thirty-four years old (M#3-p.38). Plays tennis with Kristy's mom (M#3-p.23). Attends PTA meetings (M#3-p.36).

**AUNT BUD:**

**PERSONAL INFO:**
Real name is Ellen; Mr. Craine calls her Bud (for Buddies) (M#3-p.40). Looks totally normal, with curly brown hair and big blue eyes (M#3-

p.57); has broken her leg, wears big cast (M#3-p.57). Usually rides to the Craines' on her motorcycle (M#3-p.39). Special "Bud shake" involves linking pinkies (M#3-p.40).

CRAINE PETS:

**TINKERBELL:**
Deaf white cat with blue eyes (M#3-pp.157-158).

# The DELANEYs

•

## GENERAL:

*Moved. BSC doesn't sit for them anymore.*

Kormans moved into their house (#46-p.22). Amanda and Max are good swimmers, must have neighbor at home to swim, when babysat; if kids' friends can swim the width of the pool without a rest, they're allowed to swim there (#39-p.56). Amanda and Max love to test new sitters (#39-p.53); Kristy can handle them (#39-p.32).

## HOUSE:

Ostentatious; has a fountain with a golden fish standing on its tail spouting water in the front hall (#11-p.49). The fountain cost $2,000 (#11-p.97). There are two tennis courts in the gigantic backyard, a "space control" center kitchen (#11-p.50) and a clean, all white family room (#11-p.51). Oriental carpets, gilt-framed pictures everywhere (#39-p.54). Have a new swimming pool (#39-p.56).

## AMANDA DELANEY:

### PERSONAL INFO:
Eight; mean, nasty, spoiled, and bossy (#11-p.36). Blonde hair parted evenly (#11-p.51). Shannon's neighbor (#11-p.29). She has a habit of saying how much her family's possessions cost (#11-p.97).

### EXPERIENCES:
Friends with Karen Brewer, Cici, and Meghan (#39-p.113); Karen plays Lovely Ladies with her (#39-p.69). Mal helps Amanda and Max learn that their real friends don't use them for their pool (#39-p.113). Enters Priscilla in pet show (#42-p.147).

## MAX DELANEY:

### PERSONAL INFO:
Six; mean, nasty, spoiled and bossy (#11-p.36). Blond hair and blue eyes (#11-p.51).

**EXPERIENCES:**

Friends with Timmy Hsu (#42-p.66); and Huck (#39-p.113). Enters Priscilla in pet show (#42-p.147).

## MRS. DELANEY:

**PERSONAL INFO:**

Taking real estate refresher course to go back to work and needs sitter Monday, Wednesday, and Friday afternoons for a month (#39-p.32).

## MR. DELANEY:

**PERSONAL INFO**

Partner in law firm; makes lot of money (#39-p.59).

## DELANEY PETS:

**PRISCILLA:**

Snow-white Persian cat that cost $400 (#39-p.58); gets entered in pet show (#42-p.147).

# The FELDERs

•

**HOUSE:**
Live around the corner from Claudia's house (#32-p.9). Living room is bright and sunny and has a grand piano (#32-p.35).

**SUSAN FELDER:**

**PERSONAL INFO:**
Eight (#32-p.35). Autistic savant (#32-p.38). Only child (#32-p.9) but mother is expecting another girl (#32-p.133). Has beautiful, deep brown eyes, hair almost as dark as Claudia's—soft curls to shoulders, could be a model (#32-p.36). In her own world, doesn't communicate, wrings hands, clicks tongue, rarely makes eye contact, doesn't like to be touched or hugged (#32-p.37). Can sing and play piano beautifully, can memorize songs instantly, sings with perfect pitch, but words don't mean anything to her (#32-p.39); has calendar in her head, can tell the day of the week that any date fell on, not past sixty years in the past or twenty years in the future (saw a perpetual calendar once and memorized it) (#32-p.40).

**EXPERIENCES:**
Is being transferred to a school with a strong music program, one hour from Stoneybrook (#32-p.39); Kristy, her first BSC sitter, introduces her to James Hobart, her first "real friend" (#32-p.71).

**MRS. FELDER:**

**PERSONAL INFO:**
Doesn't work (#32-p.30); pregnant with another daughter whose name will be Hope; had tests to see if the baby is okay and so far, so good (#32-p.133).

**MR. FELDER:**

**PERSONAL INFO:**
Big man, with beard, grin, and lots of curly hair (#32-p.128).

# The GARDELLAs

•

## GENERAL:

*Kristy vows that the BSC will never sit for them again (M#1-p.142).*

Full-time nanny usually takes care of the baby (M#1-p.41).

## HOUSE:
Base of the driveway has black wrought-iron fence and gate; house itself is pretty impressive: brick, with big white columns on either side of the humongous front door; a white urn stand to the right of the door, spilling over with ivy and red flowers; doorbell is brass music-box key that user must turn for chime (M#1-pp.42-43). *Inside:* main hall leads to huge living room stuffed with fancy furniture and expensive-looking lamps; a grand piano stands in one corner, with a beautiful red silk scarf on top of it (M#1-p.45). Tara's room is pink and white, with a rosebud theme; has matching crib, dresser, changing table, lampshade, and wallpaper (M#1-p.49).

## TARA GARDELLA:

### PERSONAL INFO:
Seven months old (M#1-p.41).

## MRS. GARDELLA:

### PERSONAL INFO:
Knows Claudia's mom from the library (M#1-p.40). Is horrible with names (M#1-p.44). Even though she's rich, she's just a regular person (M#1-p.45).

### EXPERIENCES:
Thinks Stacey has stolen her diamond ring (M#1-p.55); apologizes when she learns it was Mouse (M#1-p.137).

## MR. PETER GARDELLA:

### PERSONAL INFO:
Has a deep voice (M#1-p.48).

## GARDELLA PETS:

Must give them equal attention, or their feelings get hurt (M#1-p.46); they do not eat canned food (M#1-p.47).

## MOUSE:
Cat; usually eats at the dinner table with the Gardellas; even has place set for him (M#1-p.47). Stashes things around the house (M#1-p.136).

## BIRD:
Huge black bird dog with huge yellowish teeth (M#1-p.43); his bowl sits in corner of dining room, on oriental rug (M#1-p.47). Loves to retrieve things (M#1-p.48).

# The GIANELLIs

•

**GENERAL:**
Stacey is first BSC member to sit for them (#52-p.78).

**HOUSE:**
Live in the Engles' neighborhood. Sign to the left of their doorbell reads, "Child Sleeping, Please Knock" (#52-p.78).

**BOBBY GIANELLI:**

**PERSONAL INFO:**
Sometimes a bit of a bully. In Karen's class at Stoneybrook Academy (#52-p.71); takes bus home (#52-p.78); plays football, has uniform (#52-p.81).

**EXPERIENCES:**
Attends Camp BSC; has gone to a circus camp before (#86-p.34).

**ALICIA GIANELLI:**

**PERSONAL INFO:**
Just turned four (#52-p.80). Takes naps (#52-p.78); dark-haired, dark-eyed with olive skin (#52-p.79). Hates eggs (#52-p.80).

**EXPERIENCES:**
Attends Camp BSC (#86-p.33); is upset when her mother leaves (#86-p.38) and insists on staying at camp while others go on field trip, just in case her mother comes for her (#86-p.41). Eventually, she realizes she's missing out on some real fun and joins in (#86-p.117).

**MRS. GIANELLI:**

**PERSONAL INFO:**
Works away from home (#52-p.78).

**MR. GIANELLI:**

**PERSONAL INFO:**
Tall, with mustache (#52-p.78); used to be a teacher (#52-p.79).

# The HILLs

•

## GENERAL:

Dr. Johanssen is their pediatrician, recommends BSC to the Hills (#50-p.25); kids' Nanna used to baby-sit, but died recently (#50-p.44).

## HOUSE:

Live in modern house, small hallway in entrance to house, stairway to left leads up, stairway to right leads down; from hallway, can see kitchen at top of stairs (#50-p.42).

## SARA HILL:

### PERSONAL INFO:

Nine; slim, with pretty, big brown eyes, thin brown hair cut in bangs, falls to bottom of neck (#50-p.41); looks exactly like her mother (#50-pp.54-55). Artistic; Claud likes her (#50-p.66). Loves rainbows, loves to draw; room has yellow flowered curtains with matching ruffled bedspread, pictures of kittens on walls, messy, books and Barbie clothes all over floor, drawings on loose-leaf paper scattered everywhere (#50-p.45).

## EXPERIENCES:

Loves the movie *The Little Mermaid* (#50-pp.48-49). Elizabeth is friend, lives next door (#50-p.49); they make snowman and name it Enormous Hill to tease Norman about his weight (#50-p.53). Tells on Norman when he sneaks food (#50-p.46). Participates in Battle of the Bakers with two friends, Elizabeth Sayers and Brittany DePew (M#21-p.48).

## NORMAN HILL:

### PERSONAL INFO:

Seven, with short, wispy blond hair, blue eyes; fat (#50-pp.42-43). Eats lots of candy, hides food in room (#50-pp.46-47). Hates being on diets, doesn't want to go to Fat Camp (#50-p.52). Kids at school call him; Enormous Norman (#50-p.50). Thinks his parents don't like him; when he gets sad, he eats (#50-pp.99-100). Plans to lose weight by pretending he'll get sick like Stacey if he eats sweets (#50-p.157). Tells his parents that bugging him about losing weight makes him want to eat more (#50-p.156). Is looking a bit thinner than he used to be (#88-p.6). Teddy is friend at school (#50-p.70).

**EXPERIENCES:**
Has pen pal girlfriend named Brittany (#50-p.70), sends her a picture of himself (#50-p.158).

## MR. HAROLD HILL:

**PERSONAL INFO:**
Very tall; broad shoulders; almost bald with some brown hair; huge hands (#50-p.42). Works at home as a computer systems consultant (#50-p.43). Has joined the Fitness Faze Health Club (#50-p.94).

## MRS. MICHELLE HILL:

**PERSONAL INFO:**
Small; thin; looks exactly like Sara (#50-pp.54-55). Works at home as artists' representative (#50-p.94).

**EXPERIENCES:**
She and Mr. Hill try to get Norman to lose weight all the time, want him to go to Fat Camp (#50-p.52); buy exercise tape for him, tack meal plan to bulletin board in kitchen (#50-p.94); put Norman no-foods and Norman yes-foods lists on fridge (#50-p.125). After Norman tells them how he feels, they stop bugging him (#50-pp.156-157). She doesn't buy cookies, soda, and cake anymore (#50-p.157). She and Mr. Hill belong to Fitness Faze health club (#50-p.94).

# The HOBARTs

•

**GENERAL:**
From Australia, moved in to Mary Anne's old house across the street from Claudia's (#32-p.7); they all look similar with reddish-blond hair, round faces, "and a smattering of freckles across their noses" (#32-p.111); kids get teased because of their accents (#32-p.45): say "brecky" for "breakfast," "jumpers" for "sweaters," and slang words no one understands, like "rev heads" (#32-p.59). Ben and his brothers stand up to the mean kids, and they end up fitting in (#32-p.140). Claud is first BSC member to sit for James, Mathew, and Johnny (#32-p.109); They have a Nintendo Game Boy (#59-p.108).

## BEN HOBART:

**PERSONAL INFO:**
Eleven (#32-p.7), in sixth grade with Mal and Jessi at SMS (#32-p.51); red hair and glasses (#32-p.50); tall for his age (#32-p.61). Studies with Mallory (#32-p.109); nice; likes Mallory; asks her to the movies (#32-p.144).

**EXPERIENCES:**
Works for school newspaper (#59-p.136). Takes Mal to Halloween Hop (#38-p.130). Is "becoming an item" with Mal (M#2-p.11); he thinks she's a "bonzer sheila"—a terrific girl/kangaroo (M#2-p.29). Takes her to Winter Wonderland and Valentine Dances (#51-p.22); has small argument with Mal in library (#51-p.72). Doesn't speak to Mal after she bails out on caroling date; they get back together and go caroling (SS#12-p.169). Trades brothers for a night with Mal because her brothers are getting on her nerves and vice versa (#59-p.107); Hobart boys were raucous, but Mal's brothers were good for Ben (#59-pp.117-118).

## JAMES HOBART:

**PERSONAL INFO:**
Eight, in third grade with Nicky Pike at SES (#32-p.51).

135

# ● BSC Clients ●

## EXPERIENCES:

Stands up for Susan Felder when kids tease her because she's an autistic savant (he's her first real friend) (#32-p.71). Likes Carolyn Arnold; goes to Valentine's Day Masquerade Party and gives her card (#51-p.129). He and Mathew wanted to get dressed up, invite dates, and give them carnations (#51-pp.69-70), but Jessi talks them out of it, citing the difference between customs in Australia and U.S. (#51-p.71). In three-legged race at Mini-Olympics run by BSC (#55-p.80). Spends the night at Pike house during "brother trade," falls out of bed and hurts shoulder (#59-pp.117-118). Breaks his leg in two places after football accident; has to have surgery to put pins into his leg (#88-p.47); must stay in bed, so BSC makes Christmas in Summer for him (#88-from p.69).

## MATHEW HOBART:

### PERSONAL INFO:
Six (#32-p.51). Plays the violin (#56-p.37).

### EXPERIENCES:
Goes to Valentine's Day Masquerade Party (#51-p.127). Wants to be in regular race at Mini-Olympics run by BSC (#55-p.80). Plays violin in All the Children of the World (#56-p.37). Spends the night at Pike house during "brother trade" (#59-pp.117-118).

## JOHNNY HOBART:

### PERSONAL INFO:
Four (#32-p.7). Is having a life crisis, is angry that everyone is bigger, smarter, and stronger than he is (LS-p.42)

### EXPERIENCES:
Enters (plastic) weight-lifting event in Mini-Olympics; wins Cross-Country Champ Award (#55-p.135); plays drums in All the Children of the World (#56-p.38). Spends the night at Pikes during "brother trade," sleeps on bottom bunk (#59-p.110).

## MRS. HOBART:

### PERSONAL INFO:
Looks like her sons, with reddish-blonde hair and freckles (#32-p.11). Volunteers at a soup kitchen (#88-p.46). Bakes all the time and doesn't even use a mix (#88-p.68).

## MR. HOBART:

### PERSONAL INFO:
From Australia (#32-p.7).

## HOBART PETS:

### THE NEW IGUANAS:
Johnny is excited about them (#88-p.40).

136

# The HOYTs

•

## GENERAL:
Live in a tidy red house at 35 Reilly Lane (M#10-p.49). Father is Secret Service agent; the family moves around a lot. Have lived in Iowa, Oregon (M#10-p.53), New York (M#10-p.97), Texas (M#10-p.98). Don't unpack (M#10-p.54). Have secret closet that Kristy can't open (M#10-p.56). Live near the Johanssens (M#10-p.66). Family moves on as soon as father gets new assignment (M#10-p.158).

## TASHA HOYT:

### PERSONAL INFO:
Terry Hoyt's twin sister, in Mary Anne's gym class (M#10-p.22). A pretty girl with long, shiny brown hair in a braid down her back. Has gorgeous hazel eyes (M#10-p.50).

## TERRY JAMES/JOHN HOYT:

### PERSONAL INFO:
Real name is David Hawthorne (M#10-p.148). Incredibly cute, nice, and shy, new kid in Stacey's language arts and social studies classes (M#10-p.9). Has beautiful hazel eyes and shiny brown hair that flops over onto his forehead (M#10-p.10). Likes to watch baseball but has never played on a team (M#10-p.98).

### EXPERIENCES:
Goes out to a movie with Stacey (M#10-from p.94); kisses her good night (M#10-p.105).

## GEORGIE HOYT:

### PERSONAL INFO:
Little boy with brown hair and hazel eyes; wears big, horn-rimmed glasses; is very skinny, seven and a half years old (M#10-pp.51-52). Speaks very seriously; is one of the quietest kids Kristy's ever met (M#10-p.52). Loves softball, but isn't allowed to play on teams (M#10-p.53). Loves to read; likes Tintin the best (M#10-p.54).

## MRS. JANICE HOYT:

**PERSONAL INFO:**
New in town (M#10-p.24).

## MR. HOYT:

**PERSONAL INFO:**
Won't let his kids play on teams (M#10-p.53). Doesn't like to join video stores; says movies are a waste of time (M#10-p.55). Is Secret Service agent investigating counterfeiters (M#10-p.146).

# The JOHANSSENs

●

**GENERAL:**
Stacey is Charlotte's favorite sitter, usually sits for her (#13-p.4). Family has lived in Stoneybrook for generations, dating back to Charlotte's great-grandparents. (M#5-p.21). Charlotte and family go to France with Dr. Johanssen's sister, Nell (M#18-p.4).

**HOUSE:**
*Location/Outdoors:* Live on Kimball St. (#1-p.137). Around the corner from Jessi (M#18-p.26); you can see the back of her house from the Johanssens'. House sits squarely in its corner lot, with a crabapple tree in its front yard and a welcoming dried-flower wreath on the front door (M#18-p.23). There's a flagstone walk and a red mailbox with a painting of a white duck on it (M#18-p.24).

*Indoors:* To reach the living room, you walk out of the kitchen and through the dining room, turn right, go past the front door and the center hallway (where the stairs leading to the second floor are), and turn right again into the living room; all the rooms have white walls and pretty wood floors with richly colored Oriental rugs here and there (except for the kitchen, which has a dark-blue tiled floor); none of the rooms is big, but they're all cozy and comfortable; the living room has two overstuffed couches and a comfy chair that face both the fireplace and a gorgeous cabinet next to it that holds the TV and stereo (M#18-p.28).

## CHARLOTTE JOHANSSEN:

**PERSONAL INFO:**
Eight, birthday in June, can't wait to turn nine (#10-p.81); [seven #1-p.137]. Only child, used to be timid and shy (#2-p.76). Sometimes needs a lot of reassurance (M#4-p.71). Pretty; chestnut brown hair; big dark eyes and dimple in cheeks when she smiles (#3-p.40), but she does not think she's pretty (#15-p.74). Hates sports and gym class,

gets nervous in front of an audience (#55-p.73). Stacey is her favorite sitter (#13-p.4); almost like sisters (#65-p.26). Charlotte is Becca Ramsey's best friend (#75-p.53). Is supposed to stay away from sweets; had two cavities last time she went to dentist (and has two silver fillings in her molars to prove it) (M#2-p.106). Afraid of horses, swimming in the lake, boats (SS#2-p.96). Is taking piano lessons; is nervous about recital (#83-p.28). Adores Jamie Newton (M#21-p.8). Good at solving mysteries (#35-p.71). Is a Krushers' cheerleader (#38-p.110).

### SCHOOL:

Stacey thinks Charlotte is the smartest eight-year-old she's ever met (#65-p.48). Skipped into third grade after parent-teacher conference (#3-p.165); used to be quiet, sad, had no friends; year later she's happy, friendly, has a new best girlfriend each week due to Stacey's influence and skipping a grade (#10-p.77), (#13-p.4). Sophie McCann and Vanessa Pike are Charlotte's friends from class (#10-p.77); Ellie Morris was in her second grade class (#3-p.119). Theresa is her Zuni pen pal in New Mexico whose house caught fire (#44-p.51).

### LIKES AND INTERESTS:

Main interests are reading and studying (#56-p.35). Loves to be read to, though she's smart and reads well on her own (#10-p.80); reads anything from Bobbsey Twins to Roald Dahl to books for older kids, like *A Tree Grows in Brooklyn* (#29-p.109). Is beginning to paint almost as much as she reads (#31-p.91). Likes polar bears (SB-p.159). Favorite TV show is *The Cosby Show* (#3-p.137). Two of her favorite books are *Charlotte's Web* and *The Long Winter* (#35-p.29). Spaghetti and meatballs is favorite meal (#35-p.30).

### AWARDS/EVENTS:

Forgets the passage from *Charlie and the Chocolate Factory* she was supposed to recite in beauty pageant and has to be taken home in tears (#15-p.130). Wins third place in science fair for project on playing music to plants (#36-p.78). Enters Carrot in pet show (#42-p.130). Plays guitar in band performance that BSC organizes; forgets part of the music for "Tradition" (#56-pp.65, 133). In Dawn and Stacey's Save the Planet Class (#57-p.36); she and Becca decorate and sell canvas shopping bags at booth at Green Fair (#57-pp.84, 136). She and Becca don't want to be in BSC Mini-Olympics (#55-p.76); becomes official sign-maker for Mini-Olympics (#55-p.127); wins Most Creative Award (#55-p.135).

### MEDICAL:

Had tonsillitis while Stacey lived in NYC (#28-p.39); gets tonsillitis again while she's staying at Stacey's (#35-p.62).

**EXPERIENCES:**
Was taking guitar lessons (#56-p.38). Makes a little book, *The Girl Who Moved Away*, which she gives to Stacey at yard sale (#13-p.111). The first kid not to avoid Becca because she is black (#16-p.122); she and Becca become good friends after Charlotte runs out of pageant (#16-p.123). Gets invited to sit in on two BSC meetings—one normal (#35-p.44) and one emergency (#35-p.99). She and Stacey see "unexplainable" fire at the old Hennessey house (#35-p.90). Gets very worried when Stacey has to go to the hospital, thinks she may never come back (#43-p.85); becomes hypochondriac until she knows Stacey is better (#43-p.86). Member of Kids Can Do Anything Club (Kids Club) with Becca, becomes friends with Danielle Roberts (#48-pp.9, 88). Sometimes uses her mom's plastic surgical gloves as balloons (#55-p.75). Experiments with her mom's makeup during one of Stacey's sitting jobs (#65-p.50). Likes Bruce Cominsky (#65-p.51); writes him a poem, then he likes her but she's not so sure she likes him any more (#65-pp.104-105); he now has crush on Diane Dumschat (#65-p.138). Natalie Springer becomes practically inseparable from Becca and Charlotte (#78-p.137).

## DR. PEGGY JOHANSSEN:

**PERSONAL INFO:**
A doctor at Stoneybrook General Hospital (#2-p.77). Is at home on Monday afternoons (#94-p.109).

**EXPERIENCES:**
Likes Stacey a lot, helped her through a bad time with her diabetes right after Stacey's first move to Stoneybrook; not her regular doctor but always answers any questions Stacey may have about diabetes (#10-p.79); (#28-p.139).

## MR. JOHANSSEN:

**PERSONAL INFO:**
An engineer (#3-p.36).

## OTHER JOHANSSEN RELATIVES:

**BERIT MARIE HJIELHOLT JOHANSSEN:**
Charlotte's great-grandmother, who emigrated to Stoneybrook; Charlotte focuses her Heritage Day project on her; she graduated from college in Denmark; had a dimple in the same place as Charlotte; was very beautiful, with blonde hair and dark eyes (M#5-pp.21-22). Charlotte finds her diary and her locket (M#5-p.25).

## NELL:

Dr. Johanssen's older sister, an incredibly wealthy and successful art dealer, invites the Johanssens to go to France with her (M#18-p.4).

## JOHANSSEN PETS:

### CARROT:

Their pet schnauzer (#2-p.85). Gray; has a stubby little tail, hair is short all over, except for his face, where it's long and stiff; has funny, spiky eyebrows; a muscular dog, moves as if he has springs inside; always seems happy and excited (M#18-pp.25-26). Can "say his prayers" by putting his paws in lap and laying head down; Charlotte enters him in pet show (#42-p.130). Loves to be in the middle of things (M#5-p.23). Command "get out of kitchen" means "get out of here" (M#5-p.23). His favorite toy is called Mister Manny-Man, a soft white fuzzy doll he loves to chew on, carry around, and sleep with (M#18-p.29). Always sleeps later than the rest of the family (M#18-p.34). Has a bed under Mr. Johanssen's desk because he likes cavelike spaces (M#18-p.36). Food is kept in big bin inside the basement door; must add protein powder before serving (M#18-p.56). Likes to sleep beneath Mr. and Dr. Johanssen's bed; gets stuck often (M#18-pp.88-89).

# The KORMANS

•

**GENERAL:**

Moved into Delaneys' old house (#46-p.21). Jewish (#90-p.54). Kristy has baby-sat for them more than the rest of the members have (#46-p.2). Bill and Melody go to Stoneybrook Day School (#46-p.21) and always have hot dogs when baby-sat (#46-p.20); (have pizza instead once when Kristy sits for them (#57-p.115)). Kids have tough time adjusting to the huge mansion; imagine toilet gurgles to be the Toilet Monster; they must run into bed before the toilet stops flushing or the Toilet Monster will get them (#46-pp.46, 75, 136); Mary Anne makes a game out of it that cures them of their fear of the monster; now they flush the toilet a lot (#50-pp.24-25); plumber fixed pipes, Toilet Monster gone (#57-p.113). Think chocolate chips in their ice cream are moles (#53-p.74).

**HOUSE:**

House is across the street from Kristy's (#46-p.2). Delaneys' former house (*See description of mansion under Delaneys.*) Is the most mansion-like of all houses in Kristy's neighborhood (M#3-p.91). Fountain is never turned on because Skylar is scared of it (#46-p.22). Fountain is shaped like a fish standing on its tail (M#3-p.91). House isn't as ostentatious now; Kormans are much more down-to-earth than the Delaneys (#46-p.22).

**BILL KORMAN:**

**PERSONAL INFO:**

Nine (#46-p.20); goes to Stoneybrook Day School (#46-p.21).

**EXPERIENCES:**

In Save the Planet class (#57-p.38); he and Buddy work wild animal booth at Green Fair, make endangered species collages, sell birdhouses (#57-pp.85-86, 138). Participates in Battle of the Bakers with SDS friends, Greg Wilson and David Simpson (M#21-p.47).

## ● BSC Clients ●

### MELODY KORMAN:

**PERSONAL INFO:**
Seven (#46-p.20); good friends with Karen (#46-p.21); goes to Stoneybrook Day School (#46-p.21). Is afraid of thunder; scares easily (M#2-p.87).

**EXPERIENCES:**
In Save the Planet class (#57-p.38); she and Hannie work plant booth at Green Fair (#57-p.84).

### SKYLAR KORMAN:

**PERSONAL INFO:**
Year and a half, likes Cheerios (#46-p.20); very afraid of cats, calls them "tats" (#46-p.24). Likes the song, "Breaking Up Is Hard To Do" (#46-p.114). Screams quite a bit because she's teething (M#2-p.90). Loves peanut butter on graham crackers, calls peanut butter "pealut butter" (#57-p.119).

# The KUHNs

•

**GENERAL:**
Jewish (M#18-p.83). Parents are recently divorced; kids seem to be handling things well (M#4-p.3). Parents are acting civilized; Mrs. Kuhn has temporary custody, but Mr. Kuhn wants joint custody (M#4-p.5). Mr. Kuhn has temporarily moved to Texas (M#4-p.5).

**JAKE (JACOB) KUHN:**

**PERSONAL INFO:**
Eight (#20-p.54). Third-grader (#79-p.6). A little overweight (#20-p.93). Used to be called "fatso" but isn't pudgy anymore (M#4-p.26). Not a natural athlete; member of the Stars, a Saturday soccer league (#79-p.59). Needs a male presence in the house, like Logan (#79-p.98). Never used to be terribly interested in sports but now is totally into soccer (#79-p.104).

**EXPERIENCES:**
Buddy Barrett's friend (#20-p.54). Disappears after a Krushers game (M#4-p.34); found in a hole in a construction site after two days (M#4-p.116); only has a couple of bruises and a sore leg from the accident (M#4-p.127). Orders "moondust" through the mail (#58-p.68). Is jealous of Buddy's new stepfather (#79-p.32). Puts together a funny haunted house (#79-p.120).

**LAUREL KUHN:**

**PERSONAL INFO:**
Jake's sister, six, shy (#20-p.54). Is convinced that she's much more mature than Patsy (#79-p.24). Friends with Margo and Claire Pike (M#4-p.38)

**EXPERIENCES:**
Orders mood lipstick through the mail (#58-p.67).

**PATSY KUHN:**

**PERSONAL INFO:**
Five (#20-p.54).

**EXPERIENCES:**
Suzi Barrett's friend (#20-p.54); Laurel gives her sample of nail polish she ordered through mail called Neon Nails that's Day-Glo green (#58-p.66). Made junior assistant equipment manager of Krashers with Suzi and Claire (M#7-p.87).

## MR. HARRY KUHN:

**PERSONAL INFO:**
Moved to Texas after the divorce (M#4-p.5). Owns a green T-bird (M#4-p.8). Has known Dawn's mother since they were both really young (M#4-p.44). Volunteers every single year for the library's book sale (M#4-p.44).

## MRS. CAROLINE KUHN:

**PERSONAL INFO:**
Has a job (M#4-p.3).

**EXPERIENCES:**
Is not too pleased when she catches Logan baby-sitting with Mary Anne (#79-p.68); later, misunderstanding is sorted out (#79-p.103).

# The LOWELLs

•

(#56-p.124)

**GENERAL:**

*Mother is very racist, so club may not sit for them any more (#56-p.124).*

Heard about club through one of their fliers (#56-p.23). Next-door neighbor is Mr. Selznick, who's usually home during the day in case of emergency (#56-p.42). Mary Anne is first to sit for them (#56-p.25). All three kids are really pretty, look like China dolls; obedient and helpful during Mary Anne's sitting job (#56-p.25); disobedient when Claud sits for them (#56-p.54). Kids go to private school, not mentioned which one (#56-pp.27, 135). Didn't know any other kids in neighborhood; meet Hobarts when Claud sits for them (#56-p.55). Kids like to watch *Leave It to Beaver* (#56-p.30). Children may grow out of their prejudice (#56-pp.134-135).

## CAITLIN LOWELL:

**PERSONAL INFO:**
Eight (#56-p.25). Clear blue eyes, hair as blonde as Dawn's, pale complexion; wears private school uniform of blue plaid skirt, blazer, white blouse, and white tights, red shoes (#56-p.27).

**EXPERIENCES:**
She and Mackie sneak into see band performance at Newtons without mother's permission; may grow out of prejudices; seems like she really wanted to be with the rest of the kids (#56-pp.134-135).

## MACKIE (MACKENZIE) LOWELL:

**PERSONAL INFO:**
Six (#56-p.25). He has clear blue eyes, hair as blond as Dawn's, pale complexion; wears private school uniform of pressed pants, blazer, brown oxfords (#56-p.27). In first grade (#56-p.30).

**EXPERIENCES:**
He and Caitlin sneak in to see band performance without mother's permission; may grow out of prejudices; seemed like he really wanted

to be with the kids (#56-pp.134-135).

## CELESTE LOWELL:

### PERSONAL INFO:
Three (#56-p.25). Clear blue eyes, hair as blonde as Dawn's, pale complexion.

### EXPERIENCES:
Caitlin and Mackie have to "tell her about their new sitter" before she sees Claudia; stares at Claudia a lot (#56-pp.45-46).

## MRS. DENISE LOWELL:

### PERSONAL INFO:
Very organized (#56-p.25). Racist, didn't like Claudia and Jessi (#56-pp.80-81); doesn't believe in boy baby-sitters; didn't want Kristy to sit after she hears she has an adopted sister who's Vietnamese (#56-pp.89-90).

### EXPERIENCES:
Glances up and down at Mary Anne before saying hello, makes Mary Anne feel strange (#56-p.26); does the same to Claudia but is rude to her (#56-pp.42-44); doesn't even let Jessi in the door (#56-p.61). Asks for blonde, blue-eyed sitter (#56-p.88).

# The MANCUSIs

•

**GENERAL:**
Have no children but many animals (#22-p.18): Three dogs, five cats, some birds and hamsters, two guinea pigs, a snake, lots of fish, and a bunch of rabbits and turtles (#22-p.22). Live near Jessi (M#7-p.28).

**BARNEY:**
Snake (#22-p.29). Cage needs to be covered (M#7-p.23). Feeding him involves picking up insects and earthworms (M#7-p.35).

**CHERYL:**
Great Dane, obedient (#22-p.24). Huge (M#7-p.3); weighs 120 lbs. (M#7-p.33). Disappears from yard (M#7-p.37). Has dark brown spot on her shoulder, shaped like a heart (M#7-p.131).

**CROSBY:**
Orange tiger cat that can fetch like a dog (#22-p.27).

**FLUFFER-NUT, CINDY, TOTO, AND ROBERT:**
Rabbits (#22-p.29). All of them are white, fluffy, and kind of cute (M#7-p.36).

**FRANK:**
Talking bird, recites mainly lines from commercials (#22-p.27). Talks a lot, especially when lonely (M#7-p.23).

**JACQUES:**
Year-old golden retriever, follows Pooh Bear (#22-p.26). Takes a fish oil capsule after dinner (M#7-p.23).

**LING-LING:**
Siamese cat with a very loud voice (#22-p.27).

**LUCY AND RICKY:**
Guinea pigs, love to be taken out of cage for exercise (#22-p.28). Ricky makes whistling noise more often than Lucy (M#7-p.33).

**PETIE:**
A female iguana; comes from Mexico; looks like a huge lizard, with spines all down its back; won't bite (M#7-p.26).

**POOH BEAR:**
Devilish, apricot-colored poodle (#22-p.26). Eats low-cal chow (M#7-p.23).

**POWDER:**
Two-and-a-half-month-old fluffball kitten (#22-p.26).

**TOM:**
Patchy gray cat with a wicked temper (#22-p.27).

**ROSIE:**
Powder's mother (#22-p.27).

# The MARSHALLs

•

**GENERAL:**
Live on Rosedale Street, have a pet cat that's no trouble (#1-pp.101-102). Cut back on housekeeper's hours, so need sitters again (#45-p.95). The Phillips are their friends (#81-p.52).

**HOUSE:**
On Rosedale Street (#1-p.101). Have a swing and a slide in their backyard (#54-p.27). To the left of the entryway is the den, with the living room off to the right. The bedrooms are upstairs, and straight from the entryway is the kitchen and the laundry room (#81-p.50).

## NINA MARSHALL:

**PERSONAL INFO:**
Four (#7-p.73) [three #1-p.102]. Allergic to strawberries (#3-p.138). Has imaginary friend named Jimmytony (#45-p.95). Had baby blanket that was huge, grayish, with frayed edges where a satin border used to be, used to be blue, calls it Blankie, a male; took it to preschool and got teased (#54-pp.22, 25). Now it's in pieces, which Nina carries sometimes (#54-p.115).

**EXPERIENCES:**
Started preschool and goes three times a week (#54-p.23); preschool teacher is a male (#54-p.49). She and Eleanor like to play hide-and-seek, come out of hiding place giggling before anyone can find them (#45-p.98). Blankie falls apart in dryer when Dawn baby-sits; Dawn puts pieces of Blankie in Nina's shoe, under her sleeve, etc., tells her she can take it to preschool now without being teased by kids because they won't see it (#54-pp.113-115). Has Barbies (#54-p.23). Goes to talent show in Pikes' backyard with Eleanor and Dawn, brings Blankie (#54-pp.147-148).

## ELEANOR MARSHALL:

**PERSONAL INFO:**
Two (#7-p.73) [one #1-p.102]. Blonde, wavy hair with big cowlick; gigantic blue eyes (#45-p.95). Likes

to copy everything Nina says and does (#45-p.96). Now that she's two, she's past ear infections (#54-p.23). Took eardrops for infection (#1-p.102). Rubs ears when she's getting hungry (#3-p.137).

**EXPERIENCES:**
Gets entered on club's float in baby parade (#45-p.96). Goes to talent show in Pikes' backyard with Nina and Dawn (#54-p.147).

## MRS. MARSHALL:

**PERSONAL INFO:**
Takes a jazzercise class (#81-p.51); is friends with Kendra Phillips (#81-p.52). Doesn't tell the BSC members that they'll be sitting for extra kids and then doesn't pay them extra (#81-p.96). When she refuses to pay for two sitters, Stacey and Claud walk out on her (#81-p.118). Quits jazzercise, tries water aerobics (#81-p.146).

# The MARTINEZes

•

**HOUSE:**
Small and cozy (M#24-p.23). Near Miller's Park on the outskirts of Stoneybrook (M#24-p.18). Just had a fire, which started in garage (M#24-p.23). List of emergency phone numbers is on bulletin board by the phone (M#24-p.26).

**LUKE MARTINEZ:**

**PERSONAL INFO:**
Eight years old, with dark hair and dark eyes (M#24-p.23); is checkers champion of his family (M#24-p.44). Doesn't fully trust baby-sitters (M#24-p.87).

**EXPERIENCES:**
Knows something about the fire at his house but won't tell Mary Anne (M#24-p.31).

**AMALIA MARTINEZ:**

**PERSONAL INFO:**
Three years old, with dark hair, dark eyes, and big smile (M#24-p.23). Very affectionate (M#24-p.26). Loves cookies (M#24-p.82). Loves Barney (M#24-p.86).

**MRS. MARTINEZ:**

**PERSONAL INFO:**
Teaches science at SHS (M#24-p.17). Runs an after-school tutoring program at the high school (with Mr. Martinez) and teaches adult education classes in the evening (M#24-p.25). Has dark hair, dark eyes, and an infectious smile (M#24-p.23). Loves Miller's Park area and has no plans to move (M#24-p.25).

**MR. MARTINEZ:**

**PERSONAL INFO:**
Teaches science at SHS (M#24-p.17). Runs an after-school tutoring program at the high school (with Mrs. Martinez) and teaches adult education classes in the evening (M#24-p.25).

# The MASTERSes

•

**GENERAL:**
Live two blocks away from the Ramseys (#27-p.20). House is regular, kind of messy (#27-p.31). Family also lives in Los Angeles for chunk of year during Derek's taping season of *P.S. 162* (#27-p.11).

**DEREK MASTERS:**

**PERSONAL INFO:**
Eight; in Nicky Pike's third grade class at SES (#27-p.11). Plays Waldo on *P.S. 162*, a TV show (#27-p.11). Waldo in the show wears glasses but Derek has 20-20 vision (#27-p.31). Nicky Pike is his best friend in Stoneybrook (M#6-p.3). Is tutored on the set of *P.S. 162* with other kids on the show; misses being with regular kids at a normal school (M#6-p.23). Hates science; gets F's (#27-p.36). Doesn't like to talk about his show all the time (#27-p.41). Likes to play detective (M#6-p.85). Scared of kissing a girl (M#6-p.102). Looks like he's grown four inches (M#15-p.25); hasn't quite gotten used to his new gangly body

(M#15-p.37). Has a private tutor but goes back to SES (#27-p.32), where Mr. Rossi is his teacher (#27-p.77).

**EXPERIENCES:**
Career began when he was a child model, was in a lot of magazine ads and one local commercial that led to the job on *P.S. 162* (#27-p.11). Does mean things to classmates in retaliation and tells Jessi that "John" did them (#27-pp.97-98). Ends up making lots of friends (#27-pp.108, 133). Gives autographed photo of himself to Jessi that says she's the best baby-sitter he's ever had (#27-p.135). Guest stars on *Kid Detectives* (M#6-p.25). Brags that he's kissed many girls, but it's obvious that he hasn't kissed a girl in his life (M#6-pp.46-47). Has featured role in *Little Vampires*, a TV movie filmed partially in Stoneybrook (M#15-from p.14).

**TODD MASTERS:**

**PERSONAL INFO:**
Four (#27-p.19). Likes to play detective (M#6-p.85). Enjoys playing on his own (M#6-p.112).

**EXPERIENCES:**
Likes to play Candy Land game, used to call it Landy Cand (#27-p.33).

**MRS. MASTERS:**

**PERSONAL INFO:**
A nice-looking woman (#27-p.31). Always makes a point of being on the set when Derek is doing a stunt (M#15-p.52).

**EXPERIENCES:**
Has big meeting planned with Derek's agent (M#6-p.23).

**MR. MASTERS:**

**EXPERIENCES:**
He and Mrs. Masters think the going-away party is a great idea (#27-p.102). Has big meeting planned with Derek's agent (M#6-p.23).

# The NEWTONs

●

**GENERAL:**
Jamie's great-great-great-grandfather was a Native American (#56-p.67). Kids' band rehearses on Newtons' back porch and uses their electric keyboard; holds performance in their backyard (#56-pp.67, 109).

**HOUSE:**
Live on Bradford Court (#59-p.42); the Perkins' dog runs through the Newtons' yard and immediately into Claudia's yard, which is on Bradford Court; Newtons have flower bed in yard (#10-p.66). Mrs. Newton is proud of her huge, colorful flower bed (M#16-p.57). Also, close to the Pikes (#1-p.23). Swings in backyard (#1-p.23).

## JAMIE (JAMES) ANDERSON NEWTON:

**PERSONAL INFO:**
Four (#7-p.23) [three #1-p.21]. Smart (#53-p.62). Not energetic, one of club's favorite clients; Kristy, Mary Anne, and Claud sat for him even before club began (#22-p.33). Roger is best friend (#59-pp.43-44). Not a quitter (#53-p.46). Very affectionate, hardly ever cranky, adores his sitters (M#2-p.115). Attends nursery school (M#2-p.115). One of the youngest Krushers; tries hard but is afraid of the ball (M#2-p.117). At that stage where he wants to do everything himself, even though he's not great yet at things such as buckles and buttons and shoelaces (M#21-p.6). Has a chicken pox scar on his cheek (M#16-p.57). Adores Charlotte (M#21-p.8). Afraid of Halloween (#17-p.57).

**LIKES AND INTERESTS:**
Favorite sandwich is peanut butter and honey, toasted (#3-p.137). Likes Band-Aids (#17-p.48).

**EXPERIENCES:**
Calls Claudia "Claudee" (#56-p.122). Jessi reads *Georgie's Halloween* to him to help overcome his fear of Halloween (#17-p.63). Gets a new bike, red with white rac-

ing stripe (#53-p.56) with training wheels (#53-p.40); afraid of falling when twigs and leaves are in his path (#53-p.60); takes training wheels off because he thinks they're babyish (#53-p.89); he and Dawn fall down (#53-p.92); puts training wheels back on, learns to ride better (#53-p.124). Wins a squirt gun for Lucy at Sudsy's (#24-p.104). Recently had chicken pox (#31-p.44). Enters the (plastic) weight-lifting event at the Mini-Olympics run by BSC (#55-p.80). Has invisible friend named Boris who lives under the stairs of their house (#56-p.33). Cuts fingers on broken vase while Mal sits (#59-p.50). He and Lucy and his mother go to Spring Dance at Community Center, dances with his mother (#63-p.148).

## LUCY JANE NEWTON:

### PERSONAL INFO:
Jamie's baby sister (#3-p.58), seven months old in July (#7-p.23); fine dark hair and big, round, deep blue eyes (#3-p.92); (#59-p.43). Very cute and smart (#53-p.39). Has four teeth now, just grew two more (#59-p.45). Smiles often (M#2-p.115). Almost always wakes up happy (#24-p.47).

### EXPERIENCES:
Christened by a minister (#7-p.126). Recently had chicken pox (#31-p.43). Gets entered in baby parade on club's float (#45-p.46).

## MRS. NEWTON:

### PERSONAL INFO:
Well-organized (#53-p.20). Holds meeting of the Literary Circle at her house (#3-p.159).

## MR. ROGER NEWTON:
Jamie and Lucy's father (#2-p.127).

## OTHER NEWTON FAMILY MEMBERS:

### ROB FELDMAN:
Jamie's ten-year-old cousin (#23-p.53) [eight #1-p.73]; hates girls (#1-p.74). Hasn't been a full year since Claudia sat for him (#23-p.58).

### BRENDA FELDMAN:
Six, Rosie's sister (#23-p.53) [five #1-p.73]. Fussy (#1-p.74).

### ROSIE FELDMAN:
Jamie's noisy four-year-old cousin (#23-p.53) [three (#1-p.73)]. Jamie doesn't like her (#1-p.74).

### MRS. DIANE FELDMAN
Jamie's aunt (#2-p.122).

### AUNTIE NORA:
Jamie's aunt (#7-p.121).

### GRAM AND GRAMPS:
Jamie's grandparents (#7-p.127).

# The PAPADAKISes

•

**GENERAL:**
Live in Brewers' neighborhood (#11-p.19). The children don't get along with Amanda and Max Delaney (#13-p.75). Kristy usually sits for them because they live across the street from Brewers (#61-p.38). They love to "play pretend" and organize neighborhood activities; wealthy but down-to-earth (#11-p.31). Are Greek (#56-p.67). Have old Monopoly set—Kristy thinks it used to be Mrs. Papadakis's when she was young (#62-p.72). Throw a humungous family reunion (#67-p.73).

**HOUSE:**
In Brewers' area; have a huge yard, with a basketball court in the driveway and a badminton area (#67-p.73). Lou McNally's room at Papadakises is very neat — blue walls and comforter, blue-and-white chintz curtains, colorful rug (#62-p.72).

**LINNY PAPADAKIS:**

**PERSONAL INFO:**
Nine (#61-p.39) [eight #11-p.19]. He has dark hair, deep brown eyes, olive skin, terrific smile (#11-p.31). Attends Stoneybrook Academy (#86-p.34). David Michael's good friend (#11-p.19); (#62-p.6).

**EXPERIENCES:**
Paints Myrtle the Turtle and enters her in pet show (#42-p.146). Plays with Kristy's child-egg, Izzy, almost loses it (#52-pp.58-59). Wins Most Frequent Weight-Lifting Award at BSC Mini-Olympics (#55-pp.135-136). Plays in band that BSC helps organize for the kids, rehearses with Karen and Hannie playing "Miracle of Miracles" (#56-p.103). He and Hannie attend Save the Planet class (#57-p.37); he and David Michael work "It Came from Underground" demonstration and project booth at Green Fair (#57-pp.87, 134). Attends Camp BSC; has gone to a circus camp before (#86-p.34).

# ● BSC Clients ●

## HANNIE PAPADAKIS:

### PERSONAL INFO:
Seven (#33-p.44) [six #11-p.19]; dark hair, deep brown eyes, olive skin, terrific smile (#11-p.31). In same class as Karen (#11-p.36); goes to Stoneybrook Academy (#62-p.6). Good friends with Karen Brewer and Nancy Dawes; they call themselves the Three Musketeers (#61-p.38).

### EXPERIENCES:
Plays Mrs. Noswimple in Karen's game (#5-p.57) usually (#61-p.43). Stocky (#21-p.82). Pretend-married to Scott Hsu (#42-p.66). Plays harmonica in band that BSC helps organize for kids (#56-p.103). She and Linny attend Save the Planet class (#57-p.37); she and Melody work the plant booth at the Green Fair (#57-p.84). Goes to Spring Dance at Community Center, dances the sock hop with Jackie, (#63-p.147).

## SARI PAPADAKIS:

### PERSONAL INFO:
Two (#11-p.19); dark hair, deep brown eyes, olive skin, terrific smile (#11-p.19).

### EXPERIENCES:
Plays with Kristy's child-egg (#52-p.59).

## MRS. PAPADAKIS:

### PERSONAL INFO:
All three Papadakis kids look like her (#11-p.32). She and Mr. Papadakis are very thorough when leaving kids with baby-sitter (#62-p.68). Has two brothers and one sister (#67-p.73).

## MR. GEORGE PAPADAKIS:

### PERSONAL INFO:
Has two sisters (#67-p.73).

## LOU (LOUISA) MCNALLY:

### PERSONAL INFO:
Eight-year-old girl (#62-p.40); the Papadakises are her foster parents (#62-p.35). Doesn't answer to Louisa (#62-p.39); has short spiky hair slicked back on sides; wears jeans, loose sweater (#62-p.35); not very big for her age (#62-p.40); hard to tell if she's a girl (#62-p.38). Dislikes Papadakis rules (#62-p.55). Brother named Jay, eleven, wiry and strong, looks like Lou (#62-p.140). Kristy and rest of BSC agree Lou is worst kid ever (#62-p.119).

### EXPERIENCES:
Her father died not too long ago; older brother is with another foster family, mother left when Lou was baby (#62-p.38). Father taught her about Big Dipper and Orion and

**159**

could hoot like an owl (#62-p.78); can only remember her mother smelled good and was strong (#62-p.79). Stuffs Boo-Boo (Brewer cat) in a pillowcase (#62-p.116). Upset and crying while cradling one of Hannie's dolls — Dawn comforts her (#62-p.127). Had dog named Jingles but it ran away (#62-p.128). She and brother go to live with their aunt and uncle (father's brother), Mr. and Mrs. McNally, who are good with them; they give her a three-month-old black female Labrador (#62-pp.140-141); Lou names dog "Happy" (#62-p.153). Papadakises give Lou a baby doll and a football as going-away presents (#62-p.146). Kristy gives her book, *The Great Gilly Hopkins*(#62-p.151). Lou sends thank-you note to Kristy (#62-p.153).

## LOU'S FAMILY:

*Jay McNally:* Lou's brother, eleven; wiry and strong, looks a lot like Lou, has freckles and is reserved (#62-p.140). *Mr. McNally:* Jay and Lou's uncle (father's brother), shorter with kind face, he and his wife know how to act with Jay and Lou (#62-p.140); now have custody of Jay and Lou (#62-p.133). Lou calls him Uncle Mac (#62-p.153). He and Mrs. McNally don't have any kids of their own (#62-p.147). *Mrs. McNally:* Jay and Lou's aunt; tall, calm-looking woman with laugh lines at eye corners.

## PAPADAKIS PETS:

### PAT THE CAT:
Hannie's kitten, gets entered in pet show (#42-p.146).

### MYRTLE THE TURTLE:
Their pet turtle (#11-p.32).

### NOODLE THE POODLE:
Their poodle (#11-p.32). Will fetch whatever you point to (#86-p.128).

## OTHER PAPADAKIS RELATIVES:

### NIKO:
Linny's cousin; fifteen and cute (#67-p.75).

### POPPY PAPADAKIS:
Broke his hip, had to go to nursing home to recover, came down with pneumonia and is pretty sick, so Mr. and Mrs. Papadakis visit him often (#33-p.36). Recovers (#33-p.137).

# The PERKINSes

•

## GENERAL:

Move into Kristy's old house on Bradford Court (#7-p.139), which has four bedrooms (#5-p.37); lived next door to Mary Anne (before she moved), who baby-sat them a lot (#31-p.42). Girls usually race to the door when baby-sitter comes (#12-p.51); girls always color at their Barbie table — pink and white with pictures of Barbie dolls all over it (#9-p.37). Girls like to memorize and sing long songs (#33-p.83); like to "cook with real ingredients," concoct recipes of their own, like green chocolate chip cookies (#33-p.84).

## HOUSE:

Kristy's old house on Bradford Court; entire backyard fenced in for their dog, Chewy (#10-p.61); have mudroom, where dog's leash is kept (#10-p.63).

## MYRIAH PERKINS:

### PERSONAL INFO:

Six (#12-p.51) [five and a half #7-p.143]. Blonde hair, brown eyes (#9-p.33). Has Kristy's old bedroom (#9-p.32); has pictures of animals and a poster of a ballerina on her walls, and a doll house (#9-p.35). Smart, takes all kinds of lessons: ballet, tap, dancing, swimming (#9-p.10). Missing four teeth (#15-p.65), loses another tooth (#15-p.122). Has a loose tooth (M#5-p.69).

### EXPERIENCES:

Goes to Creative Theater at the Community Center on Thursdays after kindergarten, bus drops her off at corner of Bradford and Elm (#10-p.61). Can sing and tap dance; also knows ballet and gymnastics (#15-p.58). Was the baby bear in *Goldilocks* (#15-p.63). First runner-up in pageant, wins a shopping spree in Toy City (#15-p.135). Special friend is Mary Anne; Mary Anne shows her that they can see each other from their respective windows (#9-p.41); (#20-p.32). Caroline Eunice is Myriah's old Cabbage Patch doll, now it's Gabbie's and has a different name: Cindy Jane (#10-p.63). Myriah and Gabbie like to put on shows (#56-p.34).

They sing in All the Children of the World (#56-p.65).

## GABBIE PERKINS:

### PERSONAL INFO:
Nickname is The Gabbers or Gabbers (#9-p.36). Almost three (#12-p.51) [two and a half #7-p.143]; blonde hair and brown eyes (#9-p.33); smart, says cute things like "toshe me up," which means pick me up and give me a hug; calls people by their full names (#9-p.10); very huggable (#10-p.60). Likes to color and give tea parties for her dolls (#11-p.46). Loves donuts (#14-p.53).

### EXPERIENCES:
Rehearsing for play at her preschool, *The Three Piggy Opera* (#31-p.47). Has Myriah's old Cabbage Patch doll whom she now calls Cindy Jane instead of Caroline Eunice (#9-p.36). She and Myriah like to put on shows (#56-p.34). She and Myriah sing in All the Children of the World (#56-p.65). Just getting over the chicken pox (M#5-p.69).

## LAURA ELIZABETH PERKINS:

### PERSONAL INFO:
New baby (#14-p.46). Myriah liked Laurie and Gabbie liked Beth as names when mother was pregnant although parents had other choices in mind (#11-p.44).

### EXPERIENCES:
Gets entered in baby parade on club's float (#45-p.74). Just getting over the chicken pox (M#5-p.69).

## MRS. PERKINS:

### PERSONAL INFO:
Has beautiful voice and sings with choir group that has performed all over Connecticut and also in NYC and Washington, D.C. (#33-p.83).

## MR. PERKINS:

### PERSONAL INFO:
Lawyer (#33-p.83).

## PERKINS PETS:

### CHEWBACCA (CHEWY):
Perkinses' huge black Labrador; has a lot of energy, is a handful when on a walk (#9-p.35); eight months old (#9-p.33); once gets away from Claudia on a walk to meet Myriah at bus stop (#10-p.65). Loves visitors (#20-p.33). Has backyard that is fenced in (#10-p.61). Lovable but mischievous (#22-p.38); ate a tray of homemade chocolate chip cookies (#33-p.89). Can work his own hook loose; is like Houdini; you can't lock him up (M#7-p.37).

**R.C. (RAT CATCHER):**
Brown tiger cat that doesn't really catch rats, too lazy (#9-p.36).

**SOCKS SEBASTIAN PERKINS:**
Known as "Socks"; his fur is orange everywhere except his feet, which are white (SS#7-p.113).

# The PREZZIOSOs

•

**GENERAL:**
Referred to as "the P's." Friends of the Pikes (#4-p.58); not rich (#16-p.44). Go to Chatham to watch husband's college play basketball (#4-p.116).

**HOUSE:**
Live on Burnt Hill Road. Living room has a picture window (#73-p.28); hall has a mirror (#73-p.35). First-aid kit is in the linen closet upstairs (#73-p.113).

**JENNY PREZZIOSO:**

**PERSONAL INFO:**
Four (#7-p.25) [three #4-p.59]. Wears her dark brown hair in bows (#73-p.25). Bedtime is eight-thirty (M#1-p.106). Doesn't get as dressed up as she used to (#45-p.52); used to wear ribbons in hair, lacy socks, never in pants, always immaculate (#4-p.59). A spoiled brat; none of the BSC members except Mary Anne like her very much (#5-p.20). Doesn't like to be called "Jen" (#16-

p.44). Slow, picky eater (#24-p.108). Doesn't know how to share; when left alone complains bitterly (#7-p.55). Terrified of dogs (#7-p.92). Called "Angel" by her mom (#4-p.127). The kind of kid who gives baby-sitting a bad name (#34-p.9).

**POSSESSIONS:**
Has new watch but can't tell time yet (#41-p.7). Favorite toys include: a Barbie (which she calls "Hospital Barbie" because she got it when Mrs. Prezzioso was in the hospital having Andrea), a ratty old clown doll she calls Mr. Bog, and a find-the-picture book (M#1-p.73). Also has stuffed monkey named Monkey Matthew (M#1-p.76). Candy Land is her favorite game (M#2-p.53).

**EXPERIENCES:**
While Mary Anne is baby-sitting her, she comes down with a fever of 104 and is taken by ambulance to the hospital (#4-pp.121-124), where she is diagnosed as having strep throat (#4-p.136). In cross-country

race in Mini-Olympics BSC organizes (#55-p.132). Goes to Spring Dance at Community Center; wears lavender dress and corsage made of violets (#63-p.147). Knows she's being bribed by her mother with presents to prevent jealousy of the new baby; doesn't want to be a big sister (#41-p.68). When she sees new sister, she loves her (#41-p.128). Becomes "Miss Priss" again when jealous of Andrea's modeling career (#73-from p.25); then becomes Jenny-the-slob; ends up back at moderation (#73-p.136).

## ANDREA PREZZIOSO:

### PERSONAL INFO:
Not a newborn anymore, active and alert (#45-p.30); can hold head up (#45-p.55); was seven-and-a-half pounds at birth (#41-p.119). Looks like miniature version of Jenny, except that she doesn't have enough hair for bows (#73-p.25). Favorite pajamas are blue, with pink dinosaurs on them (M#1-p.103). Doesn't like diaper pins to be tight (M#2-p.49).

### EXPERIENCES:
Gets entered as "Queen Andrea" in baby parade (#45-p.81). Has been going to auditions (#73-p.51), is "the darling of the industry," gets one out of three commercials she auditions for (#73-p.58). Lands audition for Karbergers ad (#73-p.71).

## MRS. MADELEINE PREZZIOSO:

### PERSONAL INFO:
Fussy, fastidious, always polite, appears as if she just stepped out of a magazine (#4-p.59). When pregnant, knew baby was a girl (#39-p.31). Nickname for Jenny is "Angel" (#4-p.127). Is at home during the day (#86-p.29).

### EXPERIENCES:
Buys Jenny lots of presents before baby comes (#41-p.9). Gives birth to Andrea (#41-p.119). Requires club members to take infant-care course before sitting for Andrea (#45-p.30). Enters Andrea as "Queen Andrea" in baby parade, wins first place in stroller division with Kristy's help (#45-p.128); she dresses as one of the "Queen's" guards in parade (#45-p.106). Has been taking Andrea to auditions (#73-p.51). Used to be on soccer team in high school (ShS-p.123).

## MR. NICK PREZZIOSO:

### PERSONAL INFO:
Appears prim and proper but not comfortable (#4-p.59).

### EXPERIENCES:
Gives wife surprise baby shower with Mary Anne's help (#41-p.93).

## OTHER PREZZIOSO RELATIVES:

### MR. PREZZIOSO'S SISTER:
Has twin sons, two years old
(SM#1-p.62).

# The ROBERTSes

•

## DANIELLE ROBERTS:

**PERSONAL INFO:**
Nine, has leukemia, was in hospital since last summer (#48-p.7). Is now doing very, very well (#82-p.33). Hair starts to grow back, comes in red (#48-p.116). Is member of Kids Club (#48-p.63). Chemotherapy helps and she gets to come home but has to wear a wig or scarf because most of hair fell out (#48-p.46). Likes to wear T-shirt that says: "Bald is Beautiful"; small, thin face, huge brown eyes, long lashes, smiles a lot, painfully thin, dark circles under eyes (#48-p.63). Fourth- and fifth-graders uncomfortable with way she looks, third-graders don't care (#48-p.65). Befriends Becca, Charlotte, and Jessi (#48-p.88). Has two wishes: 1) to go to Disneyland, 2) to graduate from elementary school (#48-p.69). Gets tired easily after playing with Becca, Char, and Squirt (#48-pp.92-93). Likes to make jewelry (#48-p.46).

**EXPERIENCES:**
Jessi helps to grant her wish to go to Disneyland through Your Wish Is My Command (#48-p.114). Goes back to hospital for tests, not sure when she'll get to go home (#48-p.139). Writes six-year-old with leukemia (#48-p.69). Returned to Kids Can Do Anything Club in fourth grade, after spending a lot of time in the hospital and undergoing chemotherapy (#80-p.40). Her leukemia comes back, and she undergoes chemotherapy (#80-p.41). Is the best actress in the KCDAC (#80-p.84); gets a standing ovation (#80-p.139). After she crashes her parents' car, she will be free to enjoy high spirits just like any other kid but won't be allowed to abuse the privilege (#82-p.110).

## GREG ROBERTS:

**PERSONAL INFO:**
Six and a half (#48-p.96); is sometimes jealous of attention parents give to Danielle (#48-p.100).

## MRS. ROBERTS:

Hair is the same red-brown as Danielle's; she wears it in a short, sleek cap (#82-p.33).

## ROBERTS PETS:

### MR. TOES:
New kitten, all gray except for his white toes (#48-p.97).

# The RODOWSKYs

•

**GENERAL:**

Mary Anne and Logan are their first sitters (#10-p.48). The three boys all have flaming red hair and freckles, look alike (#12-p.31); (#20-p.43), and love softball (#63-p.58). Have a lot of Legos (#56-p.2). The boys know everything about cleaning (#12-p.31). Claudia decides to wear jeans whenever baby-sitting there (#12-p.34), her spill-proof, accident-proof outfit (#63-p.56). Rodowsky boys, Arnolds, and Braddocks send complimentary anonymous notes to BSC, treat them to lunch, and Jackie and Archie make portraits of them for being favorite baby-sitters (#63-pp.131, 134-135).

**HOUSE:**

Live on Reilly Lane, a few streets over from Logan's house (#10-p.47). There's nothing breakable in the rec room where the boys play; it is on the same floor as the living room (M#2-p.59). Living room is covered with the boys' artwork, professionally framed (#10-p.53). Ashley Wyeth lives next door (#12-p.37). Mr. Seger and his son Noah are also neighbors (SM#2-p.40). Not much room to play in backyard because of doghouse and windowless toolshed (#12-p.35); (#63-p.57).

**SHEA RODOWSKY:**

**PERSONAL INFO:**

Nine (#12-p.30). In Little League (#20-p.44); is an excellent player and doesn't have attitude about it (#63-p.59). Has dyslexia (reverses letters, finds it hard to recognize words and numbers) (#63-p.39) so he has to go to resource room; needs homework help from BSC (#63-pp.22, 23); is above average in intelligence (#63-p.39). Was frustrated and discouraged about dyslexia problem (#63-p.46); does better on report card, doesn't mind tutors anymore (#63-p.149). Is great with figures and measurements (M#21-p.25); has a natural talent for math (M#21-p.26).

**EXPERIENCES:**

Takes piano lessons (#12-p.108); Mrs. Schiavone is his piano teacher whose doorbell played "Over the Rainbow" before Jackie broke it (#12-p.109); says "Bullfrogs" when he messes up on the piano (#56-pp.2-3). Takes lessons at the Y (#10-p.51). Plays piano with Marilyn in band that BSC organizes (#56-p.94); played "If I Were a Rich Man" with Marilyn Arnold during performance (#56-p.132). Paints half of Bo's doghouse on the outside (#59-p.75). Mrs. Danvers is teacher (#63-p.41). Helps Claud with spelling, she helps him with homework (#63-pp.101-103); Mrs. Rodowsky specifically asks Claudia to tutor Shea (#63-p.117); Claudia and Shea make flash cards and decorate them (#63-p.121); Shea gives thank-you note to Claudia (#63-p.136). Dances fox trot with Claudia at Spring Dance at Community Center (#63-p.149). Shannon thinks he has a crush on her (M#14-p.100). Teams with Mary Anne and Claudia for the Battle of the Bakers (M#21-p.25).

## JACKIE RODOWSKY:

### PERSONAL INFO:
Seven (#10-p.47); red-haired, red cheeks, freckles (#10-p.50). Big contagious grin with one tooth missing (#12-p.97), loses tooth playing softball, likes losing teeth (#20-p.73). Looks like Alfred E. Neuman (#22-p.77). Accident prone (#11-p.19). Is called "the Walking Disaster," but the BSC members still love him

(#36-p.28). Only kid on Krushers who doesn't look neat (#20-p.101).

### DISASTERS:
Hits home run and breaks window at SES (#20-p.87). Scratches his eye with a drinking straw and has to wear an eye patch for a few days (SS#10-p.66). Has had a raisin stuck up his nose and has had his arm stuck in his pants drawer (#100-p.60). Sprains his ankle after falling from a tree and has to use a cane for awhile (#100-p.68). Has concussion after his bike hits a tree and he is not wearing a helmet; is unconscious and taken to the hospital, where fluid is drained from under his skull (#100-p.127).

### EXPERIENCES:
A pretty solid softball hitter (#63-p.58). Jessi helps him make a working volcano for the science fair (#36-p.33), but she does most of the work, and he fumbles his lines in front of the judges (#36-p.120). Has yard sale in backyard to raise money for Zuni elementary school that burned down (#44-p.80). Plays kazoo in kids' band BSC organizes (#56-p.48); thinks of name for band: All the Children of the World (#56-p.66); acts as emcee for performance (#56-pp.131-132). Tries to paint inside of Bo's doghouse while Claud is sitting; Shea paints half of the outside (#59-p.75). Goes to Spring Dance at Community Center, does sock hop with Hannie Papadakis

(#63-p.147). Plays on Krashers, shortstop or second base (M#7-p.86). Loses a tooth in the arboretum (M#19-p.87). Plays Michael Darling in *Peter Pan* (SS#9-p.124).

## ARCHIE (ARCHIBALD) RODOWSKY:

**PERSONAL INFO:**
Four (#12-p.30). Left-handed (#20-p.45).

**EXPERIENCES:**
Takes tumbling classes (#12-p.108); takes lessons at the Y (#10-p.51). Plays soccer (#36-p.31). Not on softball team yet but likes it, is a pretty good athlete (#63-p.58). Enters the (plastic) weight-lifting event in the Mini-Olympics run by BSC (#55-p.80). Plays tambourine in band that BSC organizes (#56-p.68).

## MRS. MARIEL RODOWSKY:

**PERSONAL INFO:**
Tall, thin, doesn't look like most mothers (#10-p.50). Has something good to eat on hand during sitting jobs, something not too healthy (#63-p.56).

**EXPERIENCES:**
Specifically asks for Claudia to tutor Shea (#63-p.117).

## MR. RODOWSKY:

**PERSONAL INFO:**
Father (#10-p.50).

## RODOWSKY ANIMALS:

**BO:**
Dog (#12-p.34); gets party for second birthday (#20-p.40). His doghouse is half-painted blue on the outside (#59-p.75).

**ELIZABETH:**
Jackie's male grasshopper (#10-p.52).

## OTHER RODOWSKY FAMILY MEMBERS:

**JOSEPH:**
Five; cousin visiting from Michigan (M#21-pp.82-83).

**JULIE:**
Three; cousin visiting from Michigan (M#21-pp.82-83).

# The SALEMs

•

**GENERAL:**
BSC members couldn't baby-sit until the twins were six months, now family calls fairly regularly (#52-p.34).

**HOUSE:**
Have garage (#52-p.34). Twins' nursery is bright and airy: yellow-striped curtains, bookshelf with lots of picture books, blue wooden toy chest with Winnie-the-Pooh decoration, frieze of teddy bears and balloons around middle of wall (#52-p.35).

**RICKY AND ROSE SALEM:**

**PERSONAL INFO:**
Twins, around six months old (#52-p.34); teething (#52-p.118).

**MRS. SALEM:**

**PERSONAL INFO:**
Organized (#52-p.34); switched from disposable to cloth diapers for environmental reasons (#52-p.36).

**EXPERIENCES:**
First met BSC members during infant-care course (#45-p.48). On the board of Small Animal Rescue League (#52-p.113).

# The SOBAKs

•

**HOUSE:**
Live on Cherry Valley Road (#19-p.19). Swing set by the side of the house near driveway (#19-p.36). Parents go to golf tournaments (#19-p.114).

**BETSY SOBAK:**

**PERSONAL INFO:**
Eight (#19-p.19), with brown hair (#19-p.30). When auditioning, speaks in a clear, carrying voice without reading (#91-p.59).

**EXPERIENCES:**
Used to spend most of allowance on practical jokes from McBuzz's Mail Order until parents made her quit (#19-p.34). Pranks cause Claudia to break her leg (#19-pp.37-47). Class is going to recite *Wynken, Blynken, and Nod* (#19-p.8). After tricking Mal and Dawn, she is made to see the light when Kristy, prepped by her brother Sam, embarrasses Betsy with tricks in theater (#19-p.128). Has lead role in *Alice and the Pilgrims*, Claudia's Thanksgiving play (#91-p.59).

**PAT SOBAK:**

**PERSONAL INFO:**
Betsy's sister, twenty-three years old, has a baby (#19-p.32).

**MRS. COOKIE SOBAK:**

**PERSONAL INFO:**
Member of Woman's Club (#19-p.30).

**MR. SOBAK:**

**PERSONAL INFO:**
Works at Tile Corp. (#19-p.31).

# The SPRINGERs

•

## NATALIE SPRINGER:

### PERSONAL INFO:
Seven; a friend of Karen's (#78-p.24). Has a lisp (#78-p.36), has few friends (#78-p.35). Looks a little unkempt; her socks droop around her ankles, her glasses are always a bit crooked on her nose, and her hair's a mess. But she's very sweet (#78-p.41). Goes to Stoneybrook Academy; attends Camp BSC; has gone to a circus camp before (#86-p.34).

### EXPERIENCES:
Plays Lovely Ladies with Claudia (#78-p.37). After BSC's Friendship Campaign, has more friends (#78-p.124); becomes practically inseparable from Becca and Charlotte (#78-p.137).

# The STANTON-CHAs

•

## STEPHEN STANTON-CHA:

**PERSONAL INFO:**
Seven; has sandy brown hair, short except for one longer tail in back; brown eyes have slightly Asian look to them; doesn't look like mother (M#23-pp.24-25). Biracial (half-American; half-Korean) (M#23-p.61). Shy; attends SES, but doesn't have any friends at first (M#23-pp.53-54). Teacher is Mr. Anderson (M#23-p.59). Knows karate (M#23-p.117).

**EXPERIENCES:**
Founds the Blue Ribbon Club with Jenny Prezzioso and Claire Pike after being excluded from the Slate Street Kids Club (M#23-p.109).

## MRS. NICOLE (NIKKI) STANTON-CHA:

**PERSONAL INFO:**
New owner of the Greenbrook Club (M#23-p.25). Blonde; looks a little younger than Mrs. Stevenson (M#23-p.24).

**EXPERIENCES:**
Grew up in Stoneybrook (M#23-p.28). Family once belonged to Dark Woods Country Club (M#23-p.27); Nikki didn't return to the club after her Jewish friend was discriminated against (M#23-p.29). Didn't talk to father for ten years; father stopped speaking to her after she married a Korean man (M#23-p.29). All is forgiven now (M#23-p.127).

## MR. THOMAS STANTON-CHA:

**PERSONAL INFO:**
Korean; an excellent businessman; travels often to Korea (M#23-p.29). Handsome (M#23-p.140).

## MR. PAUL R. STANTON:

**PERSONAL INFO:**
Nikki's father; Stoneybrook resident (M#23-p.29).

**EXPERIENCES:**
Didn't speak to daughter for almost ten years (M#23-p.29). Was Mayor Armstrong's "right-hand fool" (M#23-p.50) but never was convinced to join his "secret society" (M#23-p.143). Admits he's been a fool and reconciles with the rest of the family (M#23-p.127).

# The WILDERs

•

**HOUSE:**
Live at 477 Elm Street (#49-p.28). House is Cape Cod-style, off-white with green shutters, neatly cut hedges line porch; have maroon station wagon (#49-p.30). Chagall and Matisse prints on walls (#49-p.31). Basement looks like dance studio, a *barre* along each wall, floor-to-ceiling mirrors, bright lights (#49-p.38).

## ROSIE (MARY ROSE) WILDER:

**PERSONAL INFO:**
Seven (#49-p.26); often acts older (M#13-p.43); has flaming, thick red hair, freckles, hazel eyes (#49-pp.32-33). Wears tortoise-shell glasses (for reading) (#49-p.47). Has temper tantrum with parents, wants to be a normal kid (#49-p.106). Parents agree to let her be in math club and study violin and art, her favorites (#49-p.140). Skipped a grade; is in third with Nicky Pike at SES (M#11-p.90). Has TV and VCR in her own room (M#11-p.91). Has a shy streak, needs a script (M#13-p.41). Mrs.

Arnold drives her home from school (#49-p.42). Claud is Rosie's favorite sitter (#49-p.80).

**TALENT:**
Has appeared in many commercials (M#11-p.90). Takes private lessons in piano, ballet, violin, voice, and tap; in science and math clubs, advanced readers group (#49-pp.33-34). Follows strict practicing schedule (#49-p.33); has talent agent named Sandra Yu (#49-p.60); in commercial for Up'n'Out Cleaner (#49-pp.1, 45). Rehearses for Dan Beasley's talent show, *Uncle Dandy's Star Machine* (#49-p.60). Sings and plays piano on show, doesn't make one mistake (#49-p.103). Secretly draws pictures in room, Claud finds out (#49-p.93). Enters drawings of junk food at Claud's art show (#49-p.130). Is SES crossword champ, other kids tease her (#49-p.113). Asks Claud to be her art teacher (#49-p.140).

**EXPERIENCES:**
Mary Anne worries that Rosie is so busy with her lessons that she

doesn't have any friends (M#13-p.37). Janine Kishi helps her with homework (#49-pp.48, 79).

## MRS. GINGER WILDER:

### PERSONAL INFO:
Pretty, friendly face, beautiful deep brown hair; Laura Ashley dress (#49-p.31).

### EXPERIENCES:
She and Mr. Wilder push Rosie to be a star but agree to lessen her workload (#49-pp.33, 140).

## MR. GEORGE WILDER:

### PERSONAL INFO:
Wants Rosie to be famous (#49-pp.105-106). Gets home at eight or eight-thirty from work (#49-p.26).

## OTHER WILDER FAMILY MEMBERS:

### MRS. WILDER'S MOTHER:
Broke ankle, has the flu and shingles (#49-p.26).

# OTHER BSC PEOPLE

# AT STONEYBROOK MIDDLE SCHOOL

•

**ADMINISTRATORS:**

**PRINCIPAL:**
Mr. Benjamin Taylor (SS#10-p.3).

**ASSISTANT PRINCIPAL:**
Mr. Howard Kingbridge; Mary Anne's shoe comes off at Remember September dance and narrowly misses him (#10-p.92); okays Dawn's idea for school recycling center as long as students vote for it (#57-p.73); is interviewed by reporters for *Stoneybrook News* on opening day of recycling center (#57-p.103). Wins SMS Worst Dresser Award (M#4-p.130).

**SECRETARY:**
Mrs. Downey (#12-p.5); calls Stacey out of math class to tell her that her mother was taken to hospital (#58-pp.42, 44).

**JANITORS**
Mr. Halprin; helps Mary Anne (#17-p.27). Mr. Milhaus; has German accent (M#25-p.55) and speaks in a formal way (M#25-p.82). Suspect in SMS vandalism mystery (M#25-p.113). Mr. Steinmetz; former custodian; was missing a front tooth, so every time he said an "S" he whistled (#75-p.15).

**LUNCH MONITOR:**
Mrs. Ensign (#57-p.83); thinks Woody Jefferson and Trevor Sandbourne brought wine to school, but it was only cider in wine glasses (#57-p.83).

**GUIDANCE COUNSELORS:**
Mrs. Amer (#67-p.56); Dawn's mother consults Mrs. Amer regarding Dawn's big move (#67-p.57). Arranges for grief counselors to be on call after Amelia Freeman's death (#93-p.52). Mr. Seitz; Kristy talks to him about starting SMS S.A.D.D. chapter (#93-p.97).

**SCHOOL LIBRARIAN:**
Mr. Counts (#4-p.23).

**TEACHERS:**

**MR. BAILEY:**
English teacher (SS#3-p.29).

# ● Other BSC People ●

**MS. J. BELCHER:**
Mary Anne's English teacher (MAB-p.151).

**MR. BELLAFATTO:**
Deep-voiced substitute teacher for computer programming; a pretty good teacher, explains things clearly, answers questions and even cracks a few jokes (#75-p.111).

**MRS. BERNHARDT:**
Otherwise known as Dolly One; has thick blonde curly hair; is short and big-chested, with a huge smile and tons of makeup on her face (#75-p.3). Teaches Claudia's history class (#97-p.10), as well as Abby and Stacey's (#97-p.12). Chaperone on SMS trip to Hawaii (SS#13-p.65).

**MR. BLAKE:**
Dawn and Mary Anne's homeroom teacher, room #216 (#10-p.15); coach of baseball team that Logan's on (#25-p.25). Over winter vacation, takes his family skiing and sprains his ankle (#93-p.15).

**MRS. BOYDEN:**
Modern Living Class teacher for eighth-graders; assigns students to pick marriage partners (#52-p.23) and take care of child-eggs (#52-pp.44-45). Teaches Claudia's Short Takes unit called Learning to Read (#91-p.10).

**MS. BRYAN:**
Substitute home ec teacher; goes to Mischief Night Masquerade with Mr. Rothman (M#22-p.137).

**MR. CHENEY:**
Teacher, director of *Peter Pan* (SS#9-p.39).

**MR. DAVIES:**
Claudia's summer school math teacher (M#16-p.8).

**MR. DE YOUNG:**
Boys' gym teacher; holds volleyball gym class with Ms. Walden's girls' gym class (#59-p.35). Works lunch patrol (#84-p.76). Is chaperone for BSC group in Hawaii; is built a little like Jean Claude Van Damme (SS#13-p.37).

**MR. DOUGHERTY:**
Mal's creative writing teacher (#47-p.1); class of ten students meets Tuesdays and Fridays in old faculty lounge decorated with plants and bookshelves full of books (#47-p.43).

**MR. DRUBEK:**
Teacher, helps out with *Peter Pan* (SS#9-p.41).

**MRS. DWYER:**
New art teacher (M#22-p.149).

**MR. WESLEY ELLENBURG:**
Student teacher from master's program at Stoneybrook Community College who takes over Mr. Zizmore's last month of math class (#65-pp.6-7); Stacey has crush on him (#65-p.53); gives him poem, tells him she loves him (#65-pp.97, 108). Kids can call him "Wes" (#65-p.40); he looks like Tom Cruise (#65-p.37), has wavy, light brown hair; a senior at college, favorite subject is math; likes his class to be fairly informal with lots of questions and discussions (#65-pp.38-40). Twenty-two years old (#65-p.152). Taps the side of his chin when he thinks (#65-p.41). Calls on Stacey to work out hard problems (#65-p.59). Gets

highest recommendation possible (#65-p.111). Has battered silver-gray Toyota with Stoneybrook University sticker across rear windshield, calls his car "Winston" (#65-p.86). Dances with Stacey at Spring Dance (#65-p.127); tells her their age difference is too big, they need to be just friends (#65-p.132).

**MR. FISKE:**
Kristy's English teacher, younger than Watson (#45-p.35). Dances with Kristy at Spring Dance (#65-p.127). Also Stacey's English teacher (M#10-p.46). Has blond hair and a mustache; is BSC suspect in counterfeiting ring (M#10-p.89). A nice man and a pretty good teacher, even if he wears silly ties and makes terrible jokes (M#10-p.125). Cokie Mason has him for homeroom, makes fun of his clothes at lunch (M#10-p.129). Owns a battered blue Honda (M#10-p.132). Free reading time in his class is generally an excuse to hang out, as long as students keep up with reading at home (M#22-p.28).

**MS. FLOOD:**
Speaks with an Australian accent; parodied in the Sixth Grade Follies (#75-p.81).

**MRS. FREDERICKSON:**
Mal and Jessi's homeroom teacher (#14-p.12).

**MS. FROST:**
Mary Anne's math teacher (M#13-p.110). Abby's math teacher as well (#96-p.13), although Abby and Mary Anne are not in the same class (#96-p.40). Mrs. Stevenson gives her

tongue-lashing after she forces Abby to take a quiz after being out of school sick for two days (#96-p.16); now, Abby's on Ms. Frost's bad side (#96-p.17).

**MS. GARCIA:**
Receives donations for school auction from the principal's office (#62-p.92). Short Takes drama teacher for Claudia, Abby, and Stacey; Claud has heard she's decent (#91-p.27). Regretfully informs the students that play must be reworked or canceled (#91-p.95). Gives each of the students a rose from her bouquet after Thanksgiving play is performed (#91-p.111).

**MR. GEIST:**
Teaches Claudia's summer school photography class (M#16-p.1). She has a little crush on him; he has black curly hair, cool wire-rimmed glasses, is tall and lanky, with a great smile; he really inspires Claudia (M#16-p.85).

**MRS. ESTELLE GONZALEZ:**
Dawn's science teacher, instructs class to do project to save the planet (#57-p.1); students vote for her to be chairperson of recycling center (#57-p.97); asks Dawn to co-chair with her (#57-p.143). Chaperone on Hawaii trip (SS#13-p.77).

**MS. GRISWOLD:**
Kristy's science teacher who lets her retake test, but she fails it again (#53-p.118); calls Kristy's parents (#53-p.128).

**MRS. HALL:**
Claudia's English teacher (#12-p.2). Hardly ever uses students' last

names; "check" is her term for "surprise quiz" (#12-p.3). Tells Claud she's in danger of failing unless she improves spelling and vocabulary (#63-p.5). Gives extra help to Claudia, but she still fails (SM#1-p.2). Chaperone on Hawaii trip (SS#13-p.47).

**MS. HALLIDAY:**
Seventh grade gym teacher; helps with *Peter Pan* (SS#9-p.40); Mary Anne's most feared teacher—can't stand klutzes; gets along with Kristy (SS#3-p.60). Engaged, and misses fiancée when at Leicester Lodge; bonds with Mary Anne (SS#3-p.170).

**MS. HARRIS:**
Dawn's physical science teacher (#50-p.74). Unmarried, much older than Mr. Ellenburg (#65-p.129).

**COACH HALVORSEN:**
Winning basketball coach (#70-p.135).

**MR. JAZAK:**
Wears Coke-bottle glasses; parodied in the Sixth Grade Follies (#75-p.80).

**MR. LEAVITT:**
Logan's track coach (LS-p.121).

**MR. LEHRER:**
Cokie's English teacher (#46-p.59).

**MS. LEVINE:**
Stacey's homeroom teacher, who uses adjectives like "novel" (#70-p.10).

**MS. MANDEL:**
Dresses as Snow White at Halloween Hop; awards best costumes (#38-p.133).

**COACH MILLS:**
Logan's football coach (#79-p.34).

**MR. PETERS:**
Kristy's seventh grade math teacher (#2-p.18).

**MRS. PINELLI:**
Music teacher (#2-p.39). Conducts orchestra practices (#95-p.6).

**MR. REDMONT:**
Seventh grade social studies (#1-p.2) teacher, claps hands to get attention (#20-p.68).

**MRS. ROSENAUER:**
Gym instructor Mary Anne hates (#10-p.18). Dances with Mr. Zizmore at Spring Dance (#65-p.127). Works lunch patrol (#84-p.76).

**MR. MICHAEL ROTHMAN:**
Sixth grade science teacher; a tall, thin man with curly black hair (M#22-pp.47-48). Went to SMS twenty-eight years ago (M#22-p.88); was on the football team (M#22-p.89). Has an extreme fear of heights (M#22-p.107). Was one of the most popular kids at SMS; Liz Connor has a crush on him, so he accepted bet to take her to Halloween Masquerade; but he couldn't go through with it, setting off a disaster (M#22-from p.126).

**MR. SCHUBERT:**
Stacey's teacher for Math for Real Life, a Short Takes class (M#14-p.1).

**MRS. M. SIMON:**
Kristy's English teacher for one semester (#53-p.68). Mary Anne's English teacher for one semester (#93-p.17). Her voice usually takes on a faraway and dreamy quality when she's talking about poetry or a writer she really loves (#93-p.18).

**MISS STANWORTH:**
Home ec teacher, supervises Savannah and Mal for *Peter Pan* costuming; young and glamorous, she makes her own clothes and works in a professional manner (SS#9-p.86).

**MR. TROUT:**
Jessi's computer programming teacher; is a nerd (#75-p.2). Is about six feet tall, extremely skinny, with waxy black hair combed in a style right out of the 1970s. Pants are too big and always bagging over his Hush Puppies; alternates tweed jackets, wears old tattersall shirts with pocket protectors. Pronounces R's a little like W's when nervous (#75-p.7). Wears a toupee, which is fished off of his head by students (#75-p.66). Quits SMS (#75-p.109). Later writes to Jessi and explains that he's applied to a graduate program in advanced computer studies (#75-p.136).

**MS. VANDELA:**
Otherwise known as Dolly Two; has thick blonde curly hair; is short and big-chested, with a huge smile and tons of makeup on her face (#75-p.3).

**MS. WALDEN:**
Mal and Jessi's gym teacher; gives swim lessons at community pool complex as part of gym class (#55-p.28). Gym is Mondays and Wednesdays (#59-p.111). Arranged volleyball to be played with the boys (#59-p.28); calls Mal "Pike" (#59-p.35); gives Mal her first detention for not playing volleyball (#59-p.67); tells Mal to wash pinnies

instead of more detention (#59-p.93); asks boys' gym teacher to tell Chris Brooks to lighten up on Mal during volleyball (#59-p.125); does archery unit with gym class in which Mal excels (#59-pp.131, 135).

**MRS. WEGMANN:**
Claudia's summer school teacher; an old droner (SS#10-p.104).

**MR. WILLIAMS:**
Mal and Jessi's English teacher (#14-p.16). Has a pot belly (#75-p.80).

**MR. WITHUM:**
Stacey's Short Takes teacher for Project Work (M#13-p.7). Is pleasantly plump with a big, round, pink face and a cheerful smile (M#14-p.22).

**MR. WONG:**
Art teacher, supervises Mural Day (#84-p.36). Is chaperone on SMS Hawaii trip (SS#13-p.84).

**COACH WU:**
Girls' softball coach, one of the toughest coaches at SMS (#74-p.30); often blows whistle on a silver chain around her neck (#74-p.33).

**MR. ZIZMORE:**
Stacey's math teacher (#13-p.2); is detention monitor when Mal has detention for first time (#59-p.68). Stacey's class is last class of day (#65-p.8). When fed up uses big words instead of yelling (#65-p.5). Cool, patient, friendly, makes math come alive, tells Stacey she's his star student (#65-p.6). Student teacher, Wesley Ellenburg, takes over his class for last month of school (#65-p.7). Gives Ellenburg highest recommendation (#65-p.111). Dances with Mrs. Rosenaur at Spring

Dance (#65-p.127). Is teachers' representative in Board of Eduction negotiating committee (M#25-p.53).

**MR. ZORZI:**
Long-term sub for Claudia's math teacher (#40-p.5); accuses Claud of cheating on test (#40-p.34).

**STUDENTS:**

*Number in parentheses denotes grade level as of book #100; if there is no number, grade is unknown.*

**BEN ABBOTT (6):**
Auditions for the Sixth Grade Follies; recites the Gettysburg Address (#75-p.72).

**JENNIFER ABRAMS:**
Auditions for *Peter Pan* (SS#9-p.55).

**ANGELA (8):**
In Mary Anne's Modern Living class; pretend-marries Kevin; they lose their child-egg (#52-p.107).

**SUE ARCHER (8):**
Very cool girl in Dawn's science class (#50-p.75). Blonde, blue-eyed—much to Stacey's distress, Robert pays lots of attention to her on plane ride to Hawaii (SS#13-p.114) Is a big talker (SS#13-p.114).

**LAURA ARONSEN (6):**
Auditions for the Sixth Grade Follies, sings "Maybe" from *Annie* (#75-p.72).

**JEFF ATKINSON (6):**
Auditions for Sixth Grade Follies; sings the theme song from *Shining Time Station* (#75-p.72).

**CRAIG AVAZIAN (6):**
In Jessi's Short Takes class; imitates Renee Johnson (#75-p.29).

**CORINNE BAKER:**
Hangs out in SMS basketball "group" (#70-p.37); went out with Robert Brewster a few times (#70-p.87), is jealous of Stacey (#70-p.125).

**MELISSA BANKS (8):**
In Ms. Bernhardt's social studies class with Claudia (#97-p.11). Can be a little excitable (#97-p.12). Goes shopping at the Washington Mall with Claudia, Stacey, and Abby (#97-p.74). Claudia thinks she's a pest (#97-p.94), especially after they are lost together in Philadelphia (#97-p.114).

**BARBARA:**
Summer school classmate of Claudia's; wants to keep in touch (SS#10-p.107).

**SANJITA BATTS (6):**
Puerto Rican classmate of Jessi's (#75-p.4).

**KELSEY BAUMAN:**
New boy Stacey likes and asks to the Halloween Hop (#38- p.130).

**ASHLEY BEDELL (6):**
Storms off stage during the Sixth Grade Follies, saying her routine is too hard (#75-p.96).

**RON BELKIS (7):**
Boy in seventh grade; Claud thinks he is cute (#51-p.39).

**SHAWN BENEDICT:**
Female; coaxed by Kristy into competing in the cross-country ski race at Leicester Lodge (SS#3-p.199).

**AUSTIN BENTLEY (8):**
New boy in school (#6-p.34). Named after two cars, but he just

laughs when people tease him about it (LS-p.6). Goes to Halloween Hop with Cokie Mason (#38-p.132). Logan's friend; they're both on the football team (LS-p.6). Goes to Valentine's Dance with Stacey, as friends (#51-p.38). "Marries" Stacey in Modern Living class, has child-egg named "Bobby" (#52-p.69). Has been to dances and parties with Claud and Stacey, all three are just friends (#52-p.69). Stacey likes him, but he can be a wise guy (M#14-p.23); in Stacey's Short Takes class (M#14-p.23). Stacey goes with him to the Winter Wonderland Dance; doesn't love him, just thinks he's nice (SS#7-p.45). On Logan's team for Battle of the Bakers (M#21-p.25).

**EMILY BERNSTEIN (8):**
Part of Claud's old lunch group (#2-p.38); at SMS's recycling center opening, she passes out pamphlet on recycling and subscription form for *P3*, an environmental magazine (#57-pp.107-108). Very smart, the editor of the *SMS Express* (#71-p.33). A dynamo, in her own low-key, serious way (#71-p.48). Always pays attention (M#25-p.90). Re-types anti-School Spirit Month petition (#84-p.65).

**PETE BLACK (8):**
Always wears sneakers, even at dance (#51-p.105). Has grown his brown hair long over the summer; it is now down over the collar of his shirt (#99-p.66). Runs for eighth grade class president and wins (#53-pp.49, 146). Stacey's sort-of boyfriend; part of lunch crowd;

took Stacey to Halloween Hop (#3-p.25) and Final Fling (#6-p.34). Always snapping bras; snaps Dorianne Wallingford's at movies (#10-p.44); has snapped Miranda's bra (#46-p.58). Is very serious about food (#3-p.84). Does English project on Megan Rhinehart with Mary Anne, Logan, and Cokie Mason; does most of the work with Mary Anne (#46-p.93). Likes Laine Cummings (#51-p.58), takes her to Valentine Dance (#51-p.105), she dances with another boy and he almost cries (#51-p.108), she leaves him at the dance (#51-p.115). At opening day of SMS's recycling center, he passes out raffle tickets (#57-p.107). In Dawn's science class (#57-p.141). In Mary Anne's home ec class (M#4-p.89). Dresses up as clown at Awards Night (M#4-p.129). Goes to the movies with Sabrina Bouvier (#81-p.11). Falls off his bicycle and breaks his nose before the *Peter Pan* performance (SS#9-p.207). Participates in Battle of the Bakers (M#21-p.47). Went to kindergarten at SES with Kristy, Claudia, and Mary Anne (CB-p.29). Member of the football team (LS-p.48). Is becoming friends with Robert Brewster (#99-p.67). Is caught in Hawaiian helicopter crash landing with Stacey; pukes (SS#13-p.153).

**RJ BLASER (8):**
A star of the SMS basketball team, over six feet tall; wears varsity jacket (#70-p.2); hits Stacey with a snowball (#70-p.2), asks her out to a

movie (#70-p.5); likes action and silly comedy (#70-p.33). Nickname is "The Blasemeister" (#70-p.36).

**TOM BLOCK (6):**
On the Sixth Grade Follies finance committee with Jessi (#75-p.112).

**ERICA BLUMBERG (8):**
Wins Best Excuse For Not Doing Homework Award for telling her teacher that her mom has composted her report (M#4-p.130). In Modern Living class with Mary Anne and Logan (#52-p.25). In Stacey's math class with Mr. Zizmore (#65-p.62). Participates in Battle of the Bakers (M#21-p.47). In Claudia's Short Takes drama class (#91-p.29). Is going away to summer camp for several weeks (#98-p.47). Gets more baby-sitting jobs once BSC is disbanded; lives on the same block as the Newtons (#100-p.110).

**GRACE BLUME (8):**
Cokie's friend, has crush on Logan (#17-p.83); runs for class president (#53-p.23), uses video camera at candidate booth (#53-p.80), loses to Pete Black (#53-p.146). Always arranges to have as many classes as possible with Cokie (SS#9-p.57). Can actually be a decent person, once you take her away from Cokie; likes Nancy Drew mysteries; helps BSC with the Battle of the Bakers mystery (M#21-from p.75). On decorations committee for Mischief Night Masquerade with Stacey (M#22-p.30). Cokie says that Grace has "invented" a date for the dance—Ted, from Lawrenceville (M#22-p.53). But he turns up and is

really cute (M#22-p.136). For a while, Grace isn't speaking to Cokie (M#22-p.122) but they make up and are as thick as thieves again (M#22-p.148). In Ms. Bernhardt's social studies class with Claudia (#97-p.11).

**JIMMY BOULOUKOS (6):**
Sits in front of Jessi in Short Takes Computer Programming class (#75-p.29).

**SABRINA BOUVIER (8):**
BSC has never liked her and Susan Taylor because they wear too much makeup and expensive clothes, seem snobby; she and Susan are nice to Mary Anne after her makeover and haircut (#60-p.86). Goes with Carlos Mendez to SMS's January Jamboree dance (#60-p.134). Susan, her best friend, steals her boyfriend, Carlos, away from her; she goes to the movies with Pete Black instead (#81-p.11).

**ROBERT BREWSTER (8):**
Member of the SMS basketball team; hanging out at Pizza Express when he first meets Stacey—because their slices of pizza are stuck together (#70-pp.36-38). He has dark brown hair that falls over his forehead, dimples, and a smile that should have a danger sign on it (#70-p.39). Is not exactly model-gorgeous but still has deep dark eyes and broad shoulders (#76-p.9). Likes Stacey, according to Sheila MacGregor (#70-p.50). Humble, doesn't like movies like *Mall Warriors II* (#70-p.57). Goes on first date with Stacey, is very considerate

when she tells him about her diabetes (#70-p.83). Is terrible in English, but teachers let him get away with it (#70-pp.85-86). Used to go out with Corinne (#70-p.87). Quits basketball team in noble stand after Stacey is cheated out of cheerleadership (#70-p.135). Is Stacey's steady boyfriend (#76-p.2). Has summer job working on ferry between Long Island and Davis Park (#76-p.10); its name is the *Kiki* (#76-p.148). After seeing how Stacey lied to Claudia and her father, he says he doesn't trust her (#76-p.147). Soon, though, they're back together (#76-p.154). Paints house over the summer (#87-p.31). He doesn't like U4Me; has huge appetite (#87-p.33). When he gets home, there's always someone around (#94-p.2). Doesn't think the city is for him—it seems so noisy and big (#94-p.5). Has never been to a Broadway play (#94-p.9). Has been spending less and less time with his old crowd (#99-p.3). Is becoming friends with Pete Black (#99-p.67). Has more than one sister (#99-p.35). Stacey breaks up with him (#99-p.148) after learning that he's been seeing/kissing Andi Gentile (#99-p.114). He is more relaxed with Andi, and thinks he and Andi have more in common than he and Stacey (#99-p.147).

**CHRIS BROOKS (6):**
Has Mr. De Young for gym class; plays volleyball during gym with Mal and Jessi (#59-p.38); serves to Mal because he knows she'll miss the ball (#59-p.89).

**GORDON BROWN (8):**
Stopped baby-sitting for Betsy Sobak because of her practical jokes (#19-p.29). In Modern Living class with Mary Anne and Logan (#52-p.25); pretend-marries Howie Johnson because aren't enough girls in class (#52-p.26). In Mary Anne's English class; is in her Shakespeare project group (#93-p.20).

**ROSS BROWN (8):**
Stacey had crush on him, and he liked her (#43-p.105).

**ROGER BUCKNELL:**
Auditions for *Peter Pan* (SS#9-p.55).

**MARTY BUKOWSKI (8):**
Star SMS basketball player (#70-p.4); goes steady with Sheila MacGregor (#70-p.11). Nickname is "The Bukeman" (#70-p.36).

**BUTCHER BOY (8):**
Member of the Badd Boyz (LB-p.33). About five feet one and looks like he eats ice cream for every meal (LB-p.49). Picked up by police after attempting to steal from Sound Ideas; is suspended from school and ordered by juvenile court to pay a fine (LB-pp.123-125).

**CARLY:**
Girl that Claudia befriends in summer school (SS#10-p.23). Is a fantastic watercolorist and potter; has a pottery wheel in her basement (SS#10-p.24).

**MADELINE CARVER:**
Auditions for *Peter Pan* (SS#9-p.54).

**RICK CHOW (8):**
Part of Claudia's old lunch group (#2-p.39). On Decorations Committee for Mischief Night Masquerade

with Stacey (M#22-p.30). In Claudia's Short Takes drama class (#91-
p.29).

**ELISE COATES (6):**
Pretty, raven-haired girl paired
with Jessi in their synchronized
swimming class (#55-p.37); on
swim team (#55-p.39); she and Jessi
win gold medal at SMS Sports Festival (#55-p.123); will not continue
to take synchro lessons, going back
to regular swim class (#55-p.138).

**LIZ COHEN (6):**
Auditions for the Sixth Grade Follies; does the "Vitameatavegamin"
routine from *I Love Lucy* (#75-
p.72).

**KRISTIN CONDOS (6):**
In Mal and Jessi's gym class, Ms.
Walden is teacher (#55-p.28).

**CORREEN:**
Player on SMS softball team (#74-
p.61).

**JEFF CUMMINGS (8):**
In Mary Anne's English class (#93-
p.54).

**DANNI (6):**
Girl in Mal's class who barfed when
she saw fake barf Benny Ott
brought in (#14-p.125).

**DAVINA (7):**
Sings song called "Stop Pickin' on
the President" at Leicester Lodge
Talent Show (SS#3-p.141).

**JO DEFORD (8):**
Friend of the Shillaber twins during
seventh grade (#4-p.38).

**DILYS (6):**
Only sixth-grader on the SMS
softball team; joins with Kristy (#74-
p.43); must participate in "initia-

tion" task (#74-p.44); writes menac-
ing notes to try to get everyone to
confess (#74-p.133).

**MARI DRABEK (8):**
Student at Stoneybrook Art Center
(#12-p.81). In Dawn's math class;
her sculpture wins third prize ribbon (#12-p.137). On Cokie and
Grace's team for the Battle of the
Bakers (M#21-p.26). Her dad is the
desert chef at Chez Maurice; she's
been baking since she was five
years old (M#21-p.30).

**MIRANDA ELLIOT:**
Competes in Leicester Lodge ski
race (SS#3-p.194).

**FRANKLIN ENELL:**
Auditions for *Peter Pan* (SS#9-p.55).

**HEATHER EPSTEIN (8):**
One of the "bad girls" (#87-p.8). Has
short, spiky brown hair and loves
the grunge look (#87-p.25). Drinks
at U4Me concert; gets caught by security (#87-from p.109). Is now an
ex-friend of Stacey's (#87-p.137).

**MARIA FAZIO (6):**
In Jessi's Short Takes class (#75-p.6).

**NOAH FEIN (6):**
In Mr. De Young's gym class; plays
volleyball with Mal and Jessi and
rest of girls' class (#59-p.88).

**JUSTIN FORBES (8):**
Makes prank call from Atlanta Pig
Corp. to Mary Anne's party when
not invited (#10-p.116). Wins Class
Clown Award (M#4-p.130). Thinks
Mary Anne's new haircut looks
great (#60-p.65).

**BEA FOSTER (8):**
In Kristy's math class; a math whiz;
has black hair, which she wears

in a braid straight down her back; isn't much taller than Kristy; tries out with Kristy for the softball team (#74-p.32). Must participate in "initiation" task (#74-p.44).

**JASON FOX (8):**
In Stacey's math class; viewed as a dork by the basketball "group" (#70-p.39). He idolizes them, and they take advantage of him by copying his homework (#70-p.85).

**FRAN:**
In Claudia's summer school class; thinks she might have to repeat it again (SS#10-p.106).

**AMELIA FREEMAN (8):**
Killed on impact in car crash (#93-p.52). Car was hit by a drunk driver's car (#93-p.54). The entire student body and faculty of SMS attends her funeral (#93-p.86). Garden at SMS is planted in her memory (#93-p.146). Was one of the nicest and smartest girls at SMS, but she wasn't stuck up about it—in fact, she always seemed to be a bit surprised when she answered questions correctly (#93-pp.16-17). In Mary Anne's English class; was in her Shakespeare project group (#93-p.20). Had been best friends with Barbara Hirsch since second grade (#93-p.20). Was in Dawn's last period class and her science class (#57-pp.98, 141). Middle name was Louise; she played the piano; her favorite movie was *The Secret Garden*; she had a stuffed rabbit named Nibs that had slept with

her since she was a baby (#93-pp.87-88).

**JOSH FREEMAN (6):**
Amelia's younger brother (#93-p.17). Suffers some broken bones in car crash that kills Amelia (#93-p.51). Speaks movingly at groundbreaking ceremonies for garden planted in sister's honor (#93-p.146).

**G-MAN:**
Member of the Badd Boyz (LB-p.33). Isn't caught for the attempted robbery of Sound Ideas; is mad at first at Logan but then hangs up his leather jacket for good and makes some new friends (LB-p.125).

**DAVID GABEL:**
In Claudia's summer school class; called Mrs. Wegmann "Mrs. Wigwam" (SS#10-p.106).

**HELEN GALLWAY (6):**
In Mal and Jessi's gym class; very athletic (#59-p.38).

**ANDI GENTILE (8):**
One of Stacey's newest friends, also one of Robert's friends (#83-p.31). Sort of normal-looking, with dark brown hair and a wide smile (#87-p.25). Once had a career as a baby model and her parents put away a college fund out of her earnings (#83-pp.43-44). Of all the "Robert group," Stacey likes her the best (#87-p.8). She is away during the "bad girls" episode (#87-p.23). Has been seen kissing Robert while he's going out with Stacey (#99-pp.113-114); apologizes to Stacey; Stacey says she doesn't hate her (#99-p.145).

**JACQUI GRANT (8):**
One of the "bad girls" (#87-p.8). Has a constant sly grin, dark red hair streaked with green, and pale white skin; also, she wears nose jewelry (#87-p.25). Drinks at U4Me concert; gets caught by security (#87-from p.109). Is now an ex-friend of Stacey's (#87-p.137).

**ALAN GRAY (8):**
Most disgusting boy in class; sits next to Trevor in row behind Kristy in math class (#2-p.17). Lives on Rockville Court (#2-p.131). Likes Kristy but is bane of her existence, immature (#28-p.96). Wore yellow M&M's squinted between eyes at Mary Anne's surprise party and told everyone he was Little Orphan Annie (#10-p.114). Got suspended for setting off a cherry bomb in the boys' room (#43-p.105). Is Kristy's pretend-husband in Modern Living class, named child-egg son Izzy (#52-p.51). Runs for class president (#53-p.48), dresses in balloons and lets people pop them with buttons as campaign ploy (#53-p.78), loses to Pete Black (#53-p.146). In fifth grade, Kristy poured Yoo-Hoo down his shirt (#70-p.68). Sends letter about cafeteria cockroaches to *SMS Express* (#71-p.52). Claudia responds to his personal ad; his father has a post office box since he runs a mail order business from his house (#71-p.89). Has lived next to Richard Brompton all his life (#71-p.120). Helps Vanessa Pike with her haunted house; he's an expert when it comes to "gross

and disgusting" (#79-p.134). Is in Mary Anne's math class (M#13-p.110). Plays Smee in *Peter Pan* (SS#9-p.89). As "Oswald McBelch," burps on pitch to "Row, Row, Row Your Boat" at Claudia's WSTO auditions (#85-p.70). Went to kindergarten at SES with Kristy, Claudia, and Mary Anne (CB-p.29); was also with them in Mrs. Frederickson's first grade class (MAB-p.32).

**SARAH GREEN (6):**
Gets so nervous about the Sixth Grade Follies that she has to take a barf break in the girls' room (#75-p.96).

**LEW GREENBERG (8):**
On the track team; a friend of Robert's (#87-p.87). Taller than Logan, dark hair, thin, with a friendly smile and dimples (LS-p.133); called and asked Claudia out after spotting her cheering for Logan at track tryouts; she thought it was a joke and hung up (LS-p.134).

**MARGIE GREENE (8):**
SMS cheerleader, one of the most popular girls in the school (#70-p.4); is in Stacey's English class (#70-p.13).

**DAVE GRIFFIN (8):**
Dawn thinks he's cute (#51-p.40).

**BOBBY GUSTAVSON (6):**
In the Sixth Grade Follies with Jessi; visits her house for rehearsal, plans *Wayne's World*-type skit (#75-p.48).

**BRIAN HALL (8):**
Claudia responds to his personal ad (he's "Good Listener"); he came to SMS at the end of seventh grade and wasn't in any of Claudia's

classes in eighth; he's very cute— tall with sandy blond hair and an athletic build (#71-p.90). Hair is short and neat, but not too short. Goes on date with Claudia at Rosebud Cafe (#71-p.92). Clothes look pressed, and he smells lightly of cologne (#71-p.93). Old-fashioned manners (#71-p.94). Sketches model cars (#71-p.95). Likes comedy but isn't very funny (#71-p.96). Was on swim team back in Long Island; was their best butterflier (#71-p.97). Has bulgy muscles (#71-p.98). Ends up with Rose Marie Montey ("Rambling Rose") (#71-p.140).

**SANDRA HART (6):**
In Jessi's Short Takes class; reads a comic book (#75-p.6).

**TOM HAROLD (6):**
In Mr. De Young's gym class; plays volleyball with Mal and Jessi and rest of girls' gym class (#59-p.61).

**PETER HAYES (8):**
In Stacey's math class (#65-p.5). Threw his pen up at ceiling last time there was sub for math (#65-p.8). In Stacey's Short Takes class (M#13-p.5). A great athlete; has set a bunch of middle-school track records; twisted his ankle skateboarding and has to cancel appearance on Claudia's WSTO show (#85-p.101). Hangs with Robert and friends (#87-p.88). Trying out for the track team with Logan (LS-p.63); makes the cut (LS-p.125).

**JASON HENDERSON (8):**
Logan's understudy in *Peter Pan* (SS#9-p.113).

**BOBBY HENSON:**
Originally wants to play "Doe a Deer" with his armpit for Leicester Lodge talent show, then changes routine and performs Lucy's Vitameatavegamin skit (SS#3-p.183).

**BARBARA HIRSCH (8):**
In Mary Anne's English class; is in her Shakespeare project group (#93-p.20). Is really nice and had been Amelia Freeman's best friend since second grade (#93-p.20). Is in shock after Amelia is killed by drunk driver (#93-p.92).

**IRV HIRSCH (8):**
On the football team with Logan; gives him grief about dating Mary Anne (LS-p.7). In Stacey's math class; pretended to have foreign accent when there was a substitute (#65-p.8).

**LAUREN HOFFMAN (8):**
Part of Kristy's old lunch group in seventh grade (#2-p.38). Participates in Battle of the Bakers (M#21-p.47).

**ALVIN HOPPER:**
At Leicester Lodge gets call from his mother to make sure he's taking his allergy pills (SS#3-p.163).

**ICE BOX:**
Member of the Badd Boyz (LB-p.33). Built like a linebacker (LB-p.49). Picked up by police after attempting to steal from Sound Ideas; is suspended from school and ordered by juvenile court to pay a fine (LB-pp.123-125).

**PRICE IRVING (8):**
Dawn has amazing overnight crush on him, goes to Winter Wonderland

Dance with him (SS#7-p.26), then she doesn't think they have anything in common (#51-p.40).

**JACKHAMMER:**
Member of the Badd Boyz (LB-p.33).

**MALIK JAFFREY:**
Drop-dead cute SMS basketball star (#70-p.4).

**WOODY JEFFERSON (8):**
Takes Claudia to Halloween Hop (#38-p.130); he and Trevor bring Brie, pâté, cider, wine glasses, and silver to prove they don't have to eat cafeteria food to have good lunch (#57-p.83).

**BRENT JENSEN (8):**
He and Todd Long smirk at Stacey and Dawn when they hug each other at school (#57-p.30).

**GLEN JOHNSON (6):**
In Mr. De Young's gym class; plays volleyball with Mal, Jessi, and rest of girls' gym class (#59-p.39).

**HOWIE JOHNSON (8):**
Part of Claud's old lunch group in seventh grade (#2-p.39); in Modern Living class with Mary Anne (#52-p.26); "marries" Gordon Brown because there aren't any girls left in class (#52-p.26). Takes Stacey to a couple of dances, then goes out with Dorianne Wallingford (#13-p.3).

**RENEE JOHNSON (6):**
In Jessi's Short Takes class (#75-p.6).

**LILY KARP (8):**
In Claudia's social studies class; Claud doesn't know her well, but she seems smart, funny, and friendly (#97-p.74).

**ANNE KENNEDY (7):**
Girl whose Nicky Cash tickets were stolen by T-Jam and given to Logan (LB-p.111); a pretty red-haired girl, who is overjoyed when Logan gives the tickets back (LB-p.117).

**KEVIN (8):**
In Modern Living class with Mary Anne and Logan; "marries" Angela; they lose their child-egg (#52-p.107).

**CLARENCE KING (8):**
Called "King." Member of football team; gives Logan incredible grief about being a BSC member (#79-p.35). Neither modesty nor sense of humor are his strong points; hates being called "Clarence" (LS-p.1). Loses to Logan in tryouts for track team, hundred-yard dash (LS-p.125). Has become a member of the track team (LB-p.9).

**ANDREA KIRKLAND:**
Has fastest skating time at Leicester Lodge (SS#3-p.101).

**KURT:**
Boring guy who takes Claudia to movie and video arcade as part of personal ad-inspired date (#71-p.137).

**ALEXANDER KURTZMAN (8):**
Carries briefcase, wears jacket and tie, lives to obey rules (#2-p.38).

**FRANCIE LEDBETTER:**
Born the same week as Claudia in Stoneybrook (#33-p.97).

**WENDY LOESSER (6):**
Friend of Jessi's in sixth grade at SMS; doesn't have any classes with Mal; sometimes she and Jessi walk to class together (#68-p.6). Doesn't

have cable TV at her house (#68-p.9), loves horse books (#68-p.11). Has two younger sisters, ages six and eight; baby-sits sometimes for two kids down the street (#68-p.47). After "interview" with Kristy, tries out to be a replacement BSC member for Dawn (#68-p.53). After successful tryout at the Barretts, is made a BSC member (#68-p.62). Is late for meetings (#68-p.83) and sitting jobs (#68-p.90). Finally, she decides that she doesn't like the club telling her what to do, so she quits (#68-p.125). She and Jessi remain friends, though (#68-p.130).

**TODD LONG (8):**
He and Brent Jensen smirk at Stacey and Dawn when they hug each other at school (#57-p.30). In Stacey's homeroom; half the time he acts like he's in fifth grade (M#22-p.4). On decorations committee for Mischief Night Masquerade with Stacey (M#22-p.30).

**KATHLEEN LOPEZ (8):**
Girl who becomes cheerleader instead of Stacey (#70-p.130); quits after she learns that she got in by default (#70-p.140).

**SHEILA MACGREGOR (8):**
One of the "bad girls" (#87-p.8). SMS cheerleader, one of the most popular girls in the school (#70-p.4). Is very athletic (#87-p.25). Sits behind Stacey in Ms. Levine's homeroom (#70-p.10); goes steady with Marty Bukowski (#70-p.11). Wears a ring with a jewel in it; has silky, thick blonde hair (#87-p.25) and clothes

that show off her perfect figure (#70-p.11). Tells Stacey that Robert Brewster likes her (#70-p.50). Convinced her mom to let her get her nose pierced (#87-p.39). Passes around cigarette and drinks at U4Me concert (#87-p.112); gets caught by security (#87-p.115). Is now an ex-friend of Stacey's (#87-p.137).

**DENNIS MALEK:**
A.k.a. Skin, member of the Badd Boyz (LB-p.33). Has a pigmentation problem that causes white patches on his face (LB-p.60). Breaks into a locker while Logan looks on in shock (LB-p.62). Has kleptomaniac tendencies (LB-p.63). Picked up by police after attempting to steal from Sound Ideas; is suspended from school and ordered by juvenile court to pay a fine (LB-pp.123-125).

**LISA MANNHEIM (6):**
On the Sixth Grade Follies finance committee with Jessi (#75-p.112).

**ROBBIE MARA (6):**
In Mr. De Young's gym class; plays volleyball with Mal, Jessi, and rest of girls' class (#59-p.39); teases Mal during volleyball (#59-p.66).

**MARCIA:**
Good SMS softball player (#74-p.35); assigns Kristy her "initiation" task (#74-p.46).

**JAY MARSDEN (8):**
Coaxed by Kristy into joining cross-country ski race (SS#3-p.200), breaks his ankle (SS#3-p.203). Dances on crutches with Kristy at Leicester Lodge dance (SS#3-p.221).

## ● Other BSC People ●

**AMANDA MARTIN (8):**
Girl in Stacey's class who goes to Spring Dance with Sam Brewer (#65-p.110). In Stacey's English class; passes notes to her (M#22-p.26).

**COKIE (MARGUERITE) MASON (8):**
Mary Anne's "mortal enemy" (M#19-p.92). Petty, small-minded, devious, and totally unscrupulous (M#22-p.30). A cheater, a liar, the world's laziest student, and not that smart (#100-p.50). Is always looking out for Number One; her overall attitude is "What's in it for me?" (M#23-p.33). Has crush on Logan, engineers club's bad luck spree, which backfires at Old Man Hickory's stone (#17-from p.118). BSC members don't like her (#38-p.54). Sends threatening letters with fingernail clippings to Kristy to get back at her (#38-p.115). Friends with Grace, Lisa, and Bebe (#38-p.116). Her false eyelash falls in punch at Halloween Hop (#38-p.136). Got a nose job (#43-p.106). Does very little for Author's Day project on Megan Rhinehart; read jacket flap as presentation (#46-p.127). Dates Logan a few times during his break-up with Mary Anne, trying to steal him away (#46-pp.88-90). Plays Tiger Lily in *Peter Pan* (SS#9-p.89). Thinks Mary Anne looks fantastic after her haircut and makeover (#60-p.66). Donates unlimited shopping spree at Power Records in the mall for school auction (#62-p.93). Has Mr. Fiske for homeroom, makes fun of his clothes at lunch (M#10-p.129).

Embarrasses herself on the set of *Little Vampires* by dressing up to snare the not-interested Carson Fraser (M#15-p.91); invites the cast to her house for a pool party; they're all food poisoned (M#15-pp.93-97). Mildred Abbott is her grandmother, which means she's related to Christina Thomas (M#19-p.131). Always arranges to have as many classes with Grace Blume as possible (SS#9-p.57). Is a *General Hospital* devotee (SS#9-p.58). Has to drop out of the Battle of the Bakers after she comes down with a terrible case of bronchitis (M#21-p.30). On decorations committee for Mischief Night Masquerade with Stacey (M#22-p.30). Sits for the Hsus while BSC is disbanded (#100-p.115). Went to kindergarten at SES with Kristy, Claudia, and Mary Anne (CB-p.29); in second grade, she was the first person to lose a tooth during school (CB-p.61).

**KARA MAURICIO (8):**
Classmate who just got a bra (#10-p.27); in Stacey's math class last period with Mr. Zizmore (#65-p.58). In Stacey's Short Takes class last period (M#14-p.23).

**WAYNE MCCONVILLE (8):**
Drop-dead cute SMS basketball star (#70-p.4); friend of Robert's, goes out on double date with Kathleen Lopez, Robert, and Stacey (#79-p.38).

**BEVERLY MCMANIMAN (8):**
Claudia hated her in fourth grade (#7-p.76).

**LINDSAY MCMANUS:**
Competes in Leicester Lodge ski race (SS#3-p.194).

**FIONA MCRAE (6):**
Talented student in Claud's class at the art center (#12-p. 26), whose sculpture of stag wins second-prize ribbon (#12-p. 138).

**MILES (8):**
In Modern Living class with Mary Anne; "marries" Shawna Riverson; has never taken care of baby before, Shawna wants a "divorce" (#52-p.106).

**SAVANNAH MILTON (8):**
Costume designer for *Peter Pan* (SS#9-p.86).

**IRI MITSUHASHI (8):**
Japanese student who's in some of Claudia's classes; her just-friends date for the Winter Wonderland Dance (SS#7-p.14).

**ROSE MARIE MONTEY:**
A.k.a Rambling Rose (in the personals); talks incessantly, goes out with Brian Hall (#71-p.140).

**TERRY MORGAN:**
Announcer at Leicester Lodge talent show (SS#3-p.180).

**JUSTINE MOSS (6):**
Quiet and studious (#75-p.78), the shyest girl in Jessi's Short Takes class; even *she* takes part in the pranks (#75-p.28). In the Sixth Grade Follies with Jessi; visits her house for rehearsal (#75-p.46), comes up with the Mr.Trout/Klingon skit (#75-p.79).

**NATHAN:**
Short guy with thick classes, sends an ad to "Claudia's Personals";

meets Liza Shore, who is as fascinated by ancient Egypt as he is (#71-p.99).

**HARRY NOLAN:**
Wide receiver on SMS football team (LS-p.80). Makes track team for pole vault (LS-pp.117,125).

**MARK O'CONNELL (6):**
In Jessi's Short Takes class (#75-p.6).

**JANET O'NEAL (6):**
Says mean things about Mal's dad losing job (#39-p.49). In Jessi's Short Takes class (#75-p.28).

**BENNY OTT (6):**
In Jessi and Mal's homeroom (#14-p.12); from Detroit, his dad sells car parts, mother is secretary; Benny wants to become a great actor (#14-p.14). Newest kid in class until Jessi arrives (#14-p.15); a troublemaker (#14-p.125); a true goon (#55-p.32).

**MIA PAPPAS (8):**
One of the "bad girls" (#87-p.8). Tall and skinny, likes black clothes and black lipstick (#87-p.25). Drinks at U4Me concert; gets caught by security (#87-from p.109). Is now an ex-friend of Stacey's (#87-p.137).

**TROY PARKER (8):**
Wins snow-sculpture contest at Leicester Lodge (SS#3-p.124). Has been suspended for a long time; no one knows why (M#25-p.8). Everything he wears seems to clash (M#25-p.45). A Boy Scout; suspect in SMS vandalism (M#25-p.135). Color-blind (M#25-p.136). Has a chip on his shoulder the size of a log (M#25-p.137).

**JIM POIRIER:**
Member of the football team; teases Logan about being a boy baby-sitter but eventually lays off (LS-pp.48, 117). Makes track team for pole vault (LS-pp.117,125).

**JUSTIN PRICE (6):**
Dances with Mal at Leicester Lodge dance; has math with Mal (SS#3-p.215).

**RANDY RADEMACHER (6):**
In the Sixth Grade Follies with Jessi; visits her house for rehearsal (#75-p.46); does an impression of Mr. Williams-as-Elvis (#75-p.48).

**STEVE RANDAZZO:**
Tackle on the SMS football team (LS-p.80).

**DARCY REDMOND:**
SMS cheerleader, one of the most popular girls in the school (#70-p.4).

**CARY RETLIN (8):**
New kid in Stacey's English class; cute, with straight blond hair and brown eyes; totally mellow (M#22-p.26). From Oak Hill, Illinois (M#22-p.27). Seems completely at ease (M#22-p.27), with cool sense of humor (M#22-p.29). A real live wire (M#22-p.30). One of the sneakiest (and cleverest) people Kristy's ever known (M#25-p.18). The student behind the Mischief Knights, although Stacey can't prove it (M#22-p.140). Dresses as a Knight for Mischief Night Masquerade (M#22-p.138). BSC hasn't figured out quite how much trouble Cary is capable of making (SM#2-p.68). Nobody at

SMS has known him that long; he's a kind of a puzzle (M#23-p.32). Needs the money from working at the Greenbrook Club (M#23-p.34). Believes that "complications make life more interesting" (M#23-p.80). BSC can never tell whether he's giving a sincere compliment or not (M#23-p.139). Mary Anne doesn't trust him (M#24-p.48). He lives across the street from the Martinezes, by Miller's Park; has two brothers: Benson and Steig (M#24-p.48). Sends the BSC an April Fool's letter from the Stoneybrook Park System, proclaiming the area surrounding Ambrose's Sawmill will be renamed "Baby-sitters Walk" (M#24-pp.145-146). In Kristy's social studies class (M#25-p.13); erases the answers on Kristy's homework assignment (M#25-p.15) and manages to steal the watch off Kristy's wrist without her realizing it (M#25-p.17). Cary challenges the BSC to a mystery; sets up clues for them to trail (M#25-from p.16). Finds glitches in computer program (M#25-p.91). Kristy wrongly accuses him of vandalism; he must spend two hours of "quality time" with Mr. Kingbridge in order to straighten things out (M#25-p.110). In Abby's homeroom (M#25-p.128). Knows how to break into a locker (M#25-p.132). Feels he keeps the BSC from becoming complacent and boring (M#25-p.138). The war between Cary and the BSC isn't over yet (M#25-p.138). Cary stuffs

Kristy's locker with perfumed ads (M#25-p.141).

**SHAWNA RIVERSON (8):**
In Dawn and Mary Anne's homeroom (#10-p.16); locker next to Dawn's (#40-p.62); very messy locker — cups, greasy wrappers, month-old hamburgers, Styrofoam containers spilled out onto floor when she opened it (#57-p.78); likes to go to Burger Town, hates school lunches (#57-p.78). Cheats off of Claudia on math test, lets Claud take the blame (#40-pp.79-80). In Mary Anne's Modern Living class (#52-p.24); "marries" Miles, wants a "divorce" (#52-p.103). Is ostracized for not wearing yellow on class color day (#84-p.56).

**DIANA ROBERTS (8):**
Stopped sitting for Betsy Sobak because of her practical jokes (#19-p.29).

**RACHEL ROBINSON (6):**
In Mal and Jessi's sixth grade homeroom (#14-p.12); says mean things about Mal's dad losing job (#39-p.49).

**JOHN ROSEN (6):**
In Jessi's Short Takes class (#75-p.6).

**SALLY (6):**
Sits at lunch table with Rachel Robinson (#14-p.17).

**TREVOR SANDBOURNE (8):**
Most gorgeous boy in grade; jet black hair; dark, brooding eyes and freckles on nose; walks through halls looking serious and deep in thought; writes poetry for *The Literary Voice* (#2-p.10); Claud's old

boyfriend, she used to giggle about him, seemed like she liked the idea of going out with him more than she liked Trevor himself (#10-p.100), (#13-p.10); he and Woody Jefferson bring Brie, pâté, cider, wine glasses, silver to prove they don't have to eat cafeteria food to have a good lunch (#57-p.83).

**BRUCE SCHERMERHORN (8):**
In Dawn's math class, she likes him (#10-p.103). He thinks Mary Anne's new haircut, new look, is great (#60-p.65).

**SEAN (6):**
Slim, short boy with red hair and freckles (#71-p.70); writes to Claudia's Personals regarding his parents' breakup (#71-p.54). She gives him Dr. Reese's phone number (#71-p.71); he goes to her and talks things out (#71-p.139).

**MARA SEMPLE (6):**
On Sixth Grade Follies performance committee but goes to the mall instead of rehearsal at Jessi's house; her parents were awfully cold to the Ramseys when they first moved in (#75-p.47).

**CURTIS SHALLER (7):**
Goes to Valentine Dance with Jessi (#51-p.22).

**KATIE SHEA (8):**
In Dawn and Mary Anne's homeroom; berates kids who don't participate in School Spirit Month (#84-p.56).

**MARY SHERWOOD (8):**
In Dawn and Mary Anne's homeroom; berates kids who don't par-

ticipate in School Spirit Month (#84-p.56).

**MARIAH AND MIRANDA SHILLABER (8):**
Identical twins who dress alike and sit at Kristy's lunch table in seventh grade (#2-p.38). Miranda twists her ankle in gym class (#17-p.48). Miranda can't stand Pete Black because he snapped her bra in seventh grade (#46-p.58). Have new baby brother who's a year and a half old (#52-p.5).

**LIZA SHORE (7):**
Big and athletic, with purple hair; writes Personals ad to Claudia (#71-pp.57-58). Finds Nathan, a boy who is as fascinated by ancient Egypt as she is (#71-p.99).

**BRAD SIMON (8):**
Sells Abby copy of math test, calling it a "study guide"; is caught trying to do the same thing to Mary Anne (#96-p.88). The kind of guy who looks familiar without really standing out: jeans, flannel shirt, brown hair, brown eyes (#96-p.38). Has a student job in the principal's office, where the copy machine is (#96-p.92). Is suspended for cheating, and then is suspended again, this time for much longer; no one knows why (M#25-p.8).

**RODGE SOMERSET (8):**
Friend of Alan Gray's; they do a routine together for Leicester Lodge talent show (SS#3-p.142).

**JAMIE SPERLING (6):**
A girl, plays Ms. Flood in the Sixth Grade Follies (#75-p.81).

**JULIE STERN:**
Layout artist for *SMS Express* (#71-p.101). Works on anti-School Spirit Month petition (#84-p.64).

**BOB STILLMAN:**
Trying out for the track team with Logan (LS-p.63); makes the cut (LS-p.125).

**ELLIE SZILAGYI (8):**
Sits in front of Cokie in social studies class; wants to be friends with Cokie, but Cokie won't let her until her complexion clears up (SS#9-p.58).

**T-JAM (8):**
Leader of the Badd Boyz; real name is something like Theodore James; in Logan's English class, always sits in the back row and makes wisecracks (LB-p.12). Smokes (LB-p.34). Fair-haired and lean (LB-p.49). Tries to trap Logan into being a Badd Boyz member (LB-p.64). "Squank" is his way of saying "no way" (LB-p.80). Signs his name as "Jam" (LB-p.92) Picked up by police after attempting to steal from Sound Ideas; is suspended from school and ordered by juvenile court to pay a fine (LB-pp.123-125).

**TALLIE:**
SMS softball team pitcher, assigns Kristy her "initiation" task (#74-pp.61-62).

**TARIK (8):**
New guy at school, in Modern Living class with Mary Anne; "marries" Zoe (#52-p.109).

**SUSAN TAYLOR (8):**
Friends with Shawna Riverson; shops and has permed hair (#40-

p.85). BSC has never liked her and Sabrina Bouvier because they wear makeup and expensive clothes, snobby, but they're nice to Mary Anne after her makeover and haircut (#60-p.86). Carlos Mendez breaks up with Sabrina in order to go out with Susan (#81-p.11).

**THERESA:**
Girl that Claudia befriends in summer school (SS#10-p.23).

**ETHEL TINES:**
Fat girl, teased on bus (SS#3-p.226).

**HANNAH TOCE (8):**
Seems glamorous, popular, aloof; likes Mary Anne's new look (#60-p.85).

**TONYA (7):**
Seventh-grader, new member of the SMS softball team with Kristy (#74-p.43); must participate in "initiation" task (#74-p.44); inexpertly smokes cigarette (#74-p.75); takes the resulting fire in stride (#74-p.79).

**BILL TORRANCE (8):**
Cute boy in Dawn's physical science class (#50-p.75).

**ALEX TURNBULL:**
Trying out for the track team with Logan (LS-p.63).

**DORIANNE WALLINGFORD (8):**
Sat at Claudia's lunch table in seventh grade (#2-p.39); her grandparents were robbed (#2-p.40). Going out with freshman in high school (#26-p.90). Very cool, but as unathletic as Mary Anne (SS#3-p.152). Goes out with Howie Johnson after he's gone to dances with Stacey (#13-p.3).

**PENNY WELLER (8):**
SMS cheerleader, one of the most popular girls in the school (#70-p.4); is in Stacey's social studies class (#70-p.13).

**AMELIA WHITE:**
Wins snow sculpture contest at Leicester Lodge (SS#3-p.124)

**ASHLEY WYETH (8):**
Looks like a hippie; long, blonde hair in a braid; wrists loaded with silver bangle bracelets; three pierced earrings in each ear, all silver but none matching (#12-pp.6-7). Lives next door to the Rodowskys (#12-p.37). Wants to be a sculptress (#12-p.10); took lots of art classes in Chicago (#12-p.22) since she was four or five and studied at Keyes Art School when she was eight (#12-p.25). Paints or sculpts in spare time, had only one friend in Chicago (#12-p.38). Becomes Claudia's friend/mentor—they are in the same art class (#12-p.79). Parents fixing up studio for her on top floor of house (#12-p.85). Art is the only thing that truly matters to her (#12-p.119). Fire hydrant sculpture wins first prize at show (#12-p.138). Had not remained friends with Claudia, until she co-DJ's with her at WSTO (#85-p.42)—at first, their relationship is tense, but eventually they become friends again (#85-p.135). Claudia doesn't think (initially) that she has any sense of humor (#85-p.49).

**ALEX ZACHARIAS (8):**
One of Stacey's newest friends, also Robert's friend (#83-p.31). Loves

New York; often stays with an aunt who lives in Stacey's old neighborhood (#83-p.43). Parents are divorcing; Alex can't remember a time when they were happy together (#83-p.85). His dad moved out, and Alex is feeling devastated; Robert and Stacey offer support (#83-p.87). He and his mom move into a small house near Robert (#83-p.128).

**ZOE (8):**

In Modern Living class with Mary Anne and Logan; "marries" Tarik (#52-p.109).

# OTHER KIDS

•

## DANCE-RELATED:

**MARY BRAMSTEDT:**
In Jessi's dance class, plays one of the townspeople in *Coppèlia* (#16-p.25). Dances like a robot (#42-p.3); blonde (#60-p.1). Always speaks up and says what's on her mind in her own quiet way (#61-p.86). Intense, a perfectionist, not one of the best dancers (#61-p.4). Volunteers with Jessi to help teach a free six-week ballet class to less privileged kids in Stamford on Tuesdays (#61-p.2-3), gets six free lessons in exchange for the ones she misses (#61-p.3). Mindy Howard advises her to lose weight even though she doesn't need to (#61-p.9). Goes to school with Vince Parsons (#61-p.28). Faints in ballet class (#61-p.87); wants to be good ballerina, goes on rigorous diet, suffers from anorexic symptoms (#61-p.119); will go to a doctor and psychologist for help (her family goes to the counseling, too) to overcome her eating disorder (#61-p.135).

**DARCY:**
Volunteers to help with free six-week ballet class for less privileged kids at Stamford Ballet School; red hair (#61-p.29).

**CHRISTOPHER GERBER:**
Plays Franz in *Coppèlia* (#16-p.134).

**GIANMARCO:**
Little boy with huge brown eyes, is stranded at dance school with Jessi in blizzard; cries (SS#7-p.126).

**HOLLY:**
Young dance student who is stranded in blizzard; wants her mommy, daddy, Christopher, Tattoo (her collie dog), and Caboose (her baby doll) (SS#7-p.122).

**MINDY HOWARD:**
In Jessi's ballet class, tall and thin (#61-p.9); advises Mary Bramstedt to lose weight even though she's not fat (#61-p.9).

**JANE:**
In free six-week dance class at Stamford Ballet School for less privileged kids; blonde, eight years old (#61-pp.34, 50). She and Nora not enthusiastic about class (#61-p.50).

# ● Other BSC People ●

**LISA JONES:**
In Jessi's dance class; plays townsperson in *Coppèlia* (#16-p.25); one of the nicest girls in the class (#61-p.6). Plays Lilac Fairy in *Sleeping Beauty* (#42-p.10); nice (#42-p.109). When she's not at ballet, she wears jeans and sweaters (#61-p.9).

**JULIE MANSFIELD:**
One of Jessi's ballet classmates, cousin is Goober (#44-p.73).

**HILARY MORGAN:**
Twelve, in Jessi's dance class (#16-p.23); plays Chinese Doll in *Coppèlia* (#16-p.26). Always has best leotard, new toe shoes, gets hair done in French braid, Mom pushes her too much (#42-p.7); plays mean tricks on Jessi, sends her threatening notes (#42-p.140); quitting dance (#42-p.164).

**NORA:**
In free six-week dance class for less privileged kids at Stamford Ballet School; red hair, eight years old (#61-pp.34, 50); she and Jane not enthusiastic about class (#61-p.50).

**ADELE PARSONS:**
Katie Beth's deaf sister, wears two hearing aids and signs (#16-p.72); nine (#16-p.76); goes to special school for deaf in Mass.; home only on holidays, few weekends, and part of summer (#16-p.74).

**KATIE BETH PARSONS:**
Twelve, in Jessi's dance class, plays Coppèlia (#16-p.26). Taking a sign language class on Mondays at Matt's school (#16-p.132); used to be enemies with Jessi, one of Mme

Noelle's pets (#42-p.5); saves Jessi from getting hit by a piece of scenery (#42-p.120). When not at ballet, she wears tight leggings and big bold tops (#61-p.9).

**VINCE PARSONS:**
Volunteers to help with free six-week class for less privileged kids in Stamford; goes to school with Mary Bramstedt (#61-p.28); thin with tight blond curls, long narrow nose, super-straight posture, snobby-looking (#61-p.28). Nice; likes Mary Bramstedt (#61-p.56).

**DEVON RAMIREZ:**
Takes free six-week ballet class for less privileged kids in Stamford; mop of dark curls (#61-pp.29-30). Wins full scholarship (funded by Watson) for a year of ballet lessons (#61-p.138).

**RAUL:**
Volunteers to help with free six-week dance class offered to less privileged kids in Stamford (#61-p.30); Latino, olive skin, very handsome (#61-p.28).

**MARTHA ROBERTS:**
Takes free six-week dance class offered at Stamford Ballet School; quiet, dark-skinned (#61-p.34); her mom sounds like she's from the Caribbean (#61-p.129). A natural at ballet, has taken five classes before (#61-pp.94-95). Wins full scholarship (funded by Watson) to take ballet lessons for a year (#61-p.138).

**LISA SHERMER:**
Ballerina, second runner-up in pageant (#15-p.134).

**SOPHIE:**
Younger, eight-year-old, dancer (SS#7-p.67).

**CARRIE STEINFELD:**
In Jessi's dance class, in Dance of Hours in *Coppèlia* (#16-p.25); one of best and oldest dancers in class, graduating soon (#42-p.4); gets part of Bluebird of Happiness in *Sleeping Beauty* (#42-p.10). Has never had a leading role in a production (#61-p.8).

**SUE:**
Girl who volunteers to help with free six-week dance class for less privileged kids in Stamford, dark hair (#61-pp.29, 30).

**JON TSUJI:**
Volunteers to play piano for free six-week dance class at Stamford Ballet School; in his twenties (#61-p.58).

**EQUITATION-RELATED:**

**AMBER:**
In Mal's Beginning Equitation class at Kendallwood Farm, giggles when Mal gets bucked off horse (#54-p.73); invites riding class to birthday party; house is halfway between Stoneybrook and Stamford, a huge old colonial with white marble pillars around the porch and a circular driveway; has a pool (#54-pp.93, 95); calls Mal "Valerie" (#54-p.96). Mal has awful time at party, leaves early (#54-p.97); wins second place in horse show (#54-p.138).

**ALLISON ANDERS:**
In Mal's Beginning Equitation class at Kendallwood Farm; short girl with frizzy blonde hair and braces; snobby; wins first place in horse show, rides Peaches (#54-pp.60-61, 138).

**DAVID:**
Boy with glasses in Mal's Beginning Equitation class at Kendallwood Farm (#54-p.64); doesn't really like to ride, an only child (#54-p.64); shy, has dark hair (#54-pp.65, 67); wins fourth place in horse show (#54-p.138).

**KELSEY:**
Snooty blonde girl in Mal's horse-back riding class at Kendallwood Farm; wore high-collared blouses (called ratcatchers) along with other English riding togs (#54-pp.40-41, 44).

**KYLE:**
Girl in Mal's Beginning Equitation class at Kendallwood Farm (#54-p.63).

**MEGAN:**
Plump girl in Mal's Beginning Equitation class at Kendallwood Farm, has eight horses but doesn't ride too well (#54-pp.62-63).

**SIGNE:**
Girl who wins third place in Mal's Beginning Equitation class horse show (#54-p.138).

**OTHER KIDS, MIDDLE SCHOOL AGE:**

**TYLER AUSTEN:**
One of the BSC's Battle of the Bakers day care charges; Emily's older

brother; twelve; diabetic; loves baseball; doesn't need a sitter, but decides to hang with the kids (M#21-p.35).

**JILLIAN BILSKY:**
One of Kristy's cabinmates at Camp Topnotch; plays first base; log-legged and red-haired (KB-p.88). In her second year at Camp Topnotch; helps Kristy (KB-p.89).

**RICHARD BROMPTON:**
Claudia answers his personal ad (under the name "Rock"); plays rock guitar, paints, and studies eastern culture (#71-p.119). Has lived next to Alan Gray all his life (#71-p.120). Goes to all-boys Paulsen School (#71-p.121). Hair is brown, on the longish side, sort of flopping down into his eyes, which are big and brown; has a handsome face, with high cheekbones; isn't tall, but is taller than Claudia (#71-p.124). Goes on date with Claudia to the mall; spends the whole time quizzing her about Japanese culture (#71-p.126). Has a real tattoo of a skull with roses growing out of it and worms crawling on top (#71-p.127).

**GREER CARSON:**
Shannon's best friend at SDS; has long, red-brown curly hair, cut at a severe blunt angle from front to back; is serious about fashion, and she doesn't let the fact that she has to wear a uniform to school cramp her style. Also, has a big dramatic streak (ShS-p.17). Goes through troubles with Shannon's group of friends at Stoneybrook Day (SS#11-from p.173).

**ROGER CASEY:**
Really cute guy in Claudia and Kristy's sixth grade class; had curly blond hair and bright blue eyes; moved to Kansas (M#22-p.100).

**KARA FERGUISON:**
Daughter of Mr. and Mrs. Jim Ferguison of Rosedale Road; born in Stoneybrook during the same week as Claudia (#33-p.98); goes to Stoneybrook Day (#33-p.106).

**FRANNIE:**
Sixth-grader at Stoneybrook Day who becomes Sally White's latest "chosen one" (SS#11-p.185).

**KATIE GEISSINGER:**
Movie reviewer on Claudia's WSTO show (#85-p.79).

**MARIA GONZALEZ:**
Fourth grade classmate of Mary Anne's (MAB-p.100).

**AL HALL:**
Goes to Kelsey Middle School; lives in Kristy and Abby's neighborhood (#89-p.77).

**GEORGE HEWITT:**
Caller on Claudia's WSTO show; his parents are divorcing and his sister Rachel and his mother have screaming fights; Claudia refers him to Dr. Reese (#85-pp.106-108). Mother calls station, says he's getting better (#85-p.130).

**SAMANTHA HUNTER:**
Competing shortstop with Kristy at Camp Topnotch (KB-p.89).

**MEG JARDIN:**
One member of Shannon's group of friends at Stoneybrook Day (SS#11-p.173). Real name is Margaret; loves astronomy and is in Shannon's as-

tronomy unit; has a great-aunt and some relatives living in France (ShS-p.18).

**AMANDA KERNER:**
Goes to Kelsey Middle School; lives in Kristy and Abby's neighborhood (#89-p.77).

**KEVIN:**
Bart's friend from Stoneybrook Day (#95-p.34).

**LINDSEY:**
One member of Shannon's group of friends at Stoneybrook Day (SS#11-p.173).

**APRIL LIVINGSTON:**
New girl in Mary Anne's fourth grade class; has curly brown hair pulled back in a loose ponytail (MAB-p.89). Hobbies are biking, swimming, drawing cartoons, and reading; wants to be a comedian and an actress when she grows up (MAB-pp.90-91). Has a golden retriever named Alex (MAB-p.91). Mary Anne really likes her red-rimmed glasses (MAB-p.91).

**JACK LUKE:**
Fourth grade classmate of Mary Anne's (MAB-p.100).

**MARA:**
Twelve years old; older sister to Brenda and Kyle; they have been sleeping in the mall since being evicted from apartment on Sycamore Street after their mother went into the hospital; has witnessed thefts (M#14-pp.135-136).

**ROB MILLER:**
Performer on Claudia's WSTO show; tells a story and every time

he reaches a syllable that sounds like a number, he adds one to it; a Stoneybrook Day eighth-grader (#85-p.127).

**CATHY MORRIS:**
New sitter from The Baby-sitters Agency for Charlotte Johanssen (#3-p.119); gets after-school job at Polly's (#3-p.160).

**POLLY:**
One member of Shannon's group of friends at Stoneybrook Day (SS#11-p.173).

**BENSON RETLIN:**
Cary Retlin's brother; eleven years old (M#24-p.48).

**MARY ROSE:**
Girl in Claudia's fourth grade Core Group at Stamford Alternative Academy; short, with neat, shoulder-length brown hair and friendly blue eyes (CB-p.100).

**KARL SCHMAUDER:**
Goes to Kelsey Middle School; lives in Kristy and Abby's neighborhood (#89-p.77).

**JENNIFER SEARLES:**
SES classmate of Mary Anne's; Mary Anne knows her from their block (MAB-p.98).

**SETH:**
Bart's friend from Stoneybrook Day (#95-p.34).

**BILL SHEBAR:**
Movie reviewer on Claudia's WSTO show (#85-p.79).

**JOHN STEINER:**
Student at Art Center (#12-p.28), whose sculpture of a boxing cow is in the show (#12-p.137).

## BART TAYLOR:

Eighth-grader at Stoneybrook Day School; lives near Kristy; coaches Bart's Bashers, a softball team of neighborhood kids (#20-p.25); cute, with deep brown eyes, thick brown hair, and an adorable lopsided smile (#95-p.15), as well as the perfect nose (#20-p.27). Address is 65 Edgerstone Drive (SS#2-p.153). Competitive (#20-p.136). Thoughtful (M#4-p.29). Sends anonymous love letters to Kristy (#38-p.101). He and Kristy go to Halloween Hop dressed as lobsters, win Most Unusual Costume; he kisses her on the cheek after a slow dance (#38-p.134). He and Kristy like anchovies (#38-p.138). His Bashers lose World Series 8-7 to Krushers (#38-p.120). Mary Anne refers to him as the Bart-Man (#50-p.37); takes Kristy to Valentine Dance (#51-p.96). Kisses Kristy in front of everyone at Awards Night (M#4-p.131). Has a Rottweiler named Twinkle that's harmless (#20-p.76). Has little brother named Kyle (#38-p.8). Plays electric and acoustic guitar in a band, which practices in his basement (#38-p.8). Says that one of his favorite things to do is to "be with Kristy" (M#9-p.79). Kristy hardly ever sees him during the week, just for fun (SS#7-p.52). Gets stranded at her house during blizzard (SS#7-pp.52,105). Friends from SDS are Kevin and Seth (#95-p.34). Is very ticklish (#95-p.52). Watson catches Kristy and him kissing (#95-p.64); Kristy is peeved and dumps Bart without letting him get a word in edgewise (#95-p.85). Then she calls him again and says they should just be pals, not boyfriend and girlfriend (#95-p.117). Bart reluctantly goes along with it, and disinvites Kristy from the April Fools' Dance at SDS (#95-p.128). The whole thing makes Bart feel kind of lonely; he wants to stay Kristy's friend, though (#95-p.133).

## TED:

From Lawrenceville; Grace Blume's date to the Mischief Night Masquerade; she met him through her cousin (M#22-p.53). Incredibly cute, comes dressed as Prince Charming (M#22-p.136).

## JEANETTE THOMPSON:

Fourth grade classmate of Mary Anne's; fails vision test (MAB-p.103).

## SETH TURBIN:

Student at Art Center (#12-p.81).

## JACQUELINE VECCHIO:

Goes to Kelsey Middle School; lives in Kristy and Abby's neighborhood (#89-p.77).

## SALLY WHITE:

New classmate of Shannon's at Stoneybrook Day; "chooses" people to hang out with, then discards them (SS#11-from p.174). Has just moved from London, where she lived for eight months; has traveled everywhere, since her mother is some kind of movie star (SS#11-p.177). Has a hairless cat named Tallahassee (SS#11-p.182). Moved away at the end of the school year (SS#11-p.242).

## ● Other BSC People ●

**OTHER KIDS, HIGH SCHOOL AGE:**

**THE ACKERMANS:**
Friends of Charlie's (#8-p.89).

**AMY:**
Counselor in Jessi and Mal's group at Stoneybrook Day Camp at the Community Center (#76-p.55).

**ANNA ATAMIAN:**
Battle of the Bakers contestant from outside Stoneybrook; looks about fourteen (M#21-p.47). She and Rachel Kleinman are first runners-up (M#21-p.139).

**CELESTE BASKETT:**
Battle of the Bakers contestant from outside Stoneybrook (M#21-p.47).

**GERALDINE BRESLIN:**
Busperson at Rosebud; takes Logan's shift for him (SM#1-p.109).

**BRIAN:**
A friend of Sam's who auditions for Captain Hook (SS#9-p.38).

**RUSS BROMPTON:**
Richard Brompton's brother; has a long ponytail and a beat-up Chevy; drives Richard and Claudia on their ill-fated date (#71-p.125).

**JOEY CASELLA:**
Cute Boy Alert! Battle of the Bakers contestant from outside Stoneybrook; looks about fourteen (M#21-p.47).

**CATHY:**
Claudia's hospital roommate who gets no visitors; fourteen, broke an elbow requiring surgery, acts like a baby when doctors tend to her (#19-p.51).

**CHARLENE:**
Madame Minoff's assistant dance instructor (MAB-p.67).

**SINAI CHOI:**
Battle of the Bakers contestant from outside Stoneybrook; looks about thirteen; Claudia thinks she and Julie Liu are cousins (M#21-p.47).

**PATRICIA CLAYTON:**
Fifteen, Baby-sitters Agency baby-sitter (#3-p.14).

**D:**
Older member of the Badd Boyz; real name is Damon; brings the SMS Badd Boyz pizza (LB-p.36). Picked up by police after attempting to steal from Sound Ideas; is suspended from school and ordered by juvenile court to pay a fine (LB-pp.123-125).

**LUCAS DANVER:**
Plays Captain Hook in *Peter Pan* (SS#9-p.89); the most gorgeous guy in the high school (SS#9-p.90).

**TERRY DUTTON:**
Busboy at Rosebud Cafe with Logan; parents run a big animal farm that's a tourist attraction in Mercer, CT (SS#10-p.201); his dad lends Logan a horse-drawn buggy (SS#10-p.221).

**JANET GATES:**
Now in ninth grade; temporary member of BSC who dropped out of the Baby-sitters Agency and joined BSC to purposely try to give it a bad reputation; in eighth grade when BSC members were in seventh grade (#3-pp.85, 95, 106).

**209**

**GUS:**
High school senior; paints houses with Robert over the summer (#87-p.85).

**LESLIE HOWARD:**
Now in ninth grade; temporary member of BSC (#3-p.85); shaggy hair; lots of makeup, fourteen, friends with Janet Gates (#3-pp.95-96).

**RANDY JONES:**
Sam Thomas's childhood best pal (KB-p.36).

**RICK JONES:**
Charlie Thomas's childhood best pal (KB-p.36).

**KATHY:**
Girl that Sam Thomas is calling and dating; he and she bump into Stacey and Terry at Rosebud Cafe; Stacey recognizes her from *Peter Pan*; she is pretty, has red hair (M#10-pp.101-102).

**RACHEL KLEINMAN:**
Battle of the Bakers contestant from outside Stoneybrook; looks about fourteen (M#21-p.47). Father used to work for Mrs. Goode's Cookware (M#21-p.70). She and Anna Atamian are first runners-up (M#21-p.138).

**LIZ LEWIS:**
A founder of the Baby-sitters Agency, phone KL5-1162 (#3-p.7); sasses teachers, hangs around mall (#3-p.11).

**JULIE LIU:**
Battle of the Bakers contestant from outside Stoneybrook; looks about sixteen (M#21-p.47). Parents, who are instructors at a cooking school in Stamford, have very high expectations for her (M#21-pp.59-60). Bites her nails in fear that her parents will disown her if she doesn't make the final round (M#21-p.97). Is caught by the BSC kissing Marty Nisson (M#21-p.109). Drives a small red car (M#21-p.109). Claudia discovers she's older than sixteen after seeing Julie with car keys (M#21-p.109).

**LIZ:**
Assistant at Bellair's Kid Center with Stacey; going into her senior year at SHS (#87-p.67).

**GOOBER (PETER) MANSFIELD:**
Julie Mansfield's cousin (#44-p.73); did dinosaur show at carnival in Pikes' yard, kids loved him (#44-p.75). Star of high school plays in Mercer, has had part in professional production of *Shenandoah* (#44-p.73).

**DIANE MCVIE:**
Battle of the Bakers contestant; probably fifteen, but looks like she's thirty; could win prize for most makeup and longest fingernails (M#21-p.48).

**CARLOS MENDEZ:**
One of the hunkiest guys at SHS; falsely rumored at SMS that he invited Mary Anne to the Winter Dance at SHS (#60-p.88); very tall, with thick black hair and dark handsome features; goes with Sabrina Bouvier to SMS's January Jamboree dance (#60-p.134). No longer goes out with Sabrina (#83-p.77); broke up with her so he can go out with Susan Taylor, Sabrina's best friend (#81-p.11).

# ● Other BSC People ●

**JERRY MICHAELS:**
Janine's boyfriend; the most gorgeous guy Claudia's ever seen; has black hair, dressed in cool pair of jeans and beautiful blue shirt (M#6-p.92). Drives a cool little red car (M#6-p.117). Is in high school, taking advanced placement classes at the college with Janine (M#6-p.124). He likes her the way she is, not with any new look (M#6-p.125). They study a lot together (M#6-p.127). Isn't conceited; is interested in nuclear physics (M#6-p.132). Likes to send Janine notes in the mail (M#6-p.136).

**MONIQUE:**
Sophisticated private-school girl that Sam Thomas likes (#11-p.5).

**ALLIE NEWBERN:**
SDS tenth-grader; the Martinezes' former baby-sitter (M#24-p.116); Beau Robbins is her boyfriend (M#24-p.117).

**PATRICK:**
Friend of Charlie and Sam's who accompanies them when Charlie buys his car; can drive (#30-p.89).

**MICHELLE PATTERSON:**
A founder of the Baby-sitters Agency, phone KL5-7548 (#3-p.7); sasses teachers, hangs around the mall (#3-p.11). Sits for Charlotte Johanssen (#3-p.119).

**RAJ:**
Counselor in Jessi and Mal's group at Stoneybrook Day Camp at the Community Center (#76-p.55).

**REMO:**
Older member of the Badd Boyz; brings the SMS Badd Boyz pizza (LB-p.36). Picked up by police after attempting to steal from Sound Ideas; is suspended from school and ordered by juvenile court to pay a fine (LB-pp.123-125).

**BEAU ROBBINS:**
SDS tenth-grader; Allie Newbern's boyfriend (M#24-p.117). Accidentally set fire to Martinez garage and threatened Luke to keep him quiet; was blackmailed by Sam Wolf into doing further vandalism (M#24-from p.122). House is forest green, with new forest-green-brick addition (M#24-p.117); has patio in back with white wicker furniture with green cushions that match the color of the house (M#24-p.123). Arrested for vandalism (M#24-p.139).

**LINDSEY ROCKAWAY:**
A huge fan of Carson Fraser's (M#15-p.122); has stringy blonde hair, held back with barrettes (M#15-p.65). Terrorizes Derek Masters; is caught by Kristy and confesses (M#15-p.133). A very disturbed person (M#15-p.134), currently being treated at Hidden Acres, a private Massachusetts facility for disturbed adolescents (M#15-p.140).

**LAURA SANCHEZ:**
Counselor at Stoneybrook Day Camp, in Jessi and Mal's group; a tall, slim girl with large dark eyes and long, wavy hair (#76-p.55).

**SARA:**
Sixteen, long red hair, high cheekbones, Travis's girlfriend (#37-p.93); captain of the SHS swim team (#37-p.87).

# ● Other BSC People ●

**SARAH:**
Assistant at Bellair's Kid Center with Stacey; going into her senior year at SHS (#87-p.67).

**NOAH SEGER:**
High school student; son of H. Joseph Seger; neighbor to Rodowskys (SM#2-p.92). A short kid, with brown hair and an old leather bomber jacket (SM#2-p.102). With friend James, robs his own house to pay back large sum of money he owes (SM#2-p.172). No charges will be filed against him; is going to go to family counseling with his father (SM#2-p.228).

**MICKEY STONE:**
Cute Boy Alert! Battle of the Bakers contestant from outside Stoneybrook; looks about fourteen (M#21-p.47). Blond; has the *sweetest* smile (M#21-p.77). Claudia and he exchange phone numbers (M#21-p.104).

**JENNIFER STANLEY:**
Sixteen-year-old sister of Eliza Stanley; ran away from home (SecS-p.4); is now living with her uncle in New Hope (SecS-p.10) at 29 Spring Road, New Hope (SecS-p.27). Is reunited with Eliza, who sends her half of heart necklace (SecS-p.28).

**TIFFANY SWEET:**
Battle of the Bakers contestant; probably fifteen but looks like she's thirty; could win prize for most makeup and longest fingernails (M#21-p.48).

**TAMARA:**
High school freshman with spiky yellow hair who Sam takes to movies (#2-p.99).

**TRAVIS:**
Sixteen, friend of Charlie Thomas; sandy brown hair, deep blue eyes, from California, goes to SHS (#37-p.13). Drives a dark old blue Chevy with 50,000 miles on it (#37-p.36). Plays soccer, tennis, basketball, and football, belongs to lots of clubs (#37-pp.38-39). Dawn falls in love with him, but he bosses her around (#37-p.126). Buys her necklace, hair combs, suggests she cut her hair and get a third hole pierced in each ear (#37-pp.39,59). Dates Sara (#37-p.120). Dawn says good-bye to him (#37-p.126).

## OTHER KIDS, ELEMENTARY SCHOOL AGE OR YOUNGER:

**KYLE ABOU-SABH:**
Kid in Kristy's neighborhood, becomes a replacement Krusher (SS#10-p.74).

**SUSIE ALBION:**
SES third-grader; helps Claudia paint sets for Thanksgiving play (#91-p.81); mother is very suspicious of the play (#91-p.99).

**AMY:**
Little girl who lives across the street from Jessi and is angrily called home when her mother spots her in the Ramseys' yard (#14-p.108).

**ANGIE:**
"Uses" Amanda Delaney for her pool; used to be friends with Amanda (#39-p.113).

**EMILY AUSTEN:**
One of the BSC's Battle of the Bakers day care charges; eight; blonde,

straight hair; super-energetic; loves to read, make up poems, and sing songs (M#21-p.35).

**MATTHEW BAILEY:**
Kid who asks Mary Anne for a book for the Readathon (M#13-p.82).

**SIMON BEAL:**
Jeff Schafer's old classmate in Ms. Besser's class at SES (#12-p.55).

**BRUCE BOYD:**
Fifth-grader, wins Readathon (M#13-p.141).

**BRENDA:**
Six years old; see *Mara.*

**CHRIS:**
One of Bart's Bashers, shy-looking, plays outfield; on Krashers (M#7-p.86). Stuck in haunted house with Kristy and company (M#9). Has a dog named Molly (M#9-p.77).

**CICI:**
Classmate Betsy Sobak rigged bag of water to fall on (#19-p.117). Friends with Amanda Delaney and Karen Brewer (#39-p.113).

**KATIE COLLINS:**
Baby auditioning with Andrea Prezzioso at Tip-Top Talent Agency (#73-p.55).

**BRUCE COMINSKY:**
In Charlotte's class, has blue eyes and red hair; Char likes him; he says "Ew, Dumschat" every time Diane Dumschat comes near him; friend is George (#65-pp.52-53). Likes Char for short while, now has crush on Diane (#65-p.135).

**JOEY CONKLIN:**
New "walking disaster" on Burnt Hill Road; looks cute, doesn't mean to cause chaos . . . but does anyway (M#1-p.70). Hoses down the Prezziosos' front hall (M#1-p.79).

**SCOTT DANBY:**
Pike triplets' new friend (#64-p.59).

**NANCY DAWES:**
Seven; friend of Karen Brewer and Hannie Papadakis; inseparable, they call themselves the Three Musketeers (#61-p.38); lives next door to Karen's mother's house (#62-p.6). Goes to Shadow Lake with Hannie and Karen and company (SS#8-p.124). Jewish (#56-p.97). In All the Children of the World; thinks of uniform for band: red shirts and jeans (#56-p.107). Plays "Let's All Come In" with Karen and Hannie; is Princess Veronica from the Land of Harmonica (#61-p.44). The Three Musketeers build a playhouse at Brewers' house (#62-pp.9, 31, 52). Goes to Camp Mohawk (SS#2-p.46). Goes to Stoneybrook Academy; attends Camp BSC; has gone to a circus camp before (#86-p.34).

**ALEXANDRA DELONGE:**
Kid in Kristy's neighborhood, becomes a replacement Krusher (SS#10-p.74). Comes dressed in a brand-new designer outfit (SS#10-p.112).

**BRITTANY DEPEW:**
Friend of Sara Hill's; teams with her for Battle of the Bakers (M#21-p.48).

**BILLY DOBSON:**
Becca thinks he's cute (#82-p.14).

**DIANE DUMSCHAT:**
In Charlotte's class, she and Char have crushes on Bruce Cominsky, who says "Ew, Dumschat" every time Diane walks by (#65-p.53).

Bruce Cominsky has crush on her (#65-p.138).

**EJ:**
A.k.a. Eleanor Jane; bully in Marilyn and Carolyn's class; intimidates the whole neighborhood (LB-p.42).

**KIRK ENQUIST:**
Baby auditioning with Andrea Prezzioso at Tip-Top Talent Agency (#73-p.55).

**CARVER ENSIGN:**
David Michael's new friend, not allowed to visit without parental supervision (#47-p.95).

**JENNIFER EVANS:**
Sings "Friendship" on Claudia's WSTO show (#85-p.79).

**TIA FARRELL:**
Karen Brewer's friend; attends Mrs. Stone's summer playgroup (SS#13-p.90). Was raised on a big farm in Nebraska (SS#13-p.54). Falls in love with New York City and wants to see every New York movie ever made (SS#13-p.94).

**KYLE FARMER:**
One of the BSC's Battle of the Bakers charges; nine; black wavy hair, blue eyes; outgoing; makes friends easily (M#21-p.36). Tells BSC members that his sister is doing bad things, which she admits doing (M#21-p.88). Father recently left (M#21-p.89). Acts angelic but is really blaming his sister for things that he does; she goes along because he once tried to run away (M#21-p.124).

**MEGAN FARMER:**
Kyle's sister; seven; also with black hair and blue eyes; quiet and

sneaky (M#21-p.36). Admits to breaking terrarium and other bad things after her brother implicates her (M#21-p.88). Father recently left (M#21-p.89). Finally, she reveals that she is covering for Kyle, who blames her for things that he does (M#21-p.124).

**SANDY FENNING:**
Two years old (M#14-p.33); son of April Fenning, owner of Toy Town (M#14-p.30).

**PHIL FIELDS:**
Seven years old; one of Kristy's neighbors who Kristy tries to entice into joining the Krushers when they're in a player crunch; lives in a modern-looking, wooden house; plays in Challengers little league (SS#10-pp.71-72).

**FRANKIE:**
Friend of David Michael's (#5-p.99).

**RANDALL FREDERICKSON:**
Charge of Stacey's at Bellair's Kid Center; Mom is named Sandy (#87-p.128).

**ROGER FRIEDMAN:**
(#59-p.47): Jamie Newton's best friend in nursery school; five years old (#59-p.44).

**KELLIE GARCIA:**
Daughter of the head of security at Washington Mall; looks about six, with dark eyes and black hair; goes with the BSC members to plead for a day care center (M#14-p.75).

**ADRIENNE GARVEY:**
Classmate Jackie Rodowsky runs against in election to see who will take care of Snowball, class rabbit; "Ms. Perfect" (#22-p.79).

# ● Other BSC People ●

**JANNIE GILBERT:**
In Natalie Springer's class; friends with Leslie Morris and Pamela Harding (#78-p.60).

**SANDY GRAYSON:**
Caller during Junior Jeopardy, part of Claudia's WSTO show (#85-p.120).

**JERRY HANEY:**
Jeff Schafer's classmate; Jeff repeatedly gives him a black eye (#15-p.15).

**PAMELA HARDING:**
In Natalie Springer's class; friends with Leslie Morris and Jannie Gilbert (#78-p.60).

**JOSEPH HARTER:**
Three; has never been left with stranger before; is left with Stacey at the Bellair's Kid Center (#87-p.65).

**HILARY:**
Classmate whose lunch Betsy put fake barf in (#19-p.118).

**TIMMY HSU:**
Friends with Max Delaney (#39-p.68); lives down the street from Kristy; a good kid (#42-p.66). In All the Children of the World, band BSC helps organize (#56-p.97). Really rude to Druscilla (#89-p.57). Kristy says he can join the Krushers (#95-p.18).

**SCOTT HSU:**
Timmy's brother, pretend-married to Hannie (#42-p.66). In All the Children of the World, band BSC helps organize (#56-p.97). Goes to Stoneybrook Day; tried to play flute but is much better at kazoo; plays with Krusher Quartet (#89-p.119). Kristy says he can join the Krushers (#95-p.18).

**HUCK:**
Friends with Max Delaney (#39-p.68).

**JANE:**
Gives Arnold twins Raggedy Ann dolls at their birthday party (#21-p.92).

**JEROME:**
Five-year-old charge of Stacey's at Bellair's; complains that day care is for babies (#87-p.67).

**JERRY:**
A wiry nine-year-old with curly brown hair and a wicked grin (M#9-p.79). One of Bart's Bashers, plays third base. Player on Krashers (M#7-p.86); stuck in haunted mansion with Kristy and company (M#9). Has two pesty little brothers and a dog named Winter. Also has a paper route and a best friend named Bonzie, whose real name is Jimmy; likes to build forts in the woods (M#9-p.79).

**JOEY:**
One of Bart's Bashers, tall, plays first base; on Krashers (M#7-p.86); stuck in haunted house with Kristy and company (M#9). Played "Moonlight Sonata" in recital last year on piano (M#9-p.52), practices piano every day (M#9-p.53).

**JODY JONES:**
Andrew's friend (#6-p.4).

**JUSTIN:**
Classmate whose sandwich Betsy put fake ants in (#19-p.117).

**KYLE:**
Eight years old; see *Mara*.

# ● Other BSC People ●

**CHRIS LAMAR:**
Seven; goes to Stoneybrook Academy; attends Camp BSC; has gone to a circus camp before (#86-p.34).

**NICOLE LAVISTA:**
One of the BSC's Battle of the Bakers day care charges; six; hair in black curls; full of tricks; loves to draw and paint (M#21-p.35).

**TAYLOR LAVISTA:**
One of the BSC's Battle of the Bakers day care charges; Tyler's twin; three; can make a big mess (M#21-p.36).

**TYLER LAVISTA:**
One of the BSC's Battle of the Bakers day care charges; Taylor's twin; three; really wild (M#21-p.36).

**LEIF:**
In Natalie Springer's class; best friends with Lindsey; both live on Rockville Court (#78-p.60).

**LINDSEY:**
In Natalie Springer's class; best friends with Leif; both live on Rockville Court (#78-p.60).

**LIZA:**
Friend of Vanessa Pike's; tells her to wave from the Thanksgiving Parade (#69-p.7).

**MANDY:**
Dana Cheplin's best friend; lives several houses away (#94-p.51). Has short brown hair and big brown eyes (#94-p.52).

**JULIE MANSFIELD:**
Sings "Friendship" on Claudia's WSTO show (#85-p.132).

**SOPHIE MCCANN:**
Charlotte Johanssen's friend from class (#10-p.77).

**MEGHAN:**
Friends with Amanda Delaney (#39-p.113).

**RALPHIE MEISNER:**
Friends with Adam Cheplin at the Miller School; uses Adam's sleeve as a tissue (#94-p.50).

**MERRY:**
Goes to Vanessa Pike's sleepover party (#13-p.4).

**MILLICENT MONTAGUE:**
Baby auditioning with Andrea Prezzioso at Tip-Top Talent Agency (#73-p.55).

**CLARENCE MORRIS:**
In same class as Nicky Pike and Buddy Barrett; lives a couple of blocks away from the Barretts. He teases "everybody about everything," especially the boys who participate in sewing class (#66-p.147).

**ELLIE MORRIS:**
Cathy's sister, in Charlotte's class (#3-p.119).

**LESLIE MORRIS:**
A brown-haired girl, seven; in Natalie Springer's class at Stoneybrook Academy; sticks her tongue out at Natalie as she skates past; is friends with Pamela Harding and Jannie Gilbert (#78-p.60).

**KATE MUNSON:**
Lives in Kristy's neighborhood; becomes a replacement Krusher (SS#10-p.73).

**VALERIE NAMM:**
Charlotte Johanssen's "new best friend," most popular girl in fourth grade (#13-p.86).

**SHEILA NOFZIGER:**
Kid in Kristy's neighborhood; becomes a replacement Krusher (SS#10-p.74). Goes to Stoneybrook Day; takes trumpet lessons; joins the Krusher Quartet (#89-p.119).

**RICHARD OWEN:**
Kid in Kristy's neighborhood; becomes a replacement Krusher (SS#10-p.74).

**PATRICK:**
Friend of David Michael's (#5-p.99).

**PATTY:**
Seven years old; has bright red hair and freckles and a spunky personality (M#9-p.79). A Basher/Krusher (M#9-p.4); stuck in haunted mansion with Kristy and company (M#9). The Krashers can always count on her for a hit (M#9-p.78). Has three brothers and a horse named Ginger. When she grows up, she wants to have a motorcycle and be a carpenter; then, she wants to be president of the United States (M#9-p.79). Can't wash her face without a *Little Mermaid* washcloth (M#9-p.89).

**LYNN PERONE:**
Jeff Schafer's classmate at SES (#12-p.55).

**MOIRA PHILLIPS:**
Seven (#81-p.52). A dark-haired girl wearing a baseball cap; Dawn sits for the Phillips kids at the Marshalls' (#81-p.49). Mother is Kendra Phillips, a friend of Mrs. Marshall's (#81-p.52).

**BRYANT PHILLIPS:**
Moira's brother; six (#81-p.52).

**TYLER PHILLIPS:**
Moira's brother; three (#81-p.52). Splits his lip at the Marshalls' (#81-p.90).

**P. ARCHIBALD PINCKNEY:**
"Moon" for short; on the heavy side; one of Kristy's neighbors; becomes a replacement Krusher (SS#10-p.74). Plays the drums; joins the Krusher Quartet (#89-p.119).

**S. EMERSON PINCKNEY IV:**
"Quad" for short; one of the kids in Kristy's neighborhood; weighs as much as half of all the Krushers combined; doesn't want to play on Krushers (SS#10-p.73).

**DRUSCILLA PORTER:**
Seven; Mrs. ("Morbidda Destiny") Porter's granddaughter; Druscilla's parents are divorcing and mother has custody; Mrs. Porter takes care of her for some time; goes to Stoneybrook Day School (#89-p.35). Is in second grade (#89-p.39). Pale, with small red-rimmed eyes; hair is thick, black, and messed up (#89-p.37). Is taking flute lessons at school (#89-p.99). Founds the Krusher Quartet, which is later renamed Druscilla and the Dynamos (#89-p.139).

**EMILY POWERS:**
Hannah's sister; looks about three (M#14-p.112).

**HANNAH POWERS:**
Six years old; Jessi supervises her birthday party at Cinema World;

loves the Ninja Turtles; is in first grade, reads at a fifth grade reading level (M#14-p.110).

**LEA POWERS:**
Hannah's sister, one and a half years old (M#14-p.112).

**STIEG RETLIN:**
Cary Retlin's brother; lives across the street from the Martinezes and is Luke Martinez's best friend (M#24-p.48). Not supposed to see Luke for three days after they're caught lighting bottle rockets (M#24-p.70).

**ELIZABETH SAYERS:**
Friend of Sara Hill's; teams with her for Battle of the Bakers (M#21-p.48).

**DAVID SIMPSON:**
Nine; Stoneybrook Day student; friend of Bill Korman's; participates with Bill in Battle of the Bakers (M#21-p.47).

**ELIZA STANLEY:**
BSC's Santa's Helpers pen pal; eight years old; parents have just lost their jobs and her sister Jennifer has run away (SecS-p.4). Address is 40 Tenth Street, Apt. A, Freeport, CT 06900 (SecS-p.3). Is reunited with her sister; sends her half of necklace (SecS-p.28).

**STEVE:**
Classmate of Buddy Barrett's (#5-p.152).

**SARAH SUTTON:**
On Claudia's WSTO show; can say anything backward instantly (#85-p.69).

**SUKI:**
Goes to Vanessa Pike's sleepover party (#13-p.4).

**TAMMY:**
One of Jamie's sitters (#3-p.113).

**BRITTANY TAYLOR:**
Six; kid at Bellair's Kid Center; curls right up with a book (#87-p.66).

**KYLE TAYLOR:**
Bart's little brother; gets on Bart's nerves, but Bart can handle him (#38-p.8). Delivers love notes to Kristy from Bart (#38-p.104).

**TIMOTHY TAYLOR:**
Four; kid at Bellair's Kid Center; plays with toy trains (#87-p.66).

**TINA:**
Little girl at playground (#6-p.92).

**TONY:**
KCDAC member; in Mal's play as "Ed" (#80-p.134).

**RICKY TORRES:**
Used to tease Karen; they are supposed to "get married" (#41-p.48). Goes to Stoneybrook Academy; attends Camp BSC; has gone to a circus camp before (#86-p.34).

**MEL TUCKER:**
Teases the Hobart kids; short (#32-p.100); charges a dollar to neighborhood kids to see Susan Felder play the piano and perform her "calendar tricks" (#33-p.107). Teases a lot of kids who are "different"; calls Hobarts "Crocs" (M#2-p.4). Is the mysterious Mr. X who threatens/scares Dawn (M#2-p.119); the BSC decides that he's a troubled little boy who needs help more than anything (M#2-p.133). Parents are going to send him to a child psychiatrist (M#2-p.135).

**TYSON:**
SES third-grader; narrator of *Alice and the Pilgrims*; wears glasses (#91-p.79).

**ASHLEY VAUGHN:**
Classmate of Buddy's (#5-p.152).

**TIFFANY WELLS:**
Baby auditioning with Andrea Prezzioso at Tip-Top Talent Agency (#73-p.55).

**WENDY:**
Member of the KCDAC; Mal doesn't know her (#80-p.80).

**BRIAN WILLIAMS:**
Four years old; lives near the Pikes (M#23-p.55).

**GREG WILSON:**
Nine; Stoneybrook Day student; friend of Bill Korman's; participates with Bill in Battle of the Bakers (M#21-p.47).

**ZACK WOLFSON:**
With Mel Tucker, picks on kids who are "different" (M#2-p.4).

# OTHER ADULTS

•

## CLIENTS AND NEIGHBORS:

### MILDRED ABBOTT:
Christina Thomas's great-great-niece; still lives in Stoneybrook (M#19-p.59). Invites Kristy to tea; sounds very proper (M#19-p.61). Lives in elegant apartment near downtown Stoneybrook, with oriental rugs on floors and gold-framed paintings on the walls; she is tall and thin with perfectly arranged white hair; her face is stern and her blue eyes are piercing and dance when she smiles, which is fairly often (M#19-p.71). She is funny, interesting, and interested; a terrific baker (M#19-p.72). Cokie Mason is her granddaughter (M#19-p.131).

### THE BAHADURIANS:
Live at the end of Dawn's street; have a mailbox shaped like a cow (SS#7-p.85).

### THE BEHARS:
Wendy Loesser's next-door neighbors, whose baby she takes care of instead of going on BSC job (#68-p.96).

### THE BERKS:
Family where Charlotte Johanssen bought her dresser for seven dollars at a yard sale (#13-p.92).

### MR. BISCHOFF:
Gives Marilyn Arnold ride to her piano lesson (#21-p.52).

### MR. BLASER:
RJ's father, is a bigger version of RJ—tall, broad-shouldered, and handsome (#70-p.31).

### MRS. BREWSTER:
Robert's mother; has beautiful eyes (#70-p.81).

### THE CONGDONS:
Lived in house behind Pikes; moved (#13-p.58).

### ELIZABETH CONNOR:
Went to SMS twenty-eight years ago but didn't graduate (M#22-p.102). Used to live in the Johanssens' house (M#22-p.108). Was a quiet, shy, unpopular girl, with a crush on Michael Rothman (M#22-p.126). On a dare, he asked her to the Halloween Dance, then embarrassed her (M#22-p.127). Years later, she is very, very crazy and out for revenge (M#22-p.142). She is

stopped, however, and taken to a mental institution, where it is found that she'd been obsessed with what had happened to her at the dance (M#22-p.144).

**THE DODSONS:**
A family that hires sitters (#3-p.160). Need a plant-sitter while away in Florida; live down the street from Jessi (M#19-p.22). Mrs. Dodson leaves three pages of instructions for Jessi, who doesn't have a green thumb (M#19-p.35).

**MS. FARRELL:**
One of the moms who brings group of kids to Claudia's WSTO show to sing theme from *Shining Time Station* (#85-P.79).

**THE FRAMPSONS:**
Hubert, Melissa, and Cutesy (a dog); Stacey applies for pet-sitting job but is too young (#87-pp.40,45).

**MR. FONTECCHIO:**
The Martinezes' next-door neighbor; lives by Miller's Park; a tall, thin, gray-haired man with piercing blue eyes; smokes a pipe; is planning to sell house and land to Reginald Fowler; Mary Anne thinks he's a little strange (M#24-p.47). Lives with his brothers (M#24-p.84).

**BERTA FRANK:**
Eighty-nine-year-old who grew up in Stoneybrook and has sweet memories of time spent in Miller's Park; writes letter in support of BSC's crusade to save it (M#24-p.39).

**THE GIANMARCOS:**
A family that hires sitters (#3-p.160).

**MR. AND MRS. ARNOLD GOLDMAN:**
Older couple that live next door to Kishis; no children, travel a lot, robbed by Phantom Caller (#2-p.108); have garage (#65-p.80). Friendly, love children (#79-p.117). Kristy, Mary Anne, and Claud build a snowwoman on their lawn (KB-p.20).

**THE HANSONS:**
Sam and Charlie played football in their backyard (#1-p.9).

**MISS HARGREAVES:**
Mrs. McKeever's niece (#1-p.67).

**RONALD HENNESSEY:**
Used to own house at end of Elm Street that gets torn down, parts of it are saved by the historical society (#35-p.40); tells Stacey false ghost stories about house but owns up to them before his death (#35-p.133); dies in nursing home.

**RHODA HEWITT:**
George Hewitt's mother; in the middle of divorce; sends in check that saves WSTO (#85-p.129).

**THE ISAACS:**
The Robertses' neighbors, who Jessi should call if she needs any help (#82-p.77). Danielle drives her parents' car into Mrs. Isaacs' car; Mrs. Isaacs is calm, not angry (#82-pp.106-107).

**MRS. JAYDELL:**
Client Janet Gates was supposed to sit for but never did because she was trying to make the BSC look bad (#3-p.102).

# ● Other BSC People ●

**MRS. MAXINE JONES:**
Mother of Charlie and Sam's childhood friends Rick and Randy (KB-p.39).

**MRS. KATZ:**
Takes Jordan to piano lessons (#5-p.134).

**THE KELLYS:**
Family that Leslie Howard was supposed to sit for but never did because she wanted to make the BSC look bad (#3-p.100).

**MRS. MCKEEVER:**
Lives at 52 Quentin Court (#1-p.64); for club's first job, Kristy sits for her St. Bernards, Buffy and Pinky (#1-p.68).

**THE MORGANS:**
Live across street from Rodowskys; family has four boys (#10-p.136).

**MRS. MURPHY:**
The Pikes' next-door neighbor; Uncle Joe goes to her house by mistake (M#3-p.104).

**MYRTLE:**
Woman looking for person to care for her elderly mother; is offended when Stacey likens this to baby-sitting (#87-p.40).

**MR. OHDNER:**
Client of BSC (rarely mentioned); has two daughters (#10-p.44); needs sitter (#56-p.55); kids have measles (#57-p.54).

**RUPERT PEEBLES:**
Man who lived in the McGills' house before they moved in; they still get calls for him from time to time (#70-p.55).

**KENDRA PHILLIPS:**
Mother of Moira, Tyler, and Bryant; goes with Mrs. Marshall to jazzercise class (#81-p.52).

**MRS. PORTER:**
Brewers' neighbor, named Morbidda Destiny by Karen, who thinks she's a witch (#1-p.93). Wrinkled face with big nose (#1-p.94). Gray and frazzly hair, wart on end of nose, wears black dresses (#1-p.96); little scar on corner of mouth that jumps around when she speaks (#5-p.62). Doesn't like animals (#1-p.91). Lives in dark, old, run-down Victorian house (#13-p.77) that's dreary and musty (#13-p.83). Hardly ever has guests (#13-p.79); has a black cat (#13-p.83); gives apples for Halloween (#17-p.111). Daughter is getting divorced and asks Mrs. Porter to look after granddaughter, Druscilla (#89-p.35). Calls shopping "marketing"; used to live in Brooklyn (#89-p.52).

**MRS. POWERS:**
Mother of Hannah, who has birthday party at Cinema World while Jessi is working there (M#14-p.110). Other daughters are Lea and Emily; she takes the BSC number from Jessi (M#14-p.112).

**MRS. RANDAL:**
Friend of Nannie/Elizabeth; just had a heart attack (KB-p.4).

**MR. AND MRS. RANDOLPH:**
Lived across the street from Claudia; Claud, Kristy, and Mary Anne build a snowwoman on their lawn (KB-p.21).

**KEN SCHIAVONE:**
Friendly man who houses Stacey and her mom during snowstorm (SS#7-p.213); lives in Victorian house, has six-month-old baby, Mason (SS#7-p.215); he and his wife are Christmas nuts (SS#7-p.214).

**MR. H. JOSEPH SEGER:**
The Rodowskys' neighbor; Kristy and Abby witness a break-in at his house (SM#2-p.40). Wife is deceased; has one son, Noah; is a member of the Stoneybrook Business Bureau (SM#2-p.92). A short man, with brown hair combed to one side to hide bald spot; seems pretty ordinary (SM#2-p.104). The BSC stakes out his house (SM#2-p.104). Business is Seger Associates; he keeps his own hours (SM#2-p.109). The BSC members suspect he is an embezzler or a launderer (SM#2-p.109). Drives an old blue Volvo, well-maintained (SM#2-p.120). Has been robbed by his own son (SM#2-p.172); the two of them will go to family counseling (SM#2-p.228).

**MR. SELZNICK:**
The Lowells' next-door neighbor who's usually home during the day (#56-p.42).

**THE SPENCERS:**
Family that hires sitters (#3-p.160); also neighbors of Barretts (#5-p.129).

**ELVIRA STONE:**
Two-month-old goat belonging to the Stones; mother died during birth; will eat kitchen trash and mail if not supervised (#65-pp.31-32). Bony joints, big eyes, thin, pointy beard, mottled gray-white-black fur that's scraggly and dusty; fragile and sweet (#65-p.34). Loves kids (#65-p.69). Dawn and Mary Anne take care of her for three weeks in their barn (#65-pp.35,66). Mrs. Stone is careful to make sure that visitors don't overfeed her; if Mrs. Stone thinks this is going to happen, she gives Elvira a little less at feeding time (#90-p.76); has a portable pen for traveling (#90-p.77).

**MRS. STONE:**
Salt-and-pepper-haired woman who owns goat, Elvira; Dawn, and Mary Anne baby-sit Elvira for three weeks (#65-pp.30-31). Stones' farm is near the cemetery on the outskirts of town, pretty rural; farm isn't too big, has vegetable garden and barn much bigger than Spiers', rusty tractor, some chickens, horses, pigs, couple of cows; Sharon and Richard have been friendly with Stones (#65-p.33). Farm also has a quail, nine baby pigs, a goose (named Screaming Yellow Honker) (#66-pp.12,15). Owns a goose, Glynis, who thinks she's a dog (SS#10-p.60). Also, there is a lamb named Oliver Twist on the farm (SS#13-p.91). Field is leased to the Stones by Mrs. Towne (#86-p.70). Has summer play group at her farm, which Mal and Kristy help with (SS#13-p.91).

**MR. HAROLD STONE:**
Married to Mrs. Stone, owns goat named Elvira (#65-p.31).

**KARL TATE:**

One of the wealthiest men in Stoneybrook, owns property all over town (M#7-p.92). A tall, broad man with lots of thick blond hair; looks strong and healthy, like a TV wrestler (M#7-p.100). House looks like Tara in *Gone With the Wind*; pillars across the front porch and a huge fountain in the front yard (M#7-p.101). Has a pet door, which leads to the kitchen (SM#2-p.193). Office is wooden and dusty (SM#2-p.194); office windows have security locks built into the latches, the kind that have to be opened with a key; Mary Anne, Shannon, and Logan are trapped there (SM#2-p.196). Is mastermind behind dognapping ring (M#7-p.143). Is losing a bundle in the real estate market (M#7-p.143). Has been put out of business (SM#2-p.196). Suspect in stalking of BSC members (SM#2-p.206). Follows BSC to Shadow Lake; is captured by Detective Kris Renn after Abby clocks him on the head with a snowball (SM#2-p.211). Was really trying to stop the stalker (SM#2-p.224).

**MRS. TATE:**

Karl Tate's wife; drives a red Mercedes; shops a bit (M#7-p.101). Warns BSC about true stalker (SM#2-p.218). Cat is Miss Kitty (SM#2-p.218).

**MRS. TOWNE:**

Lives halfway between the Stones' farm and the Spiers' house; her house sits back on about an acre of cleared land set in the woods by the road. Stone fences mark the edges of it and line the driveway. It is a tidy old white farmhouse, with flowers, trees, and beds of vegetables around it (#66-p.15); inside, it has low ceilings and stairs leading from the front hall (#66-pp.34-35). Kitchen is big and sunny, which leads out onto an even sunnier porch filled with plants of all kinds and sizes, which she uses as a sort of greenhouse (#66-p.36). Her handiwork is evident in almost every room of the house, including the guest room (#66-p.39). Workroom is big, filled with sewing equipment (#66-p.40). Mrs. Towne is a prize-winning expert at smocking and quilting and French hand sewing (#66-p.14); she is small, hardly any taller than Mary Anne, with sharp, direct brown eyes and very short white hair that looks almost punk. Her skin is pale brown and smooth and soft; she wears jeans, a work shirt, and tennis shoes. (#66-p.34). Makes chamomile tea from own chamomile flowers (#66-p.36). Grandmother taught her how to sew, so she grew up sewing (#66-p.37). Has a son, Cal, who lives in Missouri (#66-p.41). Breaks ankle (#66-p.50); has Mary Anne help with household chores. Finally, after Mary Anne says she can't do so much, she decides to hire a housekeeper (#66-p.140). Leases a field to the Stones (#86-p.70).

**MRS. VANDERBELLEN:**

Wealthy donor who might save arboretum (M#19-p.49), but decides

not to (M#19-p.117) and then decides that she will (M#19-p.143).

**THE VANSANTS:**
Friends of Mr. and Mrs. Perkins;
live on a farm out in the country
and own a horse (SS#7-p.111).

**MARGARET WELLFLEET:**
Irate parent who complains to BSC
after she witnesses Mal allowing
Jenny Prezzioso to throw a tantrum (SS#13-p.97) Has irritable
three year-old son named Colin
(SS#13-pp.160-161) and a five- or
six-year-old daughter, Isabella
(SS#13-pp.162).

**MR. JEROME WETZLER:**
Has been writing letters to the
*Stoneybrook News*, protesting the
Mischief Night Masquerade, as well
as other school budget expenditures
(M#22-p.54). Has protest signs on his
lawn that read: "Social studies and
science? Yes! Shindigs? No!" (M#22-
p.55). Went to SMS twenty-eight
years ago (M#22-p.88). Stacey "interviews" him for information (M#22-
p.95). Writes to *Stoneybrook News*
again, to argue that school budget
should be cut further (M#25-p.80).

**MR. WILLIS:**
Lives down Claudia's street (#2-
p.100).

## INSTRUCTORS/TEACHERS:

**MS. JODY ANDREWS:**
Taylor DeWitt's teacher (#100-p.34).

**MR. ANDERSON:**
Stephen Stanton-Cha's teacher at
SES (M#23-p.59).

**ANITA:**
Instructor of the infant care course
that the club members take; husband (and instructor) is Don; son is
Ethan (#45-p.41).

**MRS. BAEHR:**
Teacher at Stoneybrook Arts Center; nice, encouraging (#12-p.22).

**MR. BARNES:**
Mal's fourth grade teacher on
whom she had a crush and under
whom she got straight A's for the
first time (#29-pp.95-96).

**MS. BESSER:**
Was Jeff's teacher at SES (#12-p.55);
gives Jeff a surprise party before
he goes to California (#15-p.105).
Helps Dawn plan fund-raiser
and sleepover for SES's pen pal
school that burned down (#44-
p.37). Buys one of Claud's junk
food paintings at art show (#49-
p.134).

**MR. BOWMAN:**
David Michael's former teacher at
SES (#6-p.40).

**MR. BRYAN:**
Rosie Wilder's private tap teacher,
as old as Claud's dad, body like a
teenager (#49-p.49).

**MARGARET COHEN:**
Teaches piano at Marilyn Arnold's
music school (#21-p.53).

**MRS. COLQUIET:**
Claudia's third grade teacher at
SES; follows Rules and wears Busi-
ness Suits (CB-p.84).

**MS. COOK:**
Margo Pike's teacher, who she's
crazy about (M#3-p.28).

# ● Other BSC People ●

## MS. COX:
Teaches synchronized swimming at the community pool complex; thin, with short darkish-blonde hair, wide smile (#55-p.34); Jessi is in her class (#55-p.35).

## MS. DANVERS:
Shannon's guidance counselor (ShS-p.90).

## MRS. DANVERS:
Shea Rodowsky's teacher (#63-p.41).

## MME DUBARRY:
Shannon's French teacher; a tall, energetic woman, who always wears bright colors and the same diamond earrings every day (ShS-p.20).

## MME DUPRE:
Teaches free six-week ballet class to less privileged kids at the Stamford Ballet School; Jessi and Mary Bramstedt volunteer to help (#61-p.2). French, much younger than Mme Noelle, in her twenties with not nearly as thick an accent; kind of pretty with grayish-blue eyes and high forehead; long brown hair in tight ponytail; normally assists Mme Noelle but conducting special class now (#61-p.27).

## MR. ECCLES:
Claudia's second grade teacher; made learning new things fun (CB-p.61).

## MS. ELLISON:
Mary Anne's fourth grade teacher; smart, pretty, self-confident, and cheerful (MAB-p.88). Other kids in class include Alan Gray and April Livingston (MAB-p.89).

## FRAN:
Counselor at playground (#6-p.92).

## MS. FRANK:
Matt Braddock's teacher (#16-p.111).

## MRS. FREDERICKSON:
First grade teacher for Claudia, Kristy, and Mary Anne; old with strange hair; yells a lot and makes Mary Anne cry (SS#11-p.73). Mary Anne doesn't like it when she yells (MAB-p.26).

## MR. HO:
Claudia's Core Group teacher at Stamford Alternative Academy (CB-p.100).

## MRS. JAMESON:
Claudia and Kristy's fourth grade teacher at SES; from the South and has a neat accent; Charlie had her (CB-p.85). Has dark brown skin, dark eyes, and speaks softly (CB-p.86); suggests that Claudia go to the Stamford Alternative Academy (CB-pp.90-91).

## MRS. JEFFRIES:
Mary Anne's second grade teacher; never raised her voice and had great ideas for helping kids learn (MAB-p.57).

## MR. KATZ:
Runs the Kids Can Do Anything Club with Mrs. Simon (#48-p.6); (#80-p.26).

## MR. KATZ:
Shannon's science teacher, who asks her to join astronomy club (SS#11-p.179).

## LAUREN KENDALL:
Riding instructor at Kendallwood Farm who teaches Mal's Beginning Equitation (#54-p.39). Has British accent; tall, slender, with straight dark hair pulled back in silver bar-

rette at neck, face tanned, green eyes, wears English riding togs of black boots, tan pants, white blouse, green jacket, velvet hunt caps (#54-pp.39-40, 42). Used to ride on an Olympic riding team (#54-p.46).

**MRS. KLEINHASSER:**
Dana Cheplin's piano teacher; lives on Acorn Place (#94-p.82). Drives Dana and Stacey to Dr. Johanssen's when Dana isn't feeling well (#94-p.110).

**MRS. KUSHEL:**
Claudia, Kristy, and Mary Anne's kindergarten teacher at SES; seemed really old to Claudia; has blonde hair, dangling down in tight ringlets; tended to shout at class (CB-p.30).

**CORLA MAGNUSSON:**
Academic coordinator of Stamford Alternative Academy; a tall woman (CB-p.97).

**COACH VICTORIA MARTIN:**
Kristy's softball coach at Camp Topnotch; Kristy thinks she's terrific (KB-p.93). Annoyed by the cabins' prank war, she says she's quitting (KB-p.106) but then comes back when the rivalry ends (KB-p.112).

**MME MINOFF:**
Seven-year-old Kristy, Mary Anne, and Claudia are in her summer beginners' ballet class; she is very strict about class dress (MAB-p.64). A tall, slender woman with black hair tied in a bun (MAB-p.68).

**MR. MOSER:**
Buddy Barrett's third grade teacher (#29-p.34). In his class, the Crows is the lowest reading group, the

Robins is the middle reading group, and the Hawks is the highest reading group; after Mal's tutorial, Buddy moves from the Crows to the Robins (#29-pp.142-143).

**MME NOELLE:**
Jessi's ballet teacher, speaks with accent, bangs a stick on the floor when students exercise at *barre* at beginning of class (#16-p.22). Older woman, teaches class in leotard, long rehearsal skirt, and dance shoes with heels (#27-p.21); a stern taskmaster (#27-p.22); used to be very intimidating to Jessi, known throughout ballet community as an excellent teacher (#42-p.5). Class comprised of ten girls (#61-p.8). Advises Mary Bramstedt to see a doctor about her eating disorder (#61-pp.119, 135). Calls Jessi "Miss Romsey" or "Mademoiselle Romsey" (M#10-p.82).

**MISS PACKETT:**
Kristy, Mary Anne, and Claudia's first grade art teacher, who wheels art cart into classrooms; disparages Claud's butterfly self-portrait and gets a talking-to from Mimi (SS#11-from p.76). Claud now knows she wasn't a very good teacher (CB-p.30).

**DR. PATEK:**
Stoneybrook Day headmistress; her office is in the administration house, but she makes a point of being around the buildings when classes are starting for the day (ShS-p.16). She calls students younger than middle-school age by their first names, then promotes them to a

more proper greeting ("Ms. Kil-bourne") in middle school (ShS-p.16).

**MRS. RANDOLPH:**
SES school nurse (MAB-p.100).

**MISS RAYMOND:**
Madeleine DeWitt's teacher (#100-p.35).

**MS. REYNOLDS:**
SES principal. Red hair; strong, kind face (#44-pp.61-62).

**MR. RILEY:**
Mme Minoff's piano player; an elderly gentleman, with glasses perched on the tip of his nose (MAB-p.68)

**MR. ROSSI:**
Teacher Derek Masters has (#27-p.77).

**MRS. SCHIAVONE:**
Shea Rodowsky's piano teacher whose doorbell played "Over the Rainbow" before Jackie broke it (#12-p.109).

**MS. SIMON:**
Runs the Kids Can Do Anything Club with Mr. Katz (#48-p.6); (#80-p.26). Once had Claudia as a student (#80-p.38).

**MS. STOTLER:**
The (temporary) principal of SES; Claire thinks she's as famous as Michael Jackson and Roseanne (M#11-p.86).

**MRS. SWALLOW:**
SES librarian (SS#11-p.149).

**MS. VAN COTT:**
Rosie Wilder's voice teacher, has long blonde hair; voice echoes when she speaks (#49-p.49).

**COACH WILLIAMS:**
Maria Kilbourne's SDS swim coach; a nice woman (ShS-p.52).

**PROFESSOR WOODLEY:**
Professor with whom Janine does her summer work-study computer job (M#16-p.9).

**MRS. WOODS:**
Charlotte's piano teacher; holds recital (#83-p.131).

**JOSEPH WOODWARD:**
Principal of elementary school on Zuni reservation in New Mexico; school burned down; sends thank-you note to kids who helped raise money for reconstruction of the school (#44-p.134).

## LAW ENFORCEMENT/GOVERNMENT:

**MS. BREEN:**
Head of security at stadium where Stacey and the bad girls are caught drinking alcohol (#87-p.115).

**OFFICER CLEARY:**
Brings Mary Anne down to the station for questioning regarding the Ambrose's Sawmill vandalism (M#24-p.52). Male; partner is Officer Pelkey (M#24-p.54).

**OFFICER DREW:**
Elderly, bald, looks like a grandfather (#2-pp.130-131).

**MRS. GRAVES:**
Lou McNally's social worker, who arranges for Lou and her brother, Jay, to live with their aunt and uncle (#62-p.133).

# ● Other BSC People ●

**SERGEANT BRIDGET IANELLI:**
Takes Logan's statement regarding the Badd Boyz (LB-p.119).

**LIEUTENANT JOFFREY:**
From the fire department, talks to Mary Anne about the library fires (M#13-p.65).

**SERGEANT JOHNSON:**
From the Stoneybrook police force; tall, with black hair and clear blue eyes; male; looks at Claudia's bank photos (M#16-p.73). Seems really friendly; listens to the BSC (M#16-p.110). Investigates robbery at Seger household (SM#2-p.40). Partner is Sgt. Tang (SM#2-p.40). Ever since his first involvement with the BSC, he's been in their corner; he's always receptive to club members who offer him suspicions, clues, or possible evidence (M#23-p.46). When he was a kid his best friend was David Follman (M#23-p.47). Questions Mary Anne about incident at Ambrose's Mill (M#24-p.58).

**SARAH KARUSH:**
President of the Stoneybrook Board of Education; looks calm and in control and acts sincere (M#25-p.52).

**MAYOR KEANE OF STONEYBROOK:**
Female (#57-p.109); gives speech at opening day of recycling center at SMS (#57-p.101).

**DETECTIVE NORTON:**
Responds to Buddy's disappearance (#5-p.141).

**RAYMOND OATES:**
Chairman of the Stoneybrook Board of Education's negotiating committee; looks like a cartoon politician, with red cheeks, a red nose, a round stomach, and perfectly combed hair; he is not even-tempered (M#25-p.52). Is independently wealthy; doesn't have to work for a living; is using SMS controversy to make a name for himself and perhaps run for mayor (M#25-p.56). Abby calls him Mr. Votes (M#25-p.58). Suspect in SMS vandalism mystery (M#25-p.113).

**MR. OLINGER:**
Federal agent who specializes in art theft; has one blue and one green eye (M#11-p.131).

**MRS. PEABODY:**
A social worker with Stoneybrook social services; picks up the vagabond mall children (M#14-p.143).

**OFFICER PELKEY:**
Officer Cleary's partner (M#24-p.54).

**CHIEF JOHN PIERCE:**
Stoneybrook police chief, comments on the dognappings (M#7-p.63).

**OFFICER SAUTER:**
Behind the desk at the Stoneybrook Police Station; gives the BSC a hard time (M#16-p.73).

**LIEUTENANT IRENE SHAY:**
Interviews the vagabond children from the Washington Mall about the mall thefts (M#14-p.141).

**OFFICER STANTON:**
Accompanies Officer Drew (#2-p.131).

**SERGEANT TANG:**
Sgt. Johnson's partner (SM#2-p.40).

## MEDICAL:

**DR. CALLOWAY:**
Pikes' doctor, who treats Mal after she falls off horse (#54-p.76).

**DR. CELENZA:**
Dentist who specializes in pulling teeth; female; Claudia has to go to her in second grade (CB-p.69). Office walls are covered with colored stars of red, green, yellow, and blue. A silver moon hangs from the ceiling. All around are pictures of smiling kids. The dentist chair looks like a rocketship (CB-p.70). Dr. Celenza wears many buttons on her white doctor's coat (CB-p.71). After the dentistry is finished, Claud gets to pick a prize out of a space helmet (CB-p.72). Dr. Celenza takes a Polaroid of all her patients (CB-p.73).

**DR. CREWS:**
Young eye doctor who prescribes Mary Anne's glasses in fourth grade (MAB-p.108).

**DR. DELLENKAMP:**
Treats Vanessa's ankle sprain (#31-p.85). Says that Emily Michelle is language-delayed (#33-p.35). Claudia's former pediatrician, to whom she goes with adoption questions (#33-p.71). Claudia started seeing her when she was two (#33-p.73). Miss Wilson is her receptionist (#33-p.73). Phone number is on the Pikes' refrigerator (#68-p.91). Treats Mal for mono (#69-p.25).

**DR. FRANK:**
Stacey's specialist in Stoneybrook (#3-p.27).

**DR. HERNANDEZ:**
Dana Cheplin's doctor (#94-p.77).

**DR. KAHN:**
The Brunos' doctor (LB-p.3).

**MISS KOPPELMAN:**
Nurse Stacey's dad hires to sit with her mom when she gets pneumonia; from a visiting nurse service in Stamford (#58-p.109).

**DR. MARCUS:**
One of Mimi's doctors (#7-p.88).

**D. RAMIREZ:**
Emergency room physician's assistant who helps Abby recover from asthma attack (#90-p.34).

**DR. REESE:**
Therapist (female) who helped Mary Anne a lot when she felt messed up (#71-p.65, CL-p.20). Standard uniform is polo shirt, sweater, and chinos (pretty preppy); she seems barely old enough to be a doctor, especially when she pulls her dark brown hair into a ponytail (#93-p.119). Is addicted to hot chocolate (#93-p.119). Claudia gives Dr. Reese's number to Sean, a boy who sends in a Personal Ad regarding his parents' break-up (#71-p.71); Sean sees her and sorts some things out (#71-p.139). Claudia gives Dr. Reese's number to George Hewitt, who calls into WSTO regarding his parents' divorce; phone number is 555-7660 (#85-p.107). Mary Anne visits Dr. Reese again after Amelia Freeman's death, to help adjust (#93-p.118). Works in new medical office building at the end of Main Street (description of office, #93-pp.118-19).

# ● Other BSC People ●

**DR. RICE:**
The Kishi family dentist; male (CB-p.68).

**DR. SMITH:**
Vet used by Thomases (#10-p.125), does not make house calls (#8-p.88); older woman with graying hair and bifocals; always talks to animals in soft, soothing voice (#11-p.23).

**DR. WEBER:**
Doctor (female) who checks Jamie Newton out after the baby-sitters' Island Adventure (SS#4-p.196).

**DR. WEST:**
Mancusis' vet to whom Jessi takes their hamster (#22-p.111).

**MISS WILSON:**
Dr. Delenkamp's receptionist (#33-p.73).

**DR. ZUCKERMAN:**
Peaches' doctor; delivers Lynn (#97-p.34).

## STONEYBROOK MANOR:

**ESTHER BARNARD:**
Karen's friend from her school's adopt-a-grandparent program (#69-p.20).

**BART BARTLESBY:**
The oldest man at SM, very vocal (#69-p.113).

**MRS. BLANCHARD:**
SM resident; elderly woman, busily arranges books for Christmas Boutique (#92-p.105).

**MRS. BROOKES:**
SM resident (#69-p.105).

**MRS. CARVER:**
SM resident; a bubble pops on her head, but she doesn't mind (#69-p.108).

**MR. CONNOR:**
Uncle Joe Pike's roommate (M#3-p.152); Uncle Joe calls him "Connor" (#92-p.65). Loud TV drives him out of the room (#92-p.65).

**MRS. FELLOWS:**
The activity director at SM (#69-p.21).

**MR. HAMILTON:**
SM resident; receives Legos in Thanksgiving basket (#69-p.111).

**MRS. KRONAUER:**
Organizes the Christmas Boutique (#92-p.39). A trim, white-haired woman with sharp blue eyes; her shoulders are slightly stooped, but she walks with a lively bounce (#92-p.60).

**MRS. LYMON:**
SM resident (#69-p.110).

**MR. MEAD:**
SM resident; drops folding table (#92-p.62).

**MR. RENQUIST:**
SM resident; lets Nicky turn the crank on his bed (#69-p.111).

**MR. RUBIN:**
SM resident; plays old upright piano (#92-p.66). Diabetic (#92-p.106).

**RUTH:**
Took care of Mr. Hennesey when he lived there (#69-p.21).

**HERMAN SCHWARTZ:**
SM resident (#69-p.105).

**MARY WRIGHT:**
SM resident (#69-p.101); receives Miss Piggy puzzle in Thanksgiving basket (#69-p.111).

## AUTHORS/ENTERTAINERS/ JOURNALISTS:

**LOUISA MAY ALCOTT:**
Nineteenth-century author to whom Mary Anne writes a fan letter (SS#11-p.151).

**TOMMY ANATOMY:**
Local actor who puts on a musical about the human body, mostly at elementary schools and playgrounds; wears a costume with the human body painted on it; an attraction at the Health Fair (LS-p.98).

**BOB ATKINSON:**
College intern at WSTO, helps Claudia and Ashley with their show (#85-p.44). A bearded, dark-blond-haired guy (#85-p.45). Parents heard the end of WWII announced on WSTO (#85-p.99).

**GEORGE BALANCHINE:**
Great ballet choreographer who wanted his corps de ballet to look alike, but since his death ballet dancers are not as overly conscious about their looks and weight (#61-p.10).

**BARBARA:**
The "mummy" who escorts Jessi and Karen out of the haunted house at Sudsy's when Karen is frightened (#24-p.101).

**DAN BEASLEY:**
Uncle Dandy on TV show in Hartford, *Uncle Dandy's Star Machine*;

lets Rosie Wilder be on show (#49-pp.63, 103).

**BILLY BLUE:**
A singer, specializing in gushy ballads, including "Your Sweet Kiss" (M#16-pp.46-48).

**FRANK BOTTOMS:**
Carson Fraser's manager; a short bald man in a shiny black running suit; is very protective of his clients (M#15-pp.30-33).

**MR. BULLOCK:**
WSTO station manager (#85-p.35). A tall, thin, gray-haired man with glasses and a great smile (#85-p.40); his office is a pigsty (#85-p.41).

**TODD BYRON:**
Actor in *Mall Warriors II*; Stacey thinks he's a great actor, even in serious movies (#70-p.33).

**NICKY CASH:**
Teenage singer who records gushy love songs; Mary Anne always cries when she listens to him; he used to be in group called 2 Hot 4 U; his real name is Reginald Fenster (LB-p.6-7). Hot new album is entitled *Dreams of You* (LB-p.78). Logan gets stolen tickets to his concert; Mary Anne is thrilled about going (LB-pp.92-94).

**CLIFF CHASE:**
Producer of *Little Vampires*; wears expensive-looking black sunglasses (M#15-p.31).

**CHERYL:**
Stuntwoman; Derek's double for *Little Vampires* (M#15-p.51).

**CAROLYN DEVRIES:**
Casting agent at Karbergers for Prezzioso auditions; her collar-

length blonde hair seems to be glued in place like a helmet (#73-p.76).

**GEORGE DELMORE:**
Henrietta Hayes's editor (#80-p.71).

**CARSON FRASER:**
Star of *Little Vampires*; has longish, wavy blond hair and sleepy-looking blue eyes (M#15-p.28); spends a lot of time complaining (M#15-p.35). Is obviously in love with himself (M#15-p.63). Favorite snack food appears to be Ritz sandwich crackers (M#15-p.105).

**THEODORE "TED" GARBER:**
Author of horror novels; guest on Claudia's WSTO show; writes the spooky, creepy, gross, and super-popular *Night Frights* series; lives in Connecticut (#85-p.115).

**CAM GEARY:**
TV star; Mary Anne's favorite actor; his favorite color is blue; Logan looks like him (M#14-p.119); a kid (#9-p.102). Dates Corrie Lalique, of *Once Upon a Dream* (#10-p.10). Mary Anne writes letter to him (CL-p.29). At Dawn's urging, he writes a personalized Christmas card to Mary Anne (SecS-p.23).

**HENRIETTA HAYES:**
Author and playwright, Mallory's new favorite (#80-p.33). A short, petite woman, wears brown-framed glasses with thick lenses, which make it hard to see her eyes. Pale face would look young except for fine wrinkles lining it. Has thick gray and brown hair that is cut to her chin and a bit on the messy side. Age is somewhere in her fifties (#80-p.58). Lives at 312 Morgan Road (#80-pp.50,56). Born in Binghamton, NY; graduated from Ithaca College (#80-p.33); letters are postmarked from Stamford (#80-p.34). Plays/books include the *Alice Anderson* series, *The Happiest Day,* and *Frog Pond Vacation* (#80-p.53). House is down a narrow dirt path through a cluster of trees; it is cozy-looking, one-story, mostly brown wood except for a stone chimney up the side. A screened-in porch on the right leads to a wooden deck with several bird feeders on it. A stone path leads to the house. (#80-p.57). The inside is simply furnished (#80-pp.59,60, 67-69). Immediately sends form letters back to writers, then reads their letters later (#80-p.62). Writes for four hours every day, then spends two more hours working on outlines for new projects (#80-p.63). Hires Mal as temporary assistant (#80-p.66). Has a cleaning lady (#80-p.69). A foster child from the age of three, when her parents and younger brother died tragically in a fire; marriage to author G. N. Rogers ended in bitter divorce. Daughter, Cassie, died at the age of eighteen, the victim of a hit-and-run driver (#80-p.91). Editor is George Delmore (#80-p.71).

**HARRY:**
The director of *Little Vampires* (M#15-p.35).

**CHAD HENRY:**
Producer/director for Channel Three TV; very tan, with huge and warm smile (#92-p.28); liaison to

Pikes for Old-fashioned Christmas Contest program; contest is for "Family First" feature in *Values AmericanStyle* show (#92-p.30). Has two kids, ages twenty-one and twenty-five (#92-p.100).

**ZEKE HILL:**
Propmaster for *Little Vampires* (M#15-p.37). A tall, skinny man with bright red hair and a face to match (M#15-p.38). Fired after real glass is substituted for break-away glass (M#15-p.56); has a very short temper (M#15-p.57). Re-hired (M#15-p.138).

**JEANNIE:**
Chad Henry's camerawoman for *Values AmericanStyle* (#92-p.55).

**JOAN:**
Casting agent at Tip-Top Talent Agency; has bright red hair, big horn-rimmed glasses, dangling earrings, and a layered black outfit (#73-p.55).

**CORRIE LALIQUE:**
Cam Geary's girlfriend; fourteen; star of *Once Upon a Dream* (#10-p.10).

**LIBBY:**
Receptionist at Tip-Top Talent Agency (#73-p.57).

**STEVE MATTHEWS:**
#1 Fan pullout idol; dark hair and deep brown eyes; Stacey prefers him to Cam Geary (M#14-p.119).

**SHEILA MAYBERRY:**
Publicist for *Little Vampires* (M#15-p.31). The only person ever dressed up on the set (M#15-p.33).

**JOHN MEAD:**
Derek Masters's driver; used to be a prizefighter (M#15-p.90).

**MISSY:**
Makeup artist for *Little Vampires*; a blonde woman in a pink smock, whom Derek thinks is the best in the business (M#15-p.26).

**AMELIA MOODY:**
Mal's favorite author (SS#11-p.145), who brings her to tears at author signing (SS#11-p.165). Author of *Nitty Gritty Meatballs* (SS#11-p.145), *Mandy Mandango Takes the Bull by the Horns* (SS#11-p.147), *The Lost Grandmother* (SS#11-p.149), and *Live from New York* (SS#11-p.162). Lives in the Adirondacks with her husband; they have two sons (SS#11-p.152); she is sixty-four years old (SS#11-p.157).

**NANCY:**
Hairdresser for *Little Vampires* (M#15-p.27).

**NESTOR:**
Another cameraman for *Values AmericanStyle* (#92-p.69).

**RAN PHILIPS:**
Assists Skyllo in singing for U4Me; has just shaved his head (#87-p.30).

**RANDOM DAN:**
DJ on radio BSC listens to (#62-p.111).

**PAMME REED:**
Author of *Bradley and the Great Chase*, speaks at Young Author's Day at SMS, autographs Mal's copy of her new book and congratulates Mal on her story (#47-p.139).

**MEGAN RINEHART:**
One of Mary Anne's favorite authors (#46-p.43); visits SMS on Author's Day and signs books for

Mary Anne, Logan, and Pete Black (#46-p.129).

**G.N. ROGERS:**
Henrietta Hayes's ex-husband, the author of "dark and forbidding" books; photo shows a frowning man with deep, worried creases on his broad forehead (#80-p.92).

**SKYLLO:**
Lead singer for U4Me; his real name is Aristotle Dukas; he has huge, vulnerable and strong eyes, which pull you out of your seat when you see them on TV; on a hunkiness scale of 1 to 10, he's a 15; his fan club has a waiting list (#87-p.28).

**MIMI SNOWDON:**
TV reporter who questions Dawn and distorts her comments about School Spirit Month (#84-p.53); works for WSBK (#84-p.102).

**MARIAN TAN:**
Editor of the *Stoneybrook News* (SS#7-p.1).

**TODD:**
Chad Henry's assistant and cameraman (#92-p.57).

**WILD BILL:**
Afternoon DJ at WSTO (M#18-p.29).

**SANDRA YU:**
Rosie Wilder's talent agent (#49-p.60).

**STONEYBROOK MERCHANTS:**

**AMBER:**
Gives Mal long-awaited haircut at salon (#21-pp.134-135).

**MRS. BALLMER:**
Works in accessories department at Bellair's; a gray-haired woman; knows Stacey's mother (#87-p.72).

**BETTY:**
Clerk at the Merry-Go-Round (M#10-p.32); catches Stacey's counterfeit bill (M#10-p.33).

**MS. BLAIR:**
Personnel director at Bellair's; young, with a friendly smile and curly hair that falls to her eyes (#87-p.47).

**NEIL DAVIS:**
Owner of Davis Diapers; a heavyset, balding man (#89-p.45). Sponsors Krushers; makes them change their name to the Diapers (#89-from p.45). Is backseat coach and too mean to the kids, so Kristy gives back his equipment and revokes his sponsorship (#89-p.131).

**GIUSEPPE DESALVIO:**
Owner of In Good Taste, a gourmet food store (#78-p.78).

**DOTTIE ELLWAY:**
Theodore III's wife; works at Ted's Tools, appears to be at home behind the counter; jokes with every customer and seems to know them all by name (M#13-p.106).

**ROSA ELLWAY:**
Theodore III's daughter; cheerful red-haired woman, runs Ellway Kennels (M#13-p.107).

**THEODORE ELLWAY III:**
Owns Ted's Tools; Miriam Ellway's brother (M#13-p.105). Has a brain like a computer when it comes to local home improvement projects (M#24-p.116).

## THEODORE ELLWAY IV:
Lives in ritzy area of town, his gardener says that he's nice (M#13-p.107).

## MARSHALL GAINES:
Family photographer for Spier/Schafer portraits (#64-p.122).

## MR. GATES:
His barbershop is around corner from SES (#6-p.105).

## ROBERT GAUTIER:
Photographer who takes portfolio shots of the Prezzioso children; studio is in old Victorian house; front parlor is stuffed with antiques and oriental rugs; dressing rooms are under the stairs (#73-p.64). He has incredible tan, jet-black hair (#73-p.66); studio has white walls, black cube to sit on, and backdrops (#73-pp.66-67).

## MRS. GROSSMAN:
Director of Kid Center at Bellair's; tall, gray-haired woman; becomes Stacey's boss (#87-p.47).

## MRS. HEMPHILL:
Works at Bellair's accessories department; is friends with Mrs. McGill and the Johanssens (M#10-p.31); passes Stacey a counterfeit bill (by accident).

## MS. JAVORSKY:
Jessi's Santa supervisor at Bellair's (SS#12-p.34).

## MS. KELLER:
Real estate agent who finds house for Stacey's mom (#28-p.86).

## ADELE LEBEQUE:
Head of Stoneybrook Day Camp; friend of Mrs. Braddock's (#76-p.55).

## OTTO:
Manager at SportsTown; a sweet man with a mustache, receding hairline, and a pot belly (#87-p.44); has a drawer filled with applications (#87-p.44).

## MRS. PEABODY:
Head judge of beauty pageant, once owned a charm school (#15-p.124).

## RON PARKER:
Small-business owner and member of good standing of the Stoneybrook Rotary Club; supports Reginald Fowler's development in Miller's Park (M#24-p.38).

## ELEANOR AND LUCAS PETERSON:
Owners of Peterson's Nurseries (SecS-p.20).

## MR. PRATT:
Assistant barber at Mr. Gates's shop; skinny, jumpy-looking (#6-p.110).

## ANDY QUIGLEY:
Owner of Quigley's Christmas Tree Nursery; a broad-shouldered old man (#92-p.90).

## MRS. QUIGLEY:
Owner of Quigley's Christmas Tree Nursery; white-haired and trim, and her eyes crinkle when she smiles (#92-pp.90-91).

## JOHN ROCKAWAY:
Head of Rockaway and Sons firm, local contractor; is really disorganized (M#15-from p.99).

## ANNA SALERNO:
Battle of the Bakers judge; owner of a fancy bakery (in Stamford) (M#21-p.127).

## DOROTHY SAWYER:
Former resident of Sawyer house (M#9-p.59). Karen, Patty, and Kristy

find her diary (M#9-p.59). In it, she writes of her plans to elope with Will Blackburn (M#9-p.64). Disappeared on June 8, 1935; is presumed dead (M#9-pp.81-82). Now runs Sew Fine (M#9-p.139); disappearance allowed her to be free, so she traveled the world and then opened store ten years ago in Stoneybrook (see M#9-p.140). Decides that it would be grand to see Will again (M#9-p.141).

**BOB SHULL:**
Owns Sound Ideas; is a friend of Mr. Bruno's from the Chamber of Commerce Softball League (LB-p.7). A tall, burly guy with blond hair and an open, friendly face (LB-p.51).

**SYLVIA STEINERT:**
The Stevensons' decorator; a dark-haired woman (#89-p.14).

**ROBERT THOMPSON:**
Manager of First Glass Inc., which fixes windows for the Pikes after Hurricane Bill (SS#10-p.224).

**JIM ZIBRESKI:**
Vice President of the Stoneybrook Bank (M#16-p.81). Wife is named Gretchen (M#16-p.82). Has a little bald spot (M#16-p.139). The BSC catches him embezzling from the bank (M#16-p.144).

## WASHINGTON MALL MERCHANTS:

**BENNY:**
Cook at Casa Grande (M#14-p.143).

**MR. BUFORD:**
New manager of Washington Mall (M#14-p.145).

**APRIL FRENNING:**
Runs Toy Town in the Washington Mall; Stacey works with her for Project Work class; a tall woman with long, curly red hair; wears an armful of silver bracelets and a big smile (M#14-p.29). Has two-year-old son, Sandy (M#14-p.30).

**MS. GARCIA:**
Head of security at Washington Mall; Kristy works with her for Project Work class (M#14-p.53). A small, wiry woman with black hair and flashing brown eyes (M#14-p.74). Has daughter, Kellie (M#14-p.75).

**JOYCE:**
Stacey's favorite hairstylist, gave her a perm (#60-pp.43, 32); works in Washington Mall (#60-p.32); gives Mary Anne short haircut, which she loves (#60-pp.45-46).

**MR. MAGEE:**
Jessi's boss at Cinema World during Project Work class (M#14-p.108).

**TED MORTON:**
Manager of the Washington Mall; has been in the job for six months (M#14-p.70). The BSC goes to him regarding the day care center; he agrees with their ideas (M#14-p.79). Can't say no to anyone, which gets him in trouble (M#14-p.123). Fired after he is implicated in the mall thefts (M#14-p.145).

**MS. MUNRO:**
Mal's manager at the BookCenter (M#14-p.37).

**MS. RICHARDS:**
Former manager of the Washington Mall; didn't want a day care center (M#14-p.70).

# ● Other BSC People ●

**SARAH:**
Part-time employee at Toy Town (M#14-p.81).

**MS. CINDY SNYDER:**
Salesperson at Lear's; helps set up the Washington Mall day care center (M#14-p.81). Likes classical music (M#14-p.106).

**SUE:**
Pierces ears of Mal, Jessi, and Claud (#21-p.128).

**MR. WILLIAMS:**
Manages the Cheese Outlet; works on day care center set-up (M#14-p.81). Likes cool old rock from the sixties (M#14-p.106). Becomes the full-time director of the day care center (M#14-p.145).

## MUSEUM/LIBRARY/ ARBORETUM/ZOO/ GREENBROOK WORKERS:

**MR. CHESTER:**
Suspicious assistant to the director of the Bedford Zoo; a short, heavy-set man; bald, wears gold-rimmed glasses (M#20-p.47).

**MS. CURETON:**
Architect working on Greenbrook Club; has flaming red hair in a mass of curls around her head (M#23-pp.35-36).

**DARCY:**
Decorator at Greenbrook Club; has straight, platinum blonde hair cut in a precise bob (M#23-pp.35-36). Only uses one name, like Madonna or Cher (M#23-p.38).

**DONALD:**
Student librarian at Stoneybrook Public Library; is in one of Janine's classes at college (#91-p.47).

**BERTHA DOW:**
Book-banner, protests at the Stoneybrook Library; is "interviewed" by Mary Anne and Kristy (M#13-pp.96-97).

**MISS MIRIAM ELLWAY:**
Works in children's section of the library (M#13-p.22). Just started work a couple of weeks ago but knows her way around; looks and acts unfriendly, with thin straight lips, thin straight gray hair, and a thin pointy nose (M#13-p.24-5).

**MS. FELD:**
Children's librarian at the Stoneybrook Public Library; the most energetic woman Mary Anne's ever seen, always doing more than one thing at a time (M#13-p.22). Her curly brown hair looks a little messy, and her sweater is missing a button; when she smiles, her green eyes light up; she loves her job (M#13-p.25).

**MRS. GOLDSMITH:**
Curator of the arboretum; gray-haired woman wearing bright pink smock (M#19-p.46).

**MS. HOBBES:**
Mr. Snipes' secretary at the Stoneybrook Museum (M#11-p.64).

**MR. KAWAJA:**
Caretaker, gardener for Greenbrook Club (M#23-p.27). Looks Asian; small and wiry, wears a black smock with many pockets (M#23-p.35). Appears to be unable to

speak (M#23-p.39). Only speaks when it's important (M#23-p.124). The Greenbrook Maze means a lot to him (M#23-p.142).

**DON NEWMAN:**
One of Claudia's favorite sculptors; has retrospective at the Stoneybrook Museum; lives nearby; sculpture is mostly abstract (see M#11-p.7). Looks like a teddy bear, with a full beard and horn-rimmed glasses (M#11-p.10). Believes that art should be touchable (M#11-p.60). Has two almost grown children; made secret compartments in his sculptures for them when they were kids (M#11-p.99). Helps Claudia trap coin thieves (M#11-p.126).

**WILL SARIES:**
Art thief who robs Stoneybrook Museum; is caught by Claudia (M#11-p.132).

**MR. SNIPES:**
Curator of the Stoneybrook Museum; doesn't usually see people on Saturdays (M#11-p.63). A skinny man, looks more like an insurance agent than a curator, with black hair, a thin black mustache, very pale skin, and small dark eyes (M#11-p.64). Robberies happened in three out of the four museums he worked at (M#11-p.73), since he was hired by museums who feel they are vulnerable to theft (M#11-p.129). Suspect in museum mystery (M#11-p.73).

**MRS. WOFSEY:**
Director of the Bedford Zoo; a pleasant woman with blonde hair in a blunt, chin-length cut (M#20-p.47).

**FAMILY FRIENDS/PARENTS' DATES/CO-WORKERS/ADULT BABY-SITTERS:**

**MRS. BRYAR:**
The Kilbournes' housekeeper (ShS-p.104).

**MRS. CUDDY:**
Former baby-sitter of Mary Anne; Kristy called her "Mrs. Cruddy"; she watched game shows and soap operas all the time; was always asking Mary Anne to do things for her, like answer her phone calls (MAB-p.61).

**MRS. CULP:**
Former Thomas housekeeper who rarely showed up (SS#11-p.26).

**TOM FIELDING:**
Watson's best friend; they haven't seen each other in a couple of years; he has a wife and four kids (#6-p.36): Katherine (five), Patrick (three), Maura (two), and Tony (eight months) (#6-p.53).

**BILL GRAUMAN:**
Bright red-haired man; friend of the Johanssens'; stays there while they are away; Stacey thinks he's a burglar (M#18-p.131).

**THEODORE "TRIP" GWYNNE:**
Goes on date with Dawn's mother (#9-pp.81-83); has round tortoise shell glasses, short blond hair, brown eyes; Dawn and Jeff call him Trip-Man (#9-p.81); they didn't like him very much.

**STU HUMBOLDT:**
Sharon's business associate, Richard's friend; lures Sharon to surprise dinner (#30-p.75).

# ● Other BSC People ●

**KELLY:**
Dawn's mother's friend who was given a baby shower at work (#15-p.39).

**MR. MAJOR:**
Friend of Aunt Cecilia (#82-p.43); Jessi and Becca think they're getting married, but really they are just in a wedding together (#82-p.98). Is a member of a group that dresses up like clowns and visits kids in hospitals; knows all kinds of cool magic tricks and balloon tricks (#90-p.45).

**MRS. MANSON:**
One of Mary Anne's baby-sitters; talked all the time about her grandchildren; they sounded as boring as she was; also drank a lot of beer on the job, which is why Mr. Spier fired her (MAB-p.61).

**MARJORIE:**
Sitter for eight-year-old Mary Anne, brought along her five-month-old baby (SS#11-p.224).

**MARY:**
Woman from Watson's office; calls often (#81-p.132).

**MRS. MILLS:**
Adult sitter for eight-year-old Mary Anne; smelled like Ivory soap and only ate dill pickles all day long (SS#11-p.223).

**PATRICIA PENNYBROOK:**
Mary Anne's sitter during fourth grade; a huge improvement over some of her other sitters (MAB-p.94).

**MRS. TATE:**
Adult sitter for eight-year-old Mary Anne; Mary Anne, Kristy, and Claudia play practical jokes on her, but she's not fazed and plays a practical joke on them (SS#11-from p.226). Drives a run-down, rust-brown car (SS#11-p.226).

## OTHER PEOPLE:

**MR. CHRISTOPHER ARMSTRONG:**
An older man; stooped and gray, who carries a cane with a silver duck's head on top (M#23-p.70). Former Stoneybrook mayor; was not well-liked; a "strong-armer" (M#23-p.50). Won golf tournament in 1942 (M#23-p.106). Confesses to being ringleader of Greenbrook Secret Society, is going to face criminal charges (M#23-p.145).

**MS. BERNSTEIN:**
Health fair chairperson (LS-p.52).

**WILL BLACKBURN:**
Tall and thin and a little stooped, with scraggly gray hair. Face is gaunt, gray eyes have no sparkle (M#9-p.30). Caretaker at haunted mansion (M#9-p.32). Dorothy Sawyer planned to elope with him, then disappeared on the night they were supposed to meet and is presumed dead (M#9-p.82). Buys the Sawyer House after Owen Sawyer dies (M#9-p.94). He used to call Dorothy "Dot" (M#9-p.112). Played center field on local baseball team forty years ago (M#9-p.118).

**PATRICIA BUNTING:**
Stout woman with iron-gray hair piled high on her head; the beauty pageant coordinator (#15-p.117).

**RABBI DORMAN:**
The Stevensons' rabbi (#96-p.10). Gives Abby and Anna their Bat

Mitzvah lessons (#96-p.11). Office is friendly and interesting and full of surprises; rabbi likes plants and both windows in his office are full of them; he is always "rescuing" stray plants (#96-p.10).

**REVEREND DOWNEY:**
Pastor at First Methodist Church; leads Amelia Freeman's funeral service (#93-p.87).

**REGINALD FOWLER:**
Very rich, very flashy developer who has "sold off Stoneybrook tree by tree," building strip malls and office buildings (M#24-p.7). Wants to build office complex where Ambrose's Sawmill stands (M#24-p.8). Arrogant (M#24-p.25). Had tried unsuccessfully to strong arm Lawrenceville into accepting one of his proposals; was accused of bribing officials (M#24-p.76). Born on January second, in Stoneybrook; was named John Wolfer until he changed his name (M#24-p.79). His mother died the day after the twins were born and his father died seven years later (M#24-p.98). Used to live in small, rustic cabin in Miller's Park (M#24-p.98). The Stoneybrook Town Council votes down his proposal (M#24-p.143).

**MR. GEIGER:**
Built all the lookalike houses in Pikes' neighborhood (#16-p.34).

**MR. HERRIOT:**
President of Mrs. Goode's Cookware (M#21-p.140).

**JANE KELLOGG:**
President of the Stoneybrook Historical Society; writes letter to *Stoneybrook News* in support of the BSC's fight against Reginald Fowler's development plans (M#24-p.38).

**MARTY NISSON:**
College intern, in charge of the Battle of the Bakers (M#21-p.21). A pretty nice guy; tall, with wavy black hair and wire-rimmed glasses—cute, but way too old for Claudia; seems ultra-organized (M#21-p.28). Rigs contest to help his girlfriend, Julie Liu (M#21-p.131).

**MRS. BETH STANLEY:**
Eliza Stanley's mother; just lost her job; oldest daughter Jennifer has run away, is living with her brother in New Hope (SecS-pp.4,10). Maiden name is Ray (SecS-pp.14). Family is reunited (SecS-p.26).

**SAMUEL WOLF:**
Reginald Fowler's twin; lives in Lawrenceville; was born on January 2nd (M#24-p.97); his mother died the day after the twins were born and his father died seven years later (M#24-p.98). Used to live in small, rustic cabin in Miller's Park (M#24-p.98). Arrested for vandalism that he caused in order to derail his brother's plans (M#24-p.139).

## FROM THE PAST:

**JULIA BERKMAN:**
Went to SMS twenty-eight years ago but didn't graduate (M#22-p.102). Transferred to a school for the performing arts (M#22-p.107).

# ● Other BSC People ●

**JACK R. BROWN:**
SMS civics teacher who died in Halloween Dance stampede twenty-eight years ago, on October 30th (M#22-p.84). Wore black-framed eyeglasses; looked serious (M#22-p.87).

**SIMON CLOCK:**
Devon Thomas's best friend, whose marriage to Christina Thomas is arranged (M#19-p.76).

**THEODORE ELLWAY:**
Died November 1943; was a big shot in Stoneybrook, made a fortune building houses, died a rich man; once owned land that the library stands upon; didn't leave his children much, wanted them to go their own way (M#13-p.103).

**DAVID FOLLMAN:**
Sergeant Johnson's childhood best friend; a reporter who investigated the secret society at Dark Woods Country Club and died in a mysterious car accident soon afterwards (M#23-pp.47-48). Ovaltine was his favorite drink (M#23-p.134). Had pieced together account of Secret Society and left it for Sgt. Johnson, with one last note (M#23-p.135).

**HERBERT FRANKS:**
Went to SMS twenty-eight years ago but didn't graduate (M#22-p.102).

**HENRY GORDON:**
Union soldier, the object of Christina Thomas's true affections; they planned to elope, but he was shipped out to PA (M#19-p.76) and killed in battle (M#19-p.78).

**ABIGAIL GRAHAM:**
Relative of Kennedy Graham's; used to live at 94 High Street (M#3-p.85).

**KENNEDY GRAHAM:**
Used to live at 94 High Street, before the Craines (M#3-p.85); is really lonely until he finds a cat and takes it in; the cat is named Tinker; after it dies, KG is never the same again (M#3-pp.86-88).

**PAUL HANCOCK:**
Sophie wrote about him in diary that Mal found in trunk that was in Stacey's attic (#29-pp.47,59); was Sophie's boyfriend in 1894 (#29-p.59).

**CASSIE HAYES:**
Henrietta Hayes's late daughter; a pretty teenaged girl with long brown hair and large brown eyes (#80-p.72). Died at eighteen, victim of a hit-and-run driver (#80-p.91).

**OLD MAN HICKORY:**
Real name: James Hickman (M#5-p.43). Club must visit his headstone at midnight (#17-p.92); James Hickman was mean, old recluse, richest and stingiest man in town; was found dead in mansion; nephew erected great headstone against uncle's wishes; gravestone is said to be haunted (#17-p.98); some people say he died of meanness (M#5-p.43). Sophie's mother's father (#29-p.61); allows people to think that his son-in-law is a gold-digging thief, even though he isn't (#29-p.124).

**SUSAN HSIA:**
Went to SMS twenty-eight years ago but didn't graduate (M#22-p.102); her family moved to Sioux Falls, South Dakota (M#22-p.107).

**STEVEN LEVY:**
Went to SMS twenty-eight years ago but didn't graduate (M#22-p.102).

**JARED MULLRAY:**
In 1810, the owners of the Schafers' farmhouse, the Mullrays, who owned a home past the Smythe property and a small farm called Wood Acres (Dawn's house), fell deeply in debt to banker Mathias Bradford. Old Man Mullray and family moved to Peacham, VT, except for thirty-year-old son Jared, who wasn't right in the head and who mysteriously disappeared. Legend has it that Jared's ghost still haunts Wood Acres in search of trinkets and things he could sell to pay back Mr. Bradford (#9-pp.88-91). In a ghost story, Dawn invents a fiancée for Jared, named Priscilla Gatlin (SS#10-p.97).

**OWEN SAWYER:**
Former resident of Sawyer House (the haunted mansion) (M#9-p.56). Didn't want his daughter, Dorothy, to marry Will Blackburn (M#9-p.62), so she planned to elope. He is devastated once she's gone and dies sixth months after she disappeared, on December 8, 1935 (M#9-p.83).

**SOPHIE:**
Twelve-year-old girl whose diary, dated 1894, Mal finds at the bottom of trunk from Stacey's attic (#29-p.47); had crush on Paul Hancock (#29-p.59); mother gives birth to a baby, Edgar, and then dies two days later (#29-p.61); father, Jared, had been unfairly accused of stealing a portrait of her mother. Old Man Hickory (her grandfather) said he was a gold digger, stopped giving

them money; her last entry says that she and her father's spirits may be uneasy and left to remain in the house, possibly haunting it (#29-pp.61-63).

**CHRISTINA THOMAS:**
Born September 7, 1845; date of death unknown. Daughter of Rachel and John Thomas (both d. 1861) of Squirelot. Disappeared 1863 (M#19-p.32) with her fortune (M#19-p.54). After her parents died, she found that she couldn't do anything with her inheritance; Devon planned to force her to marry his best friend, Simon Clock. For her part, Christina was in love with Henry Gordon, a Union soldier; they planned to elope, but he was shipped out to Pennsylvania (M#19-p.76) and killed before she got there (M#19-p.78). Looks so much like Kristy it's spooky (M#19-p.134).

**DEVON AND EDWARD THOMAS:**
Christina Thomas's younger brothers (M#19-p.40). Devon had son, Devon II, who had son, Devon III, and so on; Edward had three children, Scott, Mary, and Ellen (M#19-p.58). Devon was furious after Christina ran away; stated publicly that he was glad he was rid of her (M#19-p.78). Edward's kids donate Squirelot to be arboretum (M#19-p.108).

**DEVON THOMAS IV:**
Not really interested in family history since his contracting business got so big (M#19-p.74). Lives in California (M#19-p.139).

**JOHN AND RACHEL THOMAS:**
Died together in 1861 in freak carriage accident (M#19-p.39).

**MARK WHIPPLE:**
Went to SMS twenty-eight years ago but didn't graduate (M#22-p.102).

# PLACES

•

# TOWNS AND STREETS

•

## STONEYBROOK IN GENERAL:

Zip code: 06800. In Connecticut, closest big city is Stamford; capital, Hartford, is ninety minutes away. Borders Long Island Sound (map—SS#4-p.6). New York City is an hour or so away, by train (#69-p.3). Train from Stoneybrook arrives in Grand Central Station in NY (#76-p.45). Has one local newspaper, a radio station, a downtown area. Stoneybrook is part urban, part country, outskirts are rural (#65-p.33). Founded in 1791 (M#5-pp.40-41). Entire town was built many years ago over ancient burial grounds (#35-p.57). There was a huge storm there when older BSC members were in first grade that closed school and left the town without electricity or phone for two days (#26-p.79). Stoneybrook mail is postmarked in Stamford (#80-pp.34,49). People from Stoneybrook are called "Stoneybrookites" (M#15-p.6). Local government includes mayor (#57-p.109) and town council (M#24-p.8).

## STONEYBROOK STREET NAMES:

**ACORN PLACE:**
One of those twisting roads over by Burnt Hill Road, where the Cheplins live (#94-p.29).

**BERTRAND DRIVE:**
Where Granny and Pop-Pop live (SS#2-p.173).

**BIRCH STREET:**
Street listed in "Crimewatch" (#25-pp.22).

**BISSELL LANE:**
In Watson's neighborhood (#10-pp.39, 56).

**BRADFORD COURT:**
Where Kristy and Mary Anne used to live; Claudia lives there (58) (#1-p.7). Perkinses live in Kristy's old house; Hobarts live in Mary Anne's old house (59) (#32-p.7). The Newtons live on Bradford Court, too (#59-p.42). Lined by sycamore trees that have red and gold leaves in autumn (#78-p.7).

**BURNT HILL ROAD:**
Where Dawn/Mary Anne (177) (#4-p.35) and the Prezziosos live (#4-p.58). Logan lives there, too (689).

**CHESTNUT STREET:**
The Barrett/DeWitts move into 48 (SS#12-p.55).

**CHERRY VALLEY ROAD:**
Where the Sobaks live (#19-p.19).

**DODDS LANE:**
Street listed in "Crimewatch" (#25-p.22).

**EDGERSTOUNE DRIVE:**
In Brewers' neighborhood (#10-pp.39, 56), where Bart lives (SS#2-p.153).

**ELM STREET:**
Intersects Bradford where Community Center bus drops Myriah off (#10-p.61). Where Stacey currently lives (89) (SS#5-p.101). Wilders live there as well (477) (#49-p.28).

**FAWCETT AVENUE:**
Where Stacey used to live (#1-p.29); where Ramseys now live (612) (SS#2-p.37).

**GREEN HOUSE DRIVE:**
In Brewers' neighborhood (#10-pp.39, 56).

**HASLET AVENUE:**
In Brewers' neighborhood (#10-pp.39, 56).

**HIGH STREET:**
Near Slate Street (#5-p.135). Where the Craines live (94) (M#3-p.85).

**KIMBALL STREET:**
Johanssens live here (#1-p.137).

**LOCUST AVENUE:**
Near the Wilders' house on Elm Street (#49-p.28).

**MORGAN STREET:**
Where Henrietta Hayes lives; intersects Burnt Hill Road at 80 (#80-pp.50, 56).

**MCLELLAND ROAD:**
Where Brewers (1210) and Kilbournes live (SS#2-p.15). Where the Delaneys used to live and the Kormans now live (#46-p.21). Also where the Stevensons (1206) and Mrs. Porter (1208) live.

**OBER ROAD:**
In Brewers' neighborhood (#10-pp.39, 56).

**OLD STONEY POINT HOLLOW:**
Where Peterson's Nurseries is located (SecS-p.20).

**QUENTIN COURT:**
A few streets from Stacey's old house; the McKeevers live there (#1-p.55).

**REILLY LANE:**
The Rodowskys live here; near Brunos' house (#10-p.47). Hoyts lived there (35) (M#10-p.49).

**ROCKVILLE COURT:**
Where Alan Gray lives (#2-p.131).

**ROSEDALE ROAD:**
Where the Marshalls live (#1-p.101). Kristy has baby-sat unnamed party here (#2-p.133). Stacey's mom looks at house at 4221 (#28-p.86).

**SLATE STREET:**
Where Pikes (134) live (#5-p.21).

**SPRING STREET:**
Where Mason and Company is (#5-p.45).

**TAYLOR STREET:**
Where Mr. Spier grew up and lived until several months before Mary Anne was born (#5-p.112).

## TOWNS SURROUNDING STONEYBROOK:

**CHATHAM:**
Hour north of Stoneybrook (#4-p.116); location of Lewiston Gymnasium (#4-p.122).

**GREENPOINT ISLAND:**
Island off the coast of Stoneybrook, in Long Island Sound (map—SS#4-p.6).

**GREENVALE:**
Historic town about thirty miles from Stoneybrook. The main street is fixed up as it was two hundred years ago and there are quaint shops (#5-p.131). The Barrett-DeWitts go there on a "Mystery Tour"; they eat at The King's Arms and shop at Ye Olde Country Store (M#17-pp.48-49).

**HADDONFIELD:**
Where Pikes visit friends (#19-p.60).

**HOWARD TOWNSHIP:**
Stoneybrook's athletic arch-rivals, since the days when Sharon and Richard went to SMS (#84-p.3). Kids at HTMS go through the same School Spirit Month problems that SMS has (#84-p.92). Newspaper is the *Howard Township Sun* (#84-p.102).

**LEVITTOWN:**
Presumably in Connecticut since the Pikes go to an afternoon cocktail party there (#4-pp.88-89).

**LAWRENCEVILLE:**
North of Stoneybrook (#64-p.43); petting zoo with goats and Clydesdales in barn in Lawrenceville;

Barretts and DeWitts go there (#64-pp.44-46). Co-sponsors "Run For Your Money" fund-raiser with Stoneybrook; will give proceeds to a literacy program (#67-p.9).

**MERCER:**
Next place Phantom Caller strikes, closest town to Stoneybrook (#2-p.22). Where Terry Dutton's parents have a big animal farm, from which Logan borrows a horse-drawn buggy to convey Mary Anne home after her Sea City trip (SS#10-p.201). SMS track team faces the Mercer Junior High in competition (LB-p.5). Home of Quigley's Christmas Tree Nursery (#92-p.87).

**NEW HOPE:**
A short trip away from Stoneybrook; their All Stars play the Krashers; sisters and brothers of New Hope team sell lemonade and hot dogs (M#7-pp.124-125). Where Phantom Caller first strikes (#2-p.22).

**NINE O'CLOCK ISLAND:**
Island off the coast of Stoneybrook, in Long Island Sound, where Dawn and Claudia are marooned (map—SS#4-p.6).

**QUEENSTOWN:**
Where Aunt Cecillia moved after her husband's death, before she moved in with the Ramseys (SS#4-p.64).

**REDFIELD:**
Three miles away; the Krashers play the Redfield Raiders (M#9-p.4).

**SHERIDAN:**
Where Charlotte Johanssen bought Barbie Doll and dollhouse for two dollars at yard sale (#13-p.92).

**STAMFORD:**

Where Mrs. Brewer works (#1-p.16); closest city to Stoneybrook (#19-p.10). Where Mr. Ramsey works, where Jessi takes ballet (#16-p.7).

## OTHER TOWNS AND CITIES IN THE NORTHEAST U.S.:

**BOSTON, MA:**

Spiers and Schafers take vacation there during Jeff's visit to East Coast (#64-from p.77); if leave Stoneybrook at five A.M., can be in Boston by lunchtime (#64-p.78). Dawn, Jeff, and Mom go on whale watch on ferryboat called Queen of Nantucket; whales feed at Jeffrey's Ledge and gather at Stellwagen Bank (#64-pp.95, 98).

**DAVIS PARK, NY:**

See *Beyond Stoneybrook.*

**HAMMOND BEACH, CT.:**

Town a couple of hours from Stoneybrook, in a remote corner of CT, where the Thomases go (with Claudia) to see Charlie and Sam play in regional baseball play-offs (CB-pp.128-129); main street is Hammond Main, which runs through town; there are some tourist shops along Main, but it also has grocery stores, an old-fashioned Woolworth's, and a hardware store; there are several motels in town, mostly two stories high and made of cedar, although a couple were made of cement and painted bright tropical colors; a lot of the motels have tennis courts and pools (CB-p.135). The Thomases stay at the Sea Rose, which has neither tennis court nor swimming pool (CB-pp.136-137). Beach is on the ocean (CB-p.136) and is narrow and rocky (CB-p.138); there's a QuiK MarKet off the boardwalk (CB-p.139).

**HARTFORD, CT.:**

Where TV show *Uncle Dandy's Star Machine* is filmed (#49-pp.96-97). Capital of Connecticut.

**LAWRENCEVILLE, NJ:**

Where Toby is from (#8-p.113).

**NEW YORK, NY:**

See *Beyond Stoneybrook.*

**PINE ISLAND, ME:**

See *Beyond Stoneybrook.*

**OAKLEY, NJ:**

Where Jessi and family used to live (#14-p.35).

**OCEAN RIDGE, NY:**

Town on Fire Island, near Davis Park (#76-p.64).

**SEA CITY, NJ:**

Beach Pikes go to on vacation (#8-p.10). Plastic palm trees on main drag (#8-p.32). On a little piece of land that curls into ocean like a dog's tail (#8-p.103). See *Beyond Stoneybrook.*

**SMITHTOWN:**

Restored colonial village not too far from Sea City (#8-p.76).

# IN THE STONEYBROOK AREA

•

## COMMUNITY BUILDINGS/ ORGANIZATIONS:

**AMBROSE'S SAWMILL:**
Located in Miller's Park; Historical Society has spent much time raising money to preserve it, but developer wants to tear it down to make way for an office complex (M#24-p.8). Town council designates it an official historic landmark, which means nobody can ever change it (M#24-p.143).

**ARBORETUM:**
On the outskirts of Stoneybrook (M#19-p.36). A tree-lined, semicircular driveway leads to a gigantic, three-story brick house with huge windows trimmed in white; front entrance is formal looking, with broad steps leading to a small porch with an arched roof and wide white columns on either side. An old-fashioned greenhouse is built onto the left wing (M#19-p.45). Big wrought-iron gate leads to house and grounds (M#19-p.127). The curator is Mrs. Goldsmith (M#19-p.46), who leaves at 6 P.M. (M#19-

p.128). Greenhouse is approached through an empty living room; upstairs is closed off; greenhouse is full of plants, on shelves, on the floor, and climbing up trellises (M#19-pp.47-48). Arboretum is on the brink of closing (M#19-p.48); BSC decides to help out (M#19-from p.50). Long brick wall was covered with vines (M#19-p.103); Jessi and Dawn unearth plaque that says that the arboretum is Squirelot, given by Edward Thomas's children in memory of their grandparents and aunt (M#19-p.108). Mrs. VanderBellen decides not to buy land (M#19-p.117) then donates some money after all (M#19-143).

**BOAT DOCK:**
Where Community Center's boats are docked, in Stoneybrook, on Long Island Sound (SS#4-p.43).

**CEMETERY:**
As yet unnamed; beautiful and peaceful; where Old Hickory is buried (M#5-p.45). Main path winds through it, shaded by beautiful big trees; flowers have been

planted near many of the headstones (M#5-p.48). Mimi is buried there, in a grave covered by a small bouquet of wildflowers and yellow and white blossoms, with a simple headstone with a picture of a crane etched into it; the headstone reads: "Yamamoto," with "Mimi" underneath (M#5-pp.49-50).

## CHURCH:

On Elm Street; a small stone church, where Mrs. Woods' Beginning Students piano recital is held in common room (#83-p.131).

## DAY CARE CENTER:

For kids whose parents work; David Michael used to go there (#48-p.37); programs for babies, toddlers, preschoolers, and an after-school program for kids up to ten; Kristy volunteers there (#48-p.37); rocks Joy to sleep (#48-p.60). Center is big, rooms for all programs plus a small gym, an arts-and-crafts room, a kitchen, a nurse's office, and a playground outside; center is less busy until three o'clock (#48-p.53); Mrs. Hall is director, Randy Walker teaches toddlers, Marcia and Sandy care for the infants (#48-pp.54, 57, 59).

## FIRST CONGREGATIONAL CHURCH:

Where Claudia's cousin Lynn is christened (#97-p.138).

## FIRST METHODIST CHURCH:

Where Amelia Freeman's funeral is held (#93-p.53). Reverend Downey is pastor (#93-p.87).

## THE GREENBROOK CLUB:

Formerly the Dark Woods Country Club (M#23-p.20); closed twenty years ago and is being restarted with new owner (M#23-p.22), named Nikki Stanton-Cha (M#23-p.25). Will be open to anyone in the community, with low membership fees (M#23-p.27). Within biking distance of Mary Anne's house (M#23-p.22). Winding drive leads to imposing main building, which is built of stone and overlooks the open, rolling golf course; there are tennis courts to the right of the building, and an outdoor pool (drained for winter) lies to the right of the courts; the area is carefully landscaped, with shrubs and trees and formal garden areas complete with fountains and benches (M#23-p.24). Garden maze is old-fashioned, made of high hedges (M#23-p.38). There is a small pagodalike building near the tennis courts, as well as a maintenance shed located behind the main building (M#23-p.39). Also, there will be new changing rooms by the pool and a golf clubhouse (M#23-p.120). Bomb shelter is in center of maze (M#23-pp.129, 133). Main building's interior has large hall, dining room, cozy sitting room, fireplaces (M#23-p.25). Wine cellar is in dank, dim basement, accessible by stairs just inside the kitchen door (M#23-p.96). One room will house Greenbrook Kids Club, with Ping-Pong tables, as well as place for karate lessons (M#23.p.141). Dark Woods Country Club used to be incredibly exclusive, discriminatory (M#23-p.23). Forced to close because of lawsuits (M#23-p.2).

**THE HOUSING COUNCIL:**
Charity for the homeless, which gets prize after Stoneybrook wins the "Run For Your Money" contest (#67-p.112).

**THE HUMANE SOCIETY:**
Brings animals from pound over to Stoneybrook Manor each week for residents to play with (M#3-p.153).

**OLD FAIRGROUNDS:**
At the edge of Stoneybrook; the site of the Arts Fund Carnival (#90-p.77).

**STONEYBROOK ANIMAL SHELTER:**
Where Mary Anne gets Tigger (#10-p.128).

**STONEYBROOK ARTS CENTER:**
Claudia and Ashley attend class, work in different media (#12-p.21); portfolios are stored on shelves lining back wall of room (#12-p.23).

**STONEYBROOK BUSINESS BUREAU:**
H. Joseph Seger is member (SM#2-p.92). Members have hexagonal stickers on cars—blue is last year's, orange is this year's (SM#2-p.105).

Located in an old white house with red trim, in the middle of Stoneybrook, that has been turned into an office building; just to the right of the front hall is a room where the secretary sits behind a desk; the BSC members investigate Mr. Seger there (SM#2-pp.106-107).

**STONEYBROOK CHAMBER OF COMMERCE:**
Co-sponsors "Run For Your Money" fund-raiser with Lawrenceville, pledges winnings to an organization for the homeless (#67-p.9).

**STONEYBROOK CIVIC CENTER:**
Wonderful theater where Jessi's production of *Swan Lake* is put on (#27-p.24). Its productions are reviewed by NYC papers (#27-p.24).

**STONEYBROOK COMMUNITY CENTER:**
Has three pools in the community pool complex: Olympic-sized pool, a wading pool, and a diving pool, all outdoors (#55-p.30). Ramseys join the Community Center, Jessi takes synchronized swimming class there, Ms. Cox is teacher (#55-pp.34-35). Where Mrs. Braddock works with deaf adults (#16-p.90). Hosts Spring Dance (#63-p.8). Has Ping-Pong in game room; crafts fair sometimes out front (#76-p.12). Hosts Stoneybrook Day Camp, where Jessi and Mal work as counselors (#76-p.55). Has basketball court (#76-p.55) and an art room (#76-p.62). Offers swim-

ming and boating classes, since it is located near the Long Island Sound (SS#4-p.7).

**STONEYBROOK GENERAL HOSPITAL:**
On Rosedale Road (CL-p.3). Dr. Johanssen is doctor there (#2-p.77); where Mary Anne takes Jenny Prezzioso in an ambulance (#4-p.124). Intensive care unit on fourth floor (#37-p.47); no rules about visitors except for intensive care (#19-p.49). Mimi dies during night in the hospital (#26-p.63). Stacey's mom goes here after she collapses from pneumonia (#58-p.44). Mrs. Towne is taken here after she breaks her ankle; is put in room 211, a semi-private room where visiting hours are from three to four-thirty in the afternoon and from seven until eight-thirty at night (#66-p.53). Peaches has her baby here (#97-p.30). Maternity ward is on the fourth floor (#97-p.30). Kristy stays here after having her appendix out (CL-p.3).

**STONEYBROOK HISTORICAL SOCIETY:**
Needs money to renovate old sawmill (M#5-p.69). Heritage Day celebration is held in Miller's Park (M#5-p.99). Has big plans for site of Ambrose's Sawmill (M#24-p.29). President is Jane Kellogg (M#24-p.38).

**STONEYBROOK MANOR:**
Nursing home within walking distance from Claud's house, a rela-

tively new building, one story with lots of windows; plants and flowers along the front walkways, where people can sit outside and enjoy the sun (#35-p.116; M#3-p.150). Lobby is small and crowded; a threadbare streak has been worn into the floor by shoes and canes and wheelchairs; place is run-down (#92-p.60) Walking distance from Pikes' house (#92-p.80). Where Ronald Hennessey died (#35-p.131). Has fifty-five residents, including Mal's Uncle Joe (#69-p.70). Residents are allowed to invite family or friends to eat with them, as long as they reserve space ahead of time (M#3-p.152). The BSC puts together Thanksgiving baskets for the residents (#69-from p.96); many kids go over for carnival party (#69-p.111). Thermostat is kept turned up because residents get cold easily (#69-p.110). The Humane Society brings animals from the pound every week for residents to play with (M#3-p.153). Holds First Annual Christmas Boutique; Mrs. Krounauer is in charge (#92-p.39).

**STONEYBROOK MUSEUM:**
Recently opened; exhibits about science, history, and art; no major artists but some work by lesser-known artists (M#11-p.6). Hosts Don Newman Retrospective (M#11-p.6). Mr. Snipes is curator (M#11-p.63); Ms. Hobbes is his secretary (M#11-p.64). Coins are stolen from a display case (M#11). Museum's floors are wood; there is no big

echo-y hall and no fancy paintings in gold frames. It is just a comfortable big building with white walls and a lot of windows (M#11-p.22). Main hall has large directory that tells about displays; African mask that hangs near a display of drums (M#11-p.21). The Discovery Room has giant robot display on recycling, an area devoted to teaching kids what it feels like to live with different disabilities, and an electronic quiz board (M#11-p.24). People move to the Science Room from the Discovery Room by way of a dark "mole tunnel" (M#11-p.24). In The Science Room, a skeleton greets you; there is also a collection of fossils, shark jaws, dinosaur bones, and birds' nests laid out so that kids can pick them up and hold them; there is also a Van de Graaff generator (M#11-p.25), a climb-in kaleidoscope, and a video phone (M#11-p.26). The Music Center includes a player piano, an electric organ, and lots of smaller instruments, as well as a video screen that shows the sound waves of your voice (see M#11-p.26). A yellow hallway leads from the Music Center to the art exhibits (M#11-p.26). The Egypt Room has mummy cases, glass cases full of ancient jewelry, and hieroglyphics on the walls (M#11-p.121).

**STONEYBROOK POLICE STATION:**
Downtown (M#10-p.40). After being caught with counterfeit bill, Stacey is walked past the desk where the receptionist sits, down a hall, and into a small, stuffy interrogation room with a long table in the middle and chairs around it (M#10-p.41). Interview Room Four looks like interrogation room and is down the hall, past a water cooler and police officers working on typewriters (M#16-p.107).

**STONEYBROOK PUBLIC LIBRARY:**
Modern building, eight years old (#17-p.55); Mrs. Kishi is head librarian (#7-p.6). Mrs. Pike is a member of the trustee board (#5-p.3). On Sundays, only open for a few hours (M#11-p.72). Donald is student librarian (#91-p.47). Mrs. Kishi's office is behind the main checkout desk; black metal file cabinets stand side by side against the back wall, containing such files as clippings on local authors (#80-p.89). Library has a book sale every year (M#4-p.44). Will hold crafts fair to raise funds (M#6-p.48). Old newspapers are kept in a closet (M#10-p.71); clerks bring old magazines to person who requests them (M#10-p.75). Sometimes there are special programs in the children's room, like birdhouse making (M#10-p.83). Holds Readathon (M#13-from p.26). Built on Ellway land, on condition that if it's ever destroyed, the land reverts back to the family (M#13-pp.54-55). Has *Stoneybrook News* on microfilm as far back as 1820 (M#9-p.39). Trustee meetings are held in the Prescott Room (#5-p.3). Catalogue has been computerized (SM#2-

p.90). Children's Room is on the first floor, really two rooms. Has lots of windows, some tables, colorful posters on the walls, a puppet theater, and a big Raggedy Ann doll to lie on or snuggle with; the main room is where the fiction is shelved, where the office is, and where the main desk is. A smaller room holds the card catalog and the nonfiction (M#13-p.23). Room is fairly new (Mary Anne remembers it upstairs) (M#13-p.24). *For shelving information, see* #91-pp.47-48.

### STONEYBROOK TOWN HALL:
Near the library; a big old building made of gray stone; Mary Anne thinks it looks like a prison; has a heavy front door, a musty smell, and a quiet, hushed feeling; has an information desk and places to do research (M#5-p.86).

### STONEYBROOK UNIVERSITY:
Janine is taking classes there (#1-pp.26-27).

### STRIP MALL:
On Atlantic Avenue; where Sound Ideas is located (LB-p.49).

### TRAIN STATION:
While waiting to go to NYC, kids cluster under sign that reads NEW YORK BOUND TRAINS (M#8-p.29). Located exactly four minutes from Kristy's house (SS#6-p.17).

### WOMAN'S CLUB:
Mrs. Sobak belongs (#19-p.30).

### WSBK:
Television station; Mimi Snowdon is news reporter (#84-p.102).

### WSTO:
Radio station; 1313 on your dial (#5-p.42). Phone number is 555-WSTO (#85-p.34). Station manager is Mr. Bullock (#85-p.35). In front of the building there is a small reception area, with a young man (Max) at the desk, wearing a telephone headset (#85-p.40). From reception area there is a long hallway off of which are three doors, marked *Studio 1, Studio 2,* and *Studio 3.* The walls are thickly carpeted, as are the floors. At the end of the hallway are a conference room and the station manager's office (#85-p.41). Outside Studio 1 is red light that says On Air; inside is a room crammed with electronic equipment in every corner; shelves of tapes and CDs line the walls; one wall is glass, to see the engineer's booth (#85-pp.44-45). Was around at the end of WWII (#85-p.99). In dire financial straits, which are eased by contribution by Rhoda Hewitt (#85-pp.131-132).

## PARKS AND PLAYGROUNDS:

### BRENNER FIELD:
Where Mary Anne is supposed to pick up catnapped Tigger (#25-p.81). Pikes and other kids play kickball there (#73-p.82); must have a field with bases. Has a big

rock at its edge (#73-p.85). By the rock there is a small hedge where Peter, a fluffy brown-and-white rabbit, lives (#78-p.62). Is the home of the Official BSC Fourth of July Pre-Fireworks Festival (#98-p.124).

### CARLE PLAYGROUND:
Where Sudsy's Carnival is held (#24-p.51); a lot of tables and benches; Pikes go there (#24-p.53).

### MILLER'S PARK:
Beautiful park on the outskirts of town, with a stream and weeping willows lining the stream's banks; where Ambrose's Sawmill is located (M#24-p.8). During spring, violets bloom and animals inhabit the park (M#24-p.29). Heritage Day celebrations held there (M#5-p.99). Used to be called Carter Park (M#24-p.79). Town council rejects Reginald Fowler's development proposal and designates the park an official historic landmark, which means nobody can ever develop or change it (M#24-p.143).

## SCHOOLS:

### KELSEY MIDDLE SCHOOL:
In Brewers' area (#6-p.42); Watson and Elizabeth pay a fee to keep Kristy at SMS instead of going here. Not big enough to have an orchestra, which is why Anna and Abby go instead to SMS (#89-p.76). Some kids who go there are: Al Hall, Amanda Kerner, Jacqueline Vecchio, and Karl Schmauder (#89-p.77).

### KENDALLWOOD FARM:
Horseback riding school (English style) on the outskirts of Stoney-brook, an easy bike ride from the Pike house (#54-p.12); Lauren Kendall is riding instructor who gives Beginning Equitation classes to Mal (#54-p.39). Horses: Isabelle, a chestnut mare (#45-p.39); Pax, Mal's favorite, who's an Arabian, nearly all white with dappling of gray and delicate nostrils; Mal rides Pax in horse show and wins sixth place (#54-pp.43, 139); Gremlin, old, bucks Mal (#54-pp.70-71); Samson, gentle gelding, huge (#54-p.77); Twilight (#54-p.91); Duke (#54-p.102); Peaches (#54-p.138).

### THE MILLER SCHOOL:
Private school just outside of Stoneybrook; Dana and Adam Cheplin go to school there (#94-p.32).

### PAULSON SCHOOL:
Local all-boys school (#71-p.121).

### STONEYBROOK ACADEMY:
Linny, Hannie, and Karen attend (#11-p.36). Kristy's mom and Watson are members of the parents' council; Andrew and Emily Michelle will attend the Academy some day (#29-p.69).

## STONEYBROOK DAY SCHOOL:

Private school the Kilbournes (#11-p.36), Bart Taylor attend (#20-p.25); Kormans attend (#46-p.21), as does Druscilla Porter (#89-p.35). Not big enough to have an orchestra, which is why Anna and Abby go instead to SMS (#89-p.76). Everyone must wear uniforms to school (ShS-p.14). Shannon's uniform is blue plaid jumper over a white short-sleeved blouse (#11-p.9). On the last day of school, everyone gets to wear whatever they want (ShS-p.94). Sometimes, if a student is interested in a subject, SDS will even let a student set up a unit for credit; SDS looks like a college campus; it's made up of four red brick buildings set around a grass courtyard and connected to each other and to the administration office in the front by covered walkways. The offices are in an old house (the land for the school was donated by a woman who used to live in the house), and the gym and the track and playing fields are in the back (ShS-p.15). Most of Shannon's friends really like school (ShS-p.15). Dr. Patek is headmistress; her office is in the administration house, but she makes a point of being around the buildings when classes are starting for the day (ShS-p.16).

## STONEYBROOK ELEMENTARY SCHOOL:

David Michael and many clients' kids attend (#6-p.42); short distance from Kristy's old house (school is around corner from barbershop) (#6-p.109); across town from Kristy's new house (#20-p.93); within walking distance, but a long walk (#20-p.105). Krushers practice there Tuesdays and Saturdays (#20-p.51). Sponsors Pens Across America, national pen pal program for second- to fifth-graders; kids write to students at elementary school on Zuni reservation in New Mexico (#44-p.3). There are woods behind the school, with a little clearing (M#4-pp.104-105). Playground has a slide, jungle gym, picnic tables (M#7-p.8). Mrs. Randolph is school nurse (MAB-p.100). Principal is Ms. Reynolds (#44-pp.61-62).

## STONEYBROOK HIGH SCHOOL:

Charlie and Sam attend (#1-p.9); only high school in town (#6-p.42). The SHS store sells school supplies and memorabilia (#30-p.72); Charlie gets charm at store that was replica of SHS ring for Mary Anne to give to Dawn's mom for birthday present (#30-p.72). Has costume shop that supplies wigs for the Sixth Grade Follies (#75-p.98). Battle of the Bakers take place in SHS gym (M#21-p.29).

## STONEYBROOK MIDDLE SCHOOL:

(*See also* **SMS: Faculty and Students**)

**Location:** 358 Elm Street (M#25-p.86). Easy walk from Bradford Court (#10-p.13).

**Lunch:** Friday lunch always sloppy joes, red Jell-O with canned fruit, a dinky cup of coleslaw, milk, and a Fudgesicle (#1-p.37); hot lunches cost under a dollar (#14-p.16). Each grade has different lunch period (#46-p.95). Students aren't allowed to leave school premises for lunch (#51-p.54).

**Events:** Eighth grade class play was *Mary Poppins* (#53-p.34). Dawn organizes campaign to bring a recycling center to SMS, gives announcements over PA, passes out questionnaires (#57-p.93); Mrs. Gonzalez asks Dawn to co-chair with her (#57-p.143). Students plan and run an auction to raise money for new computers (#62-p.26). Sixth Grade Follies is held every spring (#75-p.5). Eighth Grade puts on Awards Night with funny awards (M#4-p.18). Winter Carnival Fund pays for trip to Leicester Lodge (SS#3-p.7). April is School Spirit Month (#84-p.7), which Dawn protests, helps end, and then revives on a voluntary basis (see #84, up to p.130). School system art and music programs are threatened by budget cuts (#90-p.23) but are saved by fund-raiser (#90-p.125).

**Setup:** School is not air-conditioned (#1-p.1). Girls and boys are usually separated by a movable wall in gym (#59-p.35). Old equipment shed is burned to the ground (#74-p.76). Faculty Lounge is down mysterious hallway that leads to the auditorium, with no window on the door, just a sign that says "Faculty Lounge" (M#10-p.127). The BSC members like to gather by fence at back of parking lot (M#13-pp.111-113). Fire at school is caused by electrical problems; one classroom is put out of commission (M#13-p.136). Basement has dusty old storage room, packed with ancient records (M#22-p.103); BSC members go down to basement through door marked "No Entry," which leads to dimly lit stairwell and heavy door (M#22-p.105). Sixth grade wing is at the opposite end of the building from the eighth grade wing; library is near the eighth grade wing (#14-p.12). In far corner of yard is a fat, comforting sycamore tree (#14-p.66). SMS has new job board (M#23-p.8). Room 116 is a biology classroom (M#25-p.86). Tree is planted in Mal's name on the walk near the side door (SecS-p.20).

**Publications:** *The Literary Voice* is its literary magazine (#2-p.10). The *SMS Express* is weekly (#71-p.49) SMS newspaper (*See* Magazines/Newspapers).

**Rules/Regulations:** Not allowed to put things up in lockers with tape (#12-p.77). Only one student at a time from each class is allowed to use bathroom (#51-p.55).

**Class Politics/School Gov't:** Pete Black wins as eighth grade class president (#53-p.146); Mal wins as sixth grade secretary (#53-p.145). Class president must have a B average (#53-p.9).

**Student Population:** 382, give or take a few (SS#3-p.22). Only about six black kids in school; Jessi is only black student in sixth grade (#14-p.13).

**Sports:** Basketball team is the SMS Chargers (#70-p.43). Baseball team is doing well (#84-p.2). Longtime sports arch-rival is Howard Township Middle School (#84-p.3).

**Classes:** Short Takes classes are ones in which all the students in every grade take the same special class (M#13-p.1).

**Trips:** Entire school (except Logan) goes to Leicester Lodge (SS#3-p.2). School has made deal with tour group (World Tours—#98-p.48) for discount tour packages for fifty students or more (#98-p.41). First such trip is to Hawaii (SS#13-p.1).

**Summer School:** Claudia must attend; SMS bunches all of the grades into the high school (SS#10-p.22).

**Parents Group:** Is PTO (Parent Teacher Organization) (#84-p.8).

**Homeroom:** Homerooms are divided alphabetically (M#22-p.2). Stacey's homeroom has seven rows of seats (M#22-p.1) and a loudspeaker over the door (M#22-p.5).

**Badd Boyz:** Junior version of a high school gang, at SMS (LB-p.11); led by T-Jam (LB-p.12). Other black-leather-jacket-wearing members include Skin, Ice Box, Butcher Boy, Jackhammer, and G-man (LB-p.33). Among other things, they cut school, make snotty comments in the hallway, shoplift, and steal things from lockers (LB-from p.58). Picked up by police after attempting to steal from Sound Ideas; are suspended from school and ordered by juvenile court to pay a fine (LB-pp.123-125).

**Mischief Knights:** An alias of Cary Retlin, although Stacey can't prove it (M#22-p.140). May be more than one person—nobody knows; might just be Cary. Mischief Knights pull a variety of pranks; switch books in students' lockers (M#22-p.44); steal Mrs. Simon's grade book (M#22-p.46); write messages on blackboards; put rubber chickens and toilet plungers in people's lockers; fill art cabinet with hundreds of marbles (M#22-p.47). TP the entire school and soap the windows of every car left in the teacher's parking lot; make a fake announcement over the loudspeaker about a surprise assembly with Michael Jordan (M#22-p.51). Set the school's speaker system to play the national anthem at top speed (M#25-p.9). Pranks are always signed with red "MK" (M#25-p.10).

**Memory Garden:** In courtyard at SMS; planted in honor of Amelia Freeman (#93-p.140). Barbara Hirsch and Amelia's brother Josh speak at the groundbreaking ceremonies (#93-p.146).

**Lockers:** Are numbered (#93-p.12), and combinations go right—twice to the left—right (#93-p.14).

**Stoneybrook University:** Where Janine takes classes (#1-p.27).

# ● Places ●

## RESTAURANTS:

### ARGO:
Coffee shop in downtown Stoneybrook, where Stacey and Robert go on first date (#70-p.82). Has old-fashioned booths with carefully taped-up vinyl seats and old, yellowing travel photos on the walls; it's kind of funky, but the food is great (#95-p.56).

### BURGER TOWN:
Where Shawna likes to go; hates school lunches (#57-p.78). Has double-sized burgers on Fridays; Fiesta Burger has guacamole, salsa, melted cheese, chili, and chips on the side; the Regrub ("Burger" backwards) has all of the fillings inside of the hamburger (#83-pp.72-73).

### CABBAGES AND KINGS:
Where Dawn and her mom go for wonderful tofu dinners (#23-p.10); is Dawn's favorite restaurant; she goes there with Lewis, Logan, and Mary Anne (#50-p.147).

### CHEZ MAURICE:
Fanciest restaurant in area; restaurant Claud's parents go to (#7-p.44); Dawn, Mary Anne, and Mr. Spier give Sharon's surprise birthday party here (#30-pp.74-75); Mr. Spier and Sharon take their wedding guests out to Chez Maurice after wedding, had private room (#30-p.145). Offers raffle ticket prize of a dinner for two for opening day of recycling center at SMS (#57-p.107). Mari Drabek's father is the dessert chef (M#21-p.30).

### CHICKEN WINGS:
Take-out chicken place; their ad: Speedy delivery, and service with a fryer (SS#7-p.183).

### DONUT EXPRESS:
A great place to pig out; also serves bagels (M#14-p.24).

### GOOD HUMOR MAN:
Sells fancy old-fashioned ice-cream Parlour Cone, costs a dollar (#9-p.77).

### GOOD-TIME CHARLEY'S:
Serves hamburgers, quiche, and salads, but is famous for its dessert; where Jessi and fifteen others go after *Coppèlia* (#16-p.144).

### KING KONE'S:
A store in Stoneybrook that specializes in ice cream cakes made to order (CB-p.39).

### PIETRO'S:
New Italian restaurant on the way to the mall (#93-p.40).

### PIZZA EXPRESS:
In downtown Stoneybrook, a block down from the bank (M#16-p.79). Shannon calls them to deliver pizza (#11-p.95); not always as express as they advertise (#26-p.75). Mr. Morton is owner, contributes whole wheat pizza to big sleepover (#44-pp.111-112). Doesn't deliver after eleven but does stay open until one (#78-p.97). Has a juke box (#78-p.98). Customers sit at tables and in booths; waiters and waitresses serve (#83-p.42). Has bulletin boards with events posted (M#21-p.9).

### PIZZA-TO-GO:
Closes around midnight (#78-p.97).

**RENWICK'S:**
Downtown (#12-p.65); also serves breakfast (#59-p.120). Not a fancy restaurant, but it's a fun place to eat; there are red leather booths to sit at, and the waitresses are nice (M#10-p.27). All the children's items are named after characters from Peanuts (the Lucy special = cheeseburger and fries, the Linus special = a grilled cheese sandwich) (M#10-p.28). Mary Anne and Logan go there for a candlelit dinner (LB-p.109).

**ROSEBUD CAFE:**
Downtown (#58-pp.24-25); serves more than just ice cream (#58-p.25); has real soda fountain (#58-p.31); serves salads, burgers, carrot juice; has tall stools at counter (#58-p.32). Where Arnold twins, Rodowsky boys, and Braddock kids treat BSC members for being great babysitters (#63-p.131). Logan works there (#67-p.113); is youngest busboy (SS#10-p.156); calls it "the Road Spud" (SS#10-p.130). Old-fashioned decor; hostess seats customers (#71-p.94). Rosebud Special is turkey sandwich with secret dressing (M#10-p.98). Has a neon sign outside (M#16-p.43). Another busboy is Terry Dutton (SS#10-p.201), as well as Geraldine Breslin and Carlos (SM#1-p.109).

**THELMA'S CAFE:**
A coffee house in downtown Stoneybrook, near the bank; has turquoise leather booths and waiters and waitresses who wear turquoise-and-white uniforms (M#16-pp.81-82). Where Kristy goes for a secret breakfast with her father (KB-p.126).

**TOFU EXPRESS:**
Sharon and Dawn's take-out place of choice (#86-p.78).

**TOKYO HOUSE:**
Offers take-out service; doesn't open until noon (SS#7-p.184).

**UNCLE ED'S:**
Chinese restaurant where Mary Anne and father go for take-out food (#60-p.51). Across the street from Bellair's (#87-p.73).

## STORES AND BUSINESSES:

**ACE REPAIR CO.:**
Sends man to fix Newtons' washing machine (#14-p.133).

**BABY AND COMPANY:**
In downtown Stoneybrook, on Essex Street (M#24-p.114); Claudia's favorite baby store, completely devoted to baby clothes and furniture; Karen Brewer once called it a baby museum (#78-p.48). Claudia goes there with Peaches; each crib has a girl's name on it (#78-p.49).

**BELLAIR'S DEPARTMENT STORE:**
In downtown Stoneybrook (#58-p.27); near the Merry-Go-Round (#21-p.119). Stacey's mom works there (#76-p.5); has her own office (M#10-p.29). Mr. Spier has charge card there (#10-p.85); owner is judge of beauty pageant (#15-p.124); sponsoring a Beautiful Child contest that Claire wants to

join (#15-p.143); girls' clothing on second floor reachable by escalator (#21-p.117). Escalators a big thing in Stoneybrook (M#10-p.30). Donates toys for Kids Club's toy drive at SES to give to Children's Ward at hospital (#48-p.5). Accessories department is on second floor (KB-p.23). Mrs. Hemphill works there (M#10-p.31). Jessi becomes department store Santa; Mrs. Javorsky is her supervisor (SS#12-p.34). Ms. Blair is personnel director; Mrs. Grossman is in charge of Kid Center (#87-p.47). Kid Center has play areas, with mesh-enclosed pit of plastic balls, padded tunnels, a train-and-truck corner, dollhouses, arts-and-crafts tables, and a few trikes and wagons (#87-p.48); Stacey gets a job in the Kid Center (#87-p.49). Mrs. Ballmer works in Accessories (#87-p.72). The "bad girls" shoplift there (#87-p.77). Stacey likes to shop in the Young Sophisticate section (SS#13-p.14).

**BLOOMER'S:**
Nursery on Spring Street, donates small plants for booth at Green Fair (#57-p.84).

**BOHREN'S MOVERS:**
On shirt Kristy wears (#7-p.50). Move Peaches and Russ into their new house (#78-p.133).

**BOSTWICKS:**
Huge clothing store near Stamford; Jenny is part of photo shoot for fall catalogue (#73-p.129).

**CONNECTICUT BANK AND TRUST:**
Name on pencil over Kristy's ear (#21-p.58).

**THE CONNECTICUT YANKEE GIFT SHOP:**
Sells candles (#78-p.81).

**COST-CLUB:**
Discount shopping market; Watson's a member (#69-p.98).

**DAVIS DIAPERS:**
Cloth diaper service; owned by Neil Davis, who sponsors the Krushers for a time (#89-p.45) until he becomes too pushy and Kristy says the deal is off (#89-p.131). Logo (#89-p.84).

**DEWDROP HAIR CARE:**
Sponsor of beauty pageant, "Hair products for today's youth" (#15-p.123).

**DOCTOR HERKIE'S FLEA TONIC:**
What Mary Anne considers buying for Tigger (#25-p.11).

**DT DEVELOPERS:**
Wants to buy the arboretum land and raze the arboretum (M#19-p.69). Owned by Dan and Ted (M#19-p.139).

**ELLWAY'S KENNEL:**
Run by Rosa Ellway; a place where people can leave dogs and cats while they're on vacation (M#13-p.107).

**EMBASSY THEATER:**
Revival house; Stacey goes there to see *Mary Poppins* (#6-p.96).

**FAST 'N' EASY CLEANING SERVICE:**
In Stamford, sent two women to help with party at the Pikes (#14-p.76).

**FITNESS FAZE HEALTH CLUB:**
Health club that the Hills have joined (#88-p.6).

**FUN CITY AMUSEMENT PARK:**
Pike triplets go there as often as they can; their parents now let them

ride El Monstro, a roller coaster (#64-p.53).

**FUR 'N' FEATHERS:**
Pet store on Essex Street; Mary Anne sometimes buys toys for Tigger there (M#24-p.114).

**GLORIANA'S HOUSE OF HAIR:**
Destroyed Karen Brewer's hair once; should be called Gloriana's House of Horror (#60-p.32).

**GREETINGS:**
New card shop on Essex Street (M#24-pp.113-114).

**HURLEY'S GARAGE:**
Wrong number dialed by Dawn (#5-p.92).

**IN GOOD TASTE:**
Gourmet food store; tiny with a newly shingled roof. Giuseppe DeSalvio is the owner. The shop has tight little aisles; one wall is lined with gourmet mustards; another holds exotic foods like chocolate covered grasshoppers (#78-pp.77-78).

**JUGTOWN:**
A convenience store; Matt Braddock and Jake Kuhn go there all the time to buy baseball cards; run by a man and his uncle; bells ring when you open the door; Mary Anne, Claudia, and Kristy used to go there almost every day when they were little to buy candy; has changed owners since (M#4-p.109).

**KARBERGERS:**
Large department store in Hartford; Jenny Prezzioso lands an audition for an ad there (#73-p.71).

**KULLER'S GALLERY:**
Original art gallery in Stoneybrook (#12-p.46).

**LOVE BUNDLES:**
Adoption agency through which the Brewers found Emily Michelle; Claudia calls them on her own adoption quest (#33-pp.67-8). Has only been operating for five years; places Vietnamese children only (#33-p.68).

**MCBUZZ'S MAIL ORDER:**
Company from whom Betsy Sobak buys practical jokes (#19-p.34).

**MASON AND CO.:**
On Spring Street, where Mrs. Barrett applies for job (#5-p.45).

**THE MERRY-GO-ROUND:**
Store in downtown Stoneybrook where Claud got barrettes (#2-p.46); near Bellair's (#21-p.119); Mal buys two pairs of tiny stud earrings for herself and Jessi, in the shape of open books (#21-p.120). Betty works there, catches Stacey's counterfeit bill (M#10-p.33).

**METRO-WORKS:**
Firm where Mr. Pike finds new job (#39-p.127).

**MR. STORK'S DIAPERS:**
Diaper service; truck's bells play "Rock-a-Bye Baby" (#11-p.41).

**PEMBROKE'S PARTY STORE:**
In downtown Stoneybrook, almost as big as a supermarket, loaded with oddball stuff; Mary Anne, Jessi, and the Pike kids go there to buy wacky supplies for their video for Dawn (#68-p.74); Margo shoplifts a small ring with a troll on it (#68-p.76).

**PETERSON'S NURSERIES:**
A plant nursery in Stoneybrook; has much Christmassy stuff (SS#12-

p.167). Located at 17 Old Stoney Point Hollow in Stoneybrook; owned by Eleanor and Lucas Peterson; for Secret Santa present, Logan has them plant a tree in Mallory's honor on the grounds of SMS (SecS-p.20).

**PIERRE'S DRY CLEANERS:**
On Essex Street (M#24-p.113).

**POLLY'S FINE CANDY:**
Owned by Polly, about "a hundred years old," and by younger sister (#3-p.41). Famous all across Connecticut for delicious sweets and wonderful window displays; has red-and-white awning (#69-p.34). Has gingerbread house in its window (M#10-p.27), penny counter, and cuckoo clock (#3-p.43).

**QUIGLEY'S CHRISTMAS TREE NURSERY:**
In Mercer; where Pikes (and camera crew) go to pick out a tree (#92-p.87). Andy and Mrs. Quigley are owners (#92-p.90).

**ROCKAWAY AND SONS:**
Contractor for *Little Vampires* (M#15-p.59). Owned by John Rockaway; location is lot with piles of rubble, heavy machinery, and a big trailer where the offices are located; office is incredibly disorganized (M#15-from p.99).

**SEW FINE:**
Sewing store in downtown Stoneybrook, on Essex Street (M#24-p.114); Mary Anne and Karen's mom sometimes shop there (M#9-pp.131-132). Near the pet shop (M#9-p.136). Dorothy Sawyer works there (M#9-p.139).

**THE SHS STORE:**
Sells school supplies and memorabilia (#30-p.72); Charlie gets charm that was replica of SHS ring at store for Mary Anne to give to Dawn's mom for birthday present (#30-p.72).

**SOUND IDEAS:**
Record store owned by Bob Shull, a friend of Mr. Bruno's (LB-p.7). Located in strip mall on Atlantic Avenue (LB-p.49). Badd Boyz shoplift there (LB-p.78). Storage area is in the back, with floor-to-ceiling shelves full of cassettes, records, and CDs (LB-p.78).

**SPORTSTOWN:**
In Mercer; Stacey applies for a job in its toddler center (#87-p.39). Otto is manager; a warehouse full of pinball machines, video games, batting cages, and miniature golf; toddler center is large play area (#87-p.44).

**STONEYBROOK BANK:**
Facade has vines, flowers, words, marble pillars, and beautiful old revolving doors trimmed in brass (M#16-p.44).

**STONEYBROOK CINEMA:**
Offers two free tickets to movies as part of raffle offered during opening day of SMS's recycling center (#57-p.107). Jessi and Becca buy Aunt Cecilia a coupon book for a "wedding present" (#82-p.95). Where Bart and Kristy go to see *Missing Pieces* (#95-p.36).

**STONEYBROOK JEWELER:**
Where Stacey sees a great diamond ring (M#1-p.6).

**STONEYBROOK MEGAVIDEO:**
Sharon's video store of choice (#86-p.63).

**STONEYBROOK THRIFT SHOP:**
Where Jessi searches for frames to decorate for Stoneybrook Manner Christmas Boutique (#92-p.43).

**SUDSY'S CARNIVAL:**
Where club takes the kids on Mother's Day weekend as gift to clients (#24-p.44); at parking lot near Carle Playground (#24-p.51); twenty-one kids go (#24-p.68).

**SYLPHIDE MODELS:**
Modeling agency; address is close to downtown Stoneybrook; Stacey applies for a job there (#87-p.41).

**TED'S TOOLS:**
Owned by Theodore Ellway III; an old-fashioned hardware store in downtown Stoneybrook with a million different things on the shelves; the aisles are narrow, so customers have to squeeze by each other; Dotty Ellway works behind the cash register, seems to know all of the customers by name (M#13-pp.105-106). On Main Street (M#24-p.114); Mary Anne, Mal, and Logan go there to investigate green paint clue in vandalism mystery (M#24-p.114).

**THOMPSON, THOMPSON, AND ABRAMS:**
Law firm Mr. Spier once worked for (#5-p.111).

**TILE CORP.:**
Where Mr. Sobak works (#19-p.31).

**TIP-TOP TALENT AGENCY:**
Where Mrs. Prezzioso takes Andrea for an audition; in another town on this side of Stamford, in ultra-modern building with glass doors (#73-p.53). Joan is agent (#73-p.55); Libby is receptionist (#73-p.57).

**TOY CITY:**
Where Myriah wins shopping spree as first runner-up prize in beauty pageant (#15-p.124).

**WORLD TOURS:**
Tour group offering discount packages to SMS (#98-p.48).

**WSTO:**
1313, radio station (#5-p.42); has Fifties Festival (#31-p.99). Claudia wins contest, and DJ's radio show, *For Kids Only* (#85-p.48).

**ZINGY'S:**
Downtown store that sells punk clothing (#30-p.133); salespeople there are bizarre (#47-p.124); Stacey buys outfit there to wear to fancy dinner honoring her father in NYC (#58-p.30).

**ZUZU'S PETALS:**
Flower stand just off Main Street in Stoneybrook (#78-p.80), on Essex Street (M#24-p.113).


**IN THE WASHINGTON MALL:**

Mall is the biggest one around, five levels, half hour from Stoneybrook (#3-p.70). White marble fountain (M#14-p.65) in the center of the mall shoots a spray of pink water high into the air (M#1-p.25). Hosts many Project Work Short Takes students (M#14-pp.22-23). Has been dealing with shoplifting problem (M#14). Security buttons in every store

(M#14-p.57). Succession of managers: Ms. Richards, Mr. Morton, Mr. Buford (M#14-p.145). Home of four movie theaters, a videogame arcade, a petting zoo, an exhibit area, and a little French cafe on the top level (#3-pp.70-71).

### ANTOINETTE'S SHOE TREE:
Store where Pikes get shoes (#21-p.4).

### ARTIST'S EXCHANGE:
Great art supply store; Claudia works there for Project Work class (M#14-p.25).

### BABY LOOK AT YOU NOW!:
Baby store where Becca and Jessi look for a baby tux for Squirt (#82-p.66).

### BOOKCENTER:
Really nice bookstore, with a huge children's section; Mal works there for Project Work class (M#14-p.27). Ms. Munro is manager (M#14-p.37). Children's area has pillows to lounge on, small, child-sized chairs, and stuffed animals scattered around; also has small "stage" area for puppet shows, storytellers, and story hour (M#14-p.43). Mal reads for story hour (M#14-p.44). Formerly Books by the Dozen, where Amelia Moody has author signing (SS#11-p.155).

### CASA GRANDE:
Mal and Jessi love the Super Burrito here (#47-p.121). Mary Anne and her dad go there after her makeover (#60-p.49); Spiers take Jeff there because Mexican food is his favorite (#64-p.54). Logan works

there for Project Work class (M#14-p.27). Benny is the cook (M#14-p.143).

### THE CHEESE OUTLET:
Mr. Williams is the manager (M#14-p.81) before he quits to run the day care center (M#14-p.145).

### CINEMA WORLD (CINEPLEX):
Recently renovated, really cool (#64-p.54). Spiers take Jeff there to see *The Mutant from Outer Space* (#64-p.55). On fourth floor of mall; Jessi works there for Project Work class (M#14-pp.27-28). Has program called Movie Club, a sort of frequent flyer program for films, where kids can have half price birthday parties in the afternoon (M#14-pp.109-110).

### CRITTERS:
Pet store, upstairs; Mary Anne works there for Project Work class (M#14-p.27). Robert likes to look at the iguanas there (#99-p.65).

### DANCER'S WORLD:
Special dance store in the mall; has ballet slippers, tap shoes, and sequined leotards in its window (MAB-p.63).

### DAY CARE CENTER:
BSC idea (M#14-p.61). Claudia plans design: red stripe in toddler's area, which will have table and small chairs for coloring, a trunk for dress-up clothes, and an area for block constructions; babies will go in blue corner with high chairs and cribs; biggest area will be for school-age children, colored green, with two play tables, a small library of books, an arts-and-crafts area, and a "quiet" corner (M#14-pp.87-

88). Has mats and a back room (M#14-p.133). Mr. Williams will be full-time director (M#14-p.145).

**THE DOLLAR STORE:**
Sells hairbrushes, among other things (M#14-p.86).

**DONUT DELITE:**
Donut shop (#21-p.132).

**EXERCISE SHOPPE:**
Donates mats for the day care center (M#14-p.133).

**FRIENDLY'S:**
Restaurant/ice cream place (M#1-p.29).

**THE HOMESTORE:**
Sells cribs and high chairs, among other things (M#14-p.87).

**J.C. PENNEY'S:**
Department store "anchor" (#82-p.67).

**JUST DESSERTS:**
Serves ice cream; Alan Gray works there for Project Work class (M#14-p.28).

**LAURA ASHLEY:**
Women's clothing store (#30-p.73).

**LEAR'S:**
The main department store in the mall (M#14-p.81). Home of North Pole Village (#92-p.69).

**MACY'S:**
Department store "anchor" (#82-p.67).

**NORTH POLE VILLAGE:**
Where Santa greets kids every year; it appears every Thanksgiving inside Lear's department store. When you step past Wonderland Gate, you follow a winding pathway through a snowy fantasyland. Christmas carols play over the speakers as you walk past hardworking puppet elves, clanking machinery, gingerbread houses, a reindeer stable, a post office stuffed with mail, and tinkling bells. Over it all is a blue-black rooftop with glittering stars (#92-pp.69-70).

**POWER RECORDS:**
Cokie Mason donates unlimited shopping spree there for school auction (#62-p.93).

**RITA'S BRIDAL SHOPPE:**
Full of gowns and veils (#30-p.102).

**STEVEN E:**
One of Washington Mall's fanciest clothing boutiques, very expensive (#60-p.42); Mary Anne's dad pays for half of the clothes she buys there (#60-p.51).

**SOUNDSCAPES:**
A record store (M#14-p.130).

**STUFF 'N NONSENSE:**
Where Mal and Jessi buy earrings (#47-p.123).

**TORTILLA QUEEN:**
A place to stop for nachos; really cute guy usually works there— along with a greasy-looking bald guy; window looks onto main mall thoroughfare (M#1-p.26).

**TOWN AND COUNTRY JEWELRY:**
Place where Stacey envies diamond rings (M#1-p.29).

**TOY TOWN:**
Carries regular toys and educational toys (M#14-p.24). Stacey works there for Project Work class (M#14-p.25). Run by April Frenning (M#14-p.29). Has display tables with toys for kids to play with (M#14-p.33).

## PLACES TO STAY/LIVE:

### THE GEORGE WASHINGTON:
On the outskirts of Stoneybrook; Stacey always wonders whether George Washington actually slept there; has a pool shielded by a row of bushes (M#15-p.84).

### KOZY KABINS:
On the outskirts of Stoneybrook; not that many people there (M#15-p.84).

### THE SLEEPY BEAR:
On the outskirts of Stoneybrook, busier than Kozy Kabins (M#15-p.84).

### STRATHMOORE INN:
Where Mr. Spier and Dawn's mom go for the night after their wedding, a small honeymoon (#30-p.106).

### WATERFORD GARDENS:
Apartment complex into which Nannie moves (for a little while); built in 1905 and newly remodeled, each apartment has a small living room, a kitchen, one bedroom and a bath; sliding doors lead out onto a courtyard; even in the middle of the winter, it looks like an English countryside garden with little rock paths and white trellises and wrought iron benches scattered throughout (#81-p.112).

# NEAR STONEYBROOK

•

## HAUNTED MANSIONS:

### THE SAWYER HOUSE:
On Sawyer Road (M#9-p.56). A huge, imposing brick house standing high on a hillside (M#9-p.27). Caretaker's cottage lies below (M#9-p.29). House is well-kept (M#9-p.38). A big, fancy kitchen adjoins the dining room (M#9-p.36). There's also a pool room (M#9-p.37). Kitchen has row of servants' bells (M#9-p.50). Parlor is very large, formal (M#9-p.51). Upstairs is long hallway with several described bedrooms (M#9-pp.54-56). Dorothy's room is pretty (M#9-p.59). Servants' quarters and attic are on the uppermost floor (M#9-p.65). House makes creaky settling noises at night (M#9-pp.91-95). William Blackburn bought the house after Owen Sawyer died (M#9-p.94).

## SCHOOLS:

### MERCER HIGH:
Plays basketball against Stoneybrook High (#16-p.80).

### SHERIDAN MIDDLE SCHOOL:
Basketball team is the Sheridan Wildcats, plays SMS Chargers (#70-p.43).

### SCHOOL FOR THE DEAF (IN STAMFORD):
Matt Braddock's school; an old, old building that looks like it might have once been a mansion; pretty much run like any other school—kids go to art lessons and gym classes. They eat in a cafeteria. Classes are quite small—usually not more than eight students, and the children start at very young age. Matt is in one of two second-grade classes; the children are all seven years old, but they have different degrees of hearing difficulty. Some are profoundly deaf, like Matt. A few have some hearing. Several of them can speak. They all know how to sign, but those with speech are also given speech lessons. A few are learning lip-reading (#16-pp.109-111). Big light flashes next to door when bell rings (#16-p.115).

### STAMFORD ALTERNATIVE ACADEMY (*IN STAMFORD*):

Special school that Claudia is sent to for half of fourth grade (CB-p.91). Illustrated brochure (CB-p.92). Classes are very small and students are put into classes according to their level; emphasis is on working at your own pace, not competition/comparison (CB-p.94). Corla Magnusson is the academic coordinator (CB-p.97). Main class is called Core Group (CB-p.100). Open Area is part of library, for quiet study/recreation (CB-pp.100-102). Have conferences instead of yelling in class (CB-p.112).

# THINGS

•

# KID GROUPS

•

## CAMPS:

### CAMP BSC:
BSC summer camp for charges; runs from nine A.M. to five-thirty P.M.; kids can choose half-day or full-day program; in Mary Anne and Dawn's yard, for two weeks over the summer (#86-pp.28-29). Twenty-two kids sign up (#86-p.33).

### CAMP MOHAWK:
Where BSC (Logan, but not Shannon) goes for two weeks (SS#2).

### CAMP TOPNOTCH:
Girls' sports camp that Kristy attends at age ten (KB-p.87). It specializes in softball, swimming, and tennis (KB-p.84). Kristy is in the Bluejay's Nest cabin—Patti La-Pointe is her counselor (KB-p.88). Two softball cabins/rivals are the Robins and the Bluejays; Robins wear red T-shirts or hats, while Bluejays wear blue (KB-p.90). Camp director is Mrs. Spence (KB-p.91). Victoria Martin is softball coach (KB-p.93).

## STONEYBROOK DAY CAMP:
At Stoneybrook Community Center; older counselors are fourteen to sixteen years old; junior counselors (like Jessi and Mal) are twelve or thirteen (#76-p.55).

## KID BUSINESSES:

### ABJ INCORPORATED:
Odd-job service Adam, Byron, and Jordan start after Mr. Pike loses his job (#39-p.88).

### THE BABY-SITTERS AGENCY:
The club's brief but formidable competition (#3-p.7); Janet Gates was a temporary member of BSC, thirteen, who dropped out of the Baby-sitters Agency and joined BSC to purposely try to give it a bad reputation; Janet was in eighth grade when BSC members were in seventh grade (#3-pp.85, 95, 106).

### KIDZ KITCHEN:
Kids' restaurant created during the Battle of the Bakers for day care participants; kitchen is in the SES

faculty lounge (M#21-p.80). Specialty is "bug salad," made from half a canned pear, with carrot curls for legs and raisins for eyes (M#21-p.120).

### MAKE-OVERS INC.:
Liz and Michelle's new business after Baby-sitters Agency fails (#3-p.164).

## MUSICAL GROUPS:

### ALL THE CHILDREN OF THE WORLD (ALL THE CHILDREN):
Band name for clients' kids (#56-p.65); gives performance at Newtons (#56-p.109, 130); kids wear uniform of jeans and red shirts (#56-p.107); plays and sings songs from *Fiddler on the Roof* (#56-pp.114-116); first song is "Anatevka;" also plays "Tradition" (#56-pp.114-116); asks for donations for T-shirt money; concert is a huge success (#56-p.133).

## TEAMS:

### BART'S BASHERS:
Bart Taylor's softball team, seven-to nine-year-olds (#20-p.76), older than most Krushers (M#4-p.27); twenty-one boys in T-shirts and matching red caps, four girls in snazzy cheerleader uniforms (#20-p.115). Lose in World Series to Krushers, 8-7 (#38-p.120). Players include Jerry, on third base; Joey, a tall boy on first base; and Chris, a shy-looking boy in the outfield (M#7-p.86). Also, Patty (M#9-p.4) in center field (M#9-p.8). Also, Dave and Robbie, who aren't on the Krashers (M#9-p.9). Kids are from Bart's neighborhood, a different neighborhood than most Krushers (M#9-p.78).

### CHALLENGERS:
High-end summer little league (SS#10-p.72).

### KRASHERS:
The Stoneybrook All-Star softball team, made up of some of the older members of the Krushers and the Bashers (M#7-p.48). Claire Pike protests the younger kids' exclusion (M#7-p.49). Bart and Kristy are co-coaches (M#7-p.79). Players include Jackie, Haley, Matt, Nicky from Krushers; Jerry, Joey, Chris from Bashers (M#7-p.86,120). Also Patty (M#9-p.4), a good hitter (M#9-p.78). Claire made junior assistant equipment manager, with Suzi and Patsy (M#7-p.87). Team wins against New Hope All-Stars (M#7-from p.124). Plays against the Redfield Raiders (M#9-p.2) and wins (M#9-p.9), the first game with a new lineup (M#9-p.4). Joey and Buddy make great double plays (M#9-p.78).

### KRISTY'S KRUSHERS:
Softball team organized by Kristy, named by Jackie Rodowsky (#20-p.56). For kids who are too young

or otherwise not ready for Little League (M#15-p.2). Has permission to practice at Stoneybrook Elementary on Tuesdays and Saturdays (#20-p.51). When Kristy is on SMS softball team, Stacey and Claudia try to coach (#74-p.28). Very briefly become Davis Diapers in return for new equipment, which Kristy returns after Mr. Davis proves to be too overbearing (#89-from p.45). Abby is made assistant coach (#89-p.132).

*Cheerleaders:* Vanessa Pike and Haley Braddock appointed cheerleaders with Charlotte Johanssen as helper (#20-p.84); then becomes leader because she made up all the cheers; they wear identical outfits (#20-p.100) and Charlotte joins in cheering (#20-p.127). Cheerleader outfits consist of denim skirts, sneakers, white knee socks, and Krushers Ts (#20-p.99).

*Games/Stats:* Jackie breaks principal's window with a home run (#20-p.87). They play a good game but lose to Bashers 16-11 (#20-p.131). Beat Bashers in World Series, 8-7 (#38-p.120). Balls are rarely hit past the pitcher's mound, almost never into the outfield, which makes the outfield a rather lonely place to be (M#19-p.6). Win another World Series (#89-p.138).

*Rules/Rituals:* Refreshments sold to raise money for caps, Jackie's idea (#20-p.85). Post-game Basher/

Krusher ritual is to line up to give high fives to the other team and to cheer "Two-four-six-eight! Who do we appreciate!" (M#16-p.41); Kristy calls it the Basher cheer (#89-p.44). Watson sometimes umps (#89-p.42).

*Players:* Twenty kids on team, average age 5.8 (#20-p.50); their names and softball abilities include (#20-p.50):
**Buddy Barrett** substitutes for Matt on second base for the Krashers (M#9-p.7)
**Suzi Barrett**
**Matt Braddock,** one of the best players (#53-p.99), uses sign language
**Andrew Brewer** just needs work
**Karen Brewer** just needs work; plays right field for Krashers (M#9-pp.7-8); is tired of playing in the outfield (M#19-p.5); Kristy will give her a chance at shortstop (M#19-p.10)
**Max Delaney** just needs work (has since moved away).
**Scott and Timmy Hsu** ask to join full-time and Kristy says yes (#95-p.18)
**Jacob Kuhn**
**Laurel Kuhn**
**Patsy Kuhn**
**Nina Marshall** probably just needs work
**Jamie Newton,** one of the youngest Krushers; tries hard, but is afraid of the ball (M#2-p.117)
**Hannie Papadakis** poor hitter
**Linny Papadakis** just needs work
**Claire Pike**

**Margo Pike**

**Nicky Pike** plays first base, with aid of lucky penny (M#7-p.120); pitches for Krashers (M#9-p.7)

**Gabbie Perkins** doesn't understand game yet

**Myriah Perkins** probably just needs work

**Jackie Rodowsky,** a walking disaster; shortstop or second base (M#7-p.86)

**David Michael Thomas,** a klutz; catches for the Krashers (M#9-p.7)

*Replacements:* When Kristy's in a crunch, she goes door-to-door in her neighborhood and come up with Kate Munson, Sheila Nofziger, P. Archibald "Moon" Pinckney, Kyle Abou-Sabh, Richard Owen, and Alexandra DeLonge (SS#10-p.74); they bomb in the championship against the Bashers (SS#10-p.120).

*Uniforms:* Their T-shirts are lettered in black except for Kristy's, lettered in red. Only Karen's is spelled "Crushers" (#20-p.80).

*Band:* Formed by Druscilla Porter (flute), with Moon Pinckney (drums), Sheila Nofziger (trumpet), and Scott Hsu (kazoo) (#89-p.119). First called Krusher Quartet, then the Diaper Double Duo (#89-p.123), then Druscilla and the Dynamos (#89-p.139).

**THE STARS:**
Jacob Kuhn's team in the Saturday soccer league (#79-p.59).

**OTHER:**

**THE BLUE RIBBON CLUB:**
Club that Stephen Stanton-Cha, Jenny Prezzioso, and Claire found after being excluded from the Slate Street Kids Club; members wear blue ribbons (M#23-p.109). Activities include tetherball, pogo stick, Nerf balls, Koosh balls, real badminton rackets, stilts, and a store-bought miniature golf course (M#23-p.111). Merges with SSKC to form *Slate Street Blue Ribbon Club* (M#23-p.117).

**HAPPY CHILD, INC.:**
Stamford organization that collects letters from kids to Santa and then finds people to write back (SecS-p.2).

**KIDS CAN DO ANYTHING CLUB (KIDS CLUB):**
At Stoneybrook Elementary, kids eight to ten volunteer in community (toy drive, food collection, pick up trash, etc.) (#48-p.2). Becca, Charlotte, Vanessa, Nicky, and Danielle Roberts are members; Mr. Katz and Ms. Simon are teacher-sponsors (#48-pp.8-9). Jessi volunteers there for month while Ms. Simon is away (#48-p.32). Meets in Room 164, where there's a window in the door (#80-p.26). Mallory works with them in planning a play (#80-from p.26).

**SA (SECRET AGENTS):**
Pike spy ring set up to keep eye on new neighbors (#13-p.56) with foreign accents (#13-p.59); Jordan is

Head Spy (#13-p.56) and members are awarded badges for completing missions (#13-p.61).

**SAVE THE PLANET CLASS:**
Taught by Dawn and Stacey from three-thirty to four-thirty at Stacey's once a week for six weeks (#57-pp.35-36, 39); thirteen members, all kids they baby-sit for (#57-p.38); kids organize Green Fair as a fund-raiser for SMS's recycling project (#57-pp.38, 131).

**THE SLATE STREET KIDS CLUB:**
"Country Club" that the Pike triplets put together in their yard (M#23-p.84); younger kids are excluded (M#23-p.87). Merges with Blue Rib- bon Club to form *Slate Street Blue Ribbon Club* (M#23-p.117).

**STUDENTS AGAINST DRUNK DRIVING (SADD):**
Organization that was started to ed- ucate teens about the dangers of driving under the influence of alco- hol, and to inform kids about the consequences they would face if they caused an accident (#93-p.71). After Amelia Freeman's death, Kristy and the other BSC members decide to start a Stoneybrook chap- ter (#93-p.95).

**SUMMER PLAY GROUP:**
Club's unique alternative to baby- sitting (#7-p.22).

# KID THINGS

●

*(NOTE: Things marked with an asterisk (*) are only available in Stoney-brook)*

**BOOKS:**

*Alice Anderson:* First book in Henrietta Hayes's series, in which a seventeen-year-old farm girl dreams of going to Hollywood (#80-p.7) **(*)**.

*Alice Anderson's Big Break:* The fourth Alice Anderson book, in which Alice becomes the nanny to the kids of a famous Hollywood director (#80-p.47) **(*)**.

*Alice Anderson's Greatest Challenge:* The fifth Alice Anderson book (#80-p.53) **(*)**.

*The Anderson Family Reunion:* New Alice Anderson book, which Mal inspires Henrietta Hayes to write (#80-p.129) **(*)**.

*Angelina Ballerina:* Book in Mal's Kid-Kit (M#3-p.81), by Helen Craig.

*Angus and the Ducks:* Book that Stacey reads to Henry Walker before he goes to sleep (#28-p.76); by Marjorie Flack.

*Animalia:* Taylor has it; Buddy says he read it when he was a baby (SS#12-p.197). By Graham Baese.

*Anna Karenina:* Book by Leo Tolstoy, from which Mary Anne quotes "happy families are all alike." She hasn't read it, but Janine has (#66-p.1).

*Anne of Green Gables:* By L.M. Montgomery; Mary Anne's favorite chapter book in first grade; she understands now that she identified with Anne because she didn't have a mother either (MAB-p.30).

*Babies in Space:* Book Rob Feldman reads, about scientists sending babies to other planets in rockets (#23-p.60).

*Baby Island:* Vanessa reads it on cruise (SS#1-p.107); one of Haley's favorite books (SS#4-p.2), by Carol Ryrie Brink.

*Backward Bunny:* Short book that Stacey reads to Adam Cheplin (#94-p.76).

*The Basics of Playwriting:* Book that Mallory consults while writing her play for the KCDAC (#80-p.53) **(*)**.

*Bea and Mr. Jones:* A picture book by Amy Schwartz about a kindergartner who swaps places with her father. Jessi's been saving for Squirt; puts it into her Kid-Kit (#82-p.9).

*The BFG:* Roald Dahl book that Stacey reads to Charlotte (#29-p.114).

*Black Beauty:* Jessi is reading this book by Anna Sewell for the thousandth time (M#1-p.20).

*Blueberries for Sal:* In Mary Anne's Kid-Kit; she reads it to Jenny Prezzioso; Dawn later brings it to the hospital (#4-pp.118, 125); by Robert McCloskey.

*Bone Chilling Ghost Stories:* Going-away present to Dawn from Mary Anne (#88-p.120) (*).

*The Borrowers:* Book by Mary Norton that Charlotte and Stacey have read together (#13-p.88).

*Bridge to Terebithia:* Banned book by Katherine Paterson, which Mary Anne *loved* (M#13-p.81).

*Brighty of the Grand Canyon:* Book by Marguerite Henry that Jessi and Mal have read, even though it's about a mule (#48-p.12).

*The Cat in the Hat:* Popular Dr. Seuss book that Mal reads during Story Hour at the BookCenter (M#14-p.49).

*The Catcher in the Rye:* By J.D. Salinger; Stacey thinks it's wonderful (SS#2-p.10). It is one example of Great Literature that Claudia actually likes; Mary Anne is reading it (#97-pp.81-82).

*The Cay:* by Theodore Taylor; Jeff likens his Island Adventure to its plot (SS#4-p.3).

*Charlie and the Chocolate Factory:* Book by Roald Dahl that Karen wants for Christmas (SecS-p.1).

*Charlotte's Web:* by E. B. White; one of Mary Anne's favorite books (M#4-p.92). Always a good bet to get Becca to sleep (M#8-p.61).

*The Christmas Day Kitten:* Cat book by James Herriot that Becca owns (#16-p.119).

*Christmas Tree Farm:* Book by Sandra Jordan, about a real-life family that goes to a Christmas tree farm and chops its own tree to bring home; Mal thinks it's the coolest book (#92-p.72).

*The Clue of the Tapping Heels:* One of Claudia's all-time favorite Nancy Drew books; she's read it about four times (M#16-p.52).

*The Clue of the Velvet Mask:* Nancy Drew mystery Claud has read (#22-p.42).

*The Cricket in Times Square:* Book by George Selden that Stacey inscribes and gives to Charlotte (#13-p.93).

*A Day in the Life of America:* Inspiration for *A Day in the Life of Stoneybrook.* Two hundred photographers took thousands of pictures during one twenty-four-hour period across America; the Pikes own a copy (M#16-p.36).

*A Day in the Life of Stoneybrook:* "Book" that the BSC and their clients put together for Dawn, consisting of photos taken over a day in Stoneybrook (M#16-from p.34) (*).

*Dear Mr. Henshaw:* Book by Beverly Cleary that Karen wants for Christmas (SecS-p.1).

*Deenie:* Burned banned book by Judy Blume (M#13-p.65).

*Dicey's Song:* Book by Cynthia Voigt that Mal reads (#21-p.68).

*Dr. Dredd's Wagon of Wonders:* Chapter book by Bill Brittain that scares Marilyn and Carolyn Arnold (#97-p.82).

*Dr. Dolittle:* Book by Hugh Lofting that Mal is reading (#14-p.5).

*Easy, Ivy, Overs:* Book of jump roping rhymes (#78-p.123).

*Emma:* Jane Austen novel that Kristy is reading for school (#74-p.120).

*Encyclopedia Brown:* Mystery series by Donald Sobol that Mal uses to help Buddy Barrett learn to read better (#29-p.116).

*The Enormous Crocodile:* Book by Roald Dahl that Wendy Loesser reads to the Barretts.

*Esio Trot:* By Roald Dahl; one of the cool books that Dawn and Mary Anne keep in Jeff's room for their cousin Amy (#87-p.53). Shannon carries it in her Kid-Kit (#89-p.53).

*A Fence Away from Freedom:* Book by Ellen Levine that Claudia reads about Japanese internment camps during World War II (SS#13-p.66).

*Fifty Simple Things Kids Can Do to Save the Earth:* Book by the Earth Works Group that Dawn uses for after-school ecology class she holds as part of her science project (#57-p.28).

*Find a Stranger, Say Goodbye:* Book by Lois Lowry; about a girl who finds her biological parents; Claud reads it when she begins her "great search" (#33-p.93).

*Freaky Friday:* Book by Mary Rodgers that Mal is reading and thinks is really funny (#14-p.5).

*Freckle Juice:* Book by Judy Blume that Taylor DeWitt loves (SS#12-p.196); is sure to instantly catch Greg Roberts' attention (#82-p.51). One of the cool books that Dawn and Mary Anne keep in Jeff's room for their cousin Amy (#87-p.53).

*Frog and Toad:* Jessi reads this book to Greg Roberts (#82-p.36); by Arnold Lobel.

*Frog and Toad Together:* By Arnold Lobel; Kristy reads it to Andrew and the Menders kids; it fuels Andrew's frog obsession (SM#1-p.67).

*From the Mixed Up Files of Mrs. Basil E. Frankweiler:* Newbery Award–winning book by E. L. Konigsburg that Claud is supposed to read for Mrs. Hall's class (#12-p.2).

*Georgie's Halloween:* By Robert Bright. Jessi reads this with Jamie Newton to help him overcome fear of Halloween (#17-p.63); Suzi reads it (with Stacey's help) aloud to Marnie, with many added sound effects (#66-p.93).

*Ghosts and Spooks, Chills and Thrills: Stories NOT to be Read After Dark:* Book Dawn reads (#9-p.10); contains "The Hand of the Witch" (#9-p.10), "Things Unseen" (#9-p.14), and "The Hunting of Weatherstaff Moor" (#9-p.29) (*).

*Ghosts: Fact and Fantasy:* Book that Dawn is reading (#31-p.46) (*).

*Ghosts I Have Known:* Book that Dawn is reading (M#5-p.30) (*).

*The Golden Key:* Book by George MacDonald that Mal is reading (SS#10-p.34).

*Good Money:* Book Stacey reads when she should be researching Thanksgiving (#91-p.49) (*).

*Goodnight Moon:* "Baby book" by Margaret Wise Brown that Mrs. Barrett reads to Marnie (#66-p.89). Jessi reads it to Squirt (#82-p.12).

*GOOPS and How to Be Them:* Book by G. Burgess that Mal wants to buy as reward to Buddy Barrett for his reading improvement (#29-p.144); about naughtiest kids around.

*Great Dog Tales:* Old book Dawn finds in secret passage (#9-p.64) **(*)**.

*Green Eggs and Ham:* Dr. Seuss classic that Kristy reads to kids (#6-p.78); Buddy, stumbling, reads it to Dawn (#29-p.37).

*The Grey King:* Book by Susan Cooper that Heather (in Dawn's cabin at Camp Mohawk) is reading (SS#2-p.136).

*Happy Birthday to You:* Dr. Seuss story that Stacey reads to Charlotte (#10-p.80).

*Harold and the Purple Crayon:* Book by Crockett Johnson that Claudia reads with Jamie Newton (#9-p.99). Marilyn and Carolyn Arnold request that Mary Anne read it to them (#97-p.81).

*Harriet the Spy:* Book by Louise Fitzhugh that Claudia has read; same thing happens to her when Stacey accidentally reads Claudia's personal diary instead of tutoring diary (#63-p.130); inspires Mallory into cruise-ship mischief (SS#1-p.30) as well as Leicester Lodge snooping (SS#3-p.92). Kristy wanted it to be her fourth grade play, so she could be Harriet (CB-p.104).

*Harry the Dirty Dog:* Book by Gene Zion and Margaret Bloy Graham that Suzi reads to Pow, thinking that he'll like it (#66-p.90).

*Harry's Cat's Pet Puppy:* Animal story by George Selden that Stacey reads to Charlotte (#3-p.39).

*The Haunting of Grade One:* Book that Stacey reads with Adam Cheplin (#94-p.59).

*A History of Stoneybrooke:* Tattered old book by Enos Cotterling and published by Tynedale Press in Stoneybrook in 1872 (#9-p.51) **(*)**.

*The Horse in Art:* A book of Claudia's (M#1-p.81) **(*)**.

*Horses of the World:* Book series that Jessi browses through in the library (M#10-p.84) **(*)**.

*Horton Hears a Who:* Dr. Seuss book that Mary Anne read in first grade (MAB-p.32).

*The House That Jack Built:* Traditional story that Margo recites for Little Miss Stoneybrook pageant (#15-p.77).

*I Hate English:* Claudia hears the author (Ellen Levine) interviewed on a radio show and thinks it's incredible (#85-p.54).

*Iggy's House:* Book by Judy Blume that Stacey takes to read with Charlotte when she tells her she's moving (#13-p.88).

*Impossible Charlie:* Jessi's favorite horse book (#14-p.39), by Doris Gates.

*The Indian in the Cupboard:* Book by Lynn Reid Banks that Stacey reads to the Kuhn girls (M#4-p.59).

*The Incredible Journey:* Book by Sheila Bunford that Mal's reading (#14-p.5).

*Jeff's Off-the-Wall, Krazy, Explode-Your-Sides Sense of Humor a.k.a. The Jeff Schafer Book of Funniest Jokes Ever Told, Volume One:* Joke book that Jeff is compiling (#98-pp.2, 58) (*).

*Jeremy Thatcher, Dragon Hatcher:* Cool Bruce Coville book that the Arnold twins are reading (#85-p.110).

*Julie of the Wolves:* Book by Jean Craighead George that Mary Anne loves, about a girl lost in the wilderness of Alaska (#72-p.12).

*Katie and the Sad Noise:* Book by Ruth Stiles Gannett that belonged to Charlotte Johanssen's mother; about a girl who finds (and frees) a mother dog caught in a trap (#29-p.114).

*Katy and the Big Snow:* Book by Virginia Lee Burton that Kristy reads to Karen before they're snowbound (SS#7-p.12).

*Kids Can Cook ... Naturally:* Book that Sunny gives to Dawn (#23-p.130)(*).

*"Kokolimalayas, the Bone Man":* Fantastic, scary story told by three seventh-graders on Claudia's WSTO show; story is Native American tale about a boy who defeats a monster made of bones by knowing that its heart is in its fingertip (#85-p.117).

*A Light in the Attic:* Burned banned book by Shel Silverstein (M#13-p.66).

*The Lightning Time:* Book by Gregory Maguire that reminds Mal of the Narnia Chronicles (#14-p.67).

*Little Women:* One of Dorothy Sawyer's favorite books (M#9-p.59); Mary Anne wrote Louisa May Alcott a fan letter (SS#11-p.151).

*Live from New York:* Book by Amelia Moody, Mal's favorite author, which Mal has her sign (SS#11-p.162) (*).

*The Lorax:* Environmentally themed Dr. Seuss book; Dawn gives a dramatic reading (SS#10-p.55). One of the cool books that Dawn and Mary Anne keep in Jeff's room for their cousin Amy (#87-p.53).

*The Lost Grandmother:* Book by Amelia Moody, Mal's favorite author (SS#11-p.149) (*).

*"The Lottery":* Shirley Jackson story with a surprise ending that Kristy likes a lot (#100-p.49).

*Lucy Berky and the Thanksgiving Turkey:* Funny book that Jessi takes out of the library, about a farm girl who befriends a wild turkey (#69-p.107).

*Make Way for Ducklings:* Book by Robert McCloskey that Claudia reads with Jamie Newton (#9-pp.99-100).

*Mandy Mandango Takes the Bull by the Horns:* Book by Amelia Moody, Mal's favorite author (SS#11-p.147) (*).

*Matilda:* Roald Dahl book that Jessi takes from Leicester Lodge library and gives to Pinky to read (SS#3-p.75).

*Martin and the Tooth Fairy:* Book that Adam Cheplin reads to Stacey (#94-p.84).

*The Mayor of Casterbridge:* Nannie's favorite book, by Thomas Hardy (SS#1-p.73).

*Millions of Cats:* Cat book by Wanda G'ag that Becca owns (#16-p.119).

*Misty of Chincoteague:* Horse book by Marguerite Henry that Jessi's read hundreds of times (M#8-p.63), or about eighteen times (SS#2-p.80).

*Molly's Pilgrim:* Book that Abby uses to research "real" Thanksgiving; it shows Jewish origins of festival (#91-p.49).

*A Morgan for Melinda:* Horse book by Doris Gates that Kristy reads to Charlotte to assuage her horse fears (SS#2-p.97). Mal's favorite horse book (#14-p.39).

*The Mozart Season:* Book by Virginia Euwer Woolf, which Anna has read twice (#89-p.104).

*Mr. Popper's Penguins:* Book by Richard and Florence Atwater that Charlotte and Claudia read (#25-p.68).

*Muggie Maggie:* Beverly Cleary book, which Charlotte takes out of Claudia's Kid-Kit (M#2-p.108).

*My Teacher Is an Alien:* Book by Bruce Coville that Jeff is reading; he thinks it's scary and funny (SS#12-p.75).

*The Mystery of the Ivory Charm:* A Nancy Drew mystery Claud has read (#17-p.52).

*Night Frights:* Spooky, creepy, gross, and super-popular series by Theodore "Ted" Garber, who is guest on Claudia's WSTO show (#85-p.115). Mr. Garber reads from *Night Frights Number Thirteen: Don't Get Out of Bed!* (#85-p.116) (*).

*Nitty Gritty Meatballs:* Book by Amelia Moody, Mal's favorite author (SS#11-p.145) (*).

*Number the Stars:* Book by Lois Lowry that Becca has read and recommends to Charlotte (#48-p.132).

*The Official Thomas Book of Records:* Compiles the "official statistics" of Stoneybrook kids; a Kristy Thomas Great Idea (#95-p.20) (*).

*The Owl and the Pussycat:* Edward Lear book that Stacey reads to Grace and Henry; Grace tries to recite the poem along with Stacey but keeps getting the words a little bit wrong (#28-p.75).

*Paddington Takes the Air:* In Stacey's Kid-Kit (#10-p.79); by Michael Bond.

*Pavlova:* Biography of ballet dancer Anna Pavlova, by Ellen Levine, which Jessi insists upon lending to Dawn (#98-p.38).

*Pinky Pye:* Cat book by Eleanor Estes that Becca owns (#16-p.119).

*Pippi Longstocking:* By Astrid Lindgren. Mary Anne reads it to the Pike kids (#4-p.100); Marilyn reads it to Mary Anne (#30-p.39).

*"Rainy Days and Froggy Nights":* Story written by Mallory (#14-p.10) (*).

*Rapunzel:* Mal finds a copy to read at the Craines' (M#3-p.42).

*Record Wreckers: The BSC Book of Kids' Wild, Wacko, Off-the-Wall Records:* Kristy's compilation of Stoneybrook kids' weird abilities; she wants to get it published (#95-p.120) (*).

*Sarah, Plain and Tall:* Newbery Award–winning book by Patricia MacLachlan that Claud is supposed to read for Mrs. Hall's class; Claud has time to read it because it is just fifty-eight pages long (#12-p.2).

*Sarah Morton's Day:* Great book by Kate Waters about young Pilgrim girl (#91-p.40).

*The Secret Language:* Book by Ursula Nordstrom that Mallory and Jessi liked, though old-fashioned; gives them idea to excite kids into communicating with Matt Braddock (#16-p.57).

*The Secret Garden:* Book by Frances Hodgson Burnett that Stephie is reading (SS#5-p.76); Mary Anne loves it (SS#5-p.77). Martha Menders wants to read it (SM#1-p.95).

*A Separate Peace:* Book by John Knowles that Mary Anne is reading for English (#60-p.87).

*Shiloh:* Book by Phyllis Reynolds Naylor that Kristy reads while grounded (#95-p.79).

*Short Season:* Great baseball book, according to Kristy, by Scott Eller (#89-p.104).

*The Sleepy Little Rabbit:* Story that Dawn reads to Jenny Prezzioso (M#2-p.54).

*Sneetches:* Dr. Seuss book; Margo can read the whole thing; about a character named Sylvester McMonkey McBean (LS-p.92).

*The Snowy Day:* Book by Ezra Jack Keats that Stacey reads to Henry and Grace (#28-p.75).

*Spirits, Spooks, and Ghostly Tales:* Dawn's favorite collection of ghost stories (#23-p.24). (*).

*Stone Soup:* Book that Mal reads to kids during story hour at BookCenter (see M#14-p.46).

*The Stoneybrooke Town Record:* 1864 volume is in Watson's library (M#19-p.30). In sections—first is almanac, arranged by date; other section is directory of people who lived in Stoneybrook (M#19-p.31) (*).

*The Stoneybrook Who's Who:* Copy in the public library; gives biographical information of Stoneybrook residents (SM#2-p.91) (*).

*Stormy, Misty's Foal:* Marguerite Henry horse novel; Mal has read it about eighteen times (SS#2-p.81).

*A Summer to Die:* Lois Lowry book that Mal's just begun to read, about a girl whose older sister is dying of leukemia (SS#6-p.196).

*The Tale of Peter Rabbit:* By Beatrix Potter; Claudia tries (unsuccessfully) to calm down the Newtons and Feldmans by reading it (#1-p.78). Nicky, Vanessa, Margo, and Claire turn it into a play (#4-p.100).

*Teddy Bears' Picnic:* Well-worn book of Andrew's that Emily asks Kristy to read for her (#30-p.90).

*The Tenth Good Thing About Barney:* Book by Judith Viorst; read to

Andrew's nursery school class about a family remembering its deceased pet (#1-p.124).

*There's a Nightmare in My Closet:* Book by Mercer Mayer that Mary Anne reads to the Arnold twins (#97-p.81).

*Tiffky Doofky:* By William Steig; Shannon carries a copy in her Kid-Kit (#89-p.53).

*Tik-Tok of Oz:* In Stacey's Kid-Kit (#10-p.79); by L. Frank Baum.

*Tikki Tikki Tembo:* Book that Mal reads during story hour at Book-Center (M#14-p.48).

*Time and Again:* Book by Jack Finney about a secret government project where people go back in time to change history; Jessi is reading it (#60-p.36).

*The Time Machine:* H. G. Wells Book that Carolyn Arnold's dad reads to her (#60-p.35).

*To Kill a Mockingbird:* By Harper Lee; Mary Anne can't read it often enough (#41-p.36). Stacey has test on it for English class (M#10-p.130).

*Tom Sawyer:* Burned banned book by Mark Twain (M#13-p.88).

*A Tree Grows in Brooklyn:* Book by Betty Smith that Mary Anne is reading in Sea City (#8-p.45).

*Tucker's Countryside:* Animal story by George Selden that Stacey reads to Charlotte (#3-p.39).

*Turning Thirteen:* Book by Susan Beth Pfeffer that Rabbi Dorman gives Abby and Anna before they begin their Bat Mitzvah lessons; it is about a girl who is afraid she'll lose

her best friend unless they prepare for their Bat Mitzvahs together (#96-p.11).

*The Twenty-one Balloons:* Newbery Award–winning book by William Pene DuBois that Claud is supposed to read for Mrs. Hall's class (#12-p.92).

*The Westing Game:* Great Newbery Award–winning book by Ellen Raskin that Claud is supposed to read for Mrs. Hall's class (#12-p.2).

*Where the Sidewalk Ends:* Shel Silverstein book; Claudia reads to a bunch of criers, and soon they become gigglers (#6-p.78).

*Where the Wild Things Are:* Maurice Sendak book about a boy named Max; Claudia reads it to Jamie and his cousins (#1-p.79); Stacey also reads it with Jamie (#3-p.112). Mary Anne reads it to Carolyn and Marilyn Arnold (#97-p.81).

*The Wind in the Willows:* Book for children of all ages, by Kenneth Grahame, which Charlotte puts in a basket for Stoneybrook Manor (#69-p.101). Mary Anne has read it before and is sure she'll read it again (SS#8-p.124).

*The Witch Next Door:* One of Karen's favorite books, by Norman Bridwell (#30-p.90). Karen always asks Claudia to read it to her (#16-p.88).

*The Wizard of Oz:* By L. Frank Baum; Buddy insists that his copy has better pictures than Taylor's (SS#12-p.197). In fourth grade, Mary Anne wanted to turn it into a play; Claud thought that Mary Anne would make a great Dorothy (CB-p.104).

*A Wrinkle in Time:* Madeline L'Engle book, which Mal is dying to finish (M#2-p.9). Mary Anne thinks it's exciting (#4-p.23).

*Wuthering Heights:* By Charlotte Bronte; Mary Anne has read it three times (#41-p.36); is reading it for the millionth time (M#5-p.65).

## MAGAZINES/NEWSPAPERS:

*#1 Fan:* Teen magazine that Stacey sometimes buys (M#14-p.118) (*).

*Basho-Man:* Comics that David Michael and Linny Papadakis read (#21-p.81) (*).

*Chocolate Lover's:* Magazine that Claudia reads while prepping for Battle of the Bakers (M#21-p.31).

*"Crimewatch":* Feature in the *Stoneybrook News* listing robberies and other bad stuff (#15-p.22) (*).

*Ghostly Tales:* Magazine from which Dawn orders a ghost detector (M#3-p.118) (*).

*Howard Township Sun:* Newspaper for town neighboring Stoneybrook; covers School Spirit Month bruhaha since HTMS is going through the same thing (#84-p.102) (*).

*Kumbel Catalog:* Spiers get it; sells everything; Mary Anne's favorite section is the baby supplies and furniture (#52-p.67) (*).

*The Literary Voice:* The Middle School's literary magazine (#2-p.10) (*).

*P3:* Great environmental magazine for kids, stands for "Planet-3," which is Earth (#57-p.108) (*).

*The Palo City Post:* Palo City newspaper; reporter Rhonda Leib profiles the We ♥ Kids Club (#72-pp.22, 30) (*).

*The SMS Express:* Weekly (#71-p.49) SMS newspaper; unsigned editorial is called SMS News and Views (#70-p.137); exposes basketball misdeeds; Stacey and Robert write an editorial upholding school spirit (#70-p.141). Get rid of half-page pet care column to make way for "Claudia's Personals" (#71-p.35). Has its own office (#71-p.49). Outside the office door there are a number of boxes, for personals, club announcements, finished articles, cartoons, letters to the editor, and sports schedules (#71-p.49). Inside the office, there are several desks, three computers, a photocopier, four typewriters, and an artist's slanted desk; Claudia gets an old-looking, beat-up desk (#71-p.49). Runs out of copies for the first time after "Claudia's Personals" debuts (#71-p.86). Emily Bernstein is editor, Julie Stern is layout artist (#71-p.101). Claudia starts second column, "Claudia Advises" (#71-p.118). An SMS correspondent is responsible for one article each month, a roundup of student activities; Jessi is sixth grade correspondent and writes about school play (SS#9-pp.2,3) (*).

*Space Creatures:* Comics that Jeff reads (#9-p.27) (*).

*The Stoneybrook Gazette:* Now-defunct local paper, where Claudia's birth announcement was printed (CB-p.13). Went out of business about nine years ago (#33-p.132) (*).

*The Stoneybrook News:* Local newspaper (#1-p.42); layout (SS#7-p.i); costs one dollar (SS#7-p.i). Editor is Marian Tan; address is One Stoneybrook Plaza (SS#7-p.1). Does article on opening day of SMS's recycling center, mentions Dawn three times but no photo of her; more references to Mrs. Gonzalez; Mayor Keane gives speech (#57-pp.103, 109). Interviews BSC members about their aid in solving the dognapping ring (M#7-p.145). Never writes about SMS but does have a big article about the SMS basketball team (#70-p.2). Runs photo and article about Claudia solving museum mystery (M#13-p.133). Runs article about Kristy saving Derek Masters (M#15-p.139). Runs article about BSC members entitled "Savvy Teens Find Key to Bank Mystery" (M#16-p.146). Runs banner headline, front page story about BSC Island Adventure, entitled "Connecticut Disaster Victims Tell Their Story" (SS#4-p.213); story includes photo of all the BSC members, which they hang in their rooms (SS#4-p.220). Many BSC members have letters in the paper protesting Reginald Fowler's plan to build over Miller's Park as well as articles about their crusade (M#24-from p.33) (*).

*Top Teen Starz:* Magazine which includes articles about Derek Masters, Carson Fraser, and *Little Vampires* (M#15-p.142) (*).

## TELEVISION SHOWS/MOVIES/THEATER/RADIO:

*Adventures in Babysitting:* Film Dawn watches on flight from California to Connecticut (#23-p.137).

*An Affair to Remember:* Teary movie that Stacey watches with her mom (#94-p.133).

**"Alice at the Beach":** Version of "Alice in Wonderland" that the kids in the beach day care program put on (M#12-p.111) (*).

*Alice and the Pilgrims:* Title of the uncensored play Claud, Abby, and Stacey's Short Takes drama class writes for SES third-graders; has modern character observing and commenting upon the first Thanksgiving (#91-from p.54) (*).

*An American in Paris:* Old Gene Kelly movie; Shannon watches it in preparation for her trip to Paris (ShS-p.48).

*The Brementown Musicians:* Musical in which David Michael plays a rooster (#81-p.69).

*Bringing Up Baby:* Katharine Hepburn/Cary Grant movie; Claudia goes to art house movie theater to see it with Peaches; the theater (unnamed) has an old-fashioned popcorn machine (#78-p.53).

*Buffy the Vampire Slayer:* Stupid movie that Mary Anne rents (#86-p.64).

*Car Man:* Movie that five-year-old Kristy tricks her way into seeing with Charlie, Sam, and their friends (KB-p.39). About a superhero who could turn into a car whenever he wanted to (KB-p.40) (*).

*Carrie:* Stephen King movie that scared Claudia and Stacey so much that they could barely sleep for a week afterward (M#22-p.62).

*Citizens' Court:* TV show that Claudia and Derek try to emulate in their cross examination of Janine (M#6-p.99) (*).

*The Cosby Show:* Charlotte Johanssen's favorite TV show (#3-p.137).

*Crime Court:* TV show Charlotte Johanssen watches (#29-p.111).

*Dracula:* Scary play that the BSC members see in Reese, Maine (SM#1-p.174).

*Druscilla and the Dynamos:* The Krushers' band, formed by Druscilla Porter (flute), with Sheila Nofziger (trumpet), Scott Hsu (kazoo), and Moon Pinckney (drums) (#89-p.139) (*).

*The Early Years:* Mal's play for the KCDAC; not-loosely-enough based on her own life, it is the story of a young author living in the chaotic Spike family (#80-p.75) (*).

*Emergency Room:* David Michael's favorite show (#81-p.68).

*EZ-Lite:* Radio station that Richard listens to (#89-p.82).

*For Kids Only:* Claudia and Ashley's twice-a-week WSTO radio show, which runs for a month (#85-p.48). Each show has a different theme, with four segments of fifteen minutes each (#85-p.52) (*).

*Frog Pond Vacation:* Play by Henrietta Hayes (#80-p.53) (*).

*Getting to Be a Star:* Play that Karen writes and "performs" with Amanda and Hannie in the midst of Derek Masters Fever (#27-p.62) (*).

*Ghostbusters:* Has been playing on local cable channel; inspires Ghostbuster mania that sweeps Stoneybrook's kids (M#22-p.10).

*Girls Girls Girls:* Old Elvis Presley movie that Sharon rents because it has "maximum stupid video potential" (#86-p.64).

*Gone With the Wind:* The one movie Stacey and her mom can always agree to watch together; they must have seen it about ten times (M#1-p.113).

**Great Blue Whales:** Rock group; their song "Sister Sally" is Stacey's new fave (M#22-p.5) (*).

**The Groovy Tangerine:** Band that played at ill-fated SMS Halloween Dance twenty-eight years ago (M#22-p.85) (*).

*The Happiest Day:* Play by Henrietta Hayes (#80-p.53) (*).

**"The Haunting of Pike House":** Ongoing poem by Vanessa Pike; begins with the lines "Ghosts and goblins, witches and spooks, the Pike house has all kinds of kooks" (M#22-p.35).

*Horrorville: Head's Up:* Horror movie that scares the Arnold twins (#97-p.53). They are less scared after they see *The Making of Horrorville* (#97-p.83). **(*).**

**The Insects:** Mal's favorite rock group; the carrot-topped Spider is lead singer (SS#1-p.37) **(*).**

*I Love Lucy:* Loved by both Stacey's mother and father; their favorite episode is when Lucy poses as the Maharincess of Franistan (SS#7-p.151). Bobby Henson does Vitameatavegamin routine for Leicester Lodge talent show (SS#3-p.183).

*It Came from the Snow:* Scary movie that Kristy, David Michael, and Karen watch (SM#2-p.5) **(*).**

*Kid Detectives:* Show on which a real-life mystery is acted out and then solved by someone like the victim's little brother or his best friend; Derek Masters is a guest star (M#6-p.25) **(*).**

*Little Vampires:* Derek Masters vampire TV movie, shot partially in Stoneybrook (see M#15; plot-pp.27-8) **(*).**

*Mad About Millie:* Broadway musical Laine gets tickets for as welcome back present for Stacey (#13-p.53) **(*).**

*Mall Warriors II:* Movie starring Todd Byron, which RJ Blaser takes Stacey to see; she finds it amazingly dumb; he likes it a lot (#70-p.32-33) **(*).**

*Mary Poppins:* Stacey's favorite movie; she's seen it about 65 times (#6-p.96).

*Miracle on 34th Street:* Karen and her friend Tia watch it during the summer because Tia wants to see every New York City movie ever made (SS#13-p.94).

*Monster Movie Night:* Shows *Snake Boy Loose in San Francisco*, scares Jessi and Becca to death; on channel five late at night (M#2-pp.71-72) **(*).**

*The Music Man:* Movie musical about a crooked salesman who takes money from parents saying he'll set up a boys' band; the Krusher Quartet practice reminds Kristy of this (#89-p.121).

*Once Upon a Dream:* TV show featuring Corrie Lalique (#10-p.10) **(*).**

*Out of This World:* Soap opera starring Max Morrison (#10-p.19) **(*).**

*Paris Magic:* Musical in New York City that Stacey goes to (#3-p.73).

*The Parent Trap:* Mary Anne and Dawn are absorbed by this movie (#4-p.45); Dawn watches it at least once a week (SS#2-p.17).

*Peter Pan:* SMS school play. Kristy is Peter Pan; Jackie is Michael Darling; Dawn is Wendy; Stacey and Sam are Mrs. and Mr. Darling; Jessi is cast as a pirate and then takes over for the alligator, etc. (SS#9-p.64).

*Plan Nine From Outer Space:* Ed Wood movie that Dawn rents (#86-p.64).

*Pokey Puppy:* Videos that Squirt watches (#68-p.1) **(*).**

*P.S. 162:* Becca Ramsey's favorite TV show about an inner city elementary school in L.A. starring a Stoneybrook boy, Derek Masters, whom Jessi baby-sits (#27-p.20). Derek plays Waldo, a boy with glasses and spiky hair (#20-p.31). Jessi and Mal visit the set (SS#5-p.177). *Lamont:* Boy in *P.S.162* on whom Becca has crush (#27-p.6). *Waldo:* Character on *P.S.162* who is a science whiz, and has glasses and spiked hair (#27-p.7); played by Derek Masters (#27-p.31). *Miss Pedagogue:* Teacher on *P.S. 162* (#27-p.8). *Danielle:* Played by Alison McGuire (SS#5-p.178). Another star is George Aylesworth (SS#5-p.178). Elaine Stritch makes a guest appearance (SS#5-p.179) *(*)*.

*Roman Holiday:* Audrey Hepburn/Gregory Peck movie, always makes Mary Anne weep (M#13-p.1).

*Sabrina:* Audrey Hepburn movie that Shannon wants to see before going to France (ShS-p.19).

*Sesame Street:* Emily Michelle's favorite TV show (#81-p.68).

*1776:* Claudia, Abby, and Stacey see a revival of this musical during a class trip to Philadelphia (#97-p.128).

*Smash:* Favorite rock group of Toby (#8-p.113) and Kristy and Mary Anne (#10-p.134) *(*)*.

*Spook Theatre:* TV show on Channel 47 (#2-p.80) *(*)*.

*Starlight Express:* Broadway play Laine takes club to in limo (#18-p.120). Story of a train race; all actors on roller skates (#18-p.124); at Gershwin Theatre (#18-p.125).

*Super-Girl Meets the Super-Nerds:* Play that Mallory and the triplets put on for the Pikes (#4-p.99) *(*)*.

*A Thanksgiving Play:* Censored version of Alice and the Pilgrims (#91-p.103) *(*)*.

*Third Rail:* Warm-up band for U4Me concert in Stamford; they're pretty good, but the show is dull (#87-p.108); their lead singer has the personality of a turnip (#87-p.112) *(*)*.

*Tin Can Voices:* Band that Stacey likes; they're album is *Shout It!* (SS#7-p.48) *(*)*.

*The True Adventures of Cassandra Clue/Boo Hoo, Cassandra Clue:* Live non-TV TV show that the neighborhood kids begin after their parents ban television (#96-pp.74, 97) *(*)*.

*The Twins Who Mutilated Their Baby-sitter:* Movie that the Arnold twins make with Kristy to display their knowledge of special effects (#97-p.118) *(*)*.

*U4Me:* *St*acey's current fave rock group (#87-p.4). Lead singer is Skyllo, whose real name is Aristotle Dukas (#87-p.27). Hit song is "I Don't Wanna Say Good-bye" (#87-p.30). Ran Philips is another U4Me singer—he's just shaved his head (#87-p.30). Latest album is U & Me 4 U4Me (#87-p.71). Once skipped a whole weekend at Madison Square Garden because Skyllo sneaked off to go skiing. Boys always hate U4Me (#87-p.89). Stacey and the "bad girls" go to see U4Me concert in Stamford (#87-from p.101) *(*)*.

*Uncle Dandy's Star Machine:* TV talent show in Hartford for kids; Dan Beasley is Uncle Dandy, lets Rosie Wilder be on show (#49-pp.60,63) *(*)*.

*Values AmericanStyle:* TV show for which Vanessa's essay wins Old-fashioned Christmas Contest; producer is Chad Henry; plans to follow the Pike family through their holiday season (#92-p.30). After much intrusiveness and chaos, the Pikes decline his offer and kick the camera crew out (#92-p.129) (*).

*Vertigo:* Hitchcock movie shown on BSC's flight to California (SS#5-p.19).

*Which Way's Up?:* One of Claudia's favorite TV shows, starring Donna Brinkman (SS#6-p.121) (*).

**WSBK:** Television station; Mimi Snowdon is news reporter (#84-p.102) (*).

**WSTO:** Radio station; 1313 on your dial (#5-p.42). Phone number is 555-WSTO (#85-p.34). *See Stoneybrook: Community Buildings/Organizations* (*)

## TOYS/GAMES:

**A, My Name Is Alice:** Singsong game that Claudia plays with the Newtons and other charges (see M#16-pp.58-60).

**Animals:** Game where kids imitate animals; whoever guesses the animal correctly does the next imitation (M#6-p.106).

**Backward Ball:** Just like regular softball, except you run backward around the bases (#89-p.104).

**Ballet Class:** Game in which Jessi imitates Mme Noelle, and Charlotte and Becca pretend to be grown-up ballet students (M#10-p.82).

**The Baloney Dance:** Suzi Barrett loves to do it when she's happy. Here's how to Baloney Dance: run in place, shake your hands and head really fast at the same time, and say, "Baloney baloney baloney baloney baloney!" Buddy hates it. (SS#12-p.210).

**Beauty Parlor:** Game that Hannie and Karen play where they fix their dolls' hair (SS#1-p.42).

**The Bizzer Sign:** An insult the Pike kids use when they want to annoy someone; they point index finger and say "Bzzz" (#5-p.83).

**Blast Into Superspace:** Game Nicky Pike invents (#7-pp.73-74).

**Blasto-Plane:** Jackie Rodowsky's toy that's stuck in bathroom drain (#12- p.32).

**Camping Out:** A game of Mathew Hobart's; object is to "survive the elements" while tenting in front yard (LS-p.43).

**Candy Land:** Game that Margo and Claire play (#21-p.33). Jenny Prezzioso's favorite game (M#2-p.53).

**Candy Store:** Game that Becca and Charlotte play, in which one person pretends she is the candy store owner and the other is the customer; can go on forever (#34-p.109).

**Clean Slate:** Mental game of Logan's, in which you give yourself another chance (SS#11-p.139).

**Crazy Olympics:** Game that Pikes can't resist; invent strange "events" and then compete in them (M#6-p.65).

**Dragon Kingdom:** Game that Claudia and kids play after making dragons, which involves picking a king and a queen of the dragons and then having dragon parties (M#8-p.124).

**Flamingo Fight:** Game that Mary Anne teaches Jenny Prezzioso; blindfolded, players pretend to be flamingos, hold foot with hand and hop, try to make other person fall down; can't use hands (#41-pp.124-125).

**Food Checks:** When someone yells "food check" at the table, everyone's supposed to open their mouths and display what's inside (#79-p.6).

**Fudge, Fudge, Call the Judge:** Jump-rope rhyme (#78-p.123).

**Go Fish:** Card game that Dawn plays at the Rodowskys' (M#2-p.61).

**Going Camping:** Game that Karen Brewer invented; players set up an old bedspread and chairs outside, pretend they're camping in tent (#37-p.70).

**Grandmother's House:** Memory game, in which each person says one thing that they are going to bring to grandmother's house and then has to repeat all of the things that have been said before (M#2-p.91).

**The Gross Food Game:** Maria and Shannon like to play it, coming up with the grossest combinations possible (à la a broccoli milkshake with chopped onions, or a sardine chocolate cake) (ShS-pp.1-2).

**Hot Potato:** Game in which players catch a ball and have to throw it back as soon as possible (M#8-p.91).

**I Packed My Grandmother's Trunk:** Memory game, in which everyone adds an imaginary item but only after repeating every item that's already been added (SS#12-p.63).

**Kid-Kit:** Kristy's invention; see under *Club Facts*; a box containing toys, games, books, etc., that club members sometimes bring to jobs (#3-pp.31-32).

**Let's All Come In:** Karen's hotel game (#5-pp.57-58) in which players dress up in wild outfits and are different people; four or more needed to play (#15-p.32). Characters include Mrs. Noswimple, Mrs. Mysterious, Bruce Stringbean, Darryl Blueberry, Ladonna (M#2-pp.38-9).

**Lovely Ladies:** One of Karen's favorite games; basically, the players converse as if they are very well-off, proper ladies (#78-p.37).

**Marvel in the Mist:** Super video game that Mr. McGill gives Stacey (#99-p.13)

**Mary Anne's Game of School:** Board game Mary Anne invents for kids; involves making it from September all the way around the board to June (#30-p.62).

**Memory:** A card game that Karen, Andrew, Michael, and David play;

game consists of a big stack of cards. On each is a picture — and each card has one, and only one, matching card. The cards are laid out facedown. The players take turns turning two cards over. If someone gets a pair, he or she goes again. When all the cards have been matched up, the winner is the one with the most pairs (#10-pp.95,99).

**Mudball:** Rather dirty game that the Pike boys play (M#3-p.4).

**Musical Cushions:** Version of musical chairs, played on cushions, in which instead of eliminating kids when cushions are taken away, all of the kids are told to pile onto the remaining cushions (M#14-p.113).

**Musical Rug:** Version of musical chairs played at Stacey's farewell party (#13-p.118).

**Mrs. Refrigerator:** Character having eye job in Perkins' play beauty parlor (#12-p.53).

**Mrs. Xerox:** Character having hair permed in Perkins' play beauty parlor (#12-p.53).

**Old King Cole Hole:** Third hole at Fred's Putt-Putt Course (#8-p.80).

**One Frog, Two Frog:** Natalie Springer's jump-rope rhyme (#78-p.117).

**Oogly Oogly Beast:** Neat-freak monster; Mal writes and tells stories about him, which are later turned by Kristy into an unsuccessful radio play (#85-p.9).

**Op-Talk:** Jessi teaches to Pike triplets; add "op" after each conso-

nant, spell out each word, leave vowels alone (#40-p.72).

**Operation:** Silly board game played at Leicester Lodge (SS#3-p.95).

**Pepper:** Softball practice game in which three people alternate batting and catching (M#9-p.117).

**Pictionary:** Claud owns a copy; the BSC members play it while staking out the Johanssens' house (M#18-p.120).

**Pin-the-Baby-on-the-Sitter:** Game created by Charlotte for Stacey's farewell party (#13-p.118).

**Poohsticks:** Game, popularized by Winnie the Pooh, in which sticks are thrown into stream; whoever's stick goes farthest is the winner (#14-p.90).

**Princess Power:** Video game that Haley has and Carolyn is dying to play (M#12-p.108).

**Red Light, Green Light:** Game that Claudia plays with Rodowskys (#12-p.35).

**Round Robin:** Game that Kristy's invented; nine players take the field and one goes to bat; everyone else sits on the bench. If the batter gets a hit, he/she runs the bases as far as possible. Then, when the play is dead, everybody rotates. The batter becomes the right fielder, the right fielder becomes the center fielder, and so on. The pitcher goes to the bench and a new player gets to bat (SS#10-pp.67-68).

**Sardines:** A version of hide-and-seek, only you have one hider and all the other players are seekers. When a seeker finds the hider, he doesn't just win that round of the game, he hides with the hider. The next person to find the hiders hides with them, too, and so on until one seeker is left. That seeker is the loser and starts out the next round of the game as the hider. The tricky thing when you're the hider is finding a big enough hiding place in which to fit a whole lot of other people (#30-p.55).

**Secret Agents:** Pike brothers' game in which they spy on neighbors (#13-p.56); every time you complete a mission, you get a badge; pink is easiest badge, black is hardest, and there are eight badges in between; if you earn all ten, you're named a top agent (#13-p.61). Jordan, who invented the game, has proclaimed himself head spy (#13-p.62).

**Secrets:** Game that Abby invents to get Luke Martinez to talk; to play, three or more people sit in a circle and each one tells the person to their left something they've never told anyone else before (M#24-p.85).

**Secret Santas:** Pike family tradition; everyone writes a wish on a strip of paper and tosses the paper into a hat; whoever picks the wish must make it true, being as creative as he/she wants (#92-p.112).

**Shark Attack:** Game with battery-operated Shark going across a board (M#1-p.106).

**Skatch:** Game of catch with Velcro ball and mitt (#80-p.6).

**Skip-It Rings:** Giant ankle rings, with a rope attached. Jump rope for one. (#80-p.5).

**Snail:** Spiral, hopscotch-like game (#11-p.86).

**Squiggle Ball:** A battery-operated ball that never stops moving (#80-p.6).

**Teddy Bear, Teddy Bear:** Natalie Springer's jump-rope rhyme (#78-p.116).

**The Toilet Monster:** A make-believe creature that used to terrify Bill and Melody Korman; now they talk about it just for fun (M#2-p.94).

**The Trivia Game:** Claudia hates it, plays it with Mimi and Janine anyway (#7-p.35).

**Twister:** The Pikes love to play it (M#9-p.44).

**Wandering Frog People:** Toys of Pike triplets (#9-p.26).

**Water-bomb:** Like "hot potato," with a water balloon (#67-p.43).

**Where Is Thumbkin?:** Game that Dawn plays with Marnie (#13-p.99).

**Wizard of Oz:** Game that Claudia plays with the Newtons, in which they make believe that they are characters from the MGM movie (M#9-p.73).

## PRODUCTS AND RECIPES:

**Bug-Off:** Bug spray that Mal uses (unsuccessfully) at Shadow Lake; she writes to the company and gets letter in return from Roger H. Humes, of the Consumer Relations department (SS#8-p.233). (*).

**Calladew's Perfection Shampoo:** Trial size concentrated shampoo Vanessa and Margo get in mail and use on Claire (#9-p.67) **(\*)**.

**Cuthbert Athlete's Foot Creme:** Along with sneakers after gym class, what the school's pot roast smells like to Kristy (#12-p.140) **(\*)**.

**Daddy Stew:** Casserole with hot-dog chunks; Pikes' special dish (#17-p.67).

**Day-Nite Suntan Lotion:** Product for which Abby appears in a Waikiki Beach volleyball commercial (SS#13-p.110) **(\*)**.

**Health-i-os:** Dawn's breakfast cereal of choice (M#5-p.9) **(\*)**.

**Moonlight Mist:** Stacey's new perfume (#12-p.130); smells like rosebed (#12-p.131) **(\*)**.

**Mrs. Goode's Cookware:** Sponsors Battle of the Bakers (M#21-p.1). Mary Anne's mother's cherry-chocolate cake recipe wins first prize and will be put in cookbook (M#21-p.139); will be named "Alma's Memory Cake" (M#21-p.142). Company president is Mr. Herriot (M#21-p.140) **(\*)**.

**Mrs. Brewer's Special Wake-Up Punch:** Has orange juice, lemonade, and all kinds of good stuff mixed together (M#9-p.135).

**Popcorn Picnic:** Concept from Mrs. McGill; make a batch of popcorn and put different (sometimes strange) toppings upon it (M#4-p.56).

**Smorgaspic:** A free-for-all picnic (#77-p.54).

**Sugar Snaps:** Mary Anne's breakfast cereal of choice (M#5-p.9) **(\*)**.

**Wildflower Wash:** Dawn's new shampoo (M#1-p.23) **(\*)**.

## EVENTS:

**Jack-O'-Lottery:** Lottery from which the BSC wins ten thousand dollars, enabling them to go to California (SS#5-p.13).

**Little Miss Stoneybrook:** Beauty pageant for girls five to eight that could lead to Little Miss Connecticut, Little Miss America, Little Miss World (#15-p.23). Held on a Saturday in Stoneybrook High's auditorium (#15-p.113).

**The Stoneybrook Baby Parade:** Held once every two years; parents dress babies in wild costumes to win prizes; different divisions, floats, strollers, etc.; with grand marshal and judges (#45-p.6). Slim Peabody is this year's grand marshal (#45-p.105), an old "has-been" who used to sing cowboy songs for kids.

297

# BEYOND
# STONEYBROOK

•

# IN CALIFORNIA

•

## WE ♥ KIDS CLUB FACTS:

California version of BSC founded by Sunny Winslow (Dawn's friend); other members are Maggie Blume and Jill Henderson; they give Dawn a copy of *Kids Can Cook... Naturally* and a file of handwritten recipes (#23-p.130). Also known as the "W♥KC." Initially, it doesn't have any rules or regularly scheduled meetings (#72-p.5); clients can call any of the members; Sunny has a record book at her house but doesn't use it much (#72-p.20). There aren't any officers; nobody's punctual (#72-p.20). Keeps a health-food cookbook, in which each member constantly updates a file of recipes (#72-p.21). After chaotic weeks, though, the club decides: to have regular meetings every week (without guilt trips about lateness), to keep a record book that they'll check before confirming jobs, and to have clients call only Sunny's number, during meeting hours (#72-p.126). Meetings are at Sunny's house (#77-p.15). Snacks at meetings tend towards fruits and nuts and yogurt (#77-p.20). Whitney Cater is unanimously made an honorary member and Special Helper (#77-p.136). Plans Halloween Party (M#17-p.35).

## WE ♥ KIDS CLUB MEMBERS:

### MAGGIE BLUME:

#### PERSONAL INFO:
Member of We ♥ Kids with Sunny Winslow and Jill Henderson in California (#23-p.44); blonde (#23-p.63). Has cool look, which is constantly changing; hair is short and punkish, with a thin tail in back; she usually streaks it purple or green or black; her fashion sense runs towards leather bomber jackets and lace-up black boots (#72-p.15). Tries hair in dreadlocks (SS#12-p.81). Doesn't like talking about celebrities and movie gossip (#72-p.15). Her new style is L.A.-futuristic-cyberpunk (#98-p.6).

## LIKES AND INTERESTS:

Likes ghost stories (#23-p.49); Shares Dawn's taste in natural foods (#72-p.4); is a vegetarian (SS#12-p.8). Likes really loud rock, but isn't punk (M#12-p.20). Doesn't really get into mysteries (M#12-p.63). Likes horseback riding more than surfing (M#12-p.84).

## FAMILY/HOUSE:

Her dad is in the movie business (#72-p.15). Has a little brother Zeke (M#12-pp.19-20). Lives in an enormous house, with dozens and dozens of rooms (#77-p.21), including a screening room, a gym, and a landscaped pool that looks as if someone lifted it from a tropical island and plopped it in their backyard (#72-p.15); her kitchen is so big you could Rollerblade in it (#77-p.21); Keanu Reeves once ate there (#72-p.15). Maggie lives a few blocks away from Sunny and Dawn (M#12-p.19).

## JILL HENDERSON:

### PERSONAL INFO:

Member of We ♥ Kids Club with Sunny and Maggie in California (#23-p.44); hair is dark blonde (#72-pp.14, 63). Eyes are deep, chocolate brown (#72-p.14). Quiet and serious (#72-p.14). Reminds Dawn of Mary Anne sometimes (#77-p.22).

### LIKES AND INTERESTS:

Shares Dawn's taste in natural foods (#72-p.4); is a vegetarian (SS#12-

p.8). Really likes to surf, and is seriously good at it, too (#77-p.22). Doesn't really get into mysteries (M#12-p.63). Likes horseback riding more than surfing (M#12-p.84).

### FAMILY/HOUSE:

Is the only W ♥ KC member who doesn't live in the neighborhood; her house is tucked away in the hills at the edge of town. (#72-pp.14-15); usually takes a bus to meetings (#77-p.22). Parents are divorced; she lives with her mom and her older sister, Liz; they have three ugly boxers named Spike, Shakespeare, and Smee (#72-p.15).

## SUNNY (SUNSHINE) DAYDREAM WINSLOW:

### PERSONAL INFO:

Thirteen and in eighth grade; outgoing, fun loving, and independent; has strawberry blonde hair (#72-p.14) and freckles across her upturned nose (M#12-p.19). Dawn's best friend in CA (#5-p.5) since second grade (#23-p.8). Is a vegetarian (SS#12-p.8). Always seems to be in a good mood; loves to flirt (M#12-p.19). Doesn't believe in ghosts (M#12-p.63). Walks most days to school with Dawn; routine is for Dawn to pick Sunny up; they try to change the route as often as possible (M#17-p.92).

### LIKES AND INTERESTS:

Likes ghost stories, has two shelves of them (#23-p.48). Shares Dawn's taste in natural foods (#72-p.4). Likes to surf; has carpet on bedroom floor (#72-p.13). Loves to hang out on the beach or in the surf shop and chat with the boys (M#12-p.8). Has a stuffed crocodile named Captain, her childhood companion (M#17-p.33).

**FAMILY/HOUSE:**
Lives a few houses down block from Mr. Schafer (#23-p.44). Parents were hippies (#72-p.14). Mother has lung cancer (#87-p.56).

**EXPERIENCES:**
Starts We ♥ Kids Club (#23-p.43). Invites Dawn to a club meeting (#23-p.43). Works with Dawn at special children's program on the beach, on Tuesday, Wednesday, Thursday afternoons and most Saturdays, mainly for kids with working parents (M#12-p.21). Is bruised badly in surfing accident (M#12-p.100).

# CLIENTS:

## THE AUSTINS:

Live next door to Dawn (#77-p.39). The girls play with hoses and sprinklers on their front lawn (#77-p.40).

### CLOVER AUSTIN:
Five, Daffodil's sister; neighbor of Dawn's father in California. Dawn sat for her (#9-p.8). Imaginative, outgoing (#23-p.75). Friends with Sara

and Ruby; they all pose for We ♥ Kids Club newspaper pics (#72-p.28). Is the Austin you notice first, because she lives at the top of her lungs, like Karen Brewer (#77-p.40).

### DAFFODIL AUSTIN:
Eight (#9-p.8); quiet, gangly (#23-p.75). Friends with Sara and Ruby; they all pose for We ♥ Kids Club newspaper pics (#72-p.28).

### MRS. AUSTIN:
Mr. Schafer's neighbor and client of California club (#23-p.49); a weaver with three different sized looms in her living room; used to be a flower child (#23-p.73); gives Dawn a hand-woven purse of red and deep gold, lined in silk (#23-p.128). Exhibits her weaving at crafts fairs (#77-p.128).

## THE CATERS:

Don't live far from Dawn's house (#77-p.25). Parents return from work at six (#77-p.30). House has a large broad hallway that leads to large sunny room at the back of the house (#77-p.28).

### WHITNEY CATER:
**Personal Info:** Twelve; has Down's Syndrome (#77-p.23; Down's Syndrome described on #77-p.26). A short, somewhat stocky girl, with straight brown hair, and brown eyes that seem to slant slightly at

the corners; her face is round and she has a short nose (#77-p.30). Voice is low, almost hoarse; she speaks carefully (#77-p.30). Is not very retarded; doesn't have any extreme manifestations of physical traits commonly associated with Down's Syndrome, such as retarded growth, impaired coordination, or a heart condition (#77-p.26). Is prone to ear infections; has to wear special ear plugs when she goes swimming and put drops in before and after; otherwise, has no allergies or anything that necessitates worry (#77-p.29). She is easygoing, likes to laugh, a good listener, very sympathetic and sensitive to others' moods (#77-p.28). Has been attending a special school with a summer program and is about to be switched into public school system (#77-p.23). Will continue to take special courses, work with specialists, like her speech therapist (#77-p.26). Has won many trophies for swimming (#77-p.32). Is made honorary member and Special Helper in the We ♥ Kids Club (#77-p.136).

**Likes and Interests:** Has a sweet tooth (#77-p.29). Likes animals, particularly bears and seals (#77-p.35).

**Room:** Room is typical girl's room, decorated in green and white and soft peach; a big canopy bed stands in the middle of the room with a patchwork quilt across the foot; a wide desk with a chair is by the window, next to a comfortable looking armchair. Bookshelves line one wall and on the other wall is a big poster of seals in the ocean (#77-p.32). Keeps a stack of magazines on the bottom of her bookshelf (#77-p.33). A small mirror hangs above her chest of drawers (#77-p.34). Dawn gives her a lime green stuffed panda, which she names Buster (#77-p.72).

**MR. JAMES CATER:**
Spends alternate mornings with Whitney until her camp begins (#77-p.23).

**MRS. ANNETTE CATER:**
Spends alternate mornings with Whitney until her camp begins (#77-p.23). More insightful that Mr. Cater regarding Whitney's personality (#77-p.28). Works in an office (#77-p.29).

## THE CLUNES:

Family Dawn has known for a long time; privately, she calls them "the Clones," because they look so much like one another. Each girl has short curly hair and big brown eyes. (#68-p.118). They have a large above-ground pool in their yard (#68-p.118).

**SALLY CLUNE:**
Age ten (#68-p.117).

**JENNY CLUNE:**
Age eight (#68-p.117).

**JEANETTE CLUNE:**
Age six (#68-p.118).

**THE DEWITTS:**

Two really wild kids; blast Dawn and company with sprinklers as they shoot video to send to Stoneybrook (#68-p.119). Live near Stephie; go to her school (#72-p.61). Like to play Captain Hook and Peter Pan (#72-p.63). Their living room is crammed with photos (#72-p.64)—there are the DeWitts' wedding photos, honeymoon photos from the Far East, camp-out photos, and pictures of Cynthia in various costumes (#93-p.60).

**ERICK DEWITT:**
Age eight (#72-p.61). Has a crush on Dawn (M#12-p.55). Friends with Corey McKinsey, who lives a block and a half away (#93-p.62). Steps on a nail (#93-p.63).

**RYAN DEWITT:**
Age six (#72-p.61).

**MRS. CYNTHIA DEWITT:**
An actress, has been in a ton of commercials; tall and thin, with huge brown eyes and a wonderful smile (#72-p.63). Insists that the babysitters call her Cynthia (M#17-p.12) Has an audition at Friedson/Alper Casting offices and then does voiceover at Arctic Air Studios (#93-p.60). Drives a Jeep Cherokee (#93-p.61).

**MR. DEWITT:**
*Loves* Elvis (M#17-p.68).

**THE FACKLERS:**

We ♥ Kids Club clients who call two sitters (#72-p.49).

**THE MCMULLENS:**

**CATYA MCMULLEN:**
We ♥ Kids Club client (#72-p.48).

**THE PETERSES:**

**MRS. PETERS:**
We ♥ Kids Club client (#23-p.47).

**THE ROBERTSONS:**

House is a fifteen minute walk from Dawn's (#72-p.8); house is all on one level and Spanish-style, with the rooms arranged in a square around a center courtyard; almost every room faces into the yard (SS#5-p.74).

**STEPHIE ROBERTSON:**

**Personal Info:** Eight years old (SS#5-p.223). Has asthma due to emotional stress (#68-p.120); uses an inhalator and has pills, too (full asthma description—SS#5-p.35); lost her mother at a very young age and has over-protective father (#68-

p.120); bonded with Mary Anne when the BSC came to visit; has new neighbor and friend, Margie (#68-p.120). Used to be painfully shy but is coming out of her shell (#72-p.7). Joanna, her regular nanny, usually sits for her (#72-p.6). Morning sitter is Lisa Meri (SS#5-p.74). Stephie and Dawn are almost sisters; Stephie reminds Dawn of Mary Anne (#72-p.40). Looks like her mother (#72-p.42). Loves to read, is an excellent reader (M#12-p.113). Room is young-looking, with pink bunnies everywhere and pictures on the walls of storybook characters (SS#5-p.75).

**Experiences:** Used to pretend that Joanna was her mom, but it isn't the same (#72-p.41). Writes story called "The Special Flower" in which Dawn appears as a surrogate mother-type (#72-pp.119-120).

### THE WALDENS:

**SARAH AND NATHANIEL WALDEN:**
New clients (#72-p.48)

### OTHER KIDS:

**ALANA:**
Rhymes with "pain-a"; girl in Dawn's class who is a *big* pain (#77-p.110). She and her friends are brainy show-offs (#77-p.111). She and her mother, Kayla, go out on a baseball-park date with the Schafers, to disastrous results (#77-p.115).

**KATIE BEAR:**
Beats Dawn in girls' beginners surf tournament (M#12-p.137).

**BEAU:**
Surfer dude who hangs with Stacey, Paul, Carter, Alana, and Rosemary; should have been named Wild (SS#5-p.106).

**ALANA BECKER:**
Sixteen; part of the surfer crowd that Stacey hangs out with (SS#5-p.55).

**BECKY:**
Pretty, black-haired friend of Stephie's (#72-p.118).

**ELLEN BLIEMER:**
A friend of the club who likes to play practical jokes (#72-p.21).

**ZEKE BLUME:**
Maggie's little brother; has been in a few commercials (M#12-p.20).

**DAN:**
Stacey's first surfboard instructor (SS#5-p.56).

**TIMMY FORD:**
Eight; lives across the street from the DeWitts; just moved in; has nice brown eyes and a shock of straight dark hair hanging into them; has sadness in his face (#17-p.38). Shy; his parents have separated and he's living with his dad; they don't have much money (M#17-p.39).

**JASON:**
Jeff's friend (#15-p.44).

**JOE LUHAN:**
Old classmate of Dawn's (#23-p.92).

**JUSTIN:**
In the beach day care group; tells a ghost story (M#12-p.58).

**LUKE:**
Blond friend of Jeff's; ten (#23-p.63).

**MARGIE:**
Stephie's new neighbor and friend (#68-p.120).

**COREY MCKINSEY:**
Erick DeWitt often plays at his house, which is a block and a half away (#93-p.62).

**LISA MERI:**
Stephie's morning sitter, looks between sixteen and eighteen (SS#5-p.74).

**TOM MURPHY:**
Boy on high school track team, with long brown hair; seems nice (M#17-p.85); is planning Halloween party; is carrying skateboard (M#17-p.86). Does lots of Good Samaritan deeds (M#17-pp.87-88).

**OLIVER:**
Jeff's friend, with whom he plays telephone jokes (SS#7-p.29).

**CARTER PAPE:**
Seventeen; part of the surfer crowd that Stacey hangs out with; owns her own surfboard (SS#5-p.55).

**CHIP RANSOM:**
Ninth-grader; flirts with Maggie at Vista Hills Mall (SS#12-p.8).

**PAUL RAPKIN:**
Seventeen (SS#5-p.55); part of the surfer crowd that Stacey hangs out with; drives a convertible (SS#5-p.54). Lives right down the street from Dawn; father is Dr. Rapkin (SS#5-p.59); basically a good kid (M#12-p.31). Hurt when he falls off his surfboard and it hits him in the shoulder (M#12-p.95).

**ROB:**
One of Jeff's good friends (SS#5-p.43); Jeff has a fight with him over who's the biggest Deadhead (SS#5-p.85).

**RUBY:**
Girl in Dawn/Stacey's beach day care program (M#12-p.25).

**SARA:**
Six-year-old in Dawn/Stacey's beach day care program (M#12-p.25).

**SONDRA:**
Other teen helper at beach day care program (M#12-p.26).

**ROSEMARY TANNER:**
Sixteen; part of the surfer crowd that Stacey hangs out with; owns her own surfboard (SS#5-p.55); basically a good kid (M#12-p.31); caught in the riptide, saved by lifeguards (M#12-p.96).

**TERRY:**
Intellectual boy for whom Claudia falls; good-looking, with jet-black hair, dark eyes, and a serious, handsome face (SS#5-p.46); lives between the beach and Dawn's house; has two brothers, one older and one younger; both of his parents are lawyers; loves school; hobby is reading; recently won a district-wide science fair (SS#5-pp.47-48). Has gotten hooked on Woody Allen (SS#5-p.253).

**TOM SWANSON:**
Old classmate of Dawn's; she grew up with him and Joe Luhan (#23-p.92). Has eyebrows that look like caterpillars (M#17-p.11).

**TOBY:**
Boy on high school track team, with long brown hair (M#17-p.85).

**TYLER:**
Ten-year-old in Dawn/Stacey's beach day care program (M#12-p.25).

## OTHER ADULTS:

**ALYSSA:**
Director of beach day care program (M#12-p.26).

**MRS. BANKS:**
Jill Henderson's neighbor; Smee likes to chase her cat, Tinkerbell (M#12-p.20).

**THE BATMATICS:**
Hip band that Carol listens to; "I Don't Love You Anymore" is their big hit (M#17-p.21).

**BRENDA:**
Worker at the surfside concession stand whose eyebrows are burnt off in grill accident attributed to the Surfer Ghost (M#12-p.94).

**BUCK:**
Dawn's surf instructor (M#12-p.10).

**MS. CARLENE CASEY:**
Works at Speedy Jack's; was held up in robbery (M#17-p.28).

**CHARIDA:**
Carol's friend from work (SS#12-p.108).

**JAMES L. CRUICKSHANK:**
Owner of abandoned lot that Dawn and Sunny turn into a garden; lives in Tucson (#93-p.104). Wears three-piece suit and mirrored sunglasses (#93-p.131). Gives his permission to Dawn and Sunny to maintain garden on the lot (#93-p.15).

**DEAN:**
Assistant to Alyssa, director of beach day care program (M#12-p.26). Knows a lot about marine life; wants to be a marine biologist someday (M#12-p.54).

**CLARICE DUBINA:**
One of Mr. Schafer's dates (#77-p.59). Calls Mr. Schafer "Schaf" and refers to Jeff and Dawn as "children"; Jeff, in turn, goes after her with a bumper car (#77-p.63). After she offers to go "girl stuff" shopping with Dawn, Mr. Schafer drops her off . . . for good (#77-pp.67-68).

**EVELYN FORD:**
Timmy's mother; wanted money to afford having Timmy come to live with her (M#17-p.141).

**JOHN FORD:**
Timmy's father; lives across the street from the DeWitts; separated from wife; just lost his job and is looking for a new one (M#17-p.40). Has a motorcycle; looks like a nice man but yells at a dog (M#17-p.69). Drives a black Chevy with a Frank's Franks sticker on it, which means that Dawn thinks he's a robber (M#17-from p.124).

**OFFICER GARCIA:**
Asks Dawn about the convenience store robbery; a small, black-haired woman with a gentle voice and a very serious attitude (M#17-p.28).

**GONZO:**
Surfer in jams (M#12-p.40); tries to kill Thrash (M#12-p.134).

**REVEREND GUNNESS:**
Celebrant at Schafers' wedding; female (SS#12-p.109); freckle-faced with crinkly, welcoming grin (SS#12-p.136).

**LIZ HENDERSON:**
Jill's sister; can drive (M#12-p.83).

**BARBARA HINKLEY:**
One of Mr. Schafer's dates, he meets her at a dentist's office (#77-p.68). She is not amused by Cap'n Frank's Fun Fish Fry; is instead rather picky and uptight (#77-p.70).

**JOANNA:**
Stephie's nanny, usually baby-sits for her; has dark hair and a hunk for a boyfriend (#72-p.6).

**THE JOHNSTONS:**
Friends of the Winslows; live in Oregon and named their children Vernal Equinox and Lunar Eclipse (#72-p.14).

**KAYLA:**
One of Mr. Schafer's dates (#77-p.109). Works at public relations firm, has many perks (#77-p.109). Is mother of Alana the Pain-a (#77-p.110). Used to be on fencing team in college (#77-p.112); these days, she makes do with tennis (#77-p.113).

**MR. KLEIN:**
Owns newsstand near Schafers' house (#72-p.31).

**LANCE:**
*Palo City Post* photographer, accompanies Rhonda Lieb when she interviews the We ♥ Kids Club. In his twenties, with dark brown hair

pulled back in a ponytail, with deep, luscious eyes (#72-p.28).

**RHONDA LIEB:**
Feature-story writer for the *Palo City Post*; wrote story about Maggie's dad once (#72-p.22). Looks like a college student; has short brown hair and a friendly smile (#72-p.26). Comes to interview the We ♥ Kids Club, carries cassette recorder (#72-p.26). Used to baby-sit through college; was studying to be an actress (#72-p.27).

**LYLE:**
Florist for the Schafer wedding; Claud must deal with him (SS#12-p.92).

**MARISOL:**
Chuck Raymond's director; a very tanned, very chic woman (#72-p.35).

**MRS. MCKINSEY:**
Corey's mom; drives Erick DeWitt to doctor after he steps on a nail (#93-p.66).

**CHUCK RAYMOND:**
Newscaster on local TV station (#72-p.32); interviews the We ♥ Kids Club (#72-p.35); has the bald spot on the back of his head spray painted (#72-p.35).

**KEANU REEVES:**
Actor; once had dinner at Maggie's house (#72-p.14).

**MR. ROBERTS:**
Sunny's science teacher (#23-p.47).

**LISA SCHWARTZ:**
Woman interested in hiring We ♥ Kids Club; just moved to town (#72-p.49).

**SHARI:**
Blends the smoothies at the beach-side concession stand (M#12-p.114).

**SPANKY:**
Surfer with nose ring (M#12-p.40); drops out of surfing competition for fear of being hurt (M#12-p.97).

**MS. STEVENS:**
Clerk at Ellie's Variety (M#17-p.53); dresses up in a different costume every day (M#17-p.66).

**STU:**
Chuck Raymond's assistant director (#72-p.34).

**STUART:**
Works at The Current Affair, caterer for Schafer wedding (SS#12-pp.96-97).

**MR. SWANSON:**
Dawn's English teacher at Vista (#98-p.1).

**SERGEANT SWEETZER:**
Talks to Dawn after criminal's arrest (M#17-p.127).

**TINA:**
Chuck Raymond's makeup and hair artist; a gorgeous red-haired woman (#72-p.34).

**THRASH:**
The hottest surfer around (M#12-p.10). About twenty years old and tall—maybe 6'2"—with shoulder-length white-blond hair, has three holes pierced in right ear and two in his left, wears wild-looking copper ring that looks like a snake twining around his middle finger (M#12-p.28). Calls Dawn "Kelea" (M#12-p.30). Is kind of tough, doesn't care about anything besides surfing (M#12-p.31). Wipes out and isn't found; presumed dead (M#12-p.89). Is the only surfer who can do a three-sixty (M#12-p.89). Resurfaces with dyed black buzz cut, flipping hamburgers at the concession stand (M#12-p.114). Comes back to win competition (M#12-p.137); he gives Dawn his ring (M#12-p.140).

**TJ:**
Surfer with spiked brown hair and a dangling earring (M#12-p.40).

**WANDA:**
One of the best surfers around, male or female (M#12-p.40); wiped out and was underwater for so long she almost drowned (M#12-p.96).

**KARINA WHITAKER:**
One of Mr. Schafer's dates; seems very nice (#77-p.82) then acts rudely towards Whitney, causing Dawn to brand her a big loser (#77-p.89).

**MRS. WINSLOW:**
Sunshine's mother, a former hippie; a potter who makes beautiful stoneware; is one of the warmest people Dawn knows (#72-p.14). Like a second mother to her (M#12-p.19). Has been smoking since the age of thirteen; is diagnosed with lung cancer; the doctors don't know how far it's spread (#87-p.56). Is now home from the hospital, but she has to go back from time to time for chemotherapy, which is very painful (#98-pp.7-8). Has to wear a wig; eyes look hollow and sad; her clothes hang loosely on her body (#98-p.13).

**MR. WINSLOW:**
Sunshine's father, a former hippie (#72-p.14).

**PETS:**

**SPIKE, SHAKESPEARE, AND SMEE:**
The Hendersons' dogs, all boxers; Smee likes to chase the cat next door (M#12-p.20).

## PLACES:

**TOWNS:**

**PALO CITY:**
Where Mr. Schafer lives, and Dawn and Jeff grew up (#72-p.2); near Anaheim, about two hours from San Diego (#72-p.47). John Wayne Airport is close to the Schafers' house; LAX is almost an hour away (#72-p.84). Zip code is 92800 (CL-p.13).

**SCHOOLS:**

**VISTA:**
School that Jeff and Dawn went to in CA (#15-p.41). Dawn re-enrolls there when she returns to Palo City (#72-p.3). School is a bunch of small one-story buildings grouped in a star shape around a big courtyard filled with flowering bushes and juniper trees; there are skylights in all the classrooms and a bench by a huge bougainvillea, which is Dawn's favorite spot. (#72-p.4; M#12-pp.24-25). Kids can eat lunch in the courtyard (M#17-p.54).

**TRANSPORTATION:**

**JOHN WAYNE AIRPORT:**
Close to the Schafers' house in Palo City; LAX is almost an hour away (#72-p.84).

**TOWN CENTERS:**

**PALO CITY POLICE STATION:**
A few streets away from the beach; among the regular patrol cars parked outside are several dune buggies painted in police colors; the atmosphere is more informal than in Stoneybrook; the officers wear short-sleeved uniforms and seem pretty friendly, too (except when the sitters are inquiring about the death of a surfer) (M#12-p.66).

**PALO CITY RELIEF FUND:**
Benefits earthquake victims (M#17-p.86).

**STORES/RESTAURANTS/ BUSINESSES/ATTRACTIONS:**

**BODY-SOUL JOY:**
New macrobiotic restaurant (SS#12-p.107).

**CAP'N FRANK'S FUN FISH FRY:**
Eatery where the waiters and waitresses are dressed like buccaneers, the food is served in plastic pirate ships, and the dishes all have cute little nautical names (#77-p.68), like the Schooner Sandwich and the SeaGreen delight (#77-p.69).

**CAPTAIN ROOSTER'S CHICKEN RANCH:**
Laid-back site of Claudia and Terry's final date (SS#5-p.234).

**ELLIE'S VARIETY:**
In the shopping center (M#17-p.23); sells everything from construction paper to baby T-shirts, plus lots of Halloween stuff (M#17-p.24). Mrs. Stevens is the clerk (M#17-p.63).

**FRANK'S FRANKS:**
Motto is "They're Frankly the Best!"; serves all kinds of junk food listed on orange-and-blue menu board; there's really nothing for Dawn to order (M#17-p.96); a really popular place (M#17-p.98).

**GRAUMAN'S CHINESE THEATRE:**
BSC visits there, goes down the Walk of Fame (SS#5-p.168).

**GREEN THUMB:**
Nursery that donates plants to Dawn and Sunny's lot park (#93-p.130).

**THE GROTTO:**
Fancy restaurant where Claudia and Terry go on a date; menu is in Italian (SS#5-p.66).

**THE HALLOWEEN SHOPPE:**
Only open during October; sells costumes and masks (M#17-p.55). Store looks like a little cave; every inch of wall space is covered with masks; a bunch of accessories sits on the counters (M#17-p.56).

**HANK'S FLOWER BASKET:**
Down the road from the Halloween Shoppe (M#17-p.58). A cheerful, bright, sweet-swelling place; glass cases filled with buckets of colorful flowers, tables covered with house plants, (M#17-p.59).

**HUDSON'S:**
Department store within walking distance of Dawn's house; the first things you see as you walk through the doors are the makeup and perfume counters (#77-p.74).

**KNOTT'S BERRY FARM:**
Amusement park that BSC visits (SS#5-p.187).

**KOPLER'S DRUGS:**
In the shopping center; Dawn needs hair mousse there; smells like a drug store (a mix of cologne, Band-Aids, jelly beans, and suntan lotion) (M#17-p.22).

**KOPY KWIK:**
In the shopping center (M#17-p.23).

**MAX FACTOR MUSEUM OF BEAUTY:**
Mal insists on going there (SS#5-p.54).

**MEDIEVAL TIMES:**
Theme restaurant where diners pretend the year is 1093 and that they are guests of a royal family; an arena shows sword fights and everyone wears crowns (SS#5-p.238).

**MR. KLEIN'S NEWSSTAND:**
Newsstand a few blocks from the Schafers' house (#72-p.31).

**THE NATURAL BAKER:**
The Schafers' bakery of choice (M#17-p.9).

**OCEAN INN:**
A local seafood house, really plain inside, but heaps of seafood on every plate (#77-p.60).

**(THE PALO CITY POST)**
Palo City newspaper (#72-p.22).

**SAM'S DELI:**
In the shopping center; Mr. Schafer loves their pickles (M#17-p.23).

**SIX FLAGS MAGIC MOUNTAIN:**
Amusement park that BSC goes to on last day in California (SS#5-p.235).

**SPEEDY JACK'S:**
Convenience store in the shopping center; robbed (M#17-pp.26-27). Ms. Casey works there (M#17-p.28).

**UNIVERSAL STUDIOS:**
Mr. Schafer takes the BSC there (SS#5-p.133).

**VISTA HILLS MALL:**
Where Dawn goes to buy bridesmaid dress (SS#12-p.7). Stores include:

*Carswell-Hayes:* Anchor department store in the mall; where Dawn finds bridesmaid dress (SS#12-p.13). *The Current Affair:* Small gourmet shop; caters Schafer wedding; Stuart works there (SS#12-p.97).

*Health's Angels:* Health-food snack bar (SS#12-p.8).

*SportsWest:* Sporting goods store (SS#12-p.8).

*Tito's Burritos:* Mexican food joint (SS#12-p.16).

**WALLY'S:**
Grocery store nearest to Sunny's house (SS#12-p.88).

# IN HAWAII

•

## PEOPLE:

**MR. BLANCHARD:**
Claudia's Pearl Harbor tour guide, wearing a U.S. Navy hat; was stationed at Pearl Harbor in 1941 when attack occurred; survived (SS#13-pp.70-71).

**CHAD:**
Actor in Day-Nite suntan lotion commercial whom Abby calls Mr. Dimples (SS#13-p.106).

**DANNY:**
Ten-year-old boy who helps Dawn, Mary Anne, Jessi, and Abby clean up Hawaiian beach (SS#13-p.187-188).

**KAIULANI FLORES:**
Director of Day-Nite suntan lotion commercial in which Abby appears (SS#13-p.106).

**JIM FREDERICKS:**
Helicopter pilot (SS#13-p.146). Is forced to make a crash landing (SS#13-p.155).

**EVIE HARBISON:**
Nikki's three-year-old sister (SS#13-p.130).

**JOSEPH HARBSION:**
Nikki's five-year-old brother; is lost. Blond (SS#13-p.130), brown-eyed, and dimply; Mary Anne finds him in the wrong hotel room (SS#13-p.35).

**NIKKI HARBISON:**
Evie and Joseph's seven-year-old sister; shows Mary Anne her Barbies (SS#13-p.130).

**JEANETTE:**
Younger girl who helps Dawn, Mary Anne, Jessi, and Abby clean up Hawaiian beach (SS#13-p.188).

**POHAIKEALOHA:**
Pohai, for short; ten-year-old girl who helps Dawn, Mary Anne, Jessi, and Abby clean up Hawaiian beach (SS#13-pp.187-188).

**GRANDPA SAM REYNOLDS:**
White-haired Caucasian (SS#13-p.169); met his Hawaiian wife and married right after the war; wife died a year ago and he moved in with the Reynoldses (SS#13-p.169). Has a couple of military medals as well as a citation for bravery from President Harry S Truman (SS#13-p.171). Was involved in the cleanup of Pearl Harbor (SS#13-p.181). Talks to Claudia about Pearl Harbor and her feelings of guilt for what Japan did (SS#13-p.182).

**MR. REYNOLDS:**
Co-manager of SeaView Family Resort (SS#13-p.126). A "real Hawaiian," with dark, golden skin and black hair (SS#13-p.127).

**MRS. REYNOLDS:**
Co-manager of SeaView Family Resort (SS#13-p.126). A "real Hawaiian," with dark, golden skin and black hair (SS#13-p.127).

**RAYMOND REYNOLDS:**
The Reynolds' baby (SS#13-p.168).

**SCOTT REYNOLDS:**
Eight years old (SS#13-p.168).

**LANI REYNOLDS:**
Five years old (SS#13-p.168).

**ROXANNE:**
Beet-red actress in Day-Nite suntan lotion commercial (SS#13-p.106).

**MR. YAP:**
SMS students' Honolulu tour guide; a roly-poly silver-haired man wearing flip-flops and a loud patterned shirt (SS#13-p.47).

**YUKIO:**
Younger boy who helps Dawn, Mary Anne, Jessi, and Abby clean up Hawaiian beach (SS#13-p.188).

**PLACES:**

**HALEAKALA NATIONAL PARK:**
Park where Stacey and Robert encounter *paniolos* (Hawaiian cowboys) (SS#13-p.142).

**HONOLULU:**
Among the sites the SMS students see: the Iolani Palace, the State Capitol, the Mission House Museum, the Hawaii Maritime Museum, Aloha Tower, and Chinatown (SS#13-pp.50-51).

**THE HONOLULU SURF HOTEL:**
SMS students' first hotel: a squat, rectangular, four-story, glass-and-steel building in the middle of town; not on the beach (SS#13-pp.38-39). Banyan trees have taken root in the parking lot (SS#13-p.39). Claudia, Dawn, and Mary Anne stay in Room 323; Stacey, Abby, and Jessi stay in Room 321 (SS#13-p.40). Can see the Ko-olau Mountains from the hotel window (SS#13-p.44).

**KAHIKINUI FOREST RESERVE:**
Place where Stacey's helicopter crash-lands (SS#13-p.193).

**KALAKAUA AVENUE:**
Waikiki's main drag; Stacey loves shopping there (SS#13-p.76).

**MT. TANTALUS:**
Honolulu's highest point, which Dawn, Jessi, and Logan visit (SS#13-p.84).

**PEARL HARBOR:**
Claudia is curious to see it firsthand; sees remains of the battleship *U.S.S. Arizona* (SS#13-p.67).

**THE PUNCHBOWL NATIONAL CEMETERY:**
Graveyard for American soldiers; Claudia visits there, sees part of monument, which is a long marble wall etched with maps of famous battles (SS#13-p.119).

**PUU ULAULA OVERLOOK:**
Valley overlook that leaves Stacey and Robert thunderstruck; the whole island of Manhattan could fit into the valley below (SS#13-p.117).

**SEAVIEW FAMILY RESORT:**
Oahu hotel where SMS students stay; view overlooks Kanehoe Bay, including the island used as Gilligan's Island (SS#13-pp.125-126). Located in community called Kaneoho, on the windward side of Oahu (SS#13-p.126). Hotel is huge—two swimming pools, a golf course, and a restaurant; Mr. and Mrs. Reynolds are the hotel managers (SS#13-p.126).

**TREETOP RESTAURANT:**
Dawn, Jessi, and Logan eat lunch there; it truly is built in a tree (SS#13-p.88).

**WAIKIKI BEACH:**
Beach where Abby volunteers for Day-Nite suntan lotion commercial (SS#13-p.78).

# IN KENTUCKY

•

### SEE ALSO *THE BRUNOS*

**ELLIOT:**
Little kid Logan sat for who had an accident in his pants, Logan's worst baby-sitting experience (#10-p.45).

**TINA LAWRENCE:**
Kid Logan sat for who flushed her father's necktie down the toilet (#10-p.45).

# IN MAYNARD, IOWA

•

**SEE ALSO** *THE SPIERS*

**PEOPLE:**

**BOB:**
Mary Anne's Maynard date; the grandson of one of her grandmother's friends; really, really cute (M#5-p.132). He and Mary Anne don't have much in common; all he talks about is the car he's going to buy when he's saved up enough money; is incredibly boring; eats enough for four people (M#5-p.133).

**ETHEL:**
Verna Baker's friend (MAB-p.136).

**JANET:**
Verna Baker's friend (MAB-p.136).

**MARION:**
Verna Baker's friend (MAB-p.136).

**PLACES:**

**MAYNARD, IA:**
Where Verna Baker, Mary Anne's grandmother, lives; Mary Anne goes to visit; town consists of one traffic light, a church, a bar, a feed store, and a general store; there's no movie theater, no mall, no nothing (M#5-p.129). Has a Dairy Queen, though (M#5-p.133). Landscape is as flat as a pancake (MAB-p.132).

# IN NEW YORK CITY

•

## STACEY'S FRIENDS/CLASSMATES:

**ALLISON:**
Classmate whose birthday party Stacey wants to attend, even though they don't even like each other (SB-p.136).

**CARL BAHADURIAN:**
At Stacey's party in NYC with BSC (#18-p.68).

**CAITLIN:**
Friend of Stacey's whose parents are divorced (#28-p.58); she and brother live with mother in NYC during school year and with father for vacations and summers in Chicago (#28-p.65).

**CECILE:**
Girl in Stacey's first grade class; so super proper that she always wore stockings to school; in the Beresford Ballroom Dance Academy class (SB-p.75).

**LAINE CUMMINGS:**
**Personal Info:** Stacey's former best friend (#3-p.17; #51-p.135); they were friends since they were five (#3-p.21); extra-best friends by eight; only six blocks separated their apartment buildings (SB-p.60). Laine was one of the only kids Stacey knew on her first day of Parker (SB-p.33); is a leader (#3-p.22). Fluffy brown hair (#18-p.59), permed; with brown eyes (#28-p.17). Super-smart, reads French poetry, likes foreign movies and gourmet food (has even eaten a pigeon); a bit more sophisticated than Claudia (#18-p.53; #28-p.24). Likes seltzer water and singing group called Retro (#51-pp.33-34). Has boyfriend named King, who's fifteen (#51-p.6); he calls her "Babe," she calls him "Heart" (#51-p.59).

**Family/Apartment:** Just moved to the Dakota apartments (#18-p.62). Address: 72nd and Central Park West (SS#5-p.51). Her father is big-time producer of Broadway plays who hires a limo with horn that plays first two bars of "Home on the Range (#18-pp.120-121). Has private phone line (#51-p.4). Her Aunt Mona and Uncle Edgar have condo in Florida (#51-p.6). Room has a trundle bed and guest room has two beds (SS#6-p.31).

**Experiences:** Visits Stacey when she's in the hospital in NYC, brings her fun and weird presents (#43-pp.72-73). Got job for summer as cashier at Flowers and Bows (#51-p.81). Visits Stacey during winter break for a week (#51-p.8). She goes to Valentine Dance with Pete Black at SMS, is rude, dances with another boy (#51-p.108); gets into fight with Stacey (#51-p.114); goes back to NYC night of the dance (#51-p.120). Stacey writes her, tells her she's not her best friend any more, and sends her half of their Best Friends necklace (#51-p.135).

**DEIRDRE DUNLOP:**
Old classmate of Stacey's, now going with Lowell Johnson (#3-p.156). Went to kindergarten with Stacey (SB-p.34). Was mean to Stacey when she first learned she had diabetes; they pretty much stopped being friends (SB-p.138). Has seven-year-old brother, Miles (SS#11-p.55).

**SALLY EL-MELIGI:**
Stacey's former Parker classmate who was part of her group (SS#11-p.47).

**EMILY:**
Kid from Parker Academy whom Stacey introduces to Claudia (SB-p.144).

**JIM FULTON:**
At Stacey's party in NYC with BSC (#18-p.64).

**JASON:**
Kid from Parker Academy whom Stacey introduces to Claudia (SB-p.144).

**LOWELL JOHNSTON:**
Old classmate of Stacey's; now going with Deirdre Dunlop (#3-p.156).

**KEITH:**
Friend of Stacey's in NYC whose parents are divorced (#28-p.58); he and brother spend alternate months with parents (#28-p.65).

**KING:**
Fifteen, Laine Cummings' boyfriend, attends Rudy Matthews School, across street from Laine's school (#51-p.6); calls Laine "Babe"; she calls him "Heart" (#51-p.59); long hair in ponytail (#51-p.6); hair is purple at the ends (#51-p.38).

**MISSY MANHEIM:**
Stacey's best friend in kindergarten (#13-p.22).

**READ MARCUS:**
Friend of Stacey's, girl, went to Stacey's party in NYC with BSC members; has gone out with Jim Fulton (#18-pp.64-65).

**MELISSA:**
Kid from Parker Academy whom Stacey introduces to Claudia (SB-p.144).

**RANDALL PETERSON III:**
Snobbiest boy in Stacey's first grade class; takes ballroom dance lessons at the Beresford Academy; bragged that he was going to be a senator someday; corrected people if they didn't use his whole name (SB-p.74).

**BOBBY REEDER:**
Old classmate of Stacey's who told Laine that Stacey's diabetes was contagious (#3-p.155).

**COBY REESE:**
At Stacey's party in NYC; a regular guy she's been friends with since age one (#18-p.67); star forward of basketball team (#18-p.68); exchanges numbers with Kristy (#18-p.70).

**ALLISON RITZ:**
From Stacey's past in NYC (#3-p.21); new girl from Dallas, welcomed by Stacey, then takes Stacey's place in group (SS#11-from p.52); then hated Stacey (#13-p.17).

**SAMANTHA:**
Girl in Stacey's first grade class; so super proper that she always wore stockings to school; in the Beresford Ballroom Dance Academy class (SB-p.75).

**VAL SCHIRMER:**
Stacey's former Parker classmate who was part of her group (SS#11-p.47) then hated her after diabetes incidents (#13-p.17). She and Stacey pretty much stopped being friends (SB-p.138).

**SHAYLA:**
Friend of Stacey's whose parents are divorced and live ten blocks from each other (#28-p.65); she and sister live with mother Wednesday afternoons until Saturday night and with father other times (#28-p.65).

**MARTY SHULTIS:**
Member of Stacey's school clique; leaves at the end of sixth grade (SS#11-p.47); goes to boarding school in Massachusetts (SS#11-p.49).

**PETEY SQUIRES:**
Classmate of Stacey's; in preschool, had a really messy cubby next to her neat one, would shove his stuff into hers sometimes (SB-p.19). Later, was one of Stacey's good friends at Parker (SB-p.20).

**ERIN TUKI:**
Stacey's best friend in second grade (#13-p.22).

**WILSON:**
Kid from Parker Academy whom Stacey introduces to Claudia (SB-p.144).

## CLIENTS:

**THE BARRERAS:**
Live on eighth floor of Stacey's old apartment building (#18-p.50).
**Carlos Barrera:** Nine (#18-p.50).
**Blair Barrera:** Seven (#18-p.50); favorite dinosaur is duck-billed aquatic Corythosaurus (#18-p.94).
**Cissy Barrera:** Five, can't stand Leslie Reames (#18-p.50); sturdy, playful tomboy (#18-p.86).

**THE DELUCAS:**
Haven't lived in NYC long (#18-p.51).
**Dennis Deluca:** Nine (#18-p.51).
**Sean Deluca:** Six (#18-p.51).

**THE HARRINGTONS:**
British; staying in the Baicker's apartment upstairs from Stacey's father (SS#6-p.32). Parents are diplomats (SS#6-p.34).
**Alistaire:** Seven, has perfectly combed brown hair, with bangs, and round, green eyes (SS#6-p.33).

**Rowena:** Four; has perfectly combed brown hair, with bangs, and round, green eyes (SS#6-p.33).

**Bill:** The Harringtons' bodyguard, who follows the BSC members when they sit for Alistaire and Rowena (SS#6-p.217).

**THE REAMESES:**

Live in huge twentieth-floor penthouse in Stacey's old building (#18-p.43); furnished like museum (#18-p.45); Mr. Reames calls Stacey "Anastasia" (#18-p.46).

**Leslie Reames:** Four, a little like Jenny Prezzioso (#18-p.44); small — weighed less than four pounds at birth (#18-p.45); hates dogs (#18-p.86); has wheat allergy (#18-p.86).

**Martha:** Reameses' maid (#18-p.46).

**THE UPCHURCHES:**

Live on sixteenth floor of Stacey's old building; apartment decorated in white, black, and chrome: ugly; Mr. Upchurch is divorced (#18-p.49).

**Natalie Upchurch:** Ten, sophisticated (#18-p.49); belongs to creative theater group (#18-p.50).

**Peggie Upchurch:** Eight, sophisticated (#18-p.49); belongs to creative theater group (#18-p.50).

**THE WALKERS:**

Black artists in Apt. 18E in Stacey's old building (#18-p.47); the couple gives Stacey two matted and framed pictures done by kids as going-away gift (#28-p.122); always leave out paper plates and plastic utensils when sitter is feeding kids (#28-pp.72-73). Are going to have joint exhibit at Fitzroy Gallery (#99-p.10). Apartment is filled with sculptures, wall hangings, and modern artwork (#99-p.99). Apartment rooms are in same arrangement as Stacey's old apartment, but their dining room has been turned into a studio; there are no curtains or shades on the windows; Mr. Walker's easel and chair are on the left side of the studio while Mrs. Walker's slanted desk is by the window on the right (#99-p.99)

**Mr. Walker:** Artist; has had his own show in NY (#18-p.48).

**Mrs. Gabrielle Walker:** Illustrates books (#18-p.48). Has a funny, very melodramatic way of talking — everything is Desperate! Mad! Hopeless! Fabulous! (#99-p.10). Has cut her curly, medium-length hair very short; now her cap of short black curls sets off her large, dark, carefully lined eyes and her dangling bronze earrings (#99-p.99). Is finishing a book of African-American folk stories (#99-p.100). Is very observant (#99-p.140).

**Henry Walker:** Five, shy (#18-p.48); lost briefly in American Museum of Natural History (#18-p.96).

**Grace Walker:** Three, shy (#18-p.48); never likes her parents to leave, usually cries (#28-p.71).

**THE WALTERS (*SEE ALSO QUINT WALTER, BELOW*):**

Quint's family.

**Apartment:** On the West Side, near Zabar's (M#8-p.64). Living room and dining room are the same room; big dining table is in the back near the kitchen (M#8-p.38).

**Mrs. Walter:** Soft-spoken and a little shy (M#8-p.38).

**Mr. Walter:** A chemical engineer (SS#6-p.130).

**Morgan Walter:** Quint's sister, age six; can do a cartwheel (M#8-p.38). An imp who likes to play tricks (SS#6-p.130).

**Tyler Walter:** Quint's brother, age nine (M#8-p.38). Is usually lost to the world of computers (SS#6-p.130).

## JESSI'S FRIENDS, AND OTHER DANCE PEOPLE:

### FREDERICK DUVALL:

From the New York City Ballet, teaches a special technique class to Jessi's class for a week (#57-p.54).

### QUINT WALTER:

Jessi's (now ex-)boyfriend, lives in NYC (#51-p.22). Has dark, curly hair, wide brown eyes, skin that is just slightly lighter than Jessi's, and the long, lithe body of a dancer (SS#6-p.75). Studies ballet at the Juilliard School; African-American (#61-p.85). Guys still give him a hard time about being a dancer, but he puts up with it (SS#7-p.65). Gives ballet scholarship idea to Jessi (#61-p.101). Is first boy that Jessi has kissed (M#8-p.3). Had some doubts about going to Juilliard but is really glad he did (M#8-p.39). Performs at Juilliard (M#8- p.106).

After much thought, he and Jessi mutually agree to just be friends, figuring they're too young for a long-distance relationship (M#8-p.129).

## OTHER KIDS:

### ETHAN:

Working for the Walkers and in the Fitzroy Gallery over the summer; Stacey thinks he is completely, totally gorgeous (#99-p.106). About fifteen years old; has deep blue eyes and long, almost black hair; also has high cheekbones, a straight nose, and a kind of wide mouth; wears a tiny gold hoop earring in one ear; is tall with broad shoulders (#99-p.106). Has a nice voice (#99-p.104). Would like to be an artist (#99-p.106); Mrs. Walker thinks he is gifted (#99-p.108). Is also great with kids (#99-p.107). Can Rollerblade well but isn't a show-off (#99-p.111). He and Stacey exchange phone numbers and hope to keep in touch (#99-p.142).

### BRANDON LEECH:

Lives four blocks from Laine, in apartment 3B; adopts the stray dog that Kristy found (SS#6-p.189).

### RICHIE MAGNESI:

Lives in the apartment below Stacey's father's; has a broken ankle (SS#6-p.110). His hair is brown and longish—he's let the back grow into a very chilly little tail; when he smiles, his cheeks dimple (SS#6-p.112). Is punctual beyond all reason; takes Dawn for a day on the town (SS#6-p.157).

**MORGAN SINGER:**
One of the BSC's Battle of the Bakers day care charges; eight; light brown straight hair, serious face; smart and full of fun; came all the way from New York City, along with Dana, her baby sister (M#21-p.36).

## OTHER ADULTS:

**ANITA:**
Cashier at Gristedes in NYC, in Stacey's old neighborhood (#28-pp.108-110).

**MISS ANTONIO:**
Manager of Gristedes whom Stacey doesn't like (#28-p.110).

**THE BAICKERS:**
Live upstairs from Stacey's father; lend out their apartment to the Harringtons (their cousins) (SS#6-p.32).

**DR. BARNES:**
Stacey's holistic doctor (#3-p.73); office on W. 63rd St. near Central Park West (#3-p.142).

**MRS. BARNES:**
Executive vice-president of Stacey's dad's company; company gives award ceremony in NYC in honor of Stacey's dad's promotion to vice-president (#58-p.98); she and Mr. Davis present him with a plaque (#58-p.101).

**MR. BERLENBACH:**
Stacey's teacher in NYC for her last period class; Laine has same classes with her (#28-p.59).

**DONNA BRINKMAN:**
The star of *Which Way's Up?*, spotted by Claudia on the streets of NYC (SS#6-p.121).

**MISS CHARDON:**
Taught at Parker Academy in NYC, where Stacey attended school (#13-p.15).

**MCKENZIE CLARKE:**
Claudia and Mal's instructor at the Fine Arts League of New York (SS#6-p.7). Short and slim, with thick glasses and a serious look (SS#6-p.63). Has a daughter (SS#6-p.117). Claudia thinks he likes Mal better, but really he's just challenging Claud (SS#6-p.183).

**PEG CUMMINGS:**
Laine's mother; friends with Mrs. McGill (SB-p.85).

**MRS. DANDYWORTH:**
Stacey and Laine's teacher at the Beresford Ballroom Dance Academy; is relieved that the girls' disappearance isn't her fault (SB-p.84).

**MR. DAVIS:**
President of company that Stacey's dad works for; company gives award ceremony in NYC in honor of Stacey's dad's promotion to vice president (#58-p.98); he and Mrs. Barnes present him with a plaque (#58-p.101).

**RIK DEVINE:**
Movie star; "the most gorgeous hunk ever to walk the earth"; Mr. McGill takes Stacey to meet him at the world premiere of a movie (M#2-p.105).

**FRANK:**
Actor who Jessi and Quint mistake for a jewel thief. Has thick black hair; looks strong (M#8-p.43).

**DR. PHILIP GRAHAM:**
Big authority on childhood diseases, especially diabetes; Dr. Johanssen arranges for Stacey to see him (#3-p.144); office at E. 77th and York in NYC; a tall black man with sparkling eyes and a deep voice (#3-p.146).

**ISAAC:**
Works at desk in Stacey's old building on Upper West Side (#18-p.13); always says "Have a nice day" even at night (#18-p.64).

**JAMES:**
Doorman in Stacey's old building on Upper West Side (#18-p.13).

**JUDY:**
Homeless woman on Stacey's old block on Upper West Side (#18-p.4); forty-two but looks much older (#18-p.5); calls Stacey "Missy"; often in a bad mood, screams for hours (#18-p.6); Stacey and father don't know what happened to her (#58-p.107).

**LLOYD:**
Works at desk in Stacey's old building on Upper West Side (#18-p.13).

**THE MAGNESIS:**
Live directly below Stacey's father (SS#6-p.27).

**STU MAJORS:**
Friend of Mr. McGill's; balding. Has a house in Davis Park, arranges for the McGills' vacation there (#76-p.51).

**MEDDOWS:**
Waitress who serves BSC members at Hard Rock Cafe (#18-p.34).

**MITCH:**
Robert's supervisor on the Davis Park ferry (#76-p.85).

**MISS MOSS:**
Stacey's kindergarten teacher (SB-p.33); taught her most of the games and songs she now uses with BSC clients (SB-p.34).

**PAVAROTTI:**
Famous opera singer; is among the crowd who sing "Happy Birthday" to Stacey on her fourth birthday in the Palm Court (SB-p.25).

**RED:**
Actor who Jessi and Quint mistake for a jewel thief. Has red hair and a straggly beard; looks scary (M#8-p.43). Real name is David; has a niece in Quint's ballet class (M#8-p.142).

**SALLIE:**
Woman who comes to clean Laine's apartment (SS#6-p.147).

**DR. SHERMAN:**
Fancy child psychiatrist (male) to whom Stacey's parents take her after the bed-wetting incident (SS#11-pp.61-62).

**THE SOMBERGS:**
Friends of the Pikes, who they are meeting in NYC for lunch (SS#7-p.34).

**SWEET JANE:**
Lead singer of NY club group called the Sleazebuckets; high school kids go to NY clubs to hear them; Stacey wants to put them on donation list for school auction (#62-p.95).

**DR. TIERNY:**
Vet who examines Sonny, the dog that Kristy finds (SS#6-p.153).

**TOM (MR. HANDSOME):**
Sits in aisle seat next to Dawn on flight to CA; a theater director; gives Dawn list of shows to see (#23-p.27).

**DR. WERNER:**
Stacey's specialist in NYC, a woman (#3-p.27).

**THE WILEYS:**
Friends of the Pikes, with whom they are having dinner (SS#7-p.34).

**SAMANTHA YOUNG:**
Mr. McGill's girlfriend, whom he secretly meets at Fire Island; very beautiful, with large blue eyes, wavy brown hair, and a great figure (#76-p.109). Mr. McGill calls her "Sam" sometimes (#76-p.113). Is still seeing Mr. McGill; Stacey thinks she's pretty nice (#99-p.117).

# PLACES:

## SCHOOLS:

**BERESFORD BALLROOM DANCE ACADEMY:**
Where Stacey and Laine take (and skip) dancing lessons at the age of eight (SB-p.69). On Upper East Side, 85th & Madison (SB-p.77). Classes were at four o'clock on Tuesdays (SB-p.71). Must take an elevator upstairs, then face an ornate gold-and-white sign. Inside, there is a small waiting area, with two big windows that look into the studio (SB-p.73). Music is supplied by young man at piano, with back to the waiting room; there are about twenty kids in the class (SB-p.74).

**FINE ARTS LEAGUE OF NEW YORK:**
An "open school" where Claudia and Mal take lessons (SS#6-p.2) with McKenzie Clarke (SS#6-p.5). Students call it "Falny" (SS#6-p.60). Situated in a plain building; entrance is just a set of glass double doors, with brass letters reading FALNY set above them; classrooms are huge (SS#6-p.62) with drawing tables set in a ring (SS#6-p.62).

**FITZROY GALLERY:**
Really big gallery several blocks away from where the Walkers live; famous artists show their work there; Mr. and Mrs. Walker are going to have a joint showing there (#99-p.10).

**JUILLIARD:**
One of the best music and dance schools in the world; Quint goes there and has invited Jessi to one of his performances (M#8-pp.2, 106). Located in Lincoln Center (M#8-p.102).

**PARKER ACADEMY:**
Where Stacey attended school in NY (#13-p.15). Did not require uniforms; Stacey took the subway to school (#1-p.34).

## STORES/RESTAURANTS/ MUSEUMS/ETC:

**AMERICAN MUSEUM OF NATURAL HISTORY:**
Stacey's always loved it (#76-p.22).

**BETSEY JOHNSON:**
Clothes store that Stacey thinks is Claudia's kind of place (SB-p.158).

**BLUE PAN COFFEE SHOP:**
Across street from Stacey's apartment in NYC (#13-p.136).

**CENTRAL PARK:**
Jessi is amazed by it (M#8-pp.68, 84).

**CENTRAL PARK ZOO:**
Not that big, a neat place to take kids; Morgan and Tyler like to make up names for the sea lions (M#8-p.87).

**THE CLOISTERS:**
Medieval branch of the Met, where Mal and Claudia's art class goes to sketch (SS#6-p.177).

**ERNIE'S PIZZA:**
Takeout pizza place near Deirdre's (SS#11-p.55).

**HARD ROCK CAFE:**
Where club has first meal in NYC and all buy T-shirts (#18-p.36); Stacey takes Claudia there, likes the rock and roll memorabilia on the walls and the great music they play (SB-p.161).

**HEATHE AND SONS, JEWELERS:**
Store that Jessi and Quint fear may be robbed; security guards eject them from the premises (M#8-pp.114-115).

**JOE ALLEN'S:**
One of Stacey's favorite restaurants in NYC (#3-p.157).

**JOHN'S:**
Serves the best pizza in New York; cooks it in a brick oven (SB-p.148).

**LEO'S COFFEE SHOPPE:**
Around corner from Laine's apartment building near Central Park (#3-p.157).

**THE LION'S LAIR:**
Restaurant on 70th Street (#76-p.19); hostess wears red silk suit; inside is decorated with sculptures of lions and big stone lion heads that jut out from the brick walls; outside, there is a patio and a huge rock ledge (#76-p.20).

**METROPOLITAN MUSEUM OF ART:**
Major art museum; Jessi and Quint spot Red and Frank there (M#8-p.70). Stacey loves it (#99-p.90).

**MINTER'S ICE CREAM:**
Ice cream place where Laine, Jessi, and Stacey take Rowena and Alistaire (SS#6-p.170).

**MYTHOLOGY:**
Awesome store where Claudia once bought a mirror that screams when you look at it; it closed a while ago (M#8-p.31).

**THE OYSTER BAR:**
Restaurant right in Grand Central Station, on the lower level; serves mostly fish and shellfish; Stacey's father makes reservations there (#99-p.79).

**PALM COURT:**
Restaurant in the Plaza, where Stacey goes for her fourth birthday; a very fancy place, with big palms everywhere, pink tablecloths, and gold-trimmed dishes (SB-from p.24). Mr. McGill takes Stacey,

Quint, and Jessi there, as Quint and Jessi look for Red and Frank (M#8-from p.76). People who eat there seem very wealthy (M#8-p.78). There is harp music every day at lunch, and tea sandwiches ready to order (M#8-p.79).

**THE PLAZA:**
Grand hotel, where Stacey was taken for her fourth birthday; home of *Eloise* (SB-from p.23).

**THE SALOON:**
Restaurant across the street from Lincoln Center, with roller-skating waiters and a great menu (SB-p.143).

**SHEEP MEADOW:**
Place in Central Park where Stacey loves to go; there's usually someone playing bongo drums or a guitar (SB-p.21).

**SIGN OF THE DOVE:**
Stacey's favorite restaurant, rather fancy (M#8-p.34).

**SILVER SPUR:**
Restaurant on Upper West Side in Stacey's old neighborhood (#28-p.82).

**SLEAZEBUCKETS:**
NY club group; Sweet Jane is lead singer; Stoneybrook high school kids go to NY clubs to hear them; Stacey wants to put them on donation list for school auction (#62-p.95).

**TAVERN ON THE GREEN:**
Where the BSC members go for dinner on their last night in NYC (SS#6-p.227).

**THINK BIG:**
Store that has gigantic versions of everything (M#8-p.31).

**TRIBECA BAR AND GRILL:**
Site of Allison's birthday party; "Robert DeNiro's place" (SB-p.152).

**ZABAR'S:**
Gourmet food shop on Upper West Side; Mr. McGill always stocks up there before Stacey visits (M#8-p.64).

## NEARBY TOWNS:

**DAVIS PARK, NY:**
Two-hour train ride, then a ferry ride, away from NYC; on Fire Island, where Stacey and her father go on vacation, with Claudia—and secret rendezvous with Robert Brewster. There are no cars there (#76-p.51). The McGills' house is named the Sandpiper (#76-p.52). Stores/restaurants include: The Beach Glass Gallery (#76-p.79); The Harbor Store (#76-p.78); Watch Hill, a pizza place (#76-p.81); The Casino, a somewhat fancy restaurant (#76-p.93).

# AT CAMP MOHAWK, NY

•

## PLACES:

### CAMP MOHAWK:
Map (SS#2-p.114). Camp where BSC members are counselors-in-training for two-week session (SS#2-p.4). Camp symbol is a tee-pee, which is on all uniforms (SS#2-p.8). David Michael, Karen, Haley, Matt, Jackie, Margo, Nancy Dawes, Charlotte, and Becca are campers (SS#2-pp.13,18,22,46); cabins are all wood, with bunk beds and one single for counselor (SS#2-p.33). Youngest campers are six (SS#2-p.59). Kids who can't swim are grouped as Iroquois (SS#2-p.136). Overnight campsite is about five miles from the center of Mohawk (SS#2-p.176).

### LAKE DEKANAWADA:
Lake that lies between Camp Mohawk and boys' camp (p.11); also known as Lake Dekadonka (SS#2-p.30), Lake Dukakis (SS#2-p.113), and Lake Demidonkey (SS#2-p.168).

## PEOPLE:

### AMY:
Other CIT in Dawn's cabin, went to Camp Mohawk last summer; eyes are kind of close together and her nose is pointy, so she looks like a bird; has red-blonde hair and perfect skin, seems smart (SS#2-p.58).

### CHARLENE:
Counselor in Dawn's bunk; eighteen and nice; outdoorsy, healthy (SS#2-p.58); mother becomes very sick, so Charlene has to leave camp (SS#2-p.139).

### DEBRA:
Dawn's new counselor, replaces Charlene (SS#2-p.175).

### MISS DINSMOORE:
Camp nurse (SS#2-p.148).

### FAYE AND JULIE:
Mary Anne's neighbor CITs, act very sophisticated, think Mary Anne is plain (SS#2-p.49).

### RONALD FEENIE:
Along with Harve "the Knife" Johnson, escaped convict rumored to be in the area of Camp Mohawk (SS#2-p.113) after escaping from asylum in Peacham (SS#2-p.116).

**HEATHER:**
Shy camper in Dawn's bunk; eleven; still has baby fat; parts her fine brown hair in the middle and lets it hang across her face, so she can hide behind it (SS#2-pp.60-61). Parents made her go to camp (SS#2-p.65).

**MEGHAN:**
Counselor in Claudia's cabin, tall (SS#2-p.31).

**MRS. MEANS:**
Camp director; called "Old Meanie" (SS#2-p.30).

**NONIE:**
Sassy-looking camper with long brown hair, in Stacey's bunk, has a lisp (SS#2-p.71).

**RANDI:**
Mary Anne's co-CIT, has long, long dark hair, dark eyes, and extremely cool accessories (SS#2-p.48).

**TARA:**
Mary Anne thinks she's a terror; picks on Margo Pike; has older sister, Faye, who's CIT (SS#2-p.52).

**SALLY TRONER:**
Claudia's co-CIT; wears her hair in a French braid and reminds Claudia of Stacey. Sophisticated, but probably not a snob (SS#2-p.31).

**MIKO TYRRELL:**
Female CIT with a broken leg (SS#2-p.150).

**WILL YAMAKAWA:**
Boys' camp CIT; Japanese-American, with black, black hair and dark, almond-shaped eyes and creamy skin like Claudia's; his hair is kind of punk, with the top part standing straight up (SS#2-pp.104,166). From Ashfield, NY (SS#2-p.169); his grandmother had always lived with their family; they called her Tink (p.170). He and Claudia have kept in touch—sending letter and cards and speaking every now and then on the phone (SS#3-pp.135,228).

**OTHER PEOPLE IN CLAUDIA'S BUNK:**
In Claudia's cabin: *Leann, Brandy, Jayme, Gail* (SS#2-p.32).

**OTHER PEOPLE IN DAWN'S BUNK:**
*Rachel*, who's friendly and has been going to CM since she was six (SS#2-p.59); *Shari*, short for Sharilyn, who's funny and goofy (SS#2-p.59); *Freddie*, from NYC (SS#2-p.59); *Donna*, who has gigantic ideas and plans (SS#2-p.60); *Caryn*, from Princeton, who has a million boyfriends, or so she says (SS#2-p.60); one such boyfriend is *Steve Heineman* (SS#2-p.64).

**OTHER PEOPLE IN JESSI AND MAL'S BUNK:**
*Autumn*, the counselor; *Gwen* and *Corinne*, the CITs; *Mandi, Maureen, Mary Oppenheimer*, and *Mary Travis*, the other campers, who tease Jessi and Mal for being so close (SS#2-p.40).

**OTHER PEOPLE IN KRISTY'S BUNK:**
*Jo*, her counselor, has a red/blue Mohawk (SS#2-p.91); CITs are *Lauren, Izzie*, and *Tansy*, who think Kristy's square (SS#2-p.91).

**OTHER PEOPLE IN LOGAN'S BUNK:**
*Curtis*, who's teaching the kids to play poker; *Russell*, a poet;

*Thomas*, who prefers to be called "T"; *Rick*, Logan's co-CIT, always wears Hawaiian shirts; *Henry* and *Cliff* are the CITs next door, who spend most of their time working on their tans (SS#2-p.127).

**OTHER PEOPLE IN STACEY'S BUNK:** *Barbara*, the counselor; *Joanne*, the other CIT (SS#2-p.69); *Valerie* and *Monique*, who has a sore throat (SS#2-p.72).

# IN OAKLEY, NJ:

•

**SEE ALSO** *THE RAMSEYS*

Old, settled, and comfortable neighborhood; most people have lived there since before Jessi was born, in small, crowded houses (SS#11-p.92).

## PEOPLE:

**CHELSEA:**
Three-year-old Jessi was paid to baby-sit four times in Oakley (#14-p.73).

**MRS. JASPER:**
Jessi's next-door neighbor, who lives by herself and takes care of Jessi and Becca when Squirt is born (SS#11-p.101).

**NEIL RAYMOND:**
Family members are old friends of the Ramseys; used to be kind of dorky and shy but is now sixteen, gorgeous, and full of himself (#67-p.83).

## PLACES:

**PRICE BAZAAR:**
Local food and supply store (SS#11-p.100).

**OAKLEY ELEMENTARY:**
Where Jessi went to school in New Jersey (#16-p.4).

**OAKLEY GENERAL HOSPITAL:**
Where Jessi, Becca, and Squirt were born (#16-p.2).

**WAGNER LANE:**
Where Jessi lived, and where her cousin Keisha and her family still live, at number 8320 (SS#2-p.233).

# ON THE *OCEAN PRINCESS*

•

## PEOPLE:

**ALEXANDRA (ALEX) CARMODY:**
Liar whom Mary Anne befriends; Has masses of dark, wavy hair that cascades over her shoulders and partway down her back; her figure fills out a skimpy bikini (SS#1-p.25). Tells Mary Anne that she's an orphan but has parents (SS#1-p.161) who are popular singing team for older folks—*Viv and Vernon Carmody* (SS#1-p.162).

**TIMOTHY CARMODY:**
Alexandra's brother and Claudia's secret admirer; lives in Darien (SS#1-p.121). Face is framed by curly hair, his eyes are dark, wide-set, and fringed with long lashes that are to die for (SS#1-p.122). Kisses Claudia (SS#1-p.211).

**PARKER HARRIS:**
Dawn's shipboard luv interest; has gorgeous and handsome grin, deep brown eyes, a small gap between his front teeth, light brown hair that is very straight until the ends, where it curls into little tendrils (SS#1-pp.19-20). Parents are divorced, father has custody and is remarried with two stepchildren; Parker doesn't like them at first (SS#1-p.94) but relents after trip to Disney World. Stepbrothers are named *Roddy* (age 8) and *Ricky* (age 5) (SS#1-p.152).

**MARC KUBACKI:**
Seven-year-old-boy, looks four years old (SS#1-p.63), in an impossibly small wheelchair (SS#1-p.36). Has really bad heart problem, isn't allowed to walk or run or do anything that strains his heart or makes him get out of breath (SS#1-p.64). Had major surgery and is making slow but steady recovery (SS#1-p.223).

**SPIDER:**
Lead singer for the Insects, Mal's favorite band; about twenty years old with bright red hair and missing front tooth (SS#1-p.37).

**RUDY STAPLES:**
Old man whom Kristy befriends; his wife, Gertrude, recently died (SS#1-p.73) of a heart attack (SS#1-p.75). Lives in Arizona; Kristy tries to set him up with Nannie (SS#1-p.216).

**PLACES:**

**THE *OCEAN PRINCESS:***

Cruise ship setting for SS#1; has pools, beauty parlor, barbershop, cafe, disco, stores, restaurants, and health spa (SS#1-p.13); each room has two bunk beds, two dressers, a desk, four little chairs, and everything is bolted to the floor (SS#1-p.16).

**NASSAU:**

Town on New Providence Island in the Bahamas where ship docks; Claudia goes shopping there (SS#1-p.50).

# IN SEA CITY, NJ

•

Beach that Pikes go to on vacation (#8-p.10). Have been going there for nine years (#8-p.16). Plastic palm trees on main drag (#8-p.32). On a little piece of land that curls into ocean like a dog's tail (#8-p.103). Attached to the mainland by a causeway (SS#10-p.37). First landmark on way to Sea City is billboard of purple cow; second landmark is Crabs for Grabs, a roadside restaurant (SS#10-p.38). Lifeguards are only on duty from nine A.M. to five P.M., so Pike kids are only allowed to go in the ocean during that time period (#8-p.16). There's a boardwalk with an amusement park, a movie theater, shops, and so many places to eat that you can smell Sea City before you see it (#8-p.16). No one dresses up in Sea City (#8-p.18). The next town over is Jamesport (#8-p.56). Also nearby is historic Smithtown, which looks like it's from the 1700s (#8-p.75). Postcard of Sea City (CL-p.21).

The Pikes' house—which they rent every year—is Victorian style, a big gingerbread cottage with yellow-and-white trim. There are gables and eaves and posts everywhere; there are three floors; the house faces the ocean (SS#10-p.39). Address is 12 Sandpiper Lane, Sea City, NJ 08200 (CL-p.7).

## PEOPLE:

### ALEX:
Mother's helper at Sea City who Mary Anne falls for (#8-p.102); fair-skinned, light brown hair (#8-p.47); they exchanged initialed rings with each other but didn't mean anything serious. Mary Anne didn't know Logan then (#34-p.38); tall, great smile (#34-p.68); Toby is his cousin who likes Stacey (#8-p.111); Alex won a big purple hippopotamus for Mary Anne at a ring-toss game (#34-p.96); he has girlfriend; is on a friendly basis with Mary Anne while in Sea City (#34-p.122).

### BRUCE:
Dark, curly-haired lifeguard at Sea City (#8-p.40).

**CHRIS:**
Twelve-year-old who works at Ice-Cream Palace in Sea City; gets anonymous love poems from Vanessa, who likes him, but he thinks they're from Mal (#34-p.104). Has dark eyes and curly black hair; cute (#34-p.50).

**ELLEN COOKE:**
Real estate agent in Sea City, office in little pink house surrounded by white gravel (#8-pp.24,32). Tells Pikes what to do about Hurricane Bill (SS#10-p.172).

**ELLIE (BABY), JIMMY, KENNY:**
Three kids Alex sat for who all have olive complexions and masses of black curls (#8-pp.47, 111).

**SCOTT FOLEY:**
Lifeguard Stacey has crush on; recently turned eighteen; lived in Princeton, NJ; starting college (#8-p.53); wavy blond hair, blue-eyed, tanned, muscled (#8-p.40).

**SHEILA:**
Two; Alex and Toby sit for her and her family at Sea City (#34-p.69).

**TOBY:**
Alex's cousin (#8-p.111); brown hair and eyes, a few freckles, cool clothes (#8-p.108); from Lawrenceville, NJ; fourteen, going to be a freshman; plays soccer and football; hobby is computers; has two older sisters; favorite group is Smash; favorite food is peanut butter; hates history and geography; likes math and loves telling jokes (#8-p.113); a mother's helper with Alex in Sea City for a month (#34-p.68); dates Stacey in Sea City but breaks up with her because he wants to see other people (#34-p.118). Stacey is not pleased with him (SS#10-p.43). He becomes interested in Mal; charges are Ben (eight) and Peter (six) (SS#10-p.141). Mal cancels their date (SS#10-p.218); he expresses interest in Jessi, showing that he's rather fickle in his affections (SS#10-p.227). Margo Pike sees him with an ugly girl (CL-p.22).

**PLACES:**

**BURGER GARDEN:**
Tacky-looking restaurant in Sea City surrounded by "garden" of plastic flowers with eat-out tables in shape of mushrooms and table help dressed like animals (#8-p.38). Every day there's a new Surprise Burger (#8-p.61). Fairly inexpensive (#8-p.56); serves Crazy Burgers (bacon, pickles, Swiss cheese, and orange mixture of mustard and ketchup) and Fantasy Fountain sodas (#8-pp.58, 61). Claire calls it "Gurber Garden" (SS#10-p.139). *The Enchanted Tree:* In Burger Garden in Sun City, NJ; chocolate bars "grow" on it, cost a quarter; if gold wrapper is inside you win prize; Nicky Pike wins four free dinners (#8-pp.61-62).

**CANDY HEAVEN:**
Penny candy store in Sea City (#8-p.37).

**CANDY KITCHEN:**
Candy store in Sea City (#34-p.11).

**CHILI FOTORAMA:**
On Sea City's main street (SS#10-p.86).

**CRABS FOR GRABS:**
Restaurant in Sea City (#8-p.30).

**THE DIXIE BROTHERS CIRCUS:**
Traveling circus that comes to Sea City (SS#10-p.139). Just a little tent in a vacant lot at the edge of town; outside the tent are a few rides and concession stands (SS#10-p.149). Show is "not great" one-ring affair (see SS#10-p.152).

**FRED'S PUTT-PUTT COURSE:**
Miniature golf in Sea City (#8-p.77). *Old King Cole Hole:* Third hole at Fred's Putt-Putt Course (#8-pp.79,80).

**HERCULES' HOT DOGS:**
Serves foot-long dogs in Sea City (#8-p.120).

**ICE-CREAM PALACE:**
In Sea City (#8-p.37); Chris, whom Vanessa has crush on, works there (#34-p.104). Has weird flavors, like Banana Bubble Gum (#34-p.49).

**IF THE SUIT FITS:**
Store in Sea City that sells swimwear (#8-p.100).

**KOTTON KANDY KORNER:**
Jessi wonders why they "kan't spell the name korrectly" (SS#10-p.85).

**PIZZA FALAFEL:**
On Sea City's main street, sells pizza and falafel (SS#10-p.86).

**SEA CITY ELEMENTARY SCHOOL:**
Where Pikes and company go in face of Hurricane Bill (SS#10-p.176).

**SEA CITY SAVINGS BANK:**
Local bank (SS#10-p.140).

**TAFFY N' THINGS:**
On Sea City's main street (SS#10-p.85).

**TRAMPOLINE LAND:**
In Sea City (#8-p.16), where Margo almost got sick (#35- p.102).

**TUNNEL OF LUV:**
Ride in Sea City where Toby give Stacey her first kiss (#8-p.121).

**WEINER'S WIENERS:**
New hot dog place in town, has billboard on the outskirts (SS#10-p.38).

# ON PINE ISLAND, ME

•

Sparsely populated island where McGills rent a house when Stacey's ten; there are no phones, stores, restaurants, theaters, TV, and so on (SB-from p.94). Map (SB-p.105). Only three families live there (SB-p.103). It is three-quarters of a mile long and a third of a mile wide (SB-p.113). *Notable spots include:* Pirate's Point, Blueberry Hill (SB-p.113), and Caddy's Cove, on the other side of the island (SB-p.119). *The house that the McGills stay in:* The Andersons' cabin (SB-p.111) isn't painted and is surrounded by woods; there aren't any screens on the porch; there are seventy-three rickety steps to the house (SB-p.107); the inside walls are made of thin panels of wood; the kitchen, dining area, and living area are all in one room; a counter separates the kitchen from the rest of the room (SB-p.108). There is no closet in Stacey's room, just a bunk bed (SB-p.109).

**PEOPLE:**

**THE O'CONNELLS:**
Year-round Pine Island residents; have a two-way radio (SB-p.112). Have a chicken coop, which Mara cleans out (SB-p.119).

**ALICE O'CONNELL:**
One year old; just learning to walk (at the time that Stacey's ten) (SB-p.121). Stacey's first baby-sitting job (SB-p.125).

**MARA O'CONNELL:**
Stacey's age; red-haired, freckle-faced (SB-p.111). Has lived on Pine Island all her life; she and her brother take a boat to school on the mainland (SB-p.112). Likes to sleep outdoors without a tent (SB-p.120). Drives pickup truck (SB-p.125). After she takes Mr. McGill to the hospital, Stacey considers her a first-class hero (SB-p.126). Knows the time from the position of the moon/sun (SB-p.129). Stacey never wrote to her after the McGills left Pine Island (SB-p.130).

**MR. O'CONNELL:**
Catches lobsters for a living (SB-p.115).

**MR. STANLEY:**
Boat driver who takes the McGills over to Pine Island (SB-p.102).

**TIPPY:**
The O'Connell dog, a brown mutt (SB-p.111).

# IN REESE, ME

•

A resort town, with a population of a couple of thousand people that doubles or triples during the summer (SM#1-p.19). A six-hour-plus drive from Stoneybrook; actually, nine and a half hours, with stops (SM#1-p.29). Celebrating its two hundred and fiftieth birthday (SM#1-p.55). Home to summer stock theatrical productions (SM#1-p.56).

## PLACES:

### FUDGE DEPOT:
Just sells fudge (SM#1-p.94).

### MITY KITES:
Kite store in downtown Reese (SM#1-p.94).

### THE RANDOLPH MANSION:
Four stories high, with a six-columned entranceway. Five brick chimneys pierce the sky, and there's an authentic widow's walk on the roof (SM#1-p.31). Even with sixteen people staying over, there's one whole floor not being used (SM#1-p.26). Georgio works, and sometimes sleeps, in gardener's cottage, which has electricity (SM#1-p.91).

Attic has many old things, including antique baby carriage, two sleds, a trunk of children's toys, and a large armoire (SM#1-p.132). Dumbwaiter traverses three floors (SM#1-p.165).

### REESE HISTORICAL SOCIETY:
Old brick house off of Main Street, run by Eleanor Butterfield (SM#1-p.162).

## PEOPLE/THINGS:

### THE MENDERS FAMILY:
Friends of Lisa and Seth Engle; aren't sure if they want to move out of Boston but are trying out mansion in Reese that Mr. Menders inherited from uncle (SM#1-p.19). Used to live in big apartment in Boston in new building with elevator (SM#1-p.95). Decide to move to Reese (SM#1-p.261).

*Lionel:* Fourteen (SM#1-p.33). At first, Mary Anne thinks he's pretentious and unhappy (SM#1-p.34). Wants to be an actor (SM#1-p.36). Becomes involved in Reese theater scene; coaches Jason's softball team

(SM#1-p.250). Gets a small part in *Our Town* (SM#1-p.261).

*Jill:* Ten (SM#1-p.34). Likes swimming, dressing up, dancing, summer, and teenagers; dislikes people who act like babies, winter, and being bored (SM#1-p.34). Mimics Dawn; then becomes a baby-sitter herself in Reese, for Tammy Johnson, age four (SM#1-p.260).

*Jason:* Nine (SM#1-p.33). Becomes involved in Reese softball team, which is named The Locals (SM#1-p.250).

*Martha:* Seven and shy (SM#1-p.34). Best friend from home is Louise (SM#1-p.95). Karen tries to set her up with new friends (SM#1-p.93). Ends up with three new friends in Reese (SM#1-p.262).

*Mr. Tom Menders:* A corporate businessman (SM#1-p.35), thinking of opening a health food store near Reese (SM#1-p.20).

**ELEANOR BUTTERFIELD:**
Works at the Historical Society (SM#1-p.162).

**ELTON COOPER (CHARLES RANDOLPH):**
Half of caretaker couple at Randolph Mansion; makes meals, cleans up (SM#1-p.35).

**MARGARET COOPER:**
Elton's wife, also a caretaker (SM#1-p.35); hired for the summer (SM#1-p.35); supposedly afflicted with chronic laryngitis (SM#1-p.36). In her late thirties; very pretty, with straight dark hair pulled back in a bun (SM#1-p.44).

**MILLICENT ELLSWORTH:**
Author of *A Historical Tour of Reese*, which tells the story of Reginald and Mary Randolph (SM#1-p.88). Always had a flair for the dramatic; was carried away with her stories (SM#1-p.163).

**EDWARD RANDOLPH:**
Tom Menders's great uncle, who leaves him the mansion (SM#1-p.52). According to the Tronos, he was a fine gentleman to work for (SM#1-p.170).

**LYDIA RANDOLPH:**
Elton Cooper makes up story about this Randolph descendant, saying that she was locked into back closet after having a romance with the gardener's son (SM#1-p.121).

**MARY RANDOLPH:**
According to *A Historical Tour of Reese*, mourned her husband Reginald for twenty years after his death, walking every night in a white dress onto the widow's walk of Randolph Mansion; was hurled to death by the winds in 1879 (SM#1-p.89). Town records say, however, that she died in her sleep (SM#1-p.164).

**REGINALD RANDOLPH:**
According to *A Historical Tour of Reese*, he had been a wealthy landowner and fisherman, who had owned a big fleet of fishing boats. He often captained these boats and in 1859 was lost at sea with a crew of thirteen, leaving his wife, Mary, to mourn for him (SM#1-p.89).

**SPOOKY:**
Black cat with green eyes; used to belong to Jill's great-uncle Randolph (SM#1-p.39).

**GEORGIO TRONO:**
Looks like a brooding teenage rebel loner, with straight black hair, heavy eyebrows, and a crooked smile; eyes are dark brown and alight with interest (SM#1-p.48). A flirt—especially with Claudia (SM#1-p.49). Goes to the University of Maine (SM#1-p.87). Invites Claudia to his homecoming weekend, but she points out that she's too young (SM#1-pp.258-259).

**BERTHA AND MR. TRONO:**
Georgio's grandparents; had been caretakers of the mansion when Mr. Randolph was alive (SM#1-p.49). Move back in to be caretakers for Menders family (SM#1-p.262).

# ON SHADOW LAKE, MA

•

Located in the mountains of western Massachusetts (SS#8-p.5). *In the summer,* opportunities to go boating, fishing, parasailing, waterskiing (SS#8). *In the winter,* is near downhill ski slopes and is a place for serious cross-country skiing (SM#2-p.10).

## PLACES:

### BEAVER POND:
A small pond near Shadow Lake that freezes over in the winter; Karen and David Michael want to go skating there (SM#2-p.132).

### THE LODGE:
Like a hotel, but without rooms to sleep in (SS#8-p.56); A huge wooden structure; reached by a tree-lined road that becomes a dark tunnel of leaves; adjoined by a row of smaller wooden buildings that look like stores (SS#8-p.22). One of the activity rooms has a ballet barre (SS#8-p.25). Serves dinners; is also where dances are held; dining room is enormous; also there's a ballroom, a souvenir counter, a weights-and-workout room, and several activity rooms (SS#8-p.33). Among the souvenirs sold are blue Shadow Lake baseball caps (SS#8-p.33). *In the winter:* jumping with guests (SM#2-p.133). You can sign up for activities at Information Desk (SM#2-p.133). Lodge employees wear royal blue shirts with the words *Shadow Lake Lodge Staff* embroidered on the pocket in white (SM#2-pp.133-134). Most of the staff members are very cute (SM#2-p.159).

### SHADOW LAKE:
Is so big and so deep in places that it hardly ever freezes enough to be safe for ice-skating (SM#2-p.132).

### WATSON'S CABIN:
Given to Watson by his Aunt Faith and Uncle Pierson; he spent seven summers there, from ages five to twelve (SS#8-p.2). Able to sleep twenty-five or more people; two of the bedrooms are like dorms, with wall-to-wall bunk beds; the cabin sits right on the shore of the lake; a porch runs around the cabin and the place is surrounded by trees (SS#8-p.7). A rambling, one-level

house (much too big to be called a cabin) (SS#8-p.23). The front deck looks out on the lake (SS#8-p.25). Floor plan (SS#8-p.26). Two big bedrooms with six bunk beds apiece, and two small bedrooms that can sleep two people apiece; then there's a large living/dining room (SS#8-p.27). In both bedrooms, there are braided oval rugs, white bureaus, tables made of dark wood, several windows, and neatly folded patchwork quilts at the foot of each bed (SS#8-pp.28-29). No air-conditioning; screens on windows (SS#8-p.35). Cabin's boats are the *Faith Pierson* and the *Lake Mist* (SS#8-p.156).

## PEOPLE/THINGS:

### THE BAYARD FAMILY:
At the heart of the Shadow Lake mystery (SS#8-p.137); vanished from the island on the lake; included beautiful eighteen-year-old Annie and her younger brother Ethan (SS#8-pp.139-140). Their ruined, burned-down house is still on the island (SS#8-p.167).

### BRIDGET:
Daniel's eight-year-old sister (SS#8-p.77).

### MITCH CONWAY:
Caretaker of Watson's cabin; has been there since Watson was a kid (SS#8-p.27). Very neat and responsible (SM#2-p.163).

### DANIEL:
African-American boy who Jessi befriends; stays in the cabin next to

Watson's (SS#8-p.31). Twelve years old (SS#8-p.213). Lives in Boston (SS#8-p.77). Doesn't like to read; likes basketball (SS#8-p.81). Girlfriend's name is Carol (SS#8-p.218).

### MR. FEDERMAN:
Cross guest at Shadow Lake; a thin man with a thin mouth and thinning brown hair; wears a patch over one eye which, with his mean expression, makes him look sinister (SM#2-pp.134-135).

### WOODIE KEENAN:
College-age guy with dark brown eyes and short, neatly cut, dark brown hair; guest at Shadow Lake (SM#2-p.134). Treks with BSC members to lodge in blizzard—is really Woodrow Tate, who has vowed to have revenge on BSC after they put his father behind bars (SM#2-p.223). Had become obsessed with the BSC, blaming them for family's financial downfall (SM#2-pp.224-225) has made a full confession (SM#2-pp.228).

### THE LAKE MONSTER:
Sighted occasionally, looks like the Loch Ness Monster (SS#8-p.41).

### KRIS RENN:
Short, red-haired woman; guest at Shadow Lake (SM#2-p.135). Agitated (SM#2-p.136). Stacey is pretty sure she has a gun (SM#2-p.186). Is really a detective from Special Unit, sent to capture Karl Tate for parole violations (SM#2-p.212).

### STEPHAN WEEKS:
Annie Bayard's former fiancé; now works at Shadow Lake grocery store (SS#8-pp.138-139).

# AT LEICESTER LODGE, VT

•

## PLACES/THINGS:

**CONWAY COVE:**
Town from which overturned elementary school bus originated (SS#3-p.35).

**HOOKSET CROSSING:**
Location of Leicester Lodge; population is 2,500 (SS#3-p.16).

**LEICESTER LODGE:**
In Hookset Crossing, VT (SS#3-p.1), where everyone in SMS goes for five and a half days (SS#3-p.2). A gigantic hotel in the mountains (SS#3-p.2), owned by a rich couple, Mr. and Mrs. George (SS#3-pp.7,27), who give schoolchildren an away-from-home experience; several wings are equipped as dormitories, so more than one school can be at lodge at same time (SS#3-p.7). There are candy machines on every floor and a salad bar in the dining hall (SS#3-p.14). Has library. Many people who work at lodge live/grew up in Hookset Crossing (SS#3-p.21). Vastness reminds Dawn of *The Shining* (SS#3-p.28); room is so big it can sleep fifty-six people, with two rows of bunk beds and dressers, rugs, mirrors; adjoining bathrooms (SS#3-pp.28,30). Second, third, and fourth floors are the same, connected by elevator (SS#3-p.33). The common room is where check-in is—a long, lofty room with beams in the ceiling and big easy chairs for reading (SS#3-p.34). Library is next to the common room, has books on local history (SS#3-p.62). Rumored to be haunted (SS#3-p.63)—ghost story stems from the death of a lodge visitor in the late 1930s (SS#3-p.112). Front desk has big collection of games (SS#3-p.74). Lodge was established in 1920, with huge additions built in the forties and fifties (SS#3-p.109). Georges bought the lodge in 1963 (SS#3-p.111). Boiler breaks down with great regularity all winter long (SS#3-p.111).

**WINTER WAR:**
Activity at Leicester Lodge; not mandatory; participants are divided into red team and blue team and compete in five events (SS#3-p.13).

**PEOPLE:**

**BRYCE AND GINNIE:**
Two students from Conway Cove Elementary School, for whom Mary Anne sits (SS#3-p.43). Ginnie thinks she can recite Shakespeare (SS#3-p.145).

**MARIE CASTLEMAN:**
Head housekeeper at lodge; at least seventy-five years old ; has frazzly gray hair, gold-rimmed granny glasses, and is as skinny as a wet cat; earlobes are droopy (SS#3-p.108). Has been working at lodge since 1930 (SS#3-p.109).

**PIERRE D'AMBOISE:**
According to Stacey, the world's cutest guy; his family is French, but Pierre has lived in the US his whole life; doesn't speak with an accent; doesn't speak much French; has deep brown eyes that sparkle; his voice is starting to change (SS#3-p.77). In eighth grade; lives in upstate Vermont, in Dixville Falls; takes Italian in school (SS#3-p.84). His brown hair has streaks of blond in it (SS#3-p.86). Meets Stacey after tailgating her on skis (SS#3-p.83); he is her "first meaningful crush" (SS#3-p.86). Mal observes Pierre and Stacey kissing (SS#3-p.95).

**MR. DOUGHERTY:**
CCES teacher, in the hospital for a night after braving the snow (SS#3-p.48).

**MR. AND MRS. GEORGE:**
Owners of Leicester Lodge, have a son (SS#3-p.40). Mr. George is author of *Leicester Lodge: 1920 to 1980* (SS#3-p.63).

**GUY:**
Name rhymes with "ski"; amazing-looking ski instructor; face is ruddy from being outdoors all day; hair is blond and curly, eyes pale blue; has French accent—it's luv at first sight for Claudia (SS#3-p.129). Then, Claudia's crushed when Guy introduces his wife, Domitille, and his two children, Jean and Marie (SS#3-p.196).

**JOEY:**
CCES student; has straight brown hair with big cowlick in the front; bottom middle teeth are missing, as well as side tooth on top (SS#3-p.68).

**TEENSY MOOSEMAN:**
Real name is Rebecca; is about seventy-five years old, in charge of the gardeners and handymen (SS#3-p.108).

**CURTIS OATES:**
Head cook, looks about seventy or so (SS#3-p.108). Missing a tooth (SS#3—p.110). Is in love with waitress from the dining room (SS#3-p.215).

**MS. OLSEN:**
Lodge's head ski instructor (SS#3-p.194).

**MISS WEBER:**
CCES teacher, in the hospital for a night after braving the snow (SS#3-p.48).

**PINKY WINKLER:**
Irritable student from CCES; lost her shoe, sprained her ankle (SS#3-

pp.42,55). Real name is Priscilla, and she's one bratty kid (SS#3-p.72). Is homesick (SS#3-p.154).

**OTHER CCES STUDENTS:**
Renee, Corey, Kara, Valeria, Frankie, Ian, Amber, Ryan, and Kathie (SS#3-p.119).

L. GODWIN

## About the Author

ANN MATTHEWS MARTIN was born on August 12, 1955. She grew up in Princeton, NJ, with her parents and her younger sister, Jane.

In addition to the Baby-sitters Club books, Ann has written many other books for children. Her favorite is *Ten Kids, No Pets* because she loves big families and she loves animals. Her favorite Baby-sitters Club book is *Kristy's Big Day*.

Ann M. Martin now lives in New York with her cats, Gussie and Woody. Her hobbies are reading, sewing, and needlework — especially making clothes for children.